WE COULD BE VILLAINS

THE VIGIL AND ANTE FILES
BOOK 1

WHIMSICAL PUBLISHING

This is a work of fiction. Names, characters, organizations, places, events, and incidents are either a product of the author's imagination or are used fictitiously. Any resemblance to actual persons, living or dead, or actual events is purely coincidental.

We Could be Villains
Copyright © 2022 by Megan Mccullough
All rights reserved.
No part of this book may be reproduced in any form or by any electronic or mechanical means, including information storage and retrieval systems, without written permission, except for the use of brief quotations in a book review. Please address: Whimsical Publishing, whimsicalpublishing.ca

ISBN:978-1-7780044-6-9

Edited by Micheline Ryckman & Deborah O'Carroll
Cover art and design by Micheline Ryckman & Megan McCullough

For Katie, my first writer friend. I'm with you till the end of the line.

CHAPTER 1

OFFICIAL VIGIL REPORT
FILED BY AGENT ROSEMARY COLLINS
DATES: **JAN 15 – MAY 21**
ALL RELEVANT DOCUMENTS INCLUDED
CASE #: **[REDACTED]**

JAN 15 – around 3:00 P.M. EST

Today's mission: make it through my shift without SuperCon spoilers. It was only rumored to be the most explosive VIGIL & ANTE Studios panel in history. I would have ditched work to watch the livestream, but the thought of calling out sent my stomach into knots.

Yay for being responsible, Rosemary.

Ugh, the next two hours would be an eternity.

A sharp breeze cut through my coat, and I pulled the thick fabric tighter against me as I walked quicker through the crowded New York City sidewalk. I glanced at the time on my phone. An hour until the panel and only a few minutes until my shift.

What could the huge announcement be? A third *Project Safeguard* movie? Every actor was rumored to be at the panel, so an epic new superhero team-up film made sense. The creator of

Best VIGIL Memes theorized a Degree Surge solo movie was next because he found a leaked set photo.

The suspense was killing me. I shook my head. No, I wasn't going to think about this until after work because it would make my shift feel even longer.

I put in an earbud and played my favorite showtunes. That would distract me for a while. "King of New York" blasted through my ears with its upbeat tune, and soon the loud rumble of the New York City machine disappeared. My steps matched the beat as that special Broadway joy surged through me, but I stopped short of singing along. I reserved my "performances" for my bedroom because the thought of an audience made me nauseous.

Something tickled the back of my neck. A snowflake? No, the sky was too clear. The chill crept further and further down my spine, almost like...like someone was *watching* me.

It had to be my imagination. Who was I kidding? It was nothing.

This is how people get kidnapped, Rosemary.

Why did this keep happening? It wasn't the first time this week I'd felt someone watching me. I shivered again and paused the music. Blaring horns and echoing sirens flooded my ears. The inside of my thick winter coat became hot and damp with sweat, and my gut squeezed, screaming at me that someone was on my tail. And as a seventeen-year-old girl walking alone, that was a dangerous thing.

I couldn't panic.

The smell of burnt pretzels mixed with exhaust wafted around me. Maybe I didn't have a stalker. Maybe my brain was playing tricks on me. Maybe I was anxious about the SuperCon announcement and the ensuing adorable cast interactions. Not to mention the cute meet and greet photos. And everything I was missing out on.

I glanced behind me, but there was only a sea of people

moving in unison. No one so much as looked my way. Still, I gripped my phone tighter, just in case.

No one is stalking you.

The sooner I got to work, the better.

Wait a second.

I had an idea. I quickened my pace and dodged oblivious bystanders, not willing to risk the pedestrian equivalent of road rage. I glanced back. One person matched my speed—some guy with electric blue hair. Not very covert, though my own copper waves had a similar effect. He was maybe...hmm...six feet tall with a jawline of steel only super attractive movie villains could pull off. (On principle, I refused to deem them hot.)

Someone *was* following me. I should call the police, but that would mean looking down at my phone, and it was already crowded enough—

My shoulder struck against something.

"Watch where you're going!" a gravelly voice called after me.

I sprang forward, moving even faster. "So sorry!" I stole another glance over my shoulder.

Blue Hair sped up his pace but made no eye contact. Hopefully he didn't realize I was on to him. My heart pounded.

Agh.

He was closing the gap. I needed a plan.

People in spy movies always made shaking a tail look easy.

I took in my familiar surroundings. Starbucks. The vibrant blue VIGIL & ANTE Studios billboard that always triggered my fangirl. Abandoned, graffitied building. Shady tourist trap. My knuckles tightened around my lifeline so there was no way I could drop it.

If I could just make it to work.

I jogged, then took another peek over my shoulder.

He was closer.

Our eyes locked. His were brown, all but a small sliver of ice blue peeking through the left one. Something about him struck me as familiar, but I couldn't put my finger on it.

I turned and ran harder, but the image planted itself in my head.

Okay, maybe this was just a random guy. Maybe he wasn't following me. But something about when our eyes locked... He wanted *me*.

I stole another glance.

The man was gone.

I didn't stop to see where he went. My lungs burned as I finally slowed down a block away from my job.

Had that just happened? It was like something out of a movie, only more terrifying. The feeling that something horrible is gaining on you, clawing toward the hem of your shirt. I shivered. Deep breath. I brushed a stray hair out of my eyes and walked the rest of the way to the building. My body still shook.

I nudged open the front door, a bell overhead jingling. Ah, yes, good old Ketch-A-Burger. Did I work here for the sole purpose of saving toward a SuperCon ticket? Yes. It certainly wasn't for the mediocre burgers the entire city was obsessed with.

I pushed through the line to get to the backroom. The door was barely open when the fandom-fueled screaming began. "Rosemary!"

I jumped back, heart hammering my ribcage. Oh no, Sam was not going to give me spoilers, even though the panel hadn't started yet. "H-hi, Sam."

"What do you think the big reveal is?" My co-worker grinned, peeling off his Ketch-A-Burger hat. "It'd better be another Illuman movie, because I cannot get enough of his light powers. Glowing skin and large amounts of sass? Yes, please!" Obviously I was a huge fan too, but Sam was the kind of fan who never shut up about it, even to let someone answer his own question. And when he had a theory, he *always* had to be right.

"Umm..." I blinked, mind still wrapping itself around whatever the heck he said. "Yeah, I don't know. I—I think it might be another *Project Safeguard* movie."

Sam jumped to his feet, putting him at least a foot shorter than me. "I mean, you're excited, right? You have to be excited. Everyone is. Even all the fake fans. This is going to be the biggest news since they figured out how to fake Illuman's powers in real life! Like...how can you top that kind of PR stunt? Especially because he is, without question, the *best* superhero."

I forced a chuckle. "I don't know about *that*. They're all pretty cool. I especially love Agent Liam. And Ver."

"But they aren't real superheroes." He shook his head, long brown 2000s bangs falling into his eyes. "To be a superhero you need powers. Look it up and you'll see I'm right." Oh, why did I tell him I was a fangirl?

"I don't think that's true." I shook my head and looked toward the punch-in machine. If I got fired for not clocking in on time, Mom would never let me hear the end of it. "I have to clock in though, so..."

"Anyway, I'm prepared with AirPods so I can listen while I flip burgers. No one will notice. Do you think anyone will notice? No, no one will. I'm good at hiding it."

I sighed. "Sorry, normally I'd talk but I need to clock—"

"But the AirPods? The boss won't be able to tell, right?"

"I really don't know." If I told him no, he'd argue, and if I told him yes, he'd blame me if he got in trouble. "Just please don't spoil it for me. I'm waiting to watch it until I get home."

Sam grinned, then bowed and faked a British accent. "You have my word, my lady." *Project Safeguard* reference. "Did you get it? It was a reference to—"

"Yes, Sam, I got it. Remember, no spoilers." I took off my coat and put it with my purse, hands still shaking. *Settle down. No one is going to hurt you.* I clocked in, then went to go open the door into the kitchen as it swung inside.

Cue another adrenaline rush.

"Oh! Sorry." Another one of my co-workers. "We need you on the other register. We're packed right now."

I nodded. "Sure thing." I took a deep breath, then walked

through the door. Chatter and laughter roared inside. We sure sounded busy. I turned and went up to the empty register, trying not to make eye contact with impatient customers until I logged on to the computer.

"Welcome to Ketch-A-Burger. What can I get for you today?" I looked up at the first person.

"A double cheeseburger and a large fry. Uh, lots of ketchup and no mustard." The woman looked bored to death staring at the menu screens above my head.

Next person. "Twelve-count chicken nuggets." And the next. And the next. And the next. My gaze flitted to the time in the lower left-hand corner of the screen. Four p.m.

The panel had begun, and half the world eagerly watched. There was a reason almost every VIGIL & ANTE Studios movie broke box office records.

Please no one spoil it. I glanced through the crowd, hoping I didn't hear whispered reactions. Hoping Sam didn't inevitably scream the news from the kitchen.

"Next." I glanced up as a blond-haired man stepped forward and—

His eyes.

The same heart-stopping brown as Blue Hair. Identical silvery blue in his left iris. That was an uncommon thing…right? It didn't make sense. Maybe my brain was playing tricks on me. Though both "stalkers" seemed about my age, this person had a much rounder chin. It was possible to bleach out that highlighter blue to the sand-colored surfer hair this guy had going on, but no one could magically change face shape, right? Certainly not within the last hour.

But what were the chances that two different people had the exact same eyes?

Chills crawled down my spine.

"…please." He tilted his head.

I blinked, shocked back into action. "I'm sorry, what did you say?"

"A triple cheeseburger, please."

Why was I still freaking out? He couldn't be the stalker because he looked nothing like the guy following me earlier.

Also, why would a stalker be so polite? Wait, no, that was dumb.

"Uh, could you repeat that just one more time?" I forced a smile to hide the spontaneous combustion going on in my head. Forgetting someone's order the moment after they said it is my social anxiety's worst nightmare. Yes, it happens to me way too often, but who's counting?

The man only smiled as if my mistake was no big deal, which earned another check mark in the "too nice for a stalker" column.

"Triple cheeseburger," he said.

Okay, I got it that time. I pressed buttons on the screen without looking down. "Will that be all?"

"Yes."

Deep breath. "All right, your total is $5.49."

He grimaced, reaching into his pockets. "Right. One moment." His hands emerged clutching two wads of cash. I gulped, keeping my head down as if he held something contraband. Because it was too much money.

When I dared look up, his piercing eyes were still on me instead of the bills in his hand.

"I-I'm sorry, can I help you?" I gripped the register as the world went fuzzy.

"No."

This was getting beyond weird. My instincts screamed for me to run. Still, my mind fought back. This was a public place. Three more customers lined up behind him, and almost every booth was filled, so nothing could happen to me here.

I gulped. "Then do I know you or something?"

His chin dropped as a smile played at his lips. "Not this face."

My breath caught. "What?" He *knew*. He knew about the man following me. Maybe he *was* the man following me.

Only now he shook his head. "No, you don't know me." Maybe I'd imagined his first statement. It was impossible anyway. No one could alter their appearance so drastically in that short amount of time.

"Right, umm..." I looked down at the screen again as if lost at which button to tap next. "Your cheeseburger is $5.49." My chest tightened, but I forced myself to breathe.

He thrust a few crisp bills toward me and shoved the rest into his pocket. "Here you go." The bills felt like they'd come straight from a bank. My fingers fumbled as I slipped the cash into the register and handed him change and a receipt.

"Thanks." Then he stepped to the side, clutching the receipt. And his eyes. He still stared at me. *Not this face*. What did that even mean? I shifted positions and dug fingernails into my palm as if the pain would distract me.

Someone else moved forward.

"W-welcome to Ketch-A-Burger. How can I help you?" I managed to ask, but I didn't tear my gaze from the brown-eyed man.

He stared at me as he waited for his food. But when his meal was ready, he left as though nothing had happened. His sudden departure was as strange as any of it.

I shivered. Everything about this felt wrong. Would he be waiting outside when I got off work? Maybe I should call my mom and see if she'd give me a ride home. If not, I'd ask a co-worker. I was *not* getting murdered tonight. At least not before I watched that panel.

JAN 15 – around 5:00 P.M. EST

Everywhere I looked, I searched for those haunting brown and blue eyes. If this was real, he could be anyone. A man leaned against a building talking into his phone. My heart skipped a beat. What color were his eyes? It was getting too dark to tell.

I stepped closer to Sam, hoping he didn't think it was weird.

"I get safety and stuff, but you need to chill," Sam laughed, shaking his head. "Like...you're paranoid."

"Probably," I said, shrinking back. "Girls have to worry about this stuff, though." But maybe he was right. Maybe I *was* overthinking this. One person couldn't change faces in under an hour. It was a mistake. A fluke.

Still, the guy basically confirmed it. What he said couldn't have been an accident, unless I'd imagined it.

Sam rolled his eyes, readjusting his backpack. "Okay, fine, what does this mysterious stalker look like?"

Yeah, this was the part I couldn't explain very well. I glanced at the crowded walkway behind us as the constant city chatter seemed to grow louder. "His eyes stand out the most. They're brown except for a sliver of blue in his left eye."

"So...Ironfall?" Sam raised the one eyebrow I could see behind his bangs.

My stomach lurched. "What?"

"You just described Ironfall's eyes. You know, the supervillain in *Project Safeguard*? The character literally everyone is in love with?"

"I know who he is, Sam," I said. "I just...didn't realize that." In the movie, Ironfall could change his appearance. So could my stalker, apparently. And they either had the exact same eyes, or the stalker chose to wear the same contacts both times. Unless multiple people were pulling an elaborate prank.

"Your guy must be a cosplayer," Sam said. "Which is common today because of SuperCon." That was an easy explanation, yet something still nagged at me. I was missing something. Sam straightened his shoulders. "That's right, hire me, *Criminal Minds*."

"Maybe," I breathed, still searching for an answer. It seemed too subtle for a prank. "Anyway, thanks for walking me home."

He smirked. "Anything to get my shift covered. Also, please watch the panel because I can't promise any more spoiler-free conversations. There's too much to discuss. I'm storming the VIGIL & ANTE Studios because—"

"Don't spoil it!" I sighed, then turned toward my apartment building. The sooner I was safe in there watching the comic con panel, the better.

"Then go watch it." He shook his head, motioning toward the door.

I nodded, then went inside, half-running up the three flights of stairs. The lock clicked behind me as I shut our apartment door, and I double and triple checked it in case my multi-faced stalker decided to pay a visit. *Safe at last*. Now I could finally watch the SuperCon panel. The TV blared from the corner, keeping Mom's attention like always.

I don't think watching all those design shows helped her décor taste improve.

"Looks like you got home okay." I jolted forward at my mom's voice. She stood in the kitchen chopping an onion. "I said you didn't need me to pick you up."

I nodded, glancing at the lock again. "I convinced Sam to walk me home."

She raised an eyebrow as her lips tipped upward. "Sam?"

My eyes widened. "Oh, no. He's just a co-worker. An annoying one." Why do parents immediately think you're in love when you casually mention a boy? We'd never even texted each other beyond work stuff.

"Right." She still had an amused look on her face, which meant she was convinced I liked Sam. That couldn't be farther from the truth. "Just don't let him distract you from work. You need to keep this job." She brushed an auburn strand of hair from her face.

"I know, Mom," I said. "It's not like I've gotten fired before. And he only walked me home because I agreed to take over his shift."

"Still, don't let the wrong people distract you from where you need to go. You have to be ready, and at this rate"—she looked me up and down—"you're not going to be."

I pressed my lips together as my stomach twisted.

She turned toward the sink, rolled up her sleeves, and rinsed off her knife. "You know I'm only hard on you because I love you." Yes, I knew she did, though sometimes her way of showing it cut deep.

"I know." I pressed my lips together, then escaped to my room, which wasn't much of a room anyway. It gave Harry Potter's closet a run for its money.

SuperCon, here I come.

I tossed my backpack on the floor and plopped onto my bed. What was the big announcement? Thoughts of Mom and the day melted away as I sank into the arms of my fandom. I glanced over at my *Project Safeguard* poster, grinning. Each superhero stood in a fighting stance toward the bottom of the poster. Their different colored costumes stood out against the dark New York City skyline. The large villainous figure at the top hid in the darkness, but the smirk on his sharp-featured face stood out first.

Ironfall

And then I saw his eyes.

Sam was right. They were the same. As I studied them closer, I saw more similarities than something a pair of contacts could imitate. The depth of those rich brown irises as they stared into your soul. The way you could look into their eyes and see the final piece of a mental puzzle slip into place.

They had the same powers. The same eyes. The same everything.

It was almost like my stalker *was* Ironfall.

TRANSCRIPT OF THE INTERVIEW PROCEEDINGS WITH **[REDACTED]**
SOME NAMES AND LOCATIONS REDACTED FOR SECURITY
INTERVIEW CONDUCTED ON MAY 20
LOCATION OF INTERVIEW: **[REDACTED]**
CASE #: **[REDACTED]**
PROCEEDINGS

AGENT: Would you like anything to drink? Water? Coffee? Lemonade?

[NAME REDACTED]: No, thank you, I'm good.

AGENT: All right then, you have the right to remain silent. Anything you say can and will be used against you in court. Do you understand?

[NAME REDACTED]: Yes, but I won't get a court date like most people, now will I?

AGENT: You must want to get this over with then.

[NAME REDACTED]: [inaudible]

AGENT: Did you sleep well last night?

[NAME REDACTED]: No.

AGENT: They say only the guilty sleep in jail.

[NAME REDACTED]: [chuckles] Well, you already know I'm guilty. Now you're here to pry the whole story from me to see if you can figure out whose side I'm really on. You sure you're not the one who needs that coffee?

CHAPTER 2

This was crazy. Nope. Nope. Nope. Some creepy stalker dude was playing a sick joke, or VIGIL & ANTE Studios was doing another signature marketing stunt. I wouldn't put it past them. To announce their first movie, they faked Illuman "discovering his powers," and then to reveal *Project Safeguard*, they created a superhero battle inside an empty building.

If this was a PR stunt, everyone who read the inevitable Buzzfeed article would laugh at me for freaking out. I could see the headline now: "VIGIL & ANTE STUDIOS FOOLS GIRL INTO BELIEVING IRONFALL IS REAL!"

But the alternative was even crazier: Ironfall, the supervillain in *Project Safeguard*, the most successful VIGIL & ANTE Studios movie to date, was real. And so were superpowers and the *Project Safeguard* superhero team. Cloaker could make himself look like anyone by touching them. Commander Vigil had the strength of three grown men. Degree Surge controlled temperature. Illuman's skin glowed on demand.

That didn't sound insane *at all*.

Still, the hairs on the back of my neck prickled.

I shook it off. I was probably too focused on the panel and its excitement. This whole thing was my imagination.

I glanced at the poster again. My "stalkers" could've been multiple people cosplaying and acting the part.

Okay, on that note, I needed to watch the SuperCon panel.

I stacked my bed pillows, then jumped on top. My nerves

calmed as the soft clouds enveloped me. Then I slid my laptop over and opened the Internet. I looked up SuperCon. Oh dear, dangerous move.

"VIGIL & ANTE STUDIOS ANNOUNCES—"

I jerked away and put my hand up to block it. I made it this far without spoilers, I wasn't going to ruin it now. Peeking through squinted eyes, I clicked on the website and went over to their recorded panels.

And there it was.

I grinned, then clicked on the video.

SAFEGUARDERPANELS.COM
TRANSCRIPT OF THE VIGIL & ANTE STUDIOS PANEL AT SUPERCON

Xavier Jay: Hello, SuperCon!

[Crowd cheers]

Xavier Jay: Thank you for coming out here today for the VIGIL & ANTE Studios Panel.

Noelle Atkins: I think you mean camped out all night. I saw that line, and it started forming last night. (laughs) You guys have been waiting a *long* time.

Person: (shouts) Totally worth it!

Xavier Jay: I sure hope so. In case you wandered into Hall H by mistake—which you probably didn't because there isn't even standing room—my name is Xavier Jay. You probably know me as the director of *Illuman* and *Project Safeguard*. Or you know me as Agent Liam Blake, director of VIGIL.

[Crowd cheers]

Noelle Atkins: And I'm Noelle Atkins, or, in the VIGIL & ANTE Studios movies, Agent Ver Larsen. Behind us is the wonderful cast of the original *Project Safeguard* movie. Can you believe we have all the OGs except for Cloaker? Let's give them a hand!

[Applause and cheering]

Xavier Jay: They really are as cool as the superheroes they play. Right over there we have Ruth Saxon, known on-screen as Commander Vigil.

[Ruth Saxon waves]

Noelle Atkins: Ooh, I'm excited to introduce this next one. Mason East, our very own Illuman.

[Mason East blows kisses to the crowd. Audience screams.]

Xavier Jay: Mason, I think you have a few fans here.

[Audience laughs]

Noelle Atkins: Next up, please welcome Alison Zhao, or, the superhero you know and love, Degree Surge.

Xavier Jay: Is that everyone, Noelle?

Noelle Atkins: I think so.

Xavier Jay: Wait, there's still an empty seat. Did we forget someone?

Noelle Atkins: I've heard a rumor going around that we're supposed to make an announcement.

Xavier Jay: I haven't heard that rumor! Did you hear it from a reliable source…or…?

Noelle Atkins: (nudges him playfully) Xavier, I got it from you.

Xavier Jay: Ohhhh, that announcement.

[Audience laughs]

Noelle Atkins: Are you guys ready to meet our special guest?

[Crowd screams]

Xavier Jay: I don't think they're ready. Do you think they're ready?

Noelle Atkins: No, I don't.

[Crowd cheers louder]

Xavier Jay: Now they're ready. Will you do the honors?

Noelle Atkins: Absolutely! Without further ado, please welcome...Rhett Wickford!

[Rhett enters, and the crowd goes absolutely wild. Rhett sits down.]

Noelle Atkins: That's right, everyone, the beloved villain from the first *Project Safeguard* movie, Ironfall, is coming back.

Rhett Wickford: It's true. My character, Ironfall, is back again. Get excited, everyone.

[More applause]

Xavier Jay: (gasps) Does that mean there's a third *Project Safeguard* movie?

[Standing ovation as the crowd goes wild again]

Noelle Atkins: It sure does! And to celebrate, we have a very special teaser trailer for you. But first, let's have our panel answer some questions.

Oh. My. Gosh. A third *Project Safeguard* movie. And that trailer. And Ironfall coming back? He was such a good villain in the first movie.

A thrill electrified me.

And Sam was *upset* about this? Let's be real, he was just upset at being wrong.

I wished I'd been sitting in Hall H in person. To think that before watching this, I considered the possibility that these fictional characters were real. I shook my head, laughing at my own stupidity. Would a real-life supervillain be on a comic con panel? No. It was ridiculous.

My gaze made its way back to the bright colored poster. When the new movie came out, I could get another one and—

Those eyes. Ironfall's distinct brown eyes with a sliver of icy blue. They sent another round of chills creeping down my spine.

Not the excited goosebumps from earlier, but the kind you get when something doesn't sit right.

The people following me had that exact haunting look. They used Ironfall's MO. His eyes were the one piece of reality whose appearance he couldn't manipulate. Oh my goodness, why was I still thinking about this? I'd just watched the new teaser trailer for crying out loud.

I sighed and rubbed a hand over my tired face.

Something about this kept nagging my gut.

It was probably a group of overzealous fans playing a prank. My fingers flew across the keyboard as I searched for "Ironfall cosplay contacts." The first link was another article about Ironfall making an appearance in the new movie. The rest of the relevant results that popped up looked...fake. The brown didn't have multi-dimensional golden flecks, and the blue was flat and almost too blue. I looked through a few different websites, and even found a sketchy pair on an even sketchier marketplace site. But all contacts modeled after his character appeared costume-y.

They didn't have the same depth...the look that someone was always thinking.

I looked back at the movie poster, stomach flip-flopping.

Was Ironfall real?

Rosemary, this literally makes no sense.

Someone else would have noticed him waltzing down the crowded NYC sidewalks, right? Forget the other plot holes in this outlandish conspiracy "theory." If someone else saw him, maybe it was true. But wouldn't his fangirl army have discovered this a long time ago? They'd be lined up to marry him if he existed. Not to mention the rest that wanted nothing more than to beat him in an epic battle.

Instead of turning back like a logical human being, I typed in "Ironfall sightings NYC."

The Internet slowed and slowed. I refreshed the page that wouldn't even load. Nothing came up. Absolutely nothing. The screen was blank. There were no conspiracy theories, Tumblr blogs, or even Area 51 gibberish. For the first time in history, Google itself was speechless.

My chest tightened.

Could Ironfall *actually* be real?

Then the WiFi shut off.

Oh. My. Gosh.

Not to sound like a conspiracy theorist here, but could the government censor Google searches?

It was probably the result of fans breaking the Internet in search of new leaks and hidden easter eggs.

Still, I had to know the truth.

Or maybe it was a coincidence. That was what a logical person would say.

I had to know if my theory was correct. So I grabbed the laptop, stuck it in an empty backpack, and ran out of the room. Mom leaned over the counter, now sliding chopped carrots into a salad bowl. "I'm going to Starbucks to do some research."

Her knife came down on a tomato. "Fine." She hadn't heard me.

"I'm going to Starbucks."

Still, she didn't look up. "Whatever you need to do." Was she still upset from earlier, or was she too focused to pay attention? I readjusted my backpack, then stepped closer.

"Love you, Mom," I whispered.

She nodded, but said nothing. I pressed my lips together, then turned to leave.

Hopefully she "remembered" giving me permission.

I ran down the stairs and maneuvered through the people on the sidewalk until I got to our friendly neighborhood Starbucks (a.k.a. heaven on earth). The place was narrow but deep and always smelled of freshly ground coffee beans with a little bit of chocolate, warmness (definitely a smell), and fresh pastries mixed into a perfect blend. The tan walls and incandescent lights made this place feel even cozier.

People chatted quietly around me. It was busy for an afternoon, but I was able to claim a lounge chair near the back wall. This was good because no one but me would be able to see the insane things I planned on googling. Who looks up if a *fictional* thing is real? Apparently, I do.

I opened my MacBook lid and connected to the free WiFi.

I searched the same thing as earlier. Once again, Google blanked. I gulped, glancing around, then back at my computer. There weren't cries of outrage, so the WiFi clearly hadn't gone out.

Why wasn't there a single thing about this on the Internet?

"Is someone sitting here?"

I froze.

That sounded like...

I glanced up from my laptop and gasped. Could it really be?

Tall, broad shoulders, deep reddish-brown skin, small space between his two front teeth. He looked exactly like Xavier Jay, the actor who played Agent Liam, the director of VIGIL. But... he was at SuperCon a couple hours ago. Now he wore a different outfit, one more like his character would wear. Okay, that was weird. Xavier was very into casual clothes, but the character he played wouldn't be caught dead without a tailored suit.

"Someone sitting here?" Xavier motioned to a black lounge chair to my right.

SuperCon was still going on, right? Didn't he have a meet and greet to be at or something? My stomach lurched as fangirl mode kicked in. "N-no." Then I lowered my computer screen so he wouldn't see the blank Google search.

He sat down and leaned back like he was going to relax there for a while.

Act like a normal human being.

Oh my gosh, my favorite actor was right next to me. Should I say hi? Should I destroy my computer because of my very stupid search history?

Why was he here instead of SuperCon?

Don't look at him, you'll look like a stalker.

I opened my computer again and pulled up Twitter. Why? I didn't know because I didn't even have an account, but my starstruck self couldn't think of anything else. I stole another glance.

Wait, why was he staring at my computer screen? He leaned forward, almost as if he wanted to talk to me. Why the heck would *the* Xavier Jay want to talk to me?

"What are you doing here?"

Wait, what? What was *I* doing here? What was *he* doing here? "Umm...nothing really." I gestured toward my laptop. I was clearly on Twitter. Which, yeah, I see how that was suspicious because it was the login page, but still. I couldn't admit to one of my favorite actors what I was really here to do. Because he'd probably recommend therapy. And a life. (He would be right about the last one because VIGIL & ANTE Studios was basically my life.) "Are you really Xavier Jay?"

Had I really watched a video of him speak at a con only minutes earlier?

"You tell me," he said.

What was that supposed to mean?

"Oh, uh, sorry, you just look like him," I said, my voice fumbling for a hold on reality. Okay, but this had to be him, right? They even had the same gap in their teeth. Would a doppelgänger have that? I didn't think so.

"I should," he said. "Because I am."

I gulped, then nodded. My eyes were probably bulging out of their sockets because I was now in the confirmed presence of one of my favorite actors. "Oh." It was all I could think to say.

"But you must have come here for a reason."

"My Internet went out, so I came here."

"What do you know about VIGIL?"

TRANSCRIPT OF THE INTERVIEW PROCEEDINGS WITH [REDACTED]
SOME NAMES AND LOCATIONS REDACTED FOR SECURITY
INTERVIEW CONDUCTED ON MAY 20
LOCATION OF INTERVIEW: [REDACTED]
CASE #: [REDACTED]

AGENT LIAM BLAKE: When did you first see Rosemary Collins?

[NAME REDACTED]: January 3.

AGENT LIAM BLAKE: Can you elaborate on that?

[NAME REDACTED]: I was in [LOCATION REDACTED] standing on the sidewalk nearby her family's apartment. She came outside and never even glanced my way. Not that it mattered because I was disguised.

AGENT LIAM BLAKE: You mentioned [LOCATION REDACTED]. That an area you go to a lot?

[NAME REDACTED]: No. I went there specifically to watch her.

AGENT LIAM BLAKE: So you admit to stalking her.

[NAME REDACTED]: You already know what I did, Agent Liam.

AGENT LIAM BLAKE: It's funny actually, because Rosemary has in her report that you started following her on January 15.

[NAME REDACTED]: That was only when I started dropping hints.

CHAPTER 3

I scooted away from Xavier Jay. "Well, VIGIL is in all of your movies, so..." Okay, okay, I had to remain calm. Well, as calm as I could when being questioned about a supposedly-fictional superhero organization by a guy who looked exactly like the actor who played one of my favorite characters. So yeah, not calm at all. Was everything in the VIGIL & ANTE Studios franchise real?

"I think you know what I mean." Xavier spoke in an even tone.

"That's mysterious." Oh no, did I just say that out loud?

He leaned forward. "What can I say? I'm a man of mystery." The clothes. The walk. The talk. It lined up with Agent Liam's character, not the bubbly personality of charismatic actor Xavier Jay. Xavier was king of witty remarks among the cast, but this time he didn't sound like he was joking. He sounded serious.

"Okay..."

"What's your name?"

"Rosemary," I said. "I'm kind of a huge fan."

Xavier's eyes glittered, the only thing in character about him. "Really?"

I nodded, forcing a smile to try to lighten the mood of whatever was happening right now. If VIGIL wasn't real and the Internet was watching this, hopefully they wouldn't label me as stupid quite yet.

But just like that, his seriousness returned. "A big enough fan to come out here and research our little movie studio, right?"

I sucked in a breath. He walked up when my screen was blank. How could he have known my Google search? I glanced around. There didn't seem to be any cameras, though a few people kept glancing our way as they whispered to neighboring customers. They probably recognized Xavier. I looked down at my computer. Still on Twitter. How did he—? "You weren't sitting here when I—"

"It's part of the job."

"And what job is that?"

He narrowed his eyes. "The kind that wanted me to come talk to you."

"That's still vague, even for a movie star under a strict contract." My eyebrows knit together.

"It's clear you know something, and I'm the one they sent to find out before it leaks," he said.

"Like...spoilers?"

"Sure, we'll go with that." Why did it seem like he was implying something more than spoilers? Was VIGIL real? It was impossible, yet the movie star before me wouldn't give me a straight answer.

And the people following me... "Wouldn't I get a cease and desist letter or something? Why send a literal A-list actor?" I said.

"Spoilers before the publicity stunt would really put a damper on things." Publicity stunt like Ironfall? It would fit with the new movie coming out. Yet something still didn't sit right.

"Does this spoiler have anything to do with someone parading around with Ironfall eyes?" It sounded crazy saying it out loud.

Xavier remained emotionless. "I can neither confirm nor deny." Wow. Even more vague.

"There's a guy who keeps following me. This is going to sound crazy, but please, hear me out. Each time he has a different face, yet his eyes remain the same. Brown with a sliver of blue in the left one."

Something in his face shifted, but I couldn't put my finger on what. "Has he tried contacting you?"

"No, unless you count me taking his order as 'contacting me.' Why is that important? Is he the leak?"

"Something like that. Which face was he wearing?" That's an odd way to phrase it.

"It had to be multiple guys all wearing these super realistic contact lenses. I've seen tons of cosplays, and none of them could pull off Ironfall eyes like these people could."

He leaned forward. "And these men have only been tailing you?"

I nodded. Just thinking about it sent a wave of panic through me.

He pressed his lips together. "And you're sure?" Would he say that if this was just a publicity stunt?

"I know it sounds silly. It's probably nothing, but I'm a little freaked out that people are stalking me."

"It's not silly," he said.

"What is this about?" I gulped. He wasn't making me feel better about having a stalker.

"Excuse me, sir, are you Xavier Jay?" An adorable little girl with skin a shade darker than Xavier's and two curly dark brown ponytails stood a few feet away, rocking back and forth on her toes.

I clutched my clammy hands together.

Xavier's seriousness melted away as he stood up, grinning. The switch was instantaneous, even though he still wore the character's signature suit and red tie. His shoulders loosened as the smile spread to his eyes. "Why yes I am. What's your name?"

"My name's Elizabeth!" the little girl giggled. "I can't believe you're here! You're so amazing!"

"You know, I think you have the makings of a superhero. How would you like to be an honorary junior Safeguarder?"

Her eyes widened. "Really?" she gasped. "I'm so excited for your new movie! Mommy let me watch the trailer five times."

She held up five small fingers, grinning. "And now I get to meet you!"

More and more people looked over in our direction, wide-eyed at the A-list movie star before them. Whispers became louder as people started shouting his name. I shrank into my seat, but they were all looking at the fabulous, handsome, and personable Xavier Jay.

He turned briefly to me, then held out his hand for me to shake it. I dumbly pointed to myself. He nodded, chuckling. I stood and shook his hand, but something was wedged between it. A business card?

He dropped my hand, leaving me with the paper. My eyebrows knit together. I looked down at the card.

A phone number. That was it.

Adrenaline shot through my abdomen. Why had he given me a phone number? Who was it for?

Xavier turned away, knelt down beside the girl, and took a picture with her.

"Will you take a selfie with me?" said a woman.

"Ooh, can I get one too?"

"Oh my gosh, I can't believe you're here!"

"*Project Safeguard 3* is gonna be amazing!"

"I love you so much!"

I glanced up at Xavier again, though with the growing crowd, I could barely see him. My breathing remained shaky as I packed my computer, got up, and backed away. Two screaming girls, both wearing fandom t-shirts, leapt to where I just was, eager to be a mere six feet closer to *the* Xavier Jay.

Yesterday, had I known that today I would meet one of my favorite actors, I would have died. But now I only had more questions. What was the phone number for? How did VIGIL & ANTE Studios know to send someone to me? Why did they send *the* Xavier Jay?

And the fangirl side of me kept nagging. What if VIGIL was real?

I turned the business card with the phone number in my hands. The ink glinted as the paper tilted. I twirled it once, twice.

Did Xavier Jay want me to call the number? Why was every answer he gave evasive? Was I in the middle of VIGIL & ANTE Studios' next publicity stunt? What did this have to do with those cosplayers stalking me?

I ran my fingers over the card once more before dialing the number. Who would even pick up? The marketing department? Legal? Oh no, was I about to be sued? But all I did was look up whether or not it was real, which I suppose might mean that it was real. That would be ridiculous, though.

Clearly I was missing something.

The phone rang a final time.

"Please enter your security code," said a robotic female voice.

I blinked. What? He didn't give me a security code. I looked over the smooth card once more. The phone number was the only thing written in glossy black letters. No name or instructions.

"Umm...this is Rosemary Collins," I said. Maybe that would work? "Xavier Jay gave me this number."

"Please enter your security code."

I sighed. Was there a code in invisible ink or something? And did film companies really have this tight of security?

"To leave a voicemail on this secure line, press nine."

Umm, I guess this was the right thing? I pulled the phone away from my ear and pressed the number.

"Agent Liam Blake, Director of VIGIL. Leave your name, number, and security code at the tone." There was Xavier's voice. He didn't sound like he was joking, but hadn't he said on a panel once he sometimes changed his voicemail to be something official from VIGIL as a joke?

I gulped.

The tone sounded.

"Hi, this is Rosemary Collins from Starbucks. I'm really confused about what's going on and why you gave me this number, but I thought I'd call anyway." I hung up the phone. Wow. Way to go being awkward on a voicemail. This whole thing was messing with my head, not to mention I might have left a message on a legit movie star's personal voicemail.

Oh, wow, that just sunk in.

There were so many strange things about that whole thing. The *VIGIL-is-real* narrative kept gaining evidence, but it was crazy.

Project Safeguard and the other VIGIL & ANTE Studios movies were just that: fiction.

By definition, it couldn't be real.

TRANSCRIPT OF THE INTERVIEW PROCEEDINGS
WITH IRONFALL
SOME NAMES AND LOCATIONS REDACTED FOR
SECURITY
INTERVIEW CONDUCTED ON MAY 20
LOCATION OF INTERVIEW: **[REDACTED]**
CASE #: **[REDACTED]**

AGENT LIAM BLAKE: Did you have a plan at this point?

IRONFALL: No. I just knew that I needed Rosemary.

AGENT LIAM BLAKE: When did you have everything worked out?

IRONFALL: I knew I had to go after my father's device again. I couldn't pull it off with one person, but with two, we had a chance.

AGENT LIAM BLAKE: What's your dad's name?

IRONFALL: You already know.

AGENT LIAM BLAKE: All right, I'll ask this. Explain how you initially found out about the device.

IRONFALL: I went through my dad's old files.

AGENT LIAM BLAKE: He let you do that?

IRONFALL: Well, he wasn't exactly there to stop me.

CHAPTER 4

JAN 21 – 5:23 P.M. EST

The breakroom door burst open as Sam tumbled inside, smoothing down his wrinkled uniform. I jumped back. "Oh, Rosemary! I think I know what's going to happen in *Project Safeguard 3*."

I sighed, heart drumming against my ribs. "Hi. Sorry, you scared me."

Ignoring my comment, he thrust back his 2000s pop star hair and launched into his spiel. "Okay, so I read the coolest theory, right? You know how they—?"

I stifled a groan. "Sorry, I can't stay and talk. I have to get back to work."

He raised his hands in mock surrender, but his twig-like figure still blocked my exit. "Okay, but hear me out. Ironfall, right? He's bad. He's hilarious. He's wicked smart. Anyway, I think he's going to team up with the Safeguarders." He grinned. "I mean, it makes sense if you really think about it. Besides, if he becomes an honorary Safeguarder..."

I blinked, stepping back. "That's *not* going to happen." If this guy had whatever was happening to me happen to him, his brain would explode.

"Why not? It's a great plan!" He narrowed his green eyes. "Unless you have something against the best villain ever."

Yep, that's it, sort of. "I don't have time for this right now, I'm sorry, Sam."

"Guess someone's a fake fan then." He crossed his arms. "Come on, Ironfall and Illuman on the same side? Comedy *gold*."

"We'll just have to see," I said. "Really, I do have to go back to—"

"Oh, also, you have a friend who came to surprise you," he said. "Tall dude, blond hair. Wears Ironfall contacts. Calls himself 'Nolan,' which sounds fake, but I've been watching a ton of crime shows to distract from the void of waiting for the next VIGIL & ANTE Studios movie."

My stomach dropped.

Ironfall. Or whoever was posing as him.

"Wait, is he that guy who was stalking you?" His eyes glittered. "Okay, wow, I definitely need to chill on the true crime documentaries."

I stepped past him, gripping the door handle. "It's fine. Just don't talk to him." I looked around the room, double-checking we were the only ones here. *He's dangerous.*

"Then is he your ex or something?" he said, chuckling. "Not that it's any of my business."

"Uh, I guess you could say that." I sucked in a breath. I didn't know who he was, but I was too scared to share that. "Just stay away. Far away." I gulped, turning away before Sam involved himself further. The last thing I needed was someone else in danger.

My knees felt weak as I stepped out the door. Just as I opened it, someone shoved past, jostling me against the wall. I looked back, blinking in awe. Who needed a break that badly? I looked behind me but only saw the back of his head.

Was he new? I didn't recognize him.

But the stalker guy was waiting just outside, so I made my way into the seating area. It was almost empty. My gaze flitted to a family sitting at a corner booth where a man and a woman sat with their two young kids. The man rubbed ketchup on his nose and showed it to the little girls. They giggled, the older one leaning over until she almost fell over.

If only I could warn them that there was something weird going on. I didn't know how to describe it beyond that.

I looked around. Would "Ironfall" detect my nerves?

Then I saw him standing at a high table, elbows resting on the tiled top.

Leave now. Run. Get out. There's still time.

My stomach turned. I couldn't do this. My chest tightened and fists clenched. I looked around, turning to go back to the breakroom. Back to work. Anywhere but here.

More laughter. I glanced back at the family in the corner booth. If I didn't speak with whoever this was, would he take it out on them?

"Hello."

I froze. I'd seen *Project Safeguard* enough times to recognize Rhett Wickford's smooth Ironfall voice anywhere. What was going on? And why didn't my previous stalker's voice sound like that? Slowly, I turned on my heel, trying not to shrink back. Deep breath. "Can I help you?" Did my voice shake? My toes scrunched as if anchoring my body to the ground.

The man with Ironfall's eyes leaned forward, making his muscular shoulders seem even broader underneath his tight black t-shirt. The curved jaw of his disguise relaxed, lips slightly parted. Yet his menacing eyes flashed as they scanned my appearance. Everything seemed purposeful and calculated.

I glanced back at the kitchen. "C-can I help you?" Deep breaths.

"Tell your boss you have a family emergency, then come with me," he said in a low tone.

My feet burned to move, to run away. Everything inside churned with angry tingles surging from my stomach to my constricted chest.

Another glance back. One of my co-workers took someone's order at the register, and another practiced a tap dance for his next Broadway audition. Was Sam still safe in the breakroom? They had no idea some crazy terrorist was here.

I gulped. "I'm sorry, who are you?"

He stepped closer, staring down with his endless brown and blue eyes. "Tell me, who do you think I am?"

My pulse quickened as the world seemed to go silent. "I don't know." But he certainly wanted me to think he was a fictional character.

"I'm surprised and a little disappointed." His lips tipped upward. "I wasn't trying to hide it." Was he claiming to be Ironfall?

"Oh," I said. Because I didn't know what to say to that.

"Anyway, we have business to discuss." Everything I'd eaten that day threatened to come up.

"Business? I don't know who you think I am, but I don't have *business* to talk about," I said.

"I'm sure you'll change your mind once I tell you that I've planted a bomb inside your pocket," he said.

My stomach dropped as I thrust my hands in my pockets. My fingers brushed against something cool. He was telling the truth.

How did it get there?

The man's eyes flashed. "You're not in any danger if you follow my exact instructions."

"Okay, okay, I'll come with you," I said, putting my hands out as if the gesture would stop him from making a rash decision. "I just need to talk to my boss." And Xavier Jay. But no, he would find out and blow this place to smithereens.

With a hand pressed against my stomach, I ran back to the kitchen.

"Rosemary, you okay? You don't look so good." Sam slapped a slice of cheese on a burger patty.

I shook my head. *There's a bomb in my pocket.* "I'm sick. Where's Mary?" It wasn't totally a lie.

"Breakroom," Sam said. "Hey, *feel better.*" He winked.

My eyes widened. "Really, I do feel sick." Still clutching my churning stomach, I stepped into the small room. My boss stood drinking a cup of water.

"Mary, I need to go, I'm really sick," I said. "Sorry."

The older woman looked up, lines of concern creasing her forehead. "Sure. Go home and get some rest."

"Thanks." It came out breathless. *Save me.*

Her eyebrows scrunched together. "Is something else wrong?"

"No," I lied, pressing a hand to my abdomen once more. Then before she could ask more questions, I grabbed my stuff, put on my coat, clocked out, and met the man pretending to be Ironfall.

My stalker waited near the exit. My breath caught. He nodded, that mischievous grin tugging at his lips. I glanced back at the kitchen. Please, catch my silent cry for help.

Loud cries now came from the family in the corner booth. The little one screamed in her mom's arms as the woman patted her back. The dad and older girl stood, collecting the family's trash.

Would he—?

My legs screamed to run in the other direction.

I followed him outside onto a busy sidewalk. So, so many people going about their business, heading home after another day of work. Rush hour traffic clogged the streets.

"Ironfall's" eyes bored into my soul. "Walk with me."

Five horns honked, seeming to answer for me.

For a long time, he said nothing. We fell into step with one another as my mind raced in the silence. Should I say something?

What did he want to hear? Movie Ironfall was cunning, impressed when people managed to get one step ahead of him. Was this guy the same?

I gulped.

"Okay, I'm here, now deactivate the bomb," I said, clutching the small device in my hands. The loud New York City ambiance made it difficult to hear the device's soft ticking, but I seemed to feel it in every bone of my body.

He nodded. "After you hear me out. A deal is a deal, after all."

"Who are you?"

"Ironfall," he said.

"As in, the movie..." My voice trailed off. Would he be offended if I called him a villain? "Character."

He grinned. "The one and only." Okay, he was officially insane, but I wasn't about to argue with the guy who planted a bomb on me.

"I saw your eyes," I said, shoving down the lump in my throat. Not now. I straightened, pushing back my shoulders. The frozen air didn't ease my burning lungs.

"That's what I wanted you to see." Cold. Even-toned. Stone-faced. His haunting eyes pointed dead at the black suit walking in front of us. Though his hair and face looked nothing like Rhett Wickford, the actor who played him, the way he strode down the sidewalk did.

"Right. Of course you did." I dug my nails into my cold, sweaty palm. "You've been following me for a few days now." *Don't set off the bomb.*

He looked at me, face now softening. "I'm glad you noticed."

Phew. Apparently, I'd said the right things. Anything to keep this delusional psychopath from setting off a bomb.

"How do you feel about joining my team?" His voice was low, barely audible over the invasive city ambiance.

"You're...Ironfall," I said. "I've seen the movies. You don't need a team." If he wasn't really Ironfall, he'd think I believed him, and if he was, he was good enough to take out the Safeguarders by himself. Why did he need me?

Frozen white flecks tickled my face.

"Ironfall" stopped in the middle of the sidewalk and turned to me. People funneled around us. "Good observation. But right now, you're the only person who can help me take over the country. You, Rosemary Collins, are the last piece of the puzzle." He paused, stepping closer as the crowd enveloped us. "Together, we could be villains."

I gulped. No, no, no, don't do it. I couldn't do it.

But the bomb in my pocket said otherwise.

Run.

"I did mention your parents would suffer if you refuse, right? What were their names? Marie and James Collins, I believe. Lovely names. Your mother is an interior designer, right? And your dad works at the bank. I'd hate to see them hurt." His eyes narrowed.

My breath caught. *No.* "What makes you think I care about them?" My fist clenched so tight my knuckles turned white. He couldn't see my fear.

"I've seen how they treat you, how they cast you aside. People with parents like that only crave their love more," he said. "So, yes, you care about them, and would do anything to please them. Especially something like saving their lives."

I knew they loved me in their own way. Still, I couldn't let him know how much leverage he had. "What's stopping me from going to the police?" I dug my fingernails into my hands.

He smirked. "You're too smart for that. They'd never believe you. And remember, I know who your parents are." He didn't know I had contact with Xavier Jay. "If you help me, you and your parents are perfectly safe," he said. No, I was playing with fire.

A chilling breeze cut through my coat as my chest tightened.

Would they believe me if I told them someone was crazy enough to claim they're a fictional character? Then again, after my encounter with Xavier Jay the other day, who's to say this wasn't real? Oh no, we're back to that again.

I needed more information.

"What makes me so special?" My hands quivered as I waited for an answer.

"That's for me to know and you to find out." Ironfall thrust his hands into his pockets. Why did he dodge my question?

"Wouldn't you rather have someone who's a computer whiz or a black belt or something?"

"You're what I need right now. A hacker will come later. Are you in?"

For all his outlandish claims, he didn't seem as unstable as he should. That scared me more.

Mom. Dad. I didn't have a choice. At least not right now. "Yes." The lives of my parents were in the hands of a seventeen-year-old girl.

"Ironfall" smiled, his eyes brightening. "Great. Meet me tomorrow after school at this address. I look forward to working with you." He took one hand from his jacket and reached to take mine. It was warm and dry. The corners of a piece of paper dug into my hand. "Remember, no one can know about me." His signature eyes flashed. "Now, as promised, I'll deactivate that bomb."

I handed him the small device. He fumbled around with it before slipping it into his own pocket. Then he drew back into the crowd and was gone.

I looked down at a small, business card-sized paper with an address typed, no, written on it. The handwriting was pristine.

Tomorrow after school.

Tears pricked my eyes as I folded the note.

This didn't feel real.

TRANSCRIPT OF THE INTERVIEW PROCEEDINGS
WITH IRONFALL
SOME NAMES AND LOCATIONS REDACTED FOR
SECURITY
INTERVIEW CONDUCTED ON MAY 20
LOCATION OF INTERVIEW: **[REDACTED]**
CASE #: **[REDACTED]**

AGENT LIAM BLAKE: When you revealed your true identity at Ketch-A-Burger, what was your impression of Rosemary?

IRONFALL: You know, extremely smart, pretty, a little unsure of herself, so full of potential.

AGENT LIAM BLAKE: Potential you could exploit?

IRONFALL: Well, I wouldn't use that exact word.

AGENT LIAM BLAKE: What word would you use?

IRONFALL: Tap into, I suppose. But you're right, I didn't have the purest intentions. I did use her.

AGENT LIAM BLAKE: Did you trust her?

IRONFALL: Would I have threatened her parents if I trusted her?

CHAPTER 5

JAN 22 – 3:33 P.M. EST

Following the stalker's instructions was stupid, but I wasn't about to risk my parents' lives when the group of Ironfall impersonators already planted a bomb on me.

I should have risked it and gone to the police, but the man was right. Would they believe me? And what if he found out? He knew things about me. What if he bugged my phone?

The address he gave me led to an old brick building with graffitied boards covering the windows. The front doors were faded black with splotches of gang signs painted and repainted on them. Was this really just an abandoned building?

I couldn't do this. I couldn't do this. But I couldn't turn away either.

Inhale. Exhale.

I opened the door and stepped inside.

My body electrified. Okay, not so much an abandoned building. It smelled somewhat like a Bath and Body Works, a mixture between just having been cleaned and having at least fifteen different air fresheners plugged in. The concrete floor, though dingy, seemed dirt-free. Patches of missing puke-colored paint exposed old drywall. In the center of the large room rested a bulky, beat-up particle board reception desk.

On the other side of the room, a man pounded against the boxing bag. I could just see the side profile of his face. The dark hair, the square-ish cut jaw everyone swooned over, the signature brown eyes, and the iconic black-and-silver super suit. This guy was the exact image of Rhett Wickford. The guy who played Ironfall in the movies.

Or maybe this was actually Ironfall? No, that was impossible.

Punch after punch. He hammered the bag again and again. Again and again. Arm muscles flared through his tight suit. His leg whipped around and struck with so much force the punching bag almost hit the ceiling.

My chest tightened. Whoever this was, he was good. I stepped inside and shut the door behind me, leaning against its rough wood, running over the events of the last couple days in my head. Multiple faces lined up with Ironfall's shapeshifting abilities. My interaction with Xavier Jay was weird. Xavier's voicemail box was strange. The WiFi shut down when I googled whether or not VIGIL was real.

What if all of it was real? What if the movies existed to cover it up? What if real life superhero battles were branded as publicity stunts?

I couldn't breathe.

It was impossible.

Fiction was fiction. Reality was reality.

And the reality could be that a random person with Ironfall's eyes had been stalking me, and got me to join his little terrorist thing by sticking a bomb in my pocket and threatening my parents.

The man with Ironfall's face glanced my way and slipped something from his sleeve. The projectile hurtled toward me, but I couldn't move. Couldn't even flinch. It thwacked into the door, inches from the side of my head.

I glanced over, trying to slow my pounding heart and ragged breathing. A blade. In the door. Oh my gosh.

He tried to kill me.

How?

Why?

Frozen.

Petrified.

He tried to kill me.

I looked again at the small knife protruding from the wall. It gleamed in the florescent light.

The next thing I knew, Ironfall launched his body toward me.

Adrenaline took over, but I was still too slow. Before I could put up any sort of defense, Ironfall slammed into me, throwing me on the ground. Wham! Breath knocked out of me. I wheezed, but nothing came back in. Nothing.

No air.

With a sudden rush, oxygen flooded in. I gasped and gasped, trying to counteract the hammering in my chest.

He's going to kill me.

He's going to kill me.

I thrashed against his firm grasp, but still, he pinned my arms to the ground. His face, filled with concentration and coldness, was so close to mine.

Still, I tried to wrestle out from under him. "Please don't kill me. Please please please I didn't do anything." I didn't talk to the police.

Mom and Dad. Don't hurt them too.

My breathing became more rapid until my vision started to blur. But he hadn't done anything to me. Still, I was dying.

The pressure let up on my arms. What was he doing?

"Sorry about that, I had to see what we have to work with," he said. I still lay on the floor, breathing too fast, curled up.

Because I couldn't get enough air.

Because my chest was too tight.

Because he was too much.

Because he tried to kill me.

"Are you okay?" I opened my eyes to look up at him kneeling beside me. "It was only a test. You're going to be all right." His eyebrows scrunched together with concern. It was all an act.

No, I wasn't going to be okay.

"Breathe slowly. Count to five," he said soothingly. There was nothing to do but what he said. Inhale. One. Two. Three. Four. Five. Exhale. One. Two. Three. Four. Five.

Over the next few minutes, my breathing slowed, and Ironfall sat beside me, holding my sweaty hand in his icy one.

He helped me to my feet. "Would you like some water?"

I shook my head. I wanted out of there. "What the heck were you doing?"

"I needed to see how good you are at combat and surprise attacks." He said it like it was the most normal thing in the world. Why on earth would he do something like that?

Tears stung my eyes. "Well, clearly I'm terrible at it," I said. Why choose me? I had no skills. No powers, if that part of all of this was even real. Unless he wanted to torture me.

Or he was desperate. What did he need so badly?

"That's okay, because I'm going to teach you."

"No, no." I pulled myself to my feet. "I—I need a minute." I was still shaking uncontrollably, but I stumbled away, out of his reach. Then I bolted for the door. "Ironfall" wrapped his arms around my waist, lifting me into the air. I screamed. Kicked and scratched wherever I could. "Let me go!"

"Calm down."

"I don't know what's going on or who you really are, but put me down."

"Not until I'm sure you won't run."

Blood rushed through my ears as tears filled my eyes. Comply. It was the only way.

"Rosemary. It was just a test. I had no intention of harming you."

"You threw a knife at my head!"

"I never miss."

"How am I supposed to know that?" I screamed. "And still it seems like it breaks every safety rule!"

"You've seen *Project Safeguard*, you know I don't miss."

"You're crazy!" This guy—whoever he was—was out of his mind. Why did he think attacking someone was okay?

"Look, I'm going to put you down now. Promise you won't run?"

I was getting as far from here as possible. "Y-yes." I still breathed too hard. Still thrashed around.

"I don't have to remind you what will happen to your parents if you go to the police, do I? You know what I'm capable of." Ironfall or not, I wasn't taking any chances.

He may be crazy, but he was smart. Somehow I didn't think the police alone could stop him before he...did something to Mom and Dad. I gulped.

I shook my head. "Leave them out of this, please. I'll do anything. I won't run, I promise."

"Thank you," he said. "Can't have you run off before I teach you to defend yourself." Now he chuckled. Why was the mood suddenly so light?

He slowly set me back on my feet, then turned me toward him.

"You know what, take the day," he said. "We won't get much done with you shaken up like this. I have some other villaining to do anyway."

I blinked, jerking out of his grasp. "You're letting me go?"

He nodded. "Tomorrow, same time. There won't be surprises like this waiting for you, so don't worry."

Oh, I was worrying. I backed away, trying to keep my knees from giving out. "I'll be here." *Please don't hurt my parents while I'm gone.*

"See you then, Rosemary."

I stepped away. "See you," I said. "Ironfall." My voice broke at saying the name.

What was going on here?

JAN 22 – 5:23 P.M. EST

"Please enter security code."

I groaned. "Hello? This is Rosemary Collins?"

"Please enter security code." Something clicked.

"Agent Liam Blake speaking." I think I just died. Everything was leaning towards VIGIL being real. From the first voicemail, to the changing faces, to Ironfall's face. I shivered at the thought of it, but took a deep breath to keep myself calm.

"This is Rosemary Collins, we spoke the other day. I don't know who else to turn to, and I think you probably gave me your phone number for a reason, so that's why I'm calling you." Wow, way to seem cool. Now he thought I'd never talked on the phone before.

"I—I think Ironfall just attacked me." I didn't want to admit it, but it was weirdly the most plausible explanation. That Ironfall was real. The Safeguarders were real. VIGIL was real. It was crazy. Crazy. But the things that happened, the things I'd seen. It was the only thing that made sense. "I think this is real. All of it."

And that meant Xavier Jay was really Agent Liam Blake, Director of VIGIL.

"Are you in a secure location?" he said.

"My mom's in the other room, but I don't think she can hear me." Even then, I spoke in a whisper. "I need help. He tried to kill me. I don't know what to do."

"Ironfall is real, and he's been following you." Oh my gosh, it was real. "In an hour, a car will meet you in front of the Starbucks where we met. Black Mercedes."

JAN 22 – 6:37 P.M. EST

"You can sit up front, you know." A woman's voice. I caught a glimpse of her face in the rearview mirror of the black Mercedes.

Oh. My. Goodness.

Jana Anthony, the actress who played Agent Manda.

I blinked my awe away. *Okay, Rosemary, now is not the time to fangirl.* "Oh, right." Of course I would make a fool of myself in front of another one of my favorite actors. Characters? Agents? Quickly, I switched to the front seat.

"Sorry," I said. She looked just like Agent Manda. Thick black hair pulled into a tight braid, dark skin, black leather jacket. It was as if she stepped right through the silver screen.

Her face was stone. "I can tell." Ouch. Her character was like this in the movies. Sometimes she would let out her soft side and become the team's mom, but that rarely happened. She was more of a kick butt now, talk later kind of person.

My muscles relaxed, because for the first time since I figured out Ironfall was real, I felt safe. Maybe it was because Manda never lost a fight.

She didn't talk at all during the car ride. I tried hard not to stare, because that's just creepy. (But is it okay when your favorite characters are maybe kinda sorta coming to life?)

An hour later, we arrived at, well, an apartment complex. It wasn't what I was expecting. Maybe I expected a penthouse or something more fit for a movie star. The gray brick cracked and crumbled, and it appeared to be completely...normal.

Jana opened the center console and pressed a small green button. The hood of the car shifted so the paint was dull and splotchy. How did that even happen? Until this moment, I thought *Cars 2* invented that technology.

Oh my gosh. VIGIL was real. The woman before me *was* Agent Manda. Xavier Jay was Agent Liam Blake. And my stalker was Ironfall.

It was real.

VIGIL.

All of it.

Manda parallel parked the car on the left side of the narrow, one-way street.

"Come with me," Manda said, getting out of the car. We really were the same height! A few years ago (when the doctor told me I'd stopped growing), I looked up the height of the entire VIGIL team. At 5'7", Manda was the only agent my height. And I may or may not have freaked out about that. Just like I did now.

I glanced around at my surroundings. This place was kind of shady, with rotting trash swept to the side and people loitering. I stepped closer to Manda. An older man, whose skin was so pale this was probably the first time he'd ever been outside, winked at me. Eww. No.

Manda kept her eyes dead ahead and strode to an apartment. The rickety wooden door didn't seem like it would keep out anyone who banged his fists hard enough against it. VIGIL must use the same technology for this door that they did with the car. At least, I hoped that was the case.

She sank back on her left hip. "Manda Kelly." Her voice almost sounded like a computer.

The door opened and oh my gosh. I stepped into another world. Panels—some frosted and some not—separated the small space into several rooms. Monitors covered the right side like you'd see in the TV section of Best Buy.

But most notable was the iconic "V" symbol etched into the wall. "V" for VIGIL.

Everything, it was all real. My breath caught.

I wasn't crazy.

A long table stretched from front to back of the room with more shiny computers resting on top.

At the end of the table stood Noelle Atkins. *The* Noelle Atkins. As in the actor who played Ver Larsen: the coolest hacker/scientist from the VIGIL & ANTE movies. She looked just like she did on screen with her signature blonde curls and pink manicure.

Oh. My. Gosh.

VIGIL was real, and in front of me was Agent Ver herself.

Well, I certainly hadn't expected this to happen today. Or ever.

For a moment, I couldn't move. Ver didn't have powers, unless you count a genius level IQ, but she was still one of my favorite members of the VIGIL team.

The door slid shut and Manda slipped off into another room. I just stood there trying not to appear starstruck.

Ver looked up from her computer and brushed back a strand of short, platinum blonde hair. "Hi, Rosemary. Welcome to the VIGIL headquarters. I'm Agent Veronica Larsen with VIGIL. But you can just call me Ver." She spoke fast but enunciated each word. "Like Agent Liam and Agent Manda, my job is to aid and oversee our powered operatives, but you probably already know that from the movies. If you've seen them. Have you seen them? Most people have, but I feel like I have to check. Anyway, I'm glorified tech support." Her eyes flitted to the left corner as she smiled.

A squeal rose in my throat, and that distinct jittery fangirl feeling stirred in my tight chest. "Hi!" Okay, I failed at not sounding crazy. "Sorry, I'm just a *huge* fan." A huge fan who was freaking out inside because meeting the "character" was 100000% cooler than meeting the actress. Okay, wait, did I really respond to her question with "hi"?

"Really?" Her voice squeaked a little at the end, like it does in the movies whenever she's happy. "Sorry, I always get excited when people like my character…or who I am in real life? Yeah, I'm still confused how to refer to all of this. Clearly I don't introduce my real self to people often." She waved a pen around in the air. "Our actor personas are false identities to cover for our VIGIL work, if you didn't catch that."

"It's an honor to meet you." Apparently, I couldn't think of anything smarter to say. Sometimes I thought about what I would say if I met one of my favorite actors, but those daydreams never included this specific scenario.

"Whoa." This was nothing like the enormous VIGIL

building in the movies, but it was still *awesome*. "It's real. This is all real. How is it real?"

"The headquarters isn't as elaborate as the Studios portrays, but we have a ton of science and computer equipment, along with all the surveillance stuff." Ver motioned to the wall of monitors, grinning. "We aren't lacking in the gadget department, which I am thankful for."

I turned around, taking everything in. It was so...modern and sleek. And the home of my favorite characters. "This is the coolest thing." I grinned.

Xavier—I mean Agent Liam—stepped out from behind a frosted divider, tall and commanding with his pressed suit and red tie. Manda followed close behind. Liam, Ver, and Manda together in their top-secret headquarters, standing in a circle around a table, no less. This was the stuff fanfiction was made of, and I was *here* for it (literally and figuratively).

VIGIL is real.

"How are you even real? How does the whole world not know about this? You couldn't hide something this big from the public," I said.

"With the right packaging, you'd be surprised how many people believe something is fictional. The first publicity stunt was an accident. One of our operatives, who you know as Illuman, lost control of his powers in a public place, so we swooped in with the cover story of an upcoming movie. No one even questioned it." Agent Liam crossed his arms.

"Even though he literally started glowing? There was no evidence the marketing stunts were real?" I whispered. "What about the *Project Safeguard* stunt? Weren't people in danger?" It was insane. And brilliant.

"The battle was contained to a government-owned building, no civilians in direct danger. So, yes, we can effectively keep something this big from the public, and we will for as long as the cover holds," he said.

There was a secret world of superheroes everyone fangirled over, but no one knew was real. Except me.

"You told me on the phone that Ironfall attacked you," Agent Liam said, changing the subject. He pressed his fingertips into the desk.

I nodded, glancing back at the door as if Ironfall stood there. "And he threatened to harm my parents if I didn't cooperate. He made me join his team—I don't know what to do!"

Agent Liam pressed his lips together. Ver moved closer, placing a hand on my shoulder.

"I'm so sorry, Rosemary," she said. "What can we do to help?"

I shook my head. "I don't know. He'll find out I asked you guys, a-and he'll hurt them." He'd know if I went to the police. Would he know about this too?

Agent Liam crossed his arms, leaning back on Ver's desk. "Does he trust you?"

"Definitely not," I said. "But I get the sense he doesn't trust anybody."

Manda's dark braid fell over her shoulder as she pressed her knuckles into the wood. "What do you mean he attacked you?"

Ver moved away, murmuring about still listening as she worked.

The blade.

Blurry vision.

Suffocating.

His arms pinning me down.

I gulped, shoving it away. I couldn't think about that now. "He th-threw a knife, and it stuck into the door, right here." I held a finger close to the side of my head. So close. Too close. *No air.* "And then he was..." I looked down. "He pinned me to the ground. I-it's kind of a blur. He said it was a test to see if I could fight."

"Can you fight?" Manda leaned into her left leg as she cracked her knuckles.

I shook my head, rubbing my hands together. "I thought he

wanted me dead." He would if he found out about this meeting. Too late for that now.

"Was he wearing his real face?" Agent Liam said.

"Yeah," I said. "Well, if he really looks like Rhett Wickford."

"Have you seen him use his powers like in the movie?" Ver piped up with a grin, which quickly melted away. "I'm asking purely for scientific reasons, of course. I'm kind of a superpower nerd along with a regular computer nerd."

I just shook my head.

Ver pressed her lips together. "Interesting. I've only seen him actually control reality once. Well, by that I mean I watched it through a computer screen, while the Safeguarders were doing the hard work, but whatever. From what I've seen, he usually only plays with his own appearance. Which is kind of copying Cloaker's more limited power, but that's a story for another time. Anyway, no one has ever seen him shift anything's appearance. He always does it in secret."

"Getting back on track, how long have you worked for him?" Agent Liam said.

"Two days," I said. "I don't know what to do. I don't want him to order me to kill someone or to do something bad. But I'm out of options. He'll hurt my parents if I don't do what he wants."

"He's managed to stay off VIGIL's radar since he escaped after the real-life events of *Project Safeguard*. Either he's slipping, or he needs something."

My stomach turned. "What exactly do you mean by that?" Hopefully my voice didn't sound as weak as it felt.

"A supervillain has been stalking you, and you're not dead. That's not his style," he said. "Which must mean one thing."

Fingernails dug into my flesh. "Are you saying he needs something from *me*?"

He nodded. "Tell me about your powers."

"I don't have any," I breathed. "I'm no one." There was nothing special about me, and not in the way that every teen "chosen one" says at the beginning of a film. I really was just a high school student obsessed with superhero movies and Broadway musicals. *Nothing* more. Goodness, I couldn't even get over my fear of acting on stage, even though I'd secretly dreamed of it for years.

"None?"

I shook my head.

"Interesting." He folded his hands, pressing his lips together. That's it? *Interesting?* What could Ironfall want from me? Unless he needed something badly enough to settle for an average teen. Even then, why choose me? "So why you?"

"I don't know," I said. "All I know is he did. I thought he was just insane, but now that I know he actually is Ironfall..."

"He obviously chose you for a reason," Manda said, breaking her silence. "He needs you for something."

There was a short pause, filled with the clacking of Ver's keyboard.

"How do you feel about being a double agent?" Agent Liam crossed his arms.

Manda raised her eyebrows, the first show of emotion since I'd met her. "Liam, this is a terrible idea."

"Being director means making tough calls. I don't need your permission."

She crossed her arms. "But we're part of a team, and being a team means no secrets."

"There are exceptions when you're the director, Agent Manda," he said. "We've seen how Ironfall operates. Sending someone undercover to *observe* is the best option."

"And I've seen him tactically. Liam, she has no training." Manda's large brown eyes turned hard, dark brown forehead creasing. "You can't seriously be considering this. Cloaker can shift to look like her and go undercover as usual while we get Rosemary and her family to safety." Yes, yes, please do that.

"Cloaker's on a mission." Agent Liam straightened his tie.

"I didn't know about this," Manda said.

"It's classified."

"More important than a seventeen-year-old girl's life?"

A lump formed in my throat. The only sound was of Ver's typing.

"I can't take him off that mission." He always began a movie an intimidating leader, but by the end he was more of a father figure. But this...this was next level.

"What's so important about it?"

"Everything," he emphasized. The passion in his voice...the almost desperation. It was almost as if he wanted to say but he knew the fate of the world rested on its secrecy. "You're just going to have to trust me as the director."

"Then we put her and her family in protective custody and find Ironfall ourselves." Manda stepped back as if she was ready to pace the room.

"It has to be her." He tightened his suit's red tie. "We don't know why he needs her or even what kind of threat he has on her parents. She's going in whether she's with us or not, and we need the information. We know nothing about Ironfall and his organization. It might only grow in his absence."

I shrank away, touching the desk lining the walls. Heat from mounted monitors warmed my back. Rising tension could be cut with a knife. The clacking of Ver's keyboard wasn't helping. I could only watch as they discussed my fate. They were the experts. They were my heroes. I swiped at my eyes. I couldn't cry. Not here.

I pressed my lips together, frozen.

"I don't like this." Manda shook her head.

"Are you going soft, Manda?" Agent Liam said. I shivered.

Manda's eyes darkened. "No. And you know I have your back, but I want this done right. Ironfall took out dozens of fully trained CIA agents. He nearly killed Commander Vigil." Watching them argue in person was so much more intense than in a movie.

I gulped, gripping the desk as if it anchored me to the world.

"Wouldn't Ironfall find out?" I said. "He'd see the meeting spot or whatever."

Keyboard clatter halted. "That's the beauty of technology. All you have to do is log on to our encrypted database and enter your reports. Think of it as writing a journal entry of what happened that day," Ver said. "And who knows, maybe what you write will be featured in the next VIGIL & ANTE Studios movie." She brushed a chin-length curl behind her ear.

My chest tightened. "I-it's such a big risk," I said. "How long would I have to be undercover?"

"Some deep cover missions last months," Agent Liam said. *Months.*

Manda glared. "And require special training."

"But he wouldn't suspect her," Liam said. "That's where we have the advantage."

"He already attacked her, and she couldn't defend herself." Manda raised her hands, shaking her head.

"Ironfall did say he would train me," I said, my voice soft. Why was I advocating to go back in?

Agent Liam smiled. "See, there."

"I—I don't know if I can do this," I said. "If he finds out, I can't protect myself, much less my *parents* from him."

"So he doesn't find out," Agent Liam said. "If he succeeds he won't spare you or your family."

He had a point. "I don't know." Still...

"The moment you become expendable, you're gone," he said. "This is our window to stop him before he gets that far."

I couldn't do all the things Ironfall would want me to. I couldn't watch him take over the world. I couldn't watch my parents suffer. I couldn't live with it.

Ver stepped away from her computer, offering a smile. "Remember, we'll *always* be here to back you up."

"You've seen the movies," Agent Liam said. "You know what he's capable of. His powers are similar to Cloaker's, but he can literally manipulate reality around him. His eyes are his only tell."

"That's what I'm afraid of," I said, lowering my gaze. What if I slipped?

"But you've also seen what *we're* capable of," Ver said. "We have your back."

She was right. They would. They always did. "What's stopping the Safeguarders from going in and taking him out? They're the superhero team who did it in the first *Project Safeguard*," I said.

Manda still glared.

Agent Liam sighed. "They're unavailable to us. Real life isn't like movie magic."

Was I willing to risk everything to stop Ironfall? If I didn't, who knew how many would die, including my family. Could I be responsible for that?

A lump rose in my throat.

I knew my answer.

"I'm in," I said. "I'll be your double agent." This was a terrible idea.

"Ver, set Rosemary up with the database then take her home."

She nodded.

Manda shot another glare at Agent Liam. "Let me at least show her how to defend herself against a knife."

He nodded.

"Won't Ironfall be suspicious if suddenly I know how to defend myself?" I said. I needed the training, but right now, keeping all of this a secret was in the forefront of my mind. He couldn't know. I couldn't let anything slip.

"She's right. We need a seamless story. I'll contact the CIA." Manda nodded, and they left, leaving me alone with Ver.

Her fingers flew across the keys. "So, welcome to the team. How are you feeling?" She paused. "It's all overwhelming, I know.

Crazy enough on its own, and then you add the fandom part on top."

"I think I'm okay," I said, trying to smile. "Or I will be, eventually."

"Were you a big fan?" she said, hands still clacking on the keyboard. How could she pay attention and type at the same time?

I grinned, a little bit of fangirl bubbling to the surface. "Are you kidding? You guys are my life."

"Really? I mean, that's not surprising; there are some crazy fans out there. Not that you're crazy," she laughed.

"To be honest, if I knew my mom wouldn't yell at me for being irresponsible, I'd have taken off work to livestream the SuperCon panel."

"No way," she said.

"Yep. My co-worker was hoping you'd announce another Illuman movie," I laughed. "You should have heard the grief in his voice when that wasn't the case."

She grinned, blonde curls bouncing with each bob of her head. "You know now that you're an agent I can legally give you spoilers for *Project Safeguard 3*, right? You never have to wait again. Unless you want to. Do you want to?"

I shrugged. "Actually, I hate spoilers. Though now, they might be kind of helpful so I can figure out what's even going on. Speaking of that, actually, who plays Ironfall? There's no way he could play himself."

"Don't worry, we have Cloaker play him," she said. "We grabbed some DNA off Ironfall when he attacked New York so Cloaker could make himself look just like him. Then, using a little movie magic, Cloaker was able to play both himself and Ironfall. It's also the reason you never see him and 'Rhett Wickford' together at comic con or on the red carpet. So...fun fact."

"You guys have this fake fandom thing down." I shook my head, grinning. "Imagine if the whole world knew about this." My chest hammered just thinking of it.

"Which is exactly why they can't," she said, pressing her pink lips together. "Enough politics go on here without people knowing the U.S. has superpowered individuals, which is a whole other topic."

"How has no one found out yet? I mean, you'd think there would be talk of it somewhere. Suspicions, even."

Ver only shrugged as if this was old news, barely even an issue. "Yeah. There was some speculation after Illuman's incident. The one where we announced our first movie? Anyway, I was able to come up with verified social media accounts dating back a few years. Then we sent out a press release about the movie. That shut down most speculation. The movie premiere a couple months later sealed the deal."

"How did you do it so fast?" Obviously they could in movies, but in real life? Crazy.

"I'm just that good." She tilted her chin up in mock conceit. "Just kidding. It definitely wasn't all me. Except the hacking, of course. That was me."

"Pretty sure your hacking skills are the most unrealistic part of this whole thing. And that's saying a lot," I laughed. Superheroes: real. Supervillains: real. Characters: real.

She seemed so excited. "Well, I am a fictional character, you know."

"I guess you get a pass then. But how did you keep the whole *Project Safeguard* a secret? There was an actual *threat*," I said.

"It was in such a populated area that there would be chaos if they knew. Since it happened in the secret CIA base, also known as the most fortified building in New York, we figured we could contain everything with minimal citizen risk. No need for extra danger."

"So you drafted another press release."

She nodded. "While they saved the day from the bad guys, I saved the day from the exposure of everything we worked to protect." Then she looked up from her computer, grinning. Yeah, she'd better take credit for her wizard hacking skills. "I notified the news of the second publicity stunt, and everything mopped up nicely, other than Ironfall getting away and Commander Vigil's injuries, but whatever."

"Wow." It was all I could say.

"I know our cover is over-the-top, but it's necessary. If the public knew about superheroes, so would our enemies. Then wars would be fought by people who can destroy entire cities. Nowhere would be safe. Also, I'm sure you've seen other movies where the public is scared of powered people and all that. Anyway, it's super fun to know this is real when people love the story so much."

People who loved the story. Like me. My heart leapt. "This is so cool."

"Okay, speaking of cool, I think you need a code name." She spoke so fast I barely had a moment to process what she said.

"Like a superhero name?"

"Exactly."

"But I don't have powers."

"Who cares? You're a VIGIL agent now, or you will be when you get home, so you deserve one. Besides, who knows. There might be a movie about you someday." She winked.

My eyes widened. "A superhero movie? About me?" Oh my word, that was the dream. The acting. The red carpet. The *memes*.

She glanced over, a mischievous gleam in her eyes. "I was thinking more of a trilogy."

A trilogy? Ooh, this was serious. "What superpower would they give me?"

"I don't know yet. Maybe you'll be more of a Black Widow type, known for your spy skills instead of your powers. Lots of cool action moves," she said. "Epic fighting, and some Cloaker-like espionage."

"So another Agent Manda?" But did she have a trilogy? No. (Though that's a crime because she's pretty awesome.)

Ver laughed. "I don't think anyone can beat her in a fight, so no. But you being the spy that takes down Ironfall? That's gonna turn some heads. Maybe deception is your superpower."

"I don't know about that," I said. "I'm not a liar."

She touched my shoulder, becoming the big sister every fan knows her as. "I admire that. But we need it to beat him. I believe in you, and Liam knows what he's doing. Trust him when he says this is the best plan."

I gulped. "Okay."

"Now let's find you a superhero name." She grinned. My very own superhero name. I could almost see the opening credits now.

Who did I want my pretend superhero self to be? Something detached from everything right now. The opposite of my situation.

Truthful. Selfless. *Light*.

Wait. I got it. "What do you think of Stardust?"

TRANSCRIPT OF THE INTERVIEW PROCEEDINGS
WITH IRONFALL
SOME NAMES AND LOCATIONS REDACTED FOR
SECURITY
INTERVIEW CONDUCTED ON MAY 20
LOCATION OF INTERVIEW: **[REDACTED]**
CASE #: **[REDACTED]**

AGENT LIAM BLAKE: So you got started training her?
IRONFALL: Yes.
AGENT LIAM BLAKE: Rosemary has in her report that you attacked her. Why?
IRONFALL: Well, I needed to test her reflexes and teach her to always be on guard.
AGENT LIAM BLAKE: Did you hurt her?

IRONFALL: No.

AGENT LIAM BLAKE: Was your intention to harm her?

IRONFALL: Never.

AGENT LIAM BLAKE: What were the results of your experiment?

IRONFALL: She clearly had no training. Slow reaction time, uncoordinated struggle. She dissolved into panic.

AGENT LIAM BLAKE: And how did that make you feel?

IRONFALL: Is this an interrogation or a therapy session?

AGENT LIAM BLAKE: Rosemary said you then helped her through her panic attack.

IRONFALL: That is correct.

AGENT LIAM BLAKE: Could you elaborate on why?

IRONFALL: She was my teammate, and I needed her fully functioning for us to succeed.

AGENT LIAM BLAKE: So you care about those on your side?

IRONFALL: Not at that point. My reasons were purely selfish.

CHAPTER 6

JAN 24 – 2:53 P.M.

"You look terrible," was the first thing Ironfall said to me the next time I saw him. The first time I saw him as a double agent. A spy. *I'm doing this for Mom and Dad.*

I ran my fingers through my hair that desperately needed washing. "Thanks, you too." Hopefully he didn't ask why, because I couldn't tell him he was the villain in my nightmares.

I set my bag down on the clean floor of his hideout.

"You're not still shaken up from yesterday, are you?"

I couldn't look up at him. "Well, you *are* the one who nearly blew my head off." That was too harsh. For now, I needed to choose my battles if I wanted to survive and protect my parents.

"It was a controlled exercise that won't happen again," he said.

Like I could really trust the word of a supervillain. "Right." My voice trembled. Did he know how terrified of him I was?

He stepped closer. "Soon you will be able to defend yourself against attacks of any kind." Attacks like his when he inevitably found out I worked for VIGIL? My throat squeezed. Why choose me in the first place? "Today we're going to start with..." He trailed off. "Something else is bothering you."

Yes. So many things. I looked away. Could he read my face that easily? "It's...how did you find it? This place, I mean." I couldn't breathe. Hopefully that would satisfy him.

Then Ironfall laughed. He *laughed*. It didn't seem to be in a condescending way, but in a genuine way. Which was a weird disconnect considering he was a *supervillain*. "A million dollars can get you just about anywhere you want to be."

"One *million*? Do you have someone else backing you?"

"Yes." He drew a small blade out of his sleeve and flipped it in the air, catching it again. "My knife."

I flinched, picturing it embedded in me, blood oozing from the wound. "What?"

"Assume someone else's identity, disable alarms, take down cameras, kill the security guards, plant false evidence, and you fully fund your operation." He slipped the knife back into place. "Really, most people could do it."

"Wow..." I couldn't breathe again.

"What can I say?" He smirked. "You ain't never had a friend like me."

I blinked. "Wait, did you just reference Aladdin?"

"I'm a theatre kid at heart." Again, he flashed that boyish smile everyone swooned over. I refused to swoon (mostly).

For the moment, I didn't have to pretend anything. "I love theatre too."

"Favorite musical?"

"*Anastasia*."

"I'm more of a *The Lightning Thief: The Percy Jackson Musical* kind of guy," he said. "They'd better get back on Broadway soon or I might have to threaten someone." *Threaten someone*. I gulped, trying not to shrink back. What was I supposed to say to that?

"That seems excessive."

Ironfall stepped closer, narrowing his eyes. "But effective." Was he talking about me or the producers?

No more threatening people or sneaking up behind them with daggers. I shuddered, remembering the feeling of a knife whooshing by my ear.

"Have you ever considered being in a play?" I said. Oh my gosh. Wait. I knew how to get a breather from his stifling presence and those scary knives of his. Finally audition for the school play. Which terrified me, but not as much as being with Ironfall.

His expression turned darker. I resisted the urge to run. "What are you getting at?"

"I want to audition for the school musical," I said. He'd veto this for sure. "I was planning on it before..." I motioned toward him. "Before a certain fictional character showed up."

The tips of his lips curled upward. "Sounds like fun. This isn't you getting away from me, is it?"

My eyes widened, and I quickly shook my head. "No."

"Well, sometimes in order to take over the world, you need to be an actor." He winked. "What play is it?"

"*Beauty and the Beast.*" Why was I doing this to myself? Listening to musicals was my thing, but acting on a stage terrified me. Even though I dreamed of it at night.

"I've listened to that soundtrack a few times," he said. "Maybe I'll audition with you."

No. I forced a chuckle. "I thought you were busy trying to take over the world."

"*We* are, Rosemary, but I don't want you to have all the fun without me," he said. Code for: I don't want you out of my sight.

Him around all those students. All those people who had no idea he was real. Who had no idea he could massacre them with the flick of his blade.

"Hang on a second, how old are you?" I hadn't thought about his real age before now... "Are you even high school age?" There could be a lot of issues with this real quick. I backed toward the front door.

"I'm eighteen, though just barely." He shrugged. "Why do you ask?"

"So when you first attacked New York in *Project Safeguard*..."

"I was fourteen, yes. I made myself look older so I seemed more credible." His eyes flashed. "In conclusion, I am not a creeper who tries to get in with the high schoolers."

"I'm glad," I said. Yeah, that would be...gross. "Can I ask you something else?"

His eyes glimmered. "So eager to learn all the answers."

"Why do you need my help? I'm just...me."

"That, my dear, is one of those secrets I will keep to myself. The real question is, what are yours?"

I gulped. "I keep mine close too." What threats would force me to spill them? My hands clenched together as I stepped back toward the door again. I glanced back, looking at the mark where his knife hit yesterday.

"Oh, I'll find them out." He stepped forward as his devilish grin disappeared. "I always do."

My stomach turned. Not if I could help it.

I'm an agent of VIGIL.

"Now, let's start your training," he said. "I'll make a warrior out of you yet."

JAN 25 – 4:45 P.M. EST

"Okay, so there's this meme about Ironfall and Illuman making a YouTube channel, and I think VIGIL & ANTE Studios should seriously consider it." Sam sat on the breakroom bench, sipping from his Illuman-themed water bottle.

Not this again. "You do?"

He grinned. "Think about it though. It seems out of the box, but not any more than their other publicity stunts. They'd break the internet."

"Yeah, probably." Imagine if Sam knew both characters were real. Guess what would *really* break the internet. I folded my hands, standing to my feet. My break still had ten minutes.

"Imagine the pranks they would pull together. Like, come on." He slid along the bench, reaching his arms out. "Oh, also, at some point Agent Liam interrupts them in full-on dad mode and sends them to timeout."

I sighed, looking away. "I think you're forgetting that Ironfall is the *villain*." He was the last person I wanted to talk about right now.

He shrugged. "Yeah, I know, but still, he would be amazing as a Safeguarder."

"Is that a good idea?"

He shrugged, readjusting his Ketch-A-Burger baseball cap. "Also, question. What is up with you and that friend who met you here last week?"

My eyes widened. "Uh, nothing." Nope. Absolutely nothing.

"Yeah, I'm not convinced."

"There's nothing happening between us, really." *So stop talking about him.*

"I can see right through you, but whatever. Tell me about him. He's an Ironfall cosplayer isn't he? I can spot them from a mile away." Now Sam's grin grew even wider.

"Yes, that's it. He's an Ironfall cosplayer." And definitely not the real Ironfall. My hands clutched one another. Sam couldn't find out. "And that's all you need to know."

"I've never seen eyes that real though. I mean, I've seen real eyes, obviously, but never Ironfall contacts that realistic."

Oh dear. "He gets them custom-made," I said. "But yeah, cosplay is his thing." So is murder but we don't talk about that.

"Aren't the ones in the movie CGI?"

I shrugged. "Come on, it's not like Ironfall is *real*." I chuckled, but my heart throbbed against my ribcage. He couldn't learn the truth.

"That'd be pretty great though." Sam grinned. "And then I'd get to meet Illuman. All I want is to be best friends with him."

"Don't we all?" How had people not figured out about VIGIL & ANTE Studios?

People rarely believe something presented as fiction.

Sam had no idea what he was so close to. *Stay away.*

"But seriously, what's going on between you two? You seemed a little jumpy when he came in," he said. "Wait, that weird guy following you had Ironfall eyes too, right? Are they connected?"

Now he was getting too close. "Really, Sam. I can't talk about it," I said. "Please leave it alone."

"Why does that make me want to ask more questions?"

"I believe your exact words were 'I watch too many true crime documentaries.'" I side-eyed him. Stop. Digging. Ironfall made it very clear no one could find out about him.

"Okay, yeah, but you never know who's going to turn out to be a serial killer. If this guy has red flags..."

He had giant ones. Like Olympic stadium-sized ones. It's called being a supervillain. "I know, Sam. Don't worry about it."

"Wouldn't want anyone killing the only person who gets my VIGIL & ANTE Studios obsession." He winked.

My blood chilled. "Wouldn't want anyone killing you either." But I didn't say this as a joke. He needed to stop asking questions.

"Awww, I'm touched." He clutched his hands to his chest.

"Don't let it go to your head," I said. "And by that, I mean this is none of your business."

"Okay, fine." He raised his hands in mock surrender. "I won't ask any more questions today. But that won't stop me from stalking his social media."

"I don't think he has social media."

"Maybe not, but if there's an online trace, I'll find him."

"Somehow I doubt it."

"You underestimate my computer skills," he said. "I was the one who background checked some random guy my sister was talking to and found out he was actually wanted by the FBI."

"Really?"

"Okay, not really, but I've won state in robotics every year since seventh grade, and last year the quarterback of our football team bullied me into changing his grade in biology. Dude's a jerk. Joke's on him though because my hack was so good I made it look like he did it. He got expelled and everything. Proudest moment of my life."

"That was you?" I was surprised the whole world didn't know. Maybe this guy could keep a secret when he needed to.

"Yeah," he said. "No big deal or anything. My point is, I have other ways of finding out who this dude is."

My breath caught. "Right. Just don't, please. Stay out of it."

"No promises."

JAN 28 – 3:15 P.M. EST

Okay, so I've never sung in front of anyone. Ever. It's usually only me, my reflection, and probably the neighbors that have to put up with me through the walls. Sorry, guys.

But the amount of times I've practiced "Defying Gravity" in my bedroom should have prepared me for this. Except I felt like I was going to throw up. The last thing I wanted was to puke or freeze during my audition. Or a weird combination of both.

This is literally your dream. Stop freaking out.

I had my audition papers in hand as I walked into the school auditorium. It was empty except for Mrs. Rodriguez up at the front. She smiled as she moved toward me. "Rosemary Collins, I'm glad you finally decided to audition." I was only doing this as procrastination. "Do you have any singing or acting experience?"

Motion caught the corner of my eye. My breath caught. Ironfall. He wore the same disguise as when he visited my work. He smiled and waved as his shaggy blond hair fell into his eyes. Chills. My muscles clenched.

"Rosemary?" Mrs. Rodriguez said.

Right. "Sorry, could you please repeat the question?" I said breathlessly.

"Do you have any singing or acting experience?"

I glanced at Ironfall again, then tried to focus back on the theatre teacher. "No."

"All right, I'd like for you to sing something for me. It can be anything you'd like," Mrs. Rodriguez said.

I knew which song: "Journey to the Past" from *Anastasia*. My voice shook as I sang the opening lyrics. But slowly, it grew stronger until I *felt* the words of the song. You know that breathless feeling during a musical where you feel every single voice inflection? That was what happened. I sang my heart out. I felt Ironfall watching me, but suddenly it melted away. "*...on this journey...*"

The song ended with a high note and my arms raised into the air, just like in the videos I'd seen of Christy Altomore singing it.

Breathless.

For a few moments, everything was gone.

And I loved it.

"Thank you, Rosemary. Now I'd like for you to read this script for me." She handed me a small packet of crinkled papers, then looked up at Ironfall. "Are you auditioning too?"

He looked at me. "Yes. I'm Nolan, by the way."

"Nice to meet you, Nolan. Would you mind reading the part of the Beast? Rosemary, dear, please play Belle," Mrs. Rodriguez said. Just my luck that we would play each other's love interests.

Wasn't this kind of the same as being an undercover agent? Uh, well, if I was being honest with myself, not really. Acting had a lot less at stake.

Mrs. Rodriguez handed Ironfall another stapled script.

I couldn't bring myself to look at him after that, but I felt his eyes boring into the side of my head. Then, he started saying his lines, but he wasn't merely saying them. He lived them, breathed them. I glanced over at his softening face. For a moment, I didn't see Nolan or Ironfall, I only saw the Beast. The way he said "Belle" and the way he looked back at me when he wasn't glancing at his script made me...made me believe just for a moment that all of this VIGIL and Ironfall stuff was a dream, that I was really Belle, and he my Beast.

It was my line. Everything around us—the stage, the chairs, Mrs. Rodriguez—drifted away. The script ran out of pages all too soon, thrusting me back into reality.

I ripped my gaze from Ironfall and turned back to the director. Her brown eyes shifted from Ironfall, to me, then back to Ironfall. I stole a glance at him, but he was looking at me, so my gaze dropped. For once, I could become someone else without fear of my true self showing through for Ironfall to see. A fresh breath filled my lungs.

Mrs. Rodriguez straightened her large glasses. "Thank you both for auditioning. Nolan, I still need to hear you sing, but Rosemary, you may go."

I nodded. "Thanks for putting up with my audition."

She shook her head, laughing. "I did more than put up with it, I'll tell you that much."

I went a little way up the row of chairs and turned around as Ironfall started singing "Friend Like Me."

This man could both be so normal and yet so lethal. The lyrics of the song were correct. I'd truly never had a friend like him.

If I could call him that.

I left to avoid seeing him until the next day, but he still caught up with me.

He nudged my arm. "Your acting ability wasn't something I predicted." I glanced at where he touched me and forced a smile.

"Is that a good thing?" My chest tightened.

"Yes." He nodded. "It's a very good thing."

Please let this sound natural. "I guess I'm more of a hidden actress," I said. "Meaning I memorize my favorite plays and recite them to myself in my room."

His gaze snapped to mine as his eyes lit up. "I never thought I'd meet someone else who does that. Though to be fair, anyone I could ask is dead before I get the chance to."

I gulped. "That'll do it. Why do I get that honor of being the one who isn't dead?"

Ironfall straightened, angling his body so our shoulders no longer touched as we walked. "Secrets, Rosemary, secrets."

I pressed my lips together. Now wasn't the time to push it. Because then maybe he'd ask about my own secrets. "Right, sorry."

"We're not friends."

"No, of course not." I could never consider him a friend. Not when he threatened my family.

"We're allies, both getting something out of working together. You do your part, and your parents live."

My blood froze at the mention of Mom and Dad. "I already gave you my word." Not that it meant much these days. Lying got easier with each one told, and I hated it.

Then his countenance shifted, replaced with his boyish grin that spread to his never-changing eyes. "Real people react better than blank walls, don't you think?"

"Yes," I said. As did acting with someone else. It was like… magic. "Though I'm sure my neighbors can hear me sometimes. Not sure they appreciate it as much as Mrs. Rodriguez seemed to."

"Depends on whether or not you hit the high notes."

I side-eyed him. "That's debatable."

"Then they might hate you." He held up his hand, pinching his forefinger against his thumb. "Just a bit."

I didn't know how to react to that, so I just smiled.

FEB 5 – 5:24 P.M. EST

I leaned across the table and to scoop up dirty napkins some *respectful* customer refused to throw away. Did people not realize Ketch-A-Burger was a fast-food place?

"Hi." Ironfall's smooth voice broke through the harsh din of the chain restaurant.

I jumped back, balling my hands into fists. He stood just behind me disguised as Nolan with his shaggy blond hair and oversized brown t-shirt.

"Don't sneak up on me like that," I hissed. "I clock out in a couple of minutes." What was he doing here? I planned to meet him at the hideout after work, but I didn't need an escort.

I glanced around. The restaurant was near empty right now. Except...oh no. Sam stepped out from around the register, rag and cleaner in hand. My eyes widened as I stared daggers into him. Go away. Don't notice Ironfall.

"And who might that be?"

I rubbed the table harder until the rag squeaked along the surface. "My co-worker. He never shuts up about the VIGIL & ANTE Studios movies."

"Well now, that's ironic. Maybe I should go talk—"

I whipped around, gripping his arm. "Please don't, he's already suspicious of your eyes. Or he mentioned it once."

Ironfall's lips turned up into a grin as his eyes gleamed. "He is?"

"I told him you're an Ironfall cosplayer." I glanced over. Sam hadn't walked over here yet, he was too busy clearing off a messy table in another section. I looked back at Ironfall, who still appeared amused at the whole situation.

"And what did he say to that?"

And suddenly Sam was there, holding a tray covered in trash. "I said we should meet sometime. Us fans have to stick together, am I right?"

Well, crap.

"My name is Sam." He set down the tray and stuck out his scrawny hand. This child was a twig compared to the towering human gym (and Ironfall wasn't even the most jacked guy) next to him. "Illuman is by far my favorite, but I love all the Safeguarders. You're an Ironfall guy, right?" Bro, you have *literally* no idea.

Ironfall shook his hand. "Is it that obvious?" He smirked, side-eyeing me.

"It's your eyes that gave you away. I mean how genius is it to casually cosplay with only a pair of contacts?" He waved his cleaning rag around as he spoke. Would Ironfall decide to kill him because he was sort of close to his secret?

Maybe, maybe not. But I needed to get him away. I couldn't risk it.

Now, everyone even a little close to me stood in the impact zone.

"Super cool. Look, it's time for me to clock out, and I really think we should work on our *group project*." I grabbed Sam's tray and thrust it into his arms.

"Yes, our project." Ironfall turned to me.

"Ah, a dreaded group project. My condolences," Sam said.

I stepped back. "Well, we should go."

Ironfall nodded, turning away. I followed.

Sam grabbed my arm. "Okay, he's clearly more than a crappy group project partner."

"That's all he is." I turned to him, avoiding his eyes. "I promise." Stop. Asking. Questions.

He raised an eyebrow. "You sure this guy isn't the one stalking you before?"

My stomach flipped. "Why are you so invested in this? You're the one who called *me* paranoid." He had to believe me.

"Yeah, then Mr. Ironfall Eyes showed up. He's giving me weird vibes. If you ever don't feel safe around him, call the police."

"It's not that deep, Sam. I promise you, he's not a creep." I had to convince him otherwise. I looked at Ironfall, whose forehead creased. Oh no. He knew. "Just drop it."

"Just don't want to see anyone getting hurt. Gotta be a superhero when I can," he chuckled. "This is where you thank me profusely by agreeing to cover my shifts whenever I ask."

I rolled my eyes. "Yeah, that's not gonna happen." Good, change the subject.

"Dang it. Really thought that'd work," he laughed. "Still, I'm keeping my eye on him. Couldn't find anything about him online, even on the dark web. The guy's a ghost."

I swallowed, nodding. He needed to stop asking questions. "Well, we should go work on that project." Then I stepped away, taking a deep breath before turning toward Ironfall. He started for the door, and I followed. A rush of chilly air and city noises flooded inside as we left the restaurant.

I stole a glance at Ironfall. His lips were pressed together, forehead creased in concern. "He's close to the truth."

My blood ran cold. "N-no he isn't. He's just a superfan. There are lots of those. Believe me, he just watches too many true crime documentaries. Probably thinks half of New York is made of serial killers."

He raised his eyebrows, a smirk replacing his seriousness. "Do I scream serial killer to you?"

Yes. "Nope, just supervillain."

"Glad to hear it." He laughed.

Okay, he seemed to be in a better mood. Maybe I could convince him Sam didn't know anything. "I promise, Sam's harmless. Just won't shut up about VIGIL & ANTE Studios." I rolled my eyes.

"He's jeopardizing the mission."

"How can that be jeopardizing the mission?" I said. "He doesn't know anything."

He thrust his hands into his pockets. "Don't worry about it. You have your first combat lesson today. Focus on that."

FEB 5 – 6:15 P.M. EST

"In combat, it's kill or be killed," he said. Kill like he would do to Sam. "Always be ready, and trust no one. Not even me."

I nodded. Did I have the guts to kill someone if it came down to it?

"Anticipate your opponent's next move, both on and off the battlefield. Know what makes them tick. Everyone is driven by something, and once you figure out what it is, you can better predict their actions." He squared his body toward me, spreading his feet apart, bending his knees slightly. A fighting stance? "For example, you are here because I threatened your parents, and the fear of losing them drives you. You know how powerful I am, which keeps you from going to the police."

My stomach somersaulted. "O-okay."

"Fighting is the same. Use what you know about someone to exploit their weak spots." He shifted his weight. "Like I said before, it's kill or be killed."

Kill or be killed. I dug my fingernails into my palm.

"I see the worry on your face." He chuckled. "During training, I have one strict rule: no dying."

"That's a relief." I forced a smile.

"We'll start by building your stamina, so say hello to your free personal trainer." He waved, grinning.

Breathing came easier as he became less tense. "Because PE was always my favorite," I groaned.

"Unfortunately, 'kill or be killed' requires physical strength." He shrugged, then stepped back, eyes glittering. "Besides, who doesn't want the body of a Greek god?"

Oh, we were going there. Okay. "You're one to talk." I raised an eyebrow. "You aren't exactly Illuman." Ironfall wasn't quite the shape of a limp noodle, but he wasn't ultra-chiseled either. Muscles showed through the tight sleeves of his suit, but he wasn't bulky.

"My fans beg to differ." He crossed his arms.

"I think you mean Rhett Wickford's fans." Now it was my

turn for a teasing grin.

"No, I'm pretty sure they're mine." He winked. "And don't play dumb, I know you're a fan."

"Not of *you*," I retorted. "Okay, maybe a little bit, but only because you were such a well-written character. And kind of likable." And kind of handsome. Did I just think that?

"How does the real thing compare?"

My eyes widened. "Well..." Certainly as ominous as his character. "I wasn't expecting you to be a theatre nerd." That wasn't a lie.

"I think we both found something unexpected." Why was he looking at me like that? "Anyway, let's start with some running."

"Bet you weren't expecting me to be bad at sports." I groaned. Of all the exercises, it had to be running.

"No, I knew that," he said. Wouldn't he want a warrior to help him or something? "Now let's get to work."

FEB 5 – 6:43 P.M. EST

Ugh, I hated running. Thank goodness Ironfall finally let me take a break, because I was dying. I stood back, hands on my hips as I sucked in as much air as possible. Still not enough.

My phone buzzed in my backpack. Ironfall took a swig of water, leaning against the beat-up receptionist desk. I pulled out my phone, still breathing heavily.

Oh no.

Sam.

I glanced at Ironfall again. Still drinking. I unlocked my phone and stole a look at the texts.

Sam: How's ur "group project" lol

Sam: Did Ironfall Eyes kill u?

Sam: Can u cover my shift next Thursday pls????????????????

I rolled my eyes, then made sure Ironfall was still distracted.

He couldn't know Sam still wouldn't let this situation go, at least not until he was under VIGIL's protection. I bit my lip and typed in a response.

Rosemary: I can't. Also not dead bc he's NOT a serial killer. Stop watching Criminal Minds lol

Sam: How do u KNOW he isn't a serial killer? Just sayin. For all I know, he's really Ironfall lol

I froze, staring at the screen. I needed to change the subject *now*. I stole another glance at Ironfall. Still distracted. You keep on hydrating, buddy.

Rosemary: Still not covering your shift

My heart pounded.

Sam: That's it, I'm running his face through all the criminal databases I can get into.

Rosemary: Seriously stop. Also...how???

Sam: You underestimate my stalking skills lol

My stomach flipped. What was I supposed to say to that? Every text he sent put him closer to harm's way. Closer to the truth. The *deadly* truth.

Sam: Mwahahahahaha

Sam: You'll thank me later

Sam: Hopefully by covering my shift

Sam: Or a comic con ticket would be nice

Sam: Meeting the entire Project Safeguard cast?

I sighed, then worked on another response. Should I come out and say his life was in danger? No, Ironfall would find that too close to the truth. Besides, for all I knew Sam would pretend he was a Safeguarder and Sherlock Holmes his way to the bottom of this, which would surely get him killed.

Oh, for crying out loud. I typed in another response, which I hoped would get through this stubborn boy's skull.

Rosemary: You have to stop.

"I told you he'd be a problem." I jumped at Ironfall's voice just behind me. Just behind me staring at my phone screen. To him, this was further proof Sam was close to stumbling on the truth. I clutched my other fist tight, digging fingernails into my palm.

This couldn't be happening.

"I don't think you—"

"Ask him if he's at home."

A lump bulged in my throat. "What?" Call the police. Call VIGIL. Call anybody.

"Ask him where he is." Ironfall's haunting brown and blue eyes pierced my soul. I looked away. I couldn't do this. I couldn't.

But then he'd...he'd hurt Mom and Dad.

Did I have a choice?

"Please, there has to be another way." My voice shook.

His eyes narrowed as he stepped back. "Remember our agreement."

I didn't have a choice. My fingers shook as I typed another message.

Rosemary: Are you home?

Send.

I gulped. What had I done?

Sam: Yeahhhhhh. Why?

"He...he's at home." Fear washed through my body. How did I get here? How did things go sour so quickly?

"Alone?"

I texted Sam that.

Sam: Yup. Dad's at work and sister's at her boyfriend's still

Sam: Lol she's been there for like a week

Ironfall backed away and turned.

"Where are you going?" Tears threatened to spill, but I swallowed. *Focus, Rosemary.*

"Don't follow me." His eyes darkened. A warning. "I'm taking care of this. For us. Stay here."

My chest tightened. He couldn't kill Sam. He *couldn't*.

I ran forward, stopping just a few feet from him. "Ironfall, please," I said. "He doesn't know. Surprisingly, he can actually keep a secret if his life depends on it."

And right now it did.

"Seems like quite the talker to me. Trust me, we don't want this secret getting out."

I stepped forward again. "What reason would he have to believe you're anything more than another fan?"

"This isn't up for discussion, Rosemary." And with that, the door shut behind him. I burst outside after him, but he'd already disappeared into the dark city streets.

My stomach turned as breathing became shallower. I couldn't save him. Couldn't save him.

Pull yourself together and call VIGIL.

I went back inside and pulled out my phone again. Then I dialed Agent Liam's number. Please pick up. Please.

I need you.

"Please enter security code."

Oh no, I didn't have time for this.

"This is an emergency!"

"Please enter security code."

Oh, forget it. I hung up the phone, looking around the room. Where had Ironfall gone? If I had only been a moment quicker. If I had only convinced him to stay.

Then I dialed Sam's number. He had to know what was coming.

"Hello?"

"Sam! This is Rosemary!" Breathe. Just breathe.

"If you need me to cover your shift it's a hard no."

"No, this is serious."

"Like VIGIL & ANTE Studios serious?" My blood chilled at the words. What if Ironfall was right? What if Sam *did* know? No, that was crazy.

I gulped. "You have to get somewhere safe. Someone is trying to kill you."

He laughed. "Is this a prank?"

There wasn't time for this, I needed to get moving. "Not a prank. Where do you live?"

"Weird, but okay." He explained where he lived.

I broke into a run, bursting through the door. The exhaustion from Ironfall's torture—I mean workout—melted away as adrenaline took over.

"I'm on my way. Is there a fire escape into your apartment?"

"Yeah..." he muttered.

"I'll come in that way. Don't let anyone else in."

"Wait, what's going on?"

I dodged a light pole. "He thinks you know too much."

"Who? Does this have to do with your serial-killer not-boyfriend?"

"Yes. Now hide!" *Run. Faster.* Electricity shot through my body as I pushed harder. My lungs burned, but I had to get there in time.

Before Ironfall.

Please don't let me be too late.

"You sure this isn't a joke? Because I'm like starting to freak out a bit. Should I call 911 or something?" Right, Sam was still on the line.

"No!" Because Ironfall would know, and my parents would be dead before I made it home.

"If my precious life is on the line, tell me you called in the Safeguarders," he chuckled. Really? He was joking right now?

Did he not believe there was someone coming to take him out?

"I'm almost there. Sam, your world is about to get really big."

"What's that supposed to mean?"

His building was just up ahead. *Keep going.* Okay, I was here. Around the side was a fire escape. Would Ironfall take that way? He'd probably disguise himself to get inside and go up the main entrance.

"Okay, I'm here. Coming up the fire escape now." I ended the call and thrust the phone into my pocket. The metal stairs vibrated as I pounded up each stair. Burning thighs.

Ironfall's words rang through my mind. *Kill or be killed.*

I pushed my legs harder, taking two steps at a time. I stopped just outside what was supposed to be Sam's window. He pulled open the window and crossed his arms.

"What the heck, Rosemary?" He stepped back, shaking his head.

I bit my lip, staring at the door of the small apartment. A tiny kitchen and couch lined the walls. Four doors broke up the longest wall. I assumed one led to a tiny closet bathroom, the other two led to bedrooms, and the other was the front door. Not too many places to hide. This place was barely big enough for three people to live there.

I rolled my eyes. "What part about you're about to be murdered do you not understand? Not by me, just to be clear."

"By your stalker Ironfall ex-boyfriend who I told you was a serial killer?"

"Okay, he never was and never will be my boyfriend. And not a serial killer. A supervillain."

His eyes widened, but I couldn't tell if it was from disbelief or shock. "What?"

"He's not a cosplayer. He actually *is* Ironfall."

Three loud raps sounded at the door.

We both froze.

My chest tightened.

Ironfall was here.

I pointed toward the kitchen. "Grab a sharp knife or something and hide in the bathroom. Lock the door. I'll try to talk him down." For some reason, Ironfall needed me. This was the only way. Maybe I could change his mind or at least stall him until I came up with a better plan.

Would my parents suffer for my actions? No, I couldn't think about that. Sam's life was in danger now, they would be in danger later.

"Wait, what? Like he's actually—?" Sam's voice trailed off.

I shot him a stern look. "Bathroom. Now." My heart crashed

against my ribcage. Could I talk Ironfall down? What would happen to my parents?

And what would now happen to Sam? He knew some of the truth. This could blow the operation. Maybe it would be the end.

I had to keep my parents safe, I couldn't let Sam die.

Three more knocks echoed through the near empty apartment. This kicked Sam into gear. He sprinted across the apartment as if he were suddenly trying out for the Olympics, rummaged through a drawer, and pulled out a chopping knife and a...pistol? Where had he gotten that?

He also grabbed a laptop off the counter. "Can't let him touch my baby," he muttered.

Focus, Rosemary.

Sam ran into the bathroom and shut the door. I heard the click of a lock behind me.

I crept toward the front door and cracked it open. There Ironfall stood. Dark hair. Brown and blue eyes. No disguise. "Please, no." Could he hear the fear in my voice?

"I told you not to follow me," Ironfall said, pushing the door open.

I stepped back. "Look, I'll do anything to keep my parents safe, I just can't let you—"

"Rosemary, he knows. He's a liability." His eyebrows knit together. Was that...concern?

I gulped. Don't glance at the bathroom. Don't do it, Rosemary.

How could I have let this happen?

"He doesn't know anything," I said.

"You don't know that. He's a problem."

"He won't be. You can...bribe him or something. Honestly, he's a fan. He'd probably do whatever you say."

Ironfall pressed his lips together. "And why do you think that would work?"

"It worked for me. You threaten my parents, I stay silent. I do what you want," I said. "Simple as that." The argument was too weak; I needed something else.

"And what does Sam have that I could use against him?"

My chest tightened. I didn't know. I was out of things to say. *Think, Rosemary.*

"You don't know, do you?" he said, his smooth voice taking over. "Please, Rosemary, step out into the hallway."

I gulped, digging my feet into the floor. "What are you going to do, murder everyone I come in contact with?"

"Sam is jeopardizing our mission. It isn't personal."

"Isn't it, though?" I said, now stepping toward him. He wore all black, two silver daggers clutched in his hands ready to—

Kinda felt personal.

"Stand aside." Now he had an edge in his voice. "That's an order. Remember your parents."

I clenched my hands into fists. It was Sam or my parents. Tears threatened to spill over. No, no, no, I couldn't. Why did it have to be this way?

"Rosemary..." he warned. Suddenly his voice softened. "Please, don't make this harder than it is."

That was when a gunshot fired. Ironfall reeled back as blood splattered everywhere. I looked at the bathroom door, a hole burned in the wood near the center.

I heard whimpering from the bathroom. "Oh my gosh. It was an accident!" The door flew open. "Is anyone hurt?" Sam's face was pale, the gun was nowhere in sight, he must've abandoned it in the bathroom.

Ironfall rose to his feet as a dark liquid seeped into his shirt. His jaw flared as he pressed a hand into the wound, wincing. Relief flickered for a moment, then he was solemn again as if he felt no pain. How—?

I thought he could only change the appearance of things, not reverse a gunshot wound. Something didn't add up. He should be on the floor bleeding out, not standing his ground.

He really was a psychopath.

"I-I'm sorry." Sam said. "So sorry!" His voice quivered as he clutched his computer closer to his chest. *His computer.* Ironfall said something about needing a hacker—

"Wait!" I shouted as Ironfall advanced toward Sam.

He spun on me before I could say more, a fire lit in his haunting eyes. "What were you thinking?" His voice was frighteningly low.

"I—" I couldn't breathe. "You came to kill my friend..."

His eyes flashed. "You need to trust me to do what's best for this mission, no matter what that involves. Do you understand? It's kill or be killed."

Would this mean my parents were in danger?

"Sam can join us," I blurted. "He can join our team. You mentioned needing someone good with computers, and he's a genius. Last year he hacked into the school system, changed a grade, and made someone else take the fall for it."

Ironfall blinked, but didn't lower his weapon. Blood still soaked his shirt. How badly was he hurt?

"She's right," Sam said. "And she's the only person I told about it, so I can keep a secret. Shocker to everyone, I know. I can join you in whatever dastardly thing you're planning. You just have to not kill me because that would mean I can't hack into whatever government agency you will inevitably need to access."

"I don't work with my enemies."

"Bro, I'm a fan, honestly." Sam put on his best fanboy grin.

"You also shot me," Ironfall said. I glanced down at his bloodstain.

"And I'm really sorry for that. I never meant to actually use it, I just grabbed it for intimidation—considering that you were coming to kill me—and then it just went off." Sam looked genuinely shook.

"Are you okay?" I gestured toward Ironfall's abdomen.

"It isn't bad. Doesn't even hurt."

I gulped. "You should go to a hospital." And maybe they'd

restrain him.

Ironfall raised a hand, waving his fingers as if casting a spell. "Powers, remember?"

"Can shifting the appearance of reality reverse a gunshot wound?"

"I said I'm fine," Ironfall snapped. He never answered my question.

"Good, so you'll let me live, right?" Sam said, pressing his laptop against his chest even harder. Ironfall glared at him.

I stared between them.

"Fine, you have five minutes to hack into VIGIL's system," Ironfall said. "I've been told there's loopholes in heavily redacted sections of the CIA databases. You get detected, you're dead. You alert anyone, you're dead. You do anything remotely suspicious—"

"I'm dead," Sam said. "Though getting killed by the one and only Ironfall would be a pretty cool way to die."

"Your time starts now," Ironfall said, glancing over at the clock on the wall.

Sam slammed open his laptop and started typing furiously. He typed and typed. Blood rushed in my ears. I honestly hadn't expected Ironfall to be open to it.

I waited. And waited. And waited.

"Done!" Just before the five minutes was up. "Oh my gosh, VIGIL is real too. This is the best day of my life." He flipped the screen around. "Here it is for your viewing pleasure."

"Well, Sam, it's your lucky day," Ironfall said. "But if you even think about talking to the police or VIGIL, you and your family are done."

FEB 5 – 9:39 P.M. EST
Great, now I'd dragged Sam into this.

My mind swirled as I sat back against the mountain of pillows on my bed, sliding my computer onto my lap. Yikes, even that slight movement sent shooting pain through my now-sore muscles.

How did Ironfall not need a hospital? Something didn't add up.

Using careful movements, I googled Ironfall's name.

The first headline read: *"I MET RHETT WICKFORD AFTER WAITING 12 HRS!!!!! (NOT CLICKBAIT)"*

Not what I was looking for. Moving on to the next article...

"5 Villains Who Stole the Show, as told in GIFs."

That was more like it. I clicked on the link. A bunch of villains from various movies came up. I gulped. Number three was Ironfall. *Why* were people so obsessed with him? He had funny one-liners, and he *was* cute (body of a Greek god? Not quite.)...but still...

Enough from this website.

"Ironfall Set to Return in Project Safeguard 3, VIGIL *& ANTE Studios Says in Explosive SuperCon Panel"*

I should've gone straight to my go-to meme page for all things VIGIL & ANTE Studios. Plenty of Ironfall fans hung out there. Maybe they would have some theories on his powers?

BESTVIGILMEMES.BLOGGINGLIFE.COM
FEATURING THE BEST VIGIL & ANTE STUDIOS POSTS
(DON'T @ ME)
– UNAVERAGEVIGILFAN2002

Itsmeafangirl:
VIGIL & ANTE Studios really said instead of a movie trailer let's invent a realistic glowing bodysuit and troll everyone into thinking superheroes are real :) :) :)

Comments:
Heyguys: I strive to be that extra

Shoutouttoilluman: The question is...where can I get one?

Hackerverissuperior: Not gonna lie after that I thought superpowers existed until they announced the movie. A whole 30 minutes of thinking I could sprout powers or something lol

Tiredoffakefans: we're not like other movie studios

Safeguarder4Lyfe: They got us again with Project Safeguard

Pragmaticvigilfan: Nahhh that was obviously fake. Only has the "is it real" affect the first time.

Cerealmaster58: U not wrong

level7andup: So cool how you could see the fight through the windows

Isawprojectsafeguardirl: yeah they didn't even block off the area lol. You could look right in. I was there. Didn't get an autograph though :(

Degreesurgeeeeeeeeeee: And the CIA extras?! Felt like I was inside the movie. So glad it ended up on the news so I could watch it too!

<u>*Doyouevenvigil:*</u>
Illuman probably: (power goes out) I can literally create light but that's too much work so I'm just gonna use this flashlight.

<u>*Cloakerundercover1998:*</u>
Just a friendly reminder that Degree Surge warmed up the Team's leftover pizza using her bare hands

Comments:
YougotDegreed: literally me as a superhero

Incorrectvigil:
Commander Vigil: This is serious, people.
Cloaker: *shifts into Commander Vigil* This is serious, people.

AgentAshleeeee:
The VIGIL Family Tree
Liam = dad
Commander Vigil = drill sergeant mom
Manda = quiet older sister who pretends to hate everyone
Degree Surge = ignored middle child who's a darling
Ver = baby of the family who does better in school than literally everyone
Cloaker = shapeshifting pet
Illuman = fun uncle
Comments:
Cloakda4ever: yasssss.
Imakelight: "shapeshifting pet"
ScienceyVer: i literally choked on cereal helpppppppp
shapeshiftingpet: I changed my username bc of this post lol
IlluverIsMyOTP: I need a family reunion fanfic immediately
ironDIDNTFALL: where is Ironfall on this??????????????????

---

onceuponanironfall:
Raise your hand if Ironfall's just misunderstood.

Nope. Not misunderstood. All he did was flash his perfect grin and talk in a smooth voice, which made him just likable enough to make people tempted to root for him. The writers knew what they were doing because every part of his personality was there to win you over. When he wasn't making threats. (But even then, people thought that was attractive...so who even knows anymore.)

Maybe Ironfall knew exactly what he was doing.

BESTVIGILMEMES.BLOGGINGLIFE.COM
FEATURING THE BEST VIGIL & ANTE STUDIOS POSTS
(DON'T @ ME)
– UNAVERAGEVIGILFAN2002

thatonefanficwriter:
ok but if Ironfall took over the world I'd let him

I bolted upright and gasped. Pain shot through my abs. Yikes, that hurt.

But maybe the attack on New York City wasn't a totally failed attempt, it was a foothold. Maybe Ironfall thought Earth would *willingly* let him take over. In his mind, he would rule, and we would obey because he was handsome and charismatic.

But not everyone would. I sighed.

Memes aren't that deep. But what if Ironfall thought they were?

Ohhhhhh. Maybe he thought he could get some loyal followers out of it. People who would fight for and with him. Because even if he lost the battle, he would gain supporters, maybe enough to win some sort of war. He almost won when it was just him. How much more powerful would he be with a cult-like army?

Ironfall wasn't dumb enough to believe memes, was he? Most of it was humor. Then again, a fictional character had never come to life before. Maybe his fans would fight for him.

And where did I fit in? Clearly I wasn't an Ironfall fangirl.

Ugh, I was no closer to figuring out his motives or whatever weird stuff was going on with his powers.

FEB 5 – 10:21 P.M. EST

I picked up the phone the first time it rang. "Hello?"

"This is Agent Liam. You called earlier, but I was caught up in another case," he said. Another case? I thought this was top priority. And I needed him. "What do you have to report?"

I swallowed the bulge in my throat. "Ironfall almost killed my friend." The determination on his face as he left to kill Sam haunted me.

A short pause. "Is your friend hurt? Are you hurt?"

"No, I convinced Ironfall we needed him. He's only 16, but he's good with computers. Like he broke into VIGIL in five minutes good." Hopefully that wouldn't incriminate Sam too much. It's not like Ironfall gave him a choice.

"Ver made sure our system is airtight, and you're telling me a teenager broke through her firewalls?"

My eyes widened. "It wasn't his fault, Ironfall forced him to."

"His skills must be incredible. I am glad both of you are okay. Sounds like your quick thinking saved his life. Now, tell me everything that happened," Agent Liam said. I recounted the story, voice shaking.

When I was finished, he said, "It seems Ironfall has more power than we give him credit for, especially if he just walked away from a gunshot wound. We'll need to learn more…" Agent Liam looked to floor and rubbed his chin before turning his gaze back on me. "Do you think Ironfall is going after people close to you?"

"He only attacked because Sam was close to the truth," I said. "What if my parents become suspicious? Or anyone else?"

"They will be protected. I'm assigning agents to watch your houses 24/7." His voice was firm and commanding. "Ironfall won't make a move on anyone around you without us knowing."

"He'll know you're watching us." I shivered at the thought.

"It's certainly a risk," he said.

"I want your protection, but he's going to find out," I said. "And then all of us die."

"I understand," he said. "I will make sure an agent is always within a ten-minute radius of your location."

"Thank you." I breathed a sigh of relief.

"Dispatching someone to your location now," he said. "One last thing: is Sam on our side?"

"I don't know him well enough," I said. "We go to the same high school, but I didn't meet him until I started working at Ketch-A-Burger a few months ago. He's a huge VIGIL & ANTE Studios fan, but I'm not sure which side he'd support."

"Okay." Agent Liam paused. "Don't bring him in the loop just yet. The fewer people who know you're working with us, the better. What's his name?"

"Sam Hunt."

"I'll put Ver on this. See if we can come up with his profile," Agent Liam said. "Good work, Agent Collins."

"Thank you, sir."

"Stay safe."

TRANSCRIPT OF THE INTERVIEW PROCEEDINGS
WITH IRONFALL
SOME NAMES AND LOCATIONS REDACTED FOR
SECURITY
INTERVIEW CONDUCTED ON MAY 20
LOCATION OF INTERVIEW: **[REDACTED]**
CASE #: **[REDACTED]**

AGENT LIAM BLAKE: So you decided murder was your best option?

IRONFALL: He knew too much.

AGENT LIAM BLAKE: Still, weren't you worried this would be too extreme to keep Rosemary on board with your plans?

IRONFALL: It was to protect her as much as it would me. If Sam tied her to me, well, let's face it, her life would be over too.

AGENT LIAM BLAKE: Hard to believe this was a generous act.

IRONFALL: It was purely out of survival. I figured she would see the situation the same way, between that and how I... threatened her parents.

AGENT LIAM BLAKE: And?

IRONFALL: I miscalculated. She was different than I expected. There was just something about her that drew me in, and I wasn't thinking clearly.

AGENT LIAM BLAKE: When did that start?

IRONFALL: When we auditioned for the musical.

CHAPTER 7

FEB 5 – 10:31 P.M. EST

I stretched to grab a granola bar out of the cardboard box and shut the kitchen cabinet. Oh, my poor sore muscles. Dang it, Ironfall, these workouts were killing me. Dad rustled around on the couch as the TV droned on. I unwrapped the bar and took a bite.

"...this is the seventh bank robbery-related death in five months," a TV reporter said. "However, they are not known to be related."

Chewing halted. I turned around. *Ironfall.*

The TV cut to a police chief standing at a podium. "We do have a suspect at this time." My eyes widened. My limbs electrified.

Mom came in, distracted with her phone. Why was she wearing something as nice as a plum blouse with high-waisted black slacks? She looked up at the TV.

"The identities of the victims have not been released." My stomach dropped. "As of now, only one suspect is at large. This is Erica Stein, reporting..."

Oh. My. Gosh. It was *him*. And the police believed someone else did it.

He'd do the same thing to Mom and Dad in a heartbeat.

Mom ran a hand along Dad's arm. "Hey babe, I need to head to work." He looked up and nodded.

"Mom, it's almost ten." I glanced back at the TV. *Ironfall. The robbery. Victims. Sam.* Please don't go out.

"Sorry, there's an emergency."

My eyebrows rose. "For interior design?" If any job never had an emergency, you'd think it'd be that one. Something felt off. The plastic in my hand crinkled.

"Yes." She rolled her eyes. "What would you know about how the real world works?"

"I have a job." Three, actually. And two of them were more important than she'd ever know. I did it for them. "And I know about the real world." Too much.

"Okay, well you *don't* know the things I have to do for clients." Dad shook his head, sighing.

I looked down, my hands fidgeting behind my back. "Sorry." Was anything I did enough? I thought back to Ironfall.

"What time you think you'll be home?" Dad said.

"You know how the boss gets during an emergency. It could be a while." She leaned down to press a lipstick-y kiss against his lips. They cared so much about each other yet so little about me. And I cared so *much* about them.

"Keep me updated." Dad beamed up at her.

Be safe, I wanted to say.

And then she left.

FEB 6 – 1:36 A.M. EST

I woke up wet with sweat. The ever-shining street light cast a yellow glow across my room. I sat up and checked the time on my phone. 1:36 a.m.

Just a nightmare, not that real life was much better.

My racing heart slowed, and I raked a hand through my red waves.

Lying back down, I thrust myself over to the cool side of the bed, but I still couldn't relax. Oh, forget it, I needed to get up for a little bit.

I slid out of bed and walked the memorized path to the dark kitchen. Though my apartment was asleep, the streets outside were still alive with lights and sounds. Made me feel less alone.

I grabbed a glass and filled it with water. My hands shook as I raised it to my lips.

Just a nightmare. Just a nightmare.

When I closed my eyes I still saw the knife in Ironfall's hand ready to take Sam's life. And in my dreams, ready to take Mom and Dad's lives.

The realness of the situation crashed over me again as a lump formed in my throat.

You're an agent of VIGIL.

A noise came from the lock just a few feet away from the kitchen counter. I jumped. Metal clicked. Was someone turning the knob?

I shrank back into the corner of the kitchen, setting down the glass.

Was Ironfall here to harm my parents? To prove he'd make good on his threat? To force me into submission?

To punish me for saving Sam?

Kill or be killed.

Ironfall's words echoed in the back of my mind, over and over again.

The lock jiggled again. I hadn't imagined it.

He *was* here for them.

I grabbed a knife off the counter. Wait, no, that was a bad idea. Obviously Ironfall would be way more skilled with a knife because it was his weapon of choice and I'd had very few combat lessons.

I swallowed the rising panic as my stomach churned.

In just a few seconds, the door would swing open and Ironfall would swagger in. Creaking. It was too dark. I should have turned a light on.

"Wh-who's there?" My voice trembled.

"Shh, it's me." *Ironfall*. I couldn't breathe.

In the dark I glanced in the direction of my parents' closed door. Dang it, I wasn't standing between them and Ironfall.

Don't kill them. Don't kill them.

"How do you know where I live?" Wow, that was a dumb thing to ask. Of course he knew where I lived. Probably knew my social security number too.

"I'm a villain, Rosemary. What did you expect?" He added a soft laugh to the end. Chills crept down my back. Even with the lighthearted tone, his message was clear: don't forget what villains can do.

He stepped forward so the soft glow of an outside streetlight shone on his face. He seemed relaxed, a sparkle in the blue sliver of his eye.

Get between him and my parents.

He didn't kill Sam—maybe he'd have mercy on my parents too? Slowly, I stepped closer, inching my way toward the spot blocking my parents' bedroom door.

"I didn't expect you to break into my house at two a.m.," I gulped as my voice cracked at the end.

"You'll see why soon enough." He grinned. Why did he seem so relaxed when he broke into my house?

My blood froze, but I forced myself to move faster. Crap, I still clutched the kitchen knife in my sweaty palm. My fingers tightened around the handle. So much for not fighting Ironfall with the household version of his signature weapon.

"A-are you here to hurt them?" I whispered. My chest was so tight I could barely even take in another breath. "My parents?" Don't answer that. I didn't know what I'd do if he said yes.

Another shaky breath.

Silence.

His smile morphed into a line as his gaze hardened. "Is there a reason I should?" Oh no, did I put the thought into his head? Was he now suspicious? Because there was a reason: I worked for VIGIL, and I stopped him from killing Sam.

"Well?" He straightened, taking a step closer as if he was gearing up for a fight. This was bad.

"I stopped you f-from—" I couldn't say the words out loud because my throat threatened to suffocate me. "You're going to hurt them."

I felt him step closer. I raised the knife, just a little. Just in case.

Kill or be killed.

This was him forcing me to fall in line.

I should have said nothing.

"Please don't," I said. "I promise, I've learned my lesson. Please don't hurt them."

He just stood there, tall and commanding, his silence scarier than words.

"Please, I need them," I begged. "You can't."

Kill or be killed.

Ironfall's lesson echoed through my mind.

He stood resolute, fists closed. "I can't work with someone who doesn't follow orders."

I was all that was stopping him from storming Mom and Dad's bedroom, and I had exactly an hour of fighting experience. The only thing on my side was the element of surprise. Would he expect me to fight him? Should I try to talk him down more? It hadn't worked so far.

I took a deep breath and rubbed my thumb across the warm metal of the kitchen knife. Maybe lose the knife though. Or don't?

What would Manda do?

Now or never.

I thrust the knife forward. He grabbed my wrist, twisting me around. My grip slipped, and the blade clattered to the floor. Surely Mom and Dad heard that.

Something pelted against my stomach. I gasped for air, but none came. Couldn't. Breathe. Pressure on all sides.

Air suddenly flooded my lungs, but Ironfall still pinned my arms to my sides, trapping me against himself.

"Rosemary," he hissed. "I'm not here to hurt them."

Convenient of him to say that now. I elbowed him. He grunted, but his grip only became more like steel.

"You're lying," I forced out. "That's why you're here. Because I screwed up and now you have to work with Sam."

"No." He squeezed harder. "You have to trust me on this. I am *not* here to harm your parents."

"Then you'd better start explaining." I said this as if I was the one pinning him down.

His lips moved closer to my ear. "I'm here for you, not for them."

My blood froze. "Why?" I shifted, trying to escape his grip.

"It's time to show you my real plan. And you were right: as much as I hate to let someone else on the team, we need Sam."

My breath caught. "Your real plan?" Could he be telling the truth? Or was he using this to calm me down?

"Yes. Now do you promise you won't try to stab me again?" His grip loosened. "It would be unfortunate to work with two people who tried to kill me."

There was nothing to do but agree. So I nodded. "As long as you don't take a step towards my parents."

"Not if you do as I say."

"Okay, then I promise." My entire body shook.

His arms relaxed, and I scrambled from his grasp.

"Now get dressed and follow me," he said. "I'll wait outside your apartment."

"Where are you taking me?"

"You'll know when we get there." Suddenly, his tone changed. "Now hurry up, *partner in crime*." Now he sounded playful as if we were just two friends. I gulped, stepping back to go change.

What in the world was going on?

After a final glance in Ironfall's direction, I ran to my room, changed into a sweatshirt and leggings, and grabbed my coat on the way out. Ironfall waited in the stairwell. I glanced over at my parents' doorway. How had they not woken up?

Still keeping an eye on Ironfall, I crept over to their door, cracking it open.

The bed stood perfectly made. Not one lump. Where were they? Earlier Mom said she was going out, but why wasn't she back at two a.m.? And where was Dad?

My stomach flipped.

"Rosemary?" Ironfall whispered.

I shut my parents' bedroom door again.

"Coming!" I replied. Why weren't they here? What was Ironfall going to show me?

So many questions...but hopefully in a few minutes I'd have some answers.

FEB 6 – 1:58 A.M. EST

When I locked the door behind me, Ironfall was disguised as "Nolan." He flashed a mischievous smile. I gulped. Just how fast he could change into a friendly persona (and change his appearance) was unsettling. I'm sure it was stranger to witness him shift reality in person. "How do you feel about breaking and entering?"

My stomach dropped. "What?" When would the crimes end? Sam. Mom and Dad. And now yet another...thing. How many people would he try to kill?

"Don't look so shocked."

I took a deep breath. "No one gets hurt, right?" *My, how I've lowered my standards.*

"We're not doing anything tonight. A heist takes time," he said. "Careful planning. I'm just taking you somewhere."

The bank robberies. Slit throats. He almost killed Sam. He came here to kill my parents, I was sure of it. No, no, no, I couldn't be a part of that.

"Where are you taking me?" Was he taking me to kill me?

"You'll see," he said. Then he turned, making his way down the apartment stairway. We went out into the dark city night. Sirens blared in the distance. But even in the middle of the night, people were outside. I dug my fingernails into my palms. Too many people, and none the sort I really wanted to be around, including Ironfall. Especially him. Still, I stepped faster to keep his steady pace.

He turned toward me, still walking, his voice low as he talked. "VIGIL has a vault designed to hold items they believe shouldn't get into the wrong hands." He thrust his hands into his pockets. "Something in there will ensure we gather enough loyal supporters to take over the world."

Wait...would that be enough evidence for VIGIL to arrest him? Now that he was actively planning a criminal act or something like that.

I moved closer to him as the sidewalk narrowed. "When do we start?"

He stopped at a curb as a silver car pulled up, reflecting the yellow streetlights. "Right now. I'll show you where the vault is. Don't say anything to the driver. Obviously." He winked, then opened the door to the backseat. "My lady." He gestured toward the car and gave the grandest bow I'd seen this side of Broadway.

I swallowed my fear, and forced a laugh, then got in.

"Broad Street," Ironfall told the driver. Wait, Broad Street? The same place the *Project Safeguard* publicity stunt happened? Was there some connection? Or was this his second attempt at breaching the vault?

I looked out the window as we crept along the busy street. For a few moments, I reveled in the silence, in not having to put on a facade.

Then Ironfall broke the silence. "The things you see in this city are very entertaining. Like that guy's yellow beanie with what looks like a glue stick taped to it." Wait, what? I leaned across the car, craning my neck to peer out. I caught a glimpse just as it passed out of view.

Yep. I'm not surprised. Especially because of the time of day...or time of night. There was a certain kind of people that paraded around at night. I swallowed.

I guess if I had to be out with anyone, he was the best person to be with. Because he'd keep me safe. Not that he wasn't just as scary as the rest of them.

I chuckled. "If you think this is fun, wait until you see what people wear in summer." Oh, the things I have seen.

"There's no place like this. Have you lived here your whole life?"

"Yeah." I nodded. "Same apartment too." He probably knew all this. Why ask me?

"Ooh, look, we should try that pizza place sometime. Maybe have a competition. What do you think?" He glanced over, eyes glinting in the passing streetlights.

"I think you underestimate how much I eat." That part was true. "Also, that pizza's crappy. Now, the place two blocks from here? That's the good stuff." I glanced at him as he stared back out the window with wide eyes. It was like he was seeing the city for the first time.

He grinned. "Maybe we'll try both."

For the next few minutes, he seemed content to sightsee in silence as the vehicle crawled through traffic. Why did I get the sense that he thought of me as someone more than a business partner? Maybe it was part of *his* facade. Threaten my family to hook me and use his charm to reel me in.

He almost killed them tonight.

He almost killed Sam.

I gulped, shaking the feeling. No, I wouldn't think about that. "How long have you been in New York?"

"Only a few weeks," he said. "I never stay in the same place long."

"And how long do you plan to stick around?" Also, why did he need me? Not that I could ask that in front of the driver.

"How long do you want me to stay?" That was a weird response. Of course, he had that amused tone in his voice where he was joking, pretending to be smooth, but still. Did he consider me to be more than someone to help him in his villainous pursuits? No, he was too calculating for that.

"How long do you need to be here?"

His eyes darkened. "Until the job is done."

Sometime later, the car stopped. Ironfall paid the driver, and we got out. Broad Street was as busy as ever, even with the early hours of the morning. I shivered as the crisp air sliced through my coat.

"You warm enough?"

I shook my head. "I'll be fine. Where are we going?"

Lights flashed and glowing billboards transitioned from one advertisement to the next.

"Follow me." He took the lead through the crowd. A couple blocks later, he pointed to a large, resolute looking building. The same one where the public spotted the Safeguarders fighting Ironfall. The one from the publicity stunt. It was gray with grand reliefs carved into the stone. Some sort of government building. "Welcome to New York City's top-secret CIA base. The vault is somewhere inside."

"This is your second attempt, isn't it? You tried a few years ago, but the Safeguarders stopped you," I whispered.

He nodded. "And thus, I became the most loved villain in the VIGIL & ANTE Studios cinematic universe."

"You're not wrong," I said, then paused. "Why are you trying again?"

His gaze snapped to me. "I have you."

"I'm sure an ex-con would have been more useful," I said

"Not necessarily." Ironfall pressed his lips together and

studied the gray stones. "I didn't make it very far last time. Didn't have enough clear intel."

Oh, no, I couldn't do this heist. VIGIL would take care of it. They would arrest Ironfall and my work would be done. I could go back to being a normal high school senior. I still shivered at the thought.

Ironfall placed his arm around me. "Sorry, I should have warned you that we would be outside."

"Yeah," I murmured, so aware of the pressure of his steady arm around my shoulders. "How on earth are you going to pull this off?"

"Together, with lots of research. And Sam's tech skills." He squeezed my arm. "Don't worry about a thing."

He seemed in an okay mood, so I figured it would be fine to ask a couple more questions. "Why do you want all of this?"

He smirked. "Well, wouldn't you like to know."

"Come on, you seem to know so much about me," I said. "Besides, you talk about anticipation. I'm following your own advice." A bus drove by, blocking our view.

"You don't expect your adversaries to answer your deep life questions, do you?"

"But we're not adversaries, you said so yourself, *partner in crime*." I nudged him. Maybe if I played it cool he would open up.

"Allies is *not* the same thing as friends."

"I know. But it doesn't seem like you have anyone else to share things with." I looked away. Neither did I.

He sighed. "The lives of the wicked are lonely, I suppose. It's a necessary sacrifice, that much my father drilled into me." Suddenly his figure seemed less commanding and more broken.

I nodded, keeping my eyes down. "Your father?"

Ironfall pressed his lips together, turning away. When he looked at me again, a spark lit his brown and blue eyes. "Tell you what. We'll begin preparations over pizza. How does that sound?"

I guess his dad was a touchy subject. The first one I'd noticed. "At three a.m.?"

"Why not?"

I gulped. Not like I could say no to much of anything now. "Pizza sounds great."

FEB 6 – 4:23 A.M. EST

I bolted into the apartment, my fingers quivering as I tried to pick out the correct combination for Agent Liam's phone number.

"This is Agent Liam." He sounded like he'd been asleep.

I gulped and tried to get my act together. "Agent Rosemary Collins reporting." I spoke in a hoarse whisper. "I would have waited until morning, but this is too urgent. The—uh—target is planning a heist."

"Are you in a secure location?"

Well... "I'm at home."

There was a long sigh. "The car will pick you up in an hour, same place," Agent Liam said. "Be ready with your full report."

I took a deep breath. "I will, sir. Thank you. Sorry for waking you up."

"All part of being a spy."

FEB 6 – 5:44 A.M. EST

"I would have you sit, but I don't have enough chairs." Liam paused, then sat down, rubbing his eyes. "What's your report?"

He crossed his arms, but he didn't seem hostile, it was more his ready-to-receive-information position.

"Ironfall wants me to help him steal something from the VIGIL vault."

For a few moments, he remained silent. My hands fidgeted at my sides.

He rubbed his forehead, probably because he was exhausted like me. "Do you know what he's trying to obtain?"

"You don't know? Wasn't he after something in the vault during *Project Safeguard*'s real-life event?" The heist aspect wasn't featured in the movie, probably so people wouldn't know VIGIL had a place to hold dangerous objects.

"He was, but we couldn't figure out what he needed. Is there any insight you can give us?"

"No, he only said it's something that will help him gain supporters to take over the world. Sorry."

He pressed a finger to his ear. "Ver, get me a list of every item in the VIGIL vault."

"You can arrest him now, right? On suspected burglary or something? Or for attacking Sam?" I said. "I know exactly where he's going to be tomorrow. You could take him out easily. As far as I know, I'm the only one he trusts, so you would outnumber him."

Again, he said nothing. Something was wrong. The way he swiveled back and forth in his office chair. His forefinger tapping against his cheek and his other hand readjusting his bright red tie. The way he kept glancing at his computer screen.

"The thing is, we hardly have any intel on him. Just your daily reports. There isn't a consistent pattern yet, and we must make sure we're precise before we take any sort of action..." His gaze flitted to the screen, then back to me.

Did I really hear that right? "Ironfall is going to *commit a crime*. And he's making me help him." Why wouldn't he do anything? This was the most dangerous criminal (probably ever), and Agent Liam, the director of the Vigilante Intervention and Guardianship Intelligence League was going to do *nothing?*

"You are going to have to stay undercover a while longer. Earn his trust." He pressed his lips together. "Figure out why he chose you."

"But you have a solid tip. Why won't you take it? You could get him out of the way *now*." So I didn't have to deal with this anymore. "He could hurt more people."

Liam's arms fell to his sides. "Agent Rosemary, it doesn't work like that. We play the long game until I'm authorized to bring him in."

I gritted my teeth and stood straighter. "With all due respect, sir, you never asked for clearance from anyone in the movies, even if they tried to make you. You did what you had to in order to save the world and the Safeguarders. Can't you see that we have the chance to stop Ironfall before he sheds any blood?" *Before he sheds my parents' blood.*

"Agent Collins, you don't quite understand how things work." He pressed his fingertips against each other, leaning back in his office. The Agent Liam Blake I saw on screen was so different than the one I saw now.

"I know I don't know how things work. That's why I'm probably going to blow my cover. I don't know how to act around him, and I certainly don't know how to invent a fake persona."

More tears pricked my eyes, so I turned and left the room. I wouldn't let Agent Liam know how scared I was.

TRANSCRIPT OF THE INTERVIEW PROCEEDINGS
WITH IRONFALL
SOME NAMES AND LOCATIONS REDACTED FOR
SECURITY
INTERVIEW CONDUCTED ON MAY 20

LOCATION OF INTERVIEW: [REDACTED]
CASE #: [REDACTED]

AGENT LIAM BLAKE: Let's talk about how you funded your operation. You sure you don't want any coffee?

IRONFALL: I'm all right.

AGENT LIAM BLAKE: You robbed several banks to fund yourself, is that correct?

IRONFALL: Yes.

AGENT LIAM BLAKE: Can you name them?

IRONFALL: [ANSWER REDACTED]

AGENT LIAM BLAKE: How much money did you take?

IRONFALL: I'm sure you already know that.

AGENT LIAM BLAKE: Humor me.

IRONFALL: Four million dollars.

AGENT LIAM BLAKE: That's a large sum of money.

IRONFALL: Yes, it is.

AGENT LIAM BLAKE: Autopsy reports say that the murdered were attacked from behind with a knife. They bled out due to large cuts to the throat.

IRONFALL: [inaudible]

AGENT LIAM BLAKE: You look uncomfortable. Do you need something?

IRONFALL: I don't want her to hear it.

AGENT LIAM BLAKE: Believe me, she already knows.

CHAPTER 8

Ver met me at the door, yawning. "That didn't go well, did it? Not eavesdropping, I promise. Just by the look on your face, it didn't go like you hoped."

If I said anything, tears would come. "No, it didn't."

Her face twisted. "What happened?"

"VIGIL could—" I sucked in a breath. Don't start sobbing now. "He won't do anything."

"Not defending him, but there are a lot of things different than the movies, mainly those in charge of VIGIL. The world may see Agent Liam as the big boss, but even he has to answer to people. But yeah, he takes a while to warm up to new agents, forgets how to not be a jerk, but he's as loyal as they come. I'll go talk to him." And then she stepped into the office. In the movies, Agent Liam was always the first to step up and do the right thing. Now...now he wouldn't. Was Ver different in real life too? So far, she was the same.

What was I supposed to do? How was I supposed to get out?

Wait...was Ver still wearing her pajamas?

I looked down, rubbing my tired eyes. A figure moved out of the corner of my eyes. My head whipped up and—

Then Ver came back with Agent Liam.

"Let's talk," Liam said, motioning for me to follow him. "Ver, you and Manda keep working on your assignments. The vault's inventory is top priority."

"More than sleep?" Ver said.

"More than sleep."

Ver nodded and went back to her computer. Then, Agent Liam and I returned to his office. My mind raced with questions of what he wanted to talk to me about and fear of what would happen to me.

He turned to face me. I glanced at his empty desk chair, then back to him. "I have been known to disregard protocol when the situation calls for it, but right now isn't one of those times. There is more at stake than you and your family, Agent Rosemary. If I don't play by the rules, the CIA will permanently shut us down. They've been trying for years."

I gasped. "Why? The superheroes...*Project Safeguard*... Without them protecting us, we're vulnerable to more people like Ironfall."

"That's why I have to wait for the CIA's approval. They don't believe we're necessary. Cloaker is the only active superhero, and he's..." He glanced at his computer, then back at me. "He's on a highly classified mission. The inactive ones are living the Hollywood life."

A small piece of my heart cracked. How much did the government fabricate for the audience's enjoyment? How much about my favorite characters was actually real?

And what on earth was I supposed to do now?

"Why the CIA? Are they ANTE or something?" I said.

Agent Liam pressed his lips together. "That part's classified. If I could tell you, I would, but VIGIL itself is at stake." His gaze fell to the ground. It made sense, but the Agent Liam in the movies would make sure the world was safe anyway. He'd risk everything.

"Oh." It was all I could say. Just a simple word. "They're the ones preventing you from bringing Ironfall in." My voice shook, my jaw trembling. Tears stung my eyes.

I'd have to be a double agent even longer.

"What about Sam?" I said. "Can't they arrest him on that?"

He shook his head. "They still need more information." He

pressed a finger to his ear. "Ver, what's the status on the items in the vault?"

A moment later, Ver's head popped through the door. "In your inbox. Believe me, this wasn't easy to find. You can't just rummage through old VIGIL files to get to this."

FEB 6 – 6:15 P.M. EST

I stepped into the bunker, afraid of what would come next. Because VIGIL couldn't do anything, so my mission would last even longer.

Sam wasn't here yet, and it was going to be his first day.

"Well, guess who's running late?" Ironfall turned from pounding against the punching bag. I flinched, expecting him to launch a dagger at my face.

"What? I'm on time," I said, double-checking the time on my phone.

"I meant Sam." He stepped back, rubbing his knuckles.

"Oh, right," I chuckled.

"Before he gets here, we have a problem." Ironfall unwrapped the cloth from his hands, striding toward me.

My blood ran cold. "What is it?"

He pressed his lips together. "Someone broke in last night."

I looked around, searching for anything that could be out of place, but it was immaculate. Well, as immaculate as a gross abandoned building could be. My point is that it didn't look ransacked.

Did Ironfall think it was Sam?

"Who do you think it was?"

"Someone who knew what they were doing. No fingerprints, not even a shred of evidence. These people were professionals."

Could it have been VIGIL? Would Agent Liam risk something like that? He could have just asked me details about Ironfall's hideout.

"Then how did you even know someone was here?" I gulped.

"My computer. Someone tried to access it at 1:55 a.m., and neither of us were here." Well, that wasn't unsettling at all.

"And you think it was Sam?" Oh no...

He shook his head. "No, it wasn't him. The job was too clean, and my computer wasn't breached."

"What's so important on your computer?"

Now he smirked, shaking his head. "Wouldn't you like to know?"

"I would, actually." Because maybe it would be the thing to finally get the go-ahead to arrest him.

"Just because I told you this doesn't mean I fully trust you, Rosemary."

My chest tightened. "Right, sorry."

"We need to lie low for now. I'm going to put up more security. Meanwhile, both of us need to blend in," he said.

"You mean the three of us need to blend in." Just then, Sam burst through the doorway, holding his arms wide.

"Good of you to finally join us," Ironfall muttered. "In the future, be more prompt." Tension could be cut like a knife.

To keep Sam from saying anything stupid, I hurried and said, "The cast list comes out tomorrow. Should we pull out of the school play if we land roles?" *Please say yes.*

"I think we can let that one slide. Besides"—suddenly Ironfall winked—"gotta act like a normal student and everything. Starting now." Did that explain why his mischievous side now leaked into this serious conversation?

"Oh, so you believe in fun? I thought you were all business," I teased back.

"I know how to have fun when the time calls for it, and that time is us doing the play together." Did he forget about whoever broke in? If he didn't want to talk about it, I wouldn't press.

"I don't see your logic, but I'm not going to argue." I forced a smile.

He laughed. "I'm not complaining about that. Sam, you're joining the play too." He motioned Sam over.

"I don't really act," Sam said. "In third grade I puked before playing tree number four."

Ironfall glanced at me. "You'll be a stagehand."

"I think I can handle that."

"You will handle it," Ironfall said. Then he grabbed his computer off the desk. "But I need you to find out who tried to access my computer."

"Your wish is my command, O Ironfall." Sam rolled his eyes. "Did you get it? That was a reference to *Project Safeguard*? When Illuman gets captured?"

Ironfall shot him a glare.

I stepped towards Sam, trying to play along to at least help Ironfall not look like he wanted Sam to drop dead on the spot. "And then he's like 'I'm gonna say you don't like the idea of throwing a dance party to distract the president.'" I gestured towards Ironfall.

"I don't sound like that." Ironfall shook his head, his signature boyish grin crossing his face. Okay, good, that was a start.

"Have you actually seen yourself in *Project Safeguard*? Well, Cloaker's version of you." Oh dear, did Ironfall know Cloaker played him? Would he notice the detail? I played it off with a smile. But as meticulous as Ironfall was, he had to notice.

He nodded, leaning against our hideout's ragged desk. "Saw it in theaters. Wouldn't want to miss my on-screen debut." With that stupid grin on his face, I doubted he realized my mistake.

"All right, we get it, Mr. Movie Star," Sam laughed.

I sat down across from Ironfall. If I stretched out my legs, I could touch his if I wanted to. "You have to admit, though, I definitely sounded like you."

"Why don't we watch it now, just to prove I'm right." Ironfall's eyes gleamed as he grinned.

"Aren't we supposed to be working right now though? Security and forensics and stuff?" I side-eyed him. He had a mischievous look, like it no longer mattered. Right now, he had his mind set on something else. Why watch the movie praising his sworn enemies?

"Yeah, probably," he said. "But Sam's doing all the work at the moment, and I might need to gain some acting tips from 'myself' if our names are on that cast list tomorrow."

Right. That. Auditioning seemed like a good idea at the time, but I had to focus on keeping Ironfall from learning I was a double agent. My parents' lives were on the line. The smile fell from my face.

"Did you change your mind?" he said, eyebrows scrunched together as if he was concerned. "About the play?"

I shook my head. "No, no, it's not that." Couldn't have him thinking I auditioned to stall his plans. Why did he pretend to care?

"Then what is it?" He sounded so convincing, like he really wanted to know.

I paused, pressing my lips together. I had to share. "Don't laugh, but I'm terrified of performing."

"Really? I never would've guessed." He pressed his back into the wooden desk. "Is there a story behind that?"

"Nothing interesting," I said. "Just always had a fear of it." Fear of what my parents would say. Fear of what others would say. Mom would tell me acting was a waste of time and I should put my efforts into something more productive.

"Yet you always dreamed of it." He nudged my leg with his. My breath hitched. "Look at you conquering your fears and breaking free." More like doing the less scary thing. I closed my eyes as my parents' faces flashed before me. I did all of this for them.

I sighed. "If you say so." Why was he being nice? It was more than villain banter, it seemed like he genuinely cared. Manipulation. That's what it was. But no, I couldn't show that.

He pushed himself to his feet. "You know what I think this calls for?"

"If you say a run I will fight you." I threw my head back in mock exasperation to convince him I was no longer upset.

"We're taking a break from work, remember? I think it's time for a sing-off."

"A what?"

"Where we sing our favorite showtunes together. I'll pick a song and you have to join in, and then you start. First person to not know a song loses." He reached his arm down to me.

I took his hand, and he pulled me to my feet. "You're on."

"Okay, I hate to break up whatever is happening here because I'm living for how cinematic it is, but what am I looking for?" Sam said, all but stroking Ironfall's laptop.

"Figure out who tried to break into my computer. Just don't touch my files." Ironfall narrowed his eyes.

"Right," Sam said. "I'm on it."

He opened the computer lid and typed some random stuff that apparently made sense to the computer.

"Are you going to be watching me the whole time?" Sam turned toward Ironfall.

"Yes," Ironfall said.

"What, you don't trust me?" Sam pretended to look hurt.

"I trust no one," he said. "Now do your job." He backed away, turning back to me, but still glanced over at Sam occasionally.

Would Sam try to access the files? Would he get himself killed? Would I get myself killed? I took a deep breath, waiting for the tension to break.

A few minutes later, Sam gingerly closed the lid of Ironfall's laptop. "Hate to break it to you, but there's no way to find out who accessed your computer."

Ironfall rolled his eyes, crossing his arms. "I thought you were supposed to be good at your job. Do we need to—?"

"Stop," I said, glaring at Ironfall. "Just listen to him."

He sighed, gesturing toward the computer screen. "Go on."

"Okay, so I can tell how they tried to breach, but they masked their identity too well," Sam said. "It's literally impossible to find them."

Ironfall stroked his smooth chin. "We'll have to find another way."

A grin flashed across Sam's face. "Now could I take part in this little karaoke moment? Or is that only for the inner circle?" Did he think this was some sort of fandom hangout?

The annoyed look that crossed Ironfall's face was unmatched. "It's only for people who didn't shoot—"

"Yes, join us," I interrupted. "If we're all working together, we need to treat each other with respect." My voice shook as I said it, but it was true. No matter how annoying Sam was, Ironfall had to stop thinking of him as expendable.

Because life is never expendable.

"Fine. Join us," Ironfall groaned. Wait, had he just listened to me? "But this doesn't mean I like you."

"I just sort of grow on you." Sam shrugged.

"Like a disease."

"Respect, Ironfall, respect," I muttered.

Ironfall tossed a grin my way. "Right, sorry."

"Deep down you think I'm cool, I can feel it," Sam laughed.

"Keep dreaming," Ironfall said.

Sam threw his arms wide. "Well, my dreams never included VIGIL & ANTE Studios being real, so anything is possible."

FEB 7 – 7:45 A.M. EST

Great. The cast list was supposed to come out today. That meant a group of excited students—including myself (though my emotions were a mix of terror and excitement)—hovered around an empty bulletin board outside the director's classroom.

People whispered how they hoped to get cast and being worried that their auditions "weren't good enough."

I *really* hoped I didn't get a part. Learning lines and acting *in front of people* was not what I needed right now, even though the audition was the most thrilling thing I'd ever done. I had to focus on convincing Ironfall, not an audience. Not to mention adding this on top of work and school.

At least I finally auditioned. That was something, right?

Please, don't let me get a part.

"All right, all right, everyone back up," Mrs. Rodriguez said. The crowd parted just enough for her to squeeze through. People strained their necks and wiggled toward the front to try to catch a glimpse of the paper that "held their fate." But she kept the paper clutched to her chest.

The moment she pressed the thumb tack through the freshly printed paper, the crowd pushed in. I held back, staying away from the chaos.

Oh gosh, I didn't want a part. Please, no. I couldn't add any more stress. I couldn't make any more friends for Ironfall to threaten. I shuddered thinking of what almost happened to Sam.

Murmurs and rumors spread.

"Ready to see the cast list?" Ironfall-dressed-as-Nolan suddenly showed up beside me. I jumped back.

No, I didn't want to know the cast. "I guess you decided to come to school today."

Ironfall chuckled. "I couldn't miss this." His tall figure so close made the crowd seem more stifling.

Finally, I made it up to the front. And there was my name at the very top. Right next to "Belle."

Nolan's name was the next one down.

My eyes widened, my chest constricting. No, this was terrible. But also awesome.

Beauty and the Beast. But he was a villain, I was...the double agent.

I gulped.

In a way, our parts fit.

FEB 7 – 7:55 P.M. EST

"Mom, there's something I've been meaning to talk to you about." I gulped, stepping closer to the dining room table where she sat. Oh no. Here it came.

Her eyes stayed glued to her computer screen. The computer's glow flashed through her brown eyes. "I'm busy right now." She brushed an auburn curl behind her ear as she leaned in.

"It's really important." I inhaled, taking the seat opposite her. I still don't know how she could work on those rock-hard chairs.

She looked up, piercing eyes stabbing through me. "What?" Manicured nails struck against the wooden tabletop.

Oh dear, I should've picked a better time.

"I've been thinking..." I sighed. She would rip me apart. Did I really need to quit? Ironfall. VIGIL. The play. Ironfall attacking Sam. Her life.

For everyone's safety, I had to get away.

My life had changed so much in just under a month.

"I need to quit my job," I said, closing my eyes. I braced myself. Here came the sharp words about my inevitable failure and lack of responsibility.

"And why is that?" I couldn't look at her. The clack of her nails only tightened the knot in my stomach.

"Umm...I..." I could come up with answers for a not-so-fictional supervillain—why couldn't I do the same with my own mother? "It's too much. I have a lot going on right now, and this is the least important thing on my agenda." And the most important thing to get rid of. I knew no one in theatre, but knew everyone at work, which made it the greatest risk.

She shook her head as she placed the palms of her hands together in front of her face. "In life we have to deal with a lot of things, and I wanted you to get the job so you could learn more life skills."

"You don't know the kind of pressure I'm under." Try your fandom coming to life. "It's something I think I have to do." *Or the world might pay the consequences.* I couldn't afford to fail. I couldn't afford Ironfall threatening anyone else.

Silence. She said nothing, only resumed drumming her fingernails. It's a miracle this table didn't have dents from it. A siren sounded in the distance.

"Well then, I'm busy, so decide something."

I looked up. "I can decide?"

"Yes." She said this like I should have known.

"Okay, I'm going to quit." I scooted the chair back and stood. "Thank you so much, Mom."

"I'd reconsider if I were you." And here came the disappointment.

"I'll think about it." But I'd already decided, so I ran to my room and drafted my letter of resignation.

FEB 8 – 2:57 P.M. EST

After school the next day, Ironfall and I walked to the hideout together. Sam would join us after the stagehand interest meeting. A snowflake drifted past my nose until it landed on my gray coat, melting.

"I've compiled a list of intel we need for the heist. Think blueprints, security, shift changes, habits." He sure wasn't pointing out the sights this time. "Stealth is key."

"Probably for the best." I forced a small smile. "You were a bit dramatic during your last heist."

He nudged my shoulder. "What's a heist without a little drama?"

"You play the *Mission: Impossible* theme song in your earpiece during all of them, don't you?" I chuckled.

"No, but that's a good idea," he said. "Though I don't have to pretend to be a movie character."

"But I do." I grinned.

"Hopefully you won't for long." Another smile, but something shifted in his face, sending me into panic mode. "This has to work. I can't fail again. *We can't fail.*" *And I'll kill your parents if you ruin this for me.* I could read between the lines.

The lightheartedness of before drained from the conversation.

"Then I guess I won't mess up." I gulped. My chest tightened as another weight pressed against my shoulders. I couldn't lose Mom and Dad. I couldn't.

A car alarm blared. I jumped. Ice. Slipping.

Oh n—

Arms. Ironfall gripped me until I steadied. My heart raced. I sucked in a deep breath.

"I got you. Are you okay?" he said.

I nodded. "Yeah. Thank you. I just slipped."

The horn still pulsated in the background.

He smiled, still holding me. "Anytime. I...I have your back." Had I imagined the tremble in his voice? He couldn't say he'd protect me while he threatened my parents. It didn't make sense.

He was a criminal. A murderer. And he'd take away my family at the drop of a hat.

I pulled away, setting my gaze on the VIGIL & ANTE Studios billboard. "Thanks."

"What's wrong?" he said. "Tell me."

"It's nothing." I forced a smile, but still didn't look at him. An unwanted lump formed in my throat. *Keep yourself under control.*

"If it's going to affect—" He paused, clearing his throat. "If it's going to affect our work, I need to know." Was he going to say something different? Why was he all of the sudden stumbling over his words? Where did the tremble in his voice come from? Where was the shallow banter from earlier?

I sighed, ignoring my own questions and turning back to his. I could get some of it out in the open, and it couldn't hurt too much. As long as he held my parents over me, I'd do what he wanted, until VIGIL stepped in. Yet why was it so hard?

"Rosemary?" His eyebrows knit together. He wasn't accusing me or forcing me to say something. He was *asking*. Could he read me that easily?

"You say you have my back, but you're also the one who threatened my parents if I didn't cooperate. I can't trust you." *I work for VIGIL. You can't trust me either.* I had to keep it a secret, and if he found out, me and my family would pay.

"You can trust me," he said. "You can always trust me."

"I know that's a lie." I gulped.

"Not this time." Still, he looked away. "But I understand why you don't believe me."

I couldn't take my eyes off him. What was going on in his head? Why was he acting so strange? And why, of all people, did he choose *me*?

He said nothing more until we reached his hideout.

FEB 8 – 5:23 P.M. EST

Sam and I walked toward my apartment in silence, which was weird because usually he wouldn't stop talking.

He cleared his throat. "Ironfall asked me to do some digging in VIGIL's records for the vault, but I found something else."

I froze, looking down at him. "He didn't tell me about this." What did he find? Did he know I betrayed Ironfall? How would he react? Would he tell?

He shrugged, shoving his hands into his pockets. "I don't

think he trusts you as much as you think he does. No offense or anything. I mean, he is Ironfall, the best villain—"

I cut him off. "I know he doesn't trust me. I was just saying."

"Rosemary, I know about you," he said. For the first time since the day I met him, Sam was completely serious, no trace of humor in his voice. My mouth went dry.

"You..." I breathed, trying to process what he just said.

He knew about me. VIGIL.

My parents.

"I know you work for them," he said.

"Sam, I..." I stepped forward, willing my knees not to give out. "You can't tell Ironfall. Please." My parents will die. I will die. Sam's life could be in danger too, not to mention Ironfall would disappear from VIGIL's radar. "You can't tell him."

"What's really going on?" He crossed his arms, stopping to face me. "Have you always worked for them?"

I shook my head. "I didn't think all this was real at first, but after you walked me home when I saw Ironfall stalking me, I did some research. Or I tried to; long story. Agent Liam met me, but said nothing. Slowly, I realized that everything was real, so I reached out to VIGIL again and agreed to be their double agent. Cloaker would have covered for me, but he's on another mission."

"And now you're a double agent," he breathed as if he was processing this all himself. Though the din of the New York City streets was loud, the silence between us was heavy. "That's the coolest thing I've ever heard." There was the Sam I knew.

"Sam, if you breathe a word of this to Ironfall, my parents will die." I pressed my lips together. "You can't tell him. This is the only way to stop him."

He nodded vigorously. "I won't say anything." Would he be able to keep this secret? "Remember, I framed a world-class jerk and kept that secret for a long time."

I breathed a sigh of relief. "Thank you."

Then he grinned. "So you're not as comfortable with a heist as you let on?"

I shook my head. "Absolutely not. I don't want to be doing any of this."

"It's cool and all, but this feels wrong." Sam shrugged. "I don't have a choice, though. Neither of us do."

"I know, and I'm so sorry I dragged you into this," I said. My eyes started to sting. "I tried to keep you out of it, but you kept pressing, and Ironfall found out. He came to kill you, and I had to think quick. VIGIL wouldn't answer and—"

"And I'm literally out here living my dream. Well, I would rather be working for VIGIL, but whatever, it's fine," he chuckled. "I should probably thank you. I've idolized VIGIL and the Safeguarders for way too long now. To find out it's real is the ride of a lifetime."

"You're welcome, then?" I laughed nervously.

"If I get killed, though, I'm 100 percent blaming you." His face turned serious for a split second before he broke into laughter again. He brushed his bangs from his face. How did he function with them? "My ghost will forever haunt you, especially when you get a VIGIL & ANTE Studios movie about yourself."

I shook my head. "I expect no less."

"Oh, also, please ask your VIGIL pals what information is less top-secret so I can show it to Ironfall," Sam said. "Also, if you want to ask them if I can watch the rough cut of *Project Safeguard 3*, that would be great."

"I will ask the first question only." I rolled my eyes.

It felt good to share my burden with him, no matter how scared I was that he'd accidentally let my secret slip. We laughed about fandom stuff for the rest of my walk home.

FEB 8 – 6:03 P.M. EST

The moment I got home, I ran to my room and dialed Agent Liam's number.

"Hi, this is Agent Rosemary Collins."

"Hello, Rosemary," Agent Liam said. I sighed with relief.

"Is it possible to talk to Ver? I have a computer question." Hopefully the movies didn't exaggerate her keyboard magic.

"One moment." He paused. I thought I heard a "Ver!" in the background.

"...I swear if I have to talk Commander Vigil through Instagram live one more time..." Ver muttered. Oh my gosh. If the public knew about that, imagine the hilarious fanart comics: COMMANDER VIGIL VS. TECHNOLOGY. Though it was a wonder no one had come up with something like that before since she was "old" in superhero years.

I laughed. A real, genuine laugh for the first time since this mess started. No lies behind it. Just me, fangirling. "Hi, Ver, this is Rosemary."

For a moment, I felt like I could get through this. And that wasn't just me trying to convince myself.

She gasped. "Oh, hi, Rosemary! Sorry, being the tech person is annoying when people don't ask Google first. Not you, of course. But yeah. What do you need?"

"Sam knows about me working for you, and he's on our side. He also maybe sorta broke through your firewalls and needs to know what information to keep out of Ironfall's hands," I said. Yeah, none of it would be great in his hands, but he needed *something*.

"Wait, really? How old is this kid?"

"Sixteen. I'm surprised too," I laughed.

"Looks like I'm going to be paying our newest informant a visit, then," she said. "Okay, that sounded creepy. What I mean is I'm totally recruiting him. You can never have enough computer geniuses."

I laughed. "So...the vault?"

"Yep. Just warning you that most info on the vault is off-the-books. Even I had a hard time finding it because everything was so scattered and encoded."

"Perfect. The harder it is to find, the better chance VIGIL wins. And since we're the ones getting the information, we control what he knows." Boldness surged through my bones. Rosemary – 1; Ironfall – 0. That was a first.

Why did I suddenly feel so confident? Maybe Ver's fierce attitude was bleeding into me. And Sam's too, apparently.

"You're pretty good at this, you know." I could almost see the grin on her face.

The knot in my stomach lessened as I chuckled. "Tell that to my sore muscles."

"I'm serious. For claiming to have no espionage skills, you've kept your cover well," she said. "He still has no idea?"

I pressed my lips together, passing the phone to my other hand. "Not that I know of. He's been acting weird, though. Before, he said we weren't friends, but now he's acting like we are. And how could he expect us to be friends if he's forcing me to work with him?"

"That's a pretty loaded question," she said. "But yeah, that's verifiably weird."

"He may just be lonely, but I can't shake the feeling that it's all part of his calculated plan. It has to be," I said. "But it's hard to tell if something he says or does is genuine or manipulation."

"What kind of things has he said?"

"He started to open up once, about his father, but then he shut down. Do you think he slipped up, or does he want me to think it's a touchy subject?" I sighed. "I'm so confused."

"We can be confusion buddies, then," she chuckled. "Sorry, that probably wasn't the right thing to say. Just don't lose sight of who he is." Ver paused. "But while you were talking I made a list of things to keep away from."

Wait, what? "That fast?"

"Who do you think I am? An amateur?" I could only imagine her shaking her head, trying to hold in laughter. "I know it doesn't seem like it, but VIGIL is here for you. Promise."

"I don't know how long I can do this."

"Remember what you're fighting for," she said. "That's what helps me."

"But what about when it becomes too consuming? Earlier today, saving my parents was all I could think about, and Ironfall saw it on my face," I said. "And then he asked me what was wrong, and I didn't know what to do, so I told the truth. Ver, what if I have to lie about being a double agent and he doesn't believe me?"

"You only slipped up once? You're a good liar." She paused. "Okay, I get that's supposed to be a bad thing, but when you're a spy it's a compliment."

"I hate lying," I said. "Before this I never told a lie. Now I've lied to my parents, to a supervillain. It's this web I can't escape from. Sorry, I'm spilling everything right now. You probably don't want to hear all this."

"No, it's okay. I do," she said. "We're all here for you."

"That's what he tried to tell me, in a way." I shook my head, closing my eyes. He just wanted to know my secrets for his own gain.

"Yeah, I'd trust us over him." She chuckled, muffling the line.

"I know." I gulped. "I just can't slip up again, because next time, my whole life might come crumbling down."

"Well, if it helps, the files are now on your computer. Is there anything else I can do for you?" she said.

I sighed. "Yes, actually. Did Agent Liam send anyone into Ironfall's hideout the other night?"

"Nope, our whole team was here. Why?"

I gripped my phone tighter. "Because someone did, and they tried to hack into Ironfall's computer." I shivered.

"A third party. That certainly makes things more exciting—er —interesting—er—you get what I mean."

I chuckled. "Yes, I get it. Who could they be?" I didn't need more enemies to add to my list.

"Lots of people, trust me. Fallen agents' families out for revenge, other branches of government who hate good communication, foreign nations, and a lot of other people." I pictured her shaking her head as she talked. "It could literally be anyone."

"Wow, that's not helpful."

"Hmm, it would help if you told me what's on that computer. What's he protecting?"

"He wouldn't tell me, he doesn't fully trust me yet." How was I supposed to handle this?

"Then gaining his trust is step one. Whatever you do, don't try to break into his computer yet unless you and Sam have a good opportunity. He'll figure it out just like he did with his mystery enemies."

"Okay, I can handle that." Hopefully.

TRANSCRIPT OF THE INTERVIEW PROCEEDINGS
WITH IRONFALL
SOME NAMES AND LOCATIONS REDACTED FOR SECURITY
INTERVIEW CONDUCTED ON MAY 20
LOCATION OF INTERVIEW: **[REDACTED]**
CASE #: **[REDACTED]**

AGENT LIAM BLAKE: It's interesting that you agreed to be in a play with Rosemary. I would have thought you'd focus on planning world domination.

IRONFALL: Well, we both loved theatre, and it was something I'd always wanted to do. Rosemary presented the opportunity, and I justified it by telling myself it would build trust.

AGENT LIAM BLAKE: How'd the trust thing work out?

IRONFALL: Hilarious.

CHAPTER 9

FEB 11 – 2:45 P.M. EST

Ironfall, Sam, and I entered Mrs. Rodriguez's classroom with a second wave of students. Once more, Ironfall looked like Nolan. Excited (and melodramatic) chatter echoed through the hall.

Five students had already seated themselves around two corners of the conference table, which was really two craft tables pushed together. Most seemed to know each other already.

I took a deep breath, stifled by Ironfall next to me. I'd hardly slept the night before, trying to figure out yesterday's conversation.

I wished Sam was standing between us instead of on his other side.

"Where should we sit?" I glanced at Ironfall. A dark piece of fuzz rested on his forehead. "Oh, you have something on your..." I pointed to my own face, then glanced away. Wait, would that make him think something was wrong again? Force me to say something else?

He chuckled. "Thanks." He rubbed a hand across his forehead. "Got it?"

I inspected him. The spot was gone...but his hairline seemed weird. Like it had...shifted. I blinked, then looked him up and down.

His powers made every part of his disguise look so material. Why did it suddenly seem like he was wearing a wig?

"Oh my gosh, look at that girl's shirt," Sam whispered. "The one with the blue hair."

Her bright aqua hair caught my eye first. Then I saw the face on her t-shirt. Ironfall. Bold, authoritative pose with "MISUNDERSTOOD" in obnoxious bold lettering beneath it.

My eyes widened. Well, this was awkward.

Ironfall chuckled, nudging me. "That's ironic." I looked back at his hairline, but the flaw was gone. Was it my imagination?

"I think you mean iconic." Sam grinned. "But yes, also very ironic that she's wearing it in your presence."

I couldn't take my eyes away from her shirt. So many people loved his character. Would they feel the same way if they knew he was in this very room?

"Maybe we should sit by her." Ironfall moved so close to me our shoulders touched.

"Yes!" Sam raced to the single chair on her right, but Ironfall didn't follow. Was he waiting for me to answer?

"Uh, sure," I said, forcing a smile in his general direction. Ironfall moved to sit two seats down from her. I took the one in between.

"I saw you staring at my shirt. You an Ironfall fan too?" The blue-haired girl grinned, looking straight at me.

I gulped, forcing a smile. "I suppose you could say that."

"I definitely am," Sam piped up.

"Two words: Rhett Wickford. The most beautiful man alive," the girl said.

Uh...I begged to differ. "He *is* a good actor." Played by another superhero who was *real*.

"And they're bringing him back. I miss my baby! If they ever kill him off"—she shook her head—"I'm storming VIGIL & ANTE Studios."

"You know it." Sam winked at her. Oh goodness, I think he just fell in love.

"Yeah." I glanced at the man we were talking about. "Me too."

"I'm Josie, by the way."

"Rosemary. It's nice to meet you." *Stay away from me or I might get you killed.*

"I'm Sam."

"And I'm Nolan," Ironfall said.

"Nice to meet you both. Are you two...?" She pointed at Ironfall and I.

My eyes widened. I shook my head. "No, no, no. We're just friends." Oh no. Friends was even overkill. Or was it? It's complicated, that's what it was. I glanced over at Ironfall. He just looked at me as if he was confused. Was he thinking about yesterday? Or studying me for lies? I pressed my lips together.

I wanted to sink into the floor.

"All right, good. It's always awkward when people in the cast date and inevitably break up," Josie chuckled. "It never fails."

I looked back at her as if I hadn't stared at Ironfall for a solid two seconds. Sam gave me a thumbs up. I wanted the floor to swallow me up.

"I bet," Ironfall said.

Mrs. Rodriguez stood up from her desk and walked toward the table. Thank goodness. "All right, everyone, welcome to the table read for our spring production of *Beauty and the Beast*. With such a talented cast, I have confidence this will be our best show yet. Does anyone have any questions?"

FEB 12 – 6:27 P.M. EST

Ironfall stood at the beat-up desk scrolling on his laptop as if this wasn't how we'd been spending basically all of our time since we started planning the heist. Going through top-secret CIA files wasn't as interesting as it sounded. Almost every document had something redacted (thank you, Ver), and it even left out all the action. Just lists of...stuff I didn't understand.

I'd been reading for two hours straight, and my bleary eyes still hadn't located anything related to security or the vault.

Sam groaned from across the room where his laptop was plugged in.

"What is it?" I closed my computer lid to take a break from the screen.

"I've gone over everything, and there are no records on what we'll find when we get down there. Not the metrics of the door, not the alarm system, not even the type of lock. We'll be walking in blind." He rubbed his hands together, calculating his next move. "Well, you will, because I'll be here pretending I'm Felicity Smoak."

I held a hand to my mouth to keep myself from laughing.

"I can't find anything either," Ironfall said. "Sam, get into the CIA and see what records they have. We need answers."

"Already on it." Sam attacked his computer again.

"So this is bad," I said. What would his workaround be? Something worse? Or maybe we'd have to give up the whole thing. That would be a miracle.

Ironfall sighed, looking back at his own screen. "I assume it uses some sort of biometric lock, but we have no idea what unlocks it or how to get around it."

"We could use Captain Cold's gun." I didn't have any ideas either, clearly.

"Captain Cold?"

How could he not get that? We were literally pulling a Leonard Snart-level heist. "It's a reference to *The Flash*," I chuckled.

"How can you be a literal supervillain without watching *The Flash*?" Sam piped up, not looking away from his screen.

"It is a bit of a problem," I laughed. "Can't have you only watching VIGIL & ANTE Studios movies for villain research."

"What, just me isn't good enough?" Ironfall smirked. "And are the two of you ganging up on me?"

My eyes widened. "No!"

"Yes!" Sam said, winking at me.

Ironfall shook his head, laughing. "Okay, I see how it is."

"What's the plan now?" I didn't want to know.

"We keep combing through these files," he said. "Sam, keep working on the CIA assignment. We could use some Flash speed right about now. Yes, I do know who the Flash is, I just don't have time to watch the show."

Sam turned back to his computer, and our little break was over.

"I'm almost done with my files; do you want help with yours?" Ironfall nudged me a few minutes later. Did he just…did he offer what I think he did?

"Sure, thanks." What did all this mean?

As the weather grew warmer over the next few weeks, we started planning the heist. We spent entire days hunched over blueprints and schedules. I missed so many days of school, and homework went completely out the window. He continued training me in combat, and slowly but surely, I improved in strength, stamina, and technique. It wasn't nearly as easy or epic as movie montages made it look.

Sam spent time combing through top-secret articles and learning how to deactivate cameras and alarms. Because of him, the amount I now know about advanced security systems is astounding. Still, the two of us combined didn't match the skill of any criminal mastermind Ironfall could have recruited. So why pick me?

In the midst of the darkness, there was a small glimmer of light. When I was at rehearsal, I didn't have to think about pretending to be a supervillain's accomplice. All I focused on was the stage. I think Ironfall felt the relief too. When he was there, he came alive. As if he stopped worrying about always being calculating and witty and turned into someone carefree. During those few moments between scenes, we laughed and talked about stupid stuff like normal friends would. For a few short hours, everything felt like it was as it should be. Then it would go back to "normal."

He was my friend. Sort of. Ugh, like I've said a million times, it's complicated.

MAR 5 – 11:38 A.M. EST

The chilly March air rustled my hair. Ironfall and I stood on the edge of Central Park, by Columbus Circle. It was a confusing area to drive in, but it was beautiful. If you looked one way, you could see tall buildings, and the other way, you could see the oasis itself. Benches lined the many walkways, as the city didn't usually allow people to sit on the manicured grass.

"That's it." I motioned toward the trees. "What do you think?"

He nodded, a smile growing. "It's bigger than I thought it would be."

"I can't believe you've never been here before," I said. After almost two months of him showing me his world, I figured it'd be a good idea to show him some of mine. Something that, for once, was real and not part of the mission. Maybe it would get him to trust me more.

"I guess I was waiting for someone to show me." Ironfall's grin was contagious. Right now, he seemed just like a normal guy.

"Wait till you get deeper in." I grabbed his strong hand and pulled him toward a narrow offshoot—one of my favorite routes. The trees arched over the walkway so it felt like entering a mysterious jungle. The park was a maze that drowned out the city's ever-present song. Another escape from real life.

We walked for a few minutes in silence as I took in the peace of the early spring trees.

"This is a refreshing break from the city." He closed his eyes and inhaled. The air smelled cleaner here.

"Really? I'd have thought you thrived on the chaos of it," I laughed. "Police sirens sing you to sleep, right?"

He opened his eyes and winked. "Music to my ears."

I looked away, but still felt his gaze on me. And it burned.

Then something ahead caught my attention. Auburn hair offset by a bright green coat. Mom? What was she doing here?

Ironfall couldn't see her. He didn't need to know anything more about her than he already did. And she couldn't see me with *him*. Skipping school.

I grabbed Ironfall's arm, then stepped in front of him, whipping around. "Pretend you're talking to me."

He cocked his head sideways. "I am talking to you."

"Right. But make it seem natural." Nothing about this was natural. Look at me, Ironfall. Just look at me.

"It is." He furrowed his brow. "Is something wrong?" Don't give me that innocent look.

I didn't check to see if Mom was closer. I couldn't let him see her. I couldn't let her see me.

But he'd be suspicious if I didn't explain, and I couldn't handle this right now because he was so close.

If she found out, then...then my mission was compromised. And Ironfall would murder her.

"My mom's behind us. She thinks I'm at school," I whispered, eyes wide. "Though, to be fair, I thought she was at work." My pulse echoed in my ears.

He looked past me. "Red hair, right?"

I sucked in a breath.

He tilted his head to the side. "I'm not going to hurt her, Rosemary." But he would. He stepped closer, pressing his hands on my forearms. I closed my eyes as his closeness somehow calmed my racing heart. Funny how that worked. "I...I know that I threatened them, and I'm sorry. That night...I wasn't there for revenge over what happened to your friend." His gaze dropped to his feet. All facades were off because his voice trembled.

This wasn't a lie.

It couldn't be.

"Rosemary..." His voice cracked. "I promise, I won't touch your family. No strings attached."

Speechless. Why would he say something like that? Did that mean I could get out? His hands still burned holes through my jacket and I couldn't breathe.

Ironfall rotated my body to the right. "She's passing us now." His voice was soft, quiet, almost as if he was scared. What was going through his head?

Then he turned. "We're good."

A weight lifted off my chest. I stepped back. "Sorry, that was unexpected."

"It's okay," he said, nodding. Was his claim of my parents' safety a test of loyalty? He said nothing else, but the way he stood, as if he'd been defeated, threw me off. This couldn't be a mask because he seemed so broken.

I pulled away from him to walk away.

"Coming out here with me would've been another example of you falling short, right?" he said. No hint of sarcasm or amusement in his tone.

Thoughts raced through my head, but I nodded. "She would not have been pleased, not that anything ever pleases her." I turned, and we kept walking. "Still, I try."

"My dad was hard to get along with too," he said. "Came up with some pretty interesting punishments when I messed up, which was always, if you can believe it." Was...was he opening up? He'd never allowed himself to be this vulnerable before.

"I'm sorry," I said. "What about your mom?" What on earth was even happening?

He sighed. "Never knew her, and my father refused to talk

about her. To this day, I don't know whether she died or abandoned me. I used to wonder if my father killed her." He thought *what?*

"You really believed that?" Our eyes met.

"You haven't met my father." He looked away as if ashamed. "But if he did, he had his reasons." No reason justified murder. I gulped.

"Did you go to school?"

He shook his head. "According to the government, I don't exist. Never did. So, no, I never went to school." Weird. "Don't feel bad about it; it made me who I am today." Was anything so bad that it could make such a broken monster? "Instead of taking art class I learned the art of war."

"That's..." I didn't know what to say. "Did you have friends?"

"No." He pressed his lips together. "But it had to be that way."

"Come on, even a supervillain can admit that kids need friends." I nudged him.

"My father always said you can't achieve perfection without sacrifice, and that was one of the many I had to make."

"Still, it's lonely." I offered a small, pained smile.

He looked away. "I don't think I've paid a high enough price yet."

"What do you mean?"

"Like you, I was never enough for my dad," he sighed. "He was never satisfied with my performance. Especially not after his experiments gave me powers."

Was. "Do you still have contact with him?"

"No." He looked hurt by his admission.

"Then why does it matter?" I sighed, pausing. I knew that special kind of pain. "I'm afraid that will happen with my parents too, eventually." Why did I say this? Wasn't I supposed to be more guarded than that?

"Oh?"

I looked down at the pavement. "They're so wrapped up in

each other and their work. I sometimes wonder if they care at all, or if I was just an accident they were obligated to take care of." Why was I spilling my secrets? "I just want them to love me. I know they do in their own way, they just...you know..."

"How could anyone not love you?"

My heart skipped a beat. "I—uh—thanks." No, that was dumb. Was he trying to seem nice? Did he actually mean it?

No, it was a lie. He was manipulating me.

I couldn't take this. Not now. I smiled, meeting his steady gaze. "We should start a crappy parent club."

"My father isn't as bad as I made him sound. He's a great man with vision. He wanted me to become like him—better than him even—I just wasn't strong enough. I guess I couldn't pay the price. Still can't." He looked down and cleared his throat. "That's why I have to succeed. Why *we* have to succeed. I have to show him I can do what he failed to. He needed someone close with superpowers. I can't be a failure."

"He wanted to...?" My breath caught. I couldn't finish that sentence. His dad wanted to take over the world. Was he a supervillain like his son? I swallowed, a painful lump rising in my throat.

Trees rustled in the silence that followed.

Ironfall broke eye contact as if he was nervous. "We are finishing what he started through ANTE."

I froze. *ANTE*. They were real too, and this was now so much bigger than Ironfall. In the movies, he had no connection to ANTE. They were separate villains in separate films. Cloaker barely took them down in his movie, and when they resurfaced in *Project Safeguard 2*, the entire superhero team was involved.

But in reality, Ironfall's father was connected to them.

"And...and..." But he stopped, looking away.

"And what?" I said, stepping closer to him. "You can tell me." What was he so scared to say? My hands quivered.

A sharp wind whipped across my face, breaking our conversation. I shivered. The nerves taut throughout my body only made me chillier.

"Are you cold?" His voice was still tender, the juxtaposition between monster and man.

"I'll be okay." I turned my face from him. "What were you going to say?" My voice was soft. Breathless. Scared to know the answer.

"Never mind." His face turned hard, and I knew not to press.

I gulped. "Well, let's sit in the sun." Were my words too stiff? Too awkward? Forced? As if I hated the fact that both he and his father were supervillains?

Still, Ironfall slowed his pace and moved closer so our shoulders pressed together. I tensed. My head jumbled itself with truth and lies.

If you get too close, he's going to find you out.
And he's going to hurt Mom and Dad.
He's a killer.
He's a monster.
He's broken.
He's working for ANTE.
What did he decide against saying?

"Do you think this is a good spot?" His sudden cheery words made me jump. He'd picked one of the few areas you could sit on the grass.

"Yeah," I said. *He's working with ANTE.*

How could I stop ANTE? With VIGIL on the verge of being shut down...

My knees weakened, so I hurried and sat down, opening my script to a random page to hide my thoughts.

I needed to tell Agent Liam about this as soon as possible.

"No one's ever listened to me before," he said. "Thank you."

I forced a smile. "You can tell me anything." Another lie.

"I know you have no reason to trust me, but you can do the same with me." What happened to us not being friends?

I stared holes into my script. "What scene do you want to

start with?" Then the conversation dipped back into the comfortable friendly banter we shared, but my mind raced with what had just happened.

MAR 5 – 10:11 P.M. EST

"This is Rosemary Collins. Another emergency," I said into the phone, glancing behind me as was now my habit. "I don't know how or why, but Ironfall is collaborating with ANTE."

Silence. A soft buzz came from the phone. "Are you sure he said ANTE?"

"Yes, why?"

"This is bigger than we thought." Did I imagine the waver in his voice, or was he worried? "I knew they were coming back. The CIA denied it, but I had a hunch. Their clutches are now deep within government agencies."

"How do you know?" I said.

His voice became hushed. "Cloaker is on a deep cover mission."

My eyes widened. "He's inside ANTE?"

"Yes," Agent Liam said. "That's why I couldn't pull him out to take your place."

"If ANTE is in everything..." I blinked. They could rise up and overthrow everything. And Ironfall was working for them and they were all over the CIA...

"He would know about you." It was as if Agent Liam read my mind. My stomach twisted. Ironfall knew. He had to. My parents... But something wasn't quite right.

"He would've found out the moment I became an agent," I said. "Right?" Still, that thought didn't comfort me.

"You're right. Something about this doesn't add up." He paused. "Keep him placated for now, and watch your back. I'll see what I can do to get the Safeguarders back together just in case, but don't get your hopes up." Then I heard a muffled, "... Ver, get me the CIA."

The Safeguarders—the superheroes I grew up watching on TV.

He cleared his throat. "You're a good agent, Rosemary. I'd hate to see this go south." Was...was Dad-Liam peeking through?

A smile tugged at the corners of my mouth. "I'll try my best, sir." A small amount of hope glimmered in my future. The Safeguarders would fix everything. And I would finally be safe.

A few hours later, my phone rang again.

"Hello?" My heart pounded.

"This is Agent Liam." He paused. "The Safeguarders are a no-go."

My chest caved. "Oh."

"The CIA claims Cloaker dismantled the terrorist organization years ago. They call Ironfall's claim of working with them a scare-tactic."

"But it's not," I said. "Can you get in contact with Cloaker? See what he knows?"

"No. Last time I was able to make contact was the same day Sam was attacked."

"Which explains why you didn't answer the phone." I gulped.

"Yes. Now we wait and see what everyone is planning," Agent Liam said. "We have to proceed carefully, because VIGIL and the world are at stake."

"Just tell me what to do," I said.

"Ver designed an untraceable thumb drive to clone Ironfall's computer. From there, they can work their magic and we'll get access to whatever he's keeping on there. You just have to keep the USB plugged in for five minutes. It'd better have some insight into what's going on."

MAR 31 – 9:37 P.M. EDT

I clutched the paper advertising *Beauty and the Beast* as I approached the sofa where Dad sat reading. My grip tightened, wrinkling the paper further. Deep breath.

I'd put this off since the cast list came out.

The apartment creaked.

Dad sighed, but didn't look up from his book. "What do you need?"

"Actually, I wanted to tell you about something." Interrupting his reading time was a dangerous game, but there were rarely other opportunities between his strange work hours and his determination to forget I existed.

"Okay. What is it?"

The flier crinkled again. "I got the lead role in the school musical."

"That's great." Yep, he didn't hear a word of what I just said.

I thrust the sheet above his novel to gain his full attention. "The dates are April 15–17, and the shows start at 7:30."

He swatted my hand away. "I have to work."

Uh-huh. Sure. "Doesn't the bank close at five?"

"Yes, but I need to stay late to do paperwork," Dad said.

"It's still a few weeks away; couldn't you take a night off or come on the weekend?" I knew better than to invite him. Yet in case something went wrong, I wanted to spend as much time with him and Mom as possible, even if they didn't like it.

"This is not up for discussion."

If he knew I risked my life spying on a supervillain for him, would he decide differently? Would he pay more attention to me?

Would he even care?

I swallowed. "Please, consider it. The cast is very talented. Some of them are headed for Broadway." Or they would be if they actually learned their lines.

I'd already lost my father in the pages of whatever he was reading.

"Good talk, Dad." I reached over the back of the couch and placed the flier on a cushion. Maybe he'd see it later and change his mind.

I doubted it.

The thumb drive weighed heavy in my pocket as more time went by. I tried, I really did, but I was never alone with his computer.

If Ironfall knew I worked for VIGIL, he never showed it. Never let it come between us, as weird as that was. Because he treated me like his friend. Like he had my back. Like he'd protect me.

During my waking moments, my mind raced, trying to find flaws in our nearly finished heist plan.

It was scary who I was becoming. Just a couple months ago, I was a shy nobody who didn't know what she wanted to do with her life. Now I was a full-fledged theatre kid who knew how to rob a top-secret facility. Each moment with Ironfall became less and less stressful because it was a routine. An eerily comfortable one.

Lying to him became somewhat easier, but I had to remain vigilant. Otherwise Mom and Dad would pay the price.

APRIL 13 – 4:42 P.M. EDT

Both the heist and the show drew near, so lines, plans, and that stupid thumb drive packed my head. While different scenes were being rehearsed for their final times, I went back and forth between practicing lines and running through the heist for loopholes.

For the last few days, something within our plan hadn't sat right with me. A detail was off. In my head I played through the part where we made our way down to the vault and assessed the lock. We had a fifteen-minute window to do that. Then—

"...next year?" Josie's voice brought me back to the auditorium. She sat sideways in the red theater chair, facing me.

"What?"

"Are you planning on majoring in theatre next year?" she asked.

I only shrugged. That wasn't exactly something I could answer right now. For one, I had way more important things to think about. And then I was buried in so many lies I didn't know what I should tell her.

"What college are you going to?" she said. That wasn't one I'd rather respond to.

"I don't know." Honestly, that was the least of my worries. "You?"

Josie shrugged and glanced back at Mrs. Rodriguez, who was currently acting out her vision for how the Beast should be portrayed, even though she was too short to look like much of a Beast. Ironfall stood a few feet away from her with a smug look on his face.

"Not sure yet. I'm thinking of NYU..."

I only stared. "Sorry, I zoned out for a sec." How had we missed the shift change? Then there'd be twice as many guards there.

Josie laughed. "I do that all the time. Especially in chemistry." She rolled her eyes, which almost matched her striking hair.

"Sorry, there's a lot on my plate." I didn't have time to think about this. I needed to fix the hole in our scheme.

"I know what you mean. At first, I was jealous of you for getting Belle, but now I'm happy," she said. "There's so much senior stuff, it's ridiculous. Senior quote, applying to college, graduation announcements, deciding what to do for the rest of your life. Why so much pressure?"

I stole another glance at Ironfall. He covered his mouth to hide obvious laughter at Mrs. Rodriguez motioning wildly through the air. Our eyes met again, his glittering in the stage light.

"Save me," Ironfall mouthed. Josie and I giggled.

A few minutes later, Mrs. Rodriguez quit pretending she could act like the Beast and gave Ironfall his part back. "All right, I need everyone up here for the Gaston scene."

Josie rose to leave.

"Hey," Ironfall said, suddenly nearby. Josie giggled, inching closer to him. "Talking about me?"

"Nope, just college and the future and stuff." She twirled a blue curl around her finger, suddenly taking the part of her character: one of the silly girls who fawned and squealed over Gaston.

Ironfall raised his eyebrows at me.

I smiled a little. "Yep. It's true."

"I bet you're going into theatre." Josie still focused on Ironfall-dressed-as-Nolan. "You probably already have a Broadway gig lined up."

"I need *all* actors in the Gaston scene." The director turned her eye upon Josie. "We're getting close to the performance, people."

"Sorry, gotta go." Then Josie ran onto the stage.

The moment she was out of earshot, I moved to the seat directly next to his.

Ironfall looked back at the stage, then laughed. "I think Rodriguez has a very specific vision, don't you?"

But I couldn't contain it any longer. The final puzzle piece. "I figured it out!" I squealed. Everyone on stage turned to stare. Yikes. Too loud. I bit my lip, then leaned in to whisper. "We're going to run into security during a shift change. That's what we've been missing." A grin crossed my face, eyes wide with anticipation of his response.

The cast started rehearsing again.

Ironfall rubbed his forehead. "Gah, how did I miss that?" He threw his arms wide and wrapped his arms around me. The next thing I knew, he spun me in the air as I clutched his neck. My feet brushed against the next row.

"You're brilliant!" he exclaimed. "I knew they wanted you for a reason." He stopped, setting me back on my feet.

I froze.

They. As in ANTE?

"Who's they?" And why choose me?

He just stared, eyes wide and chest rising and falling as if he'd just spilled a secret.

"Rosemary, come step in for Jane!" Mrs. Rodriguez shouted from the stage.

I couldn't leave now, not after Ironfall dropped a bomb like that. But I had to leave without the answer that plagued me since the beginning.

Why me?

TRANSCRIPT OF THE INTERVIEW PROCEEDINGS
WITH IRONFALL
SOME NAMES AND LOCATIONS REDACTED FOR
SECURITY
INTERVIEW CONDUCTED ON MAY 20
LOCATION OF INTERVIEW: **[REDACTED]**
CASE #: **[REDACTED]**

AGENT LIAM BLAKE: Were you trying to manipulate Rosemary that day in Central Park?

IRONFALL: No.

AGENT LIAM BLAKE: So when you said you wouldn't hurt her parents, you were telling the truth. Weren't you afraid that when she was free from your threat she would stop helping you?

IRONFALL: I was terrified.

AGENT LIAM BLAKE: So why did you do it?

IRONFALL: I knew that if I was forcing her, it wouldn't be real.

AGENT LIAM: What wouldn't be real?

IRONFALL: Everything, Agent Liam. Everything.

CHAPTER 10

APRIL 14 – 3:35 P.M. EDT

After the last three months, I still hated running. The drills Ironfall and I did together were pure torture, even after so much practice. Sure, I always felt better after, but yeah, it wasn't fun.

I gulped down a glass of water. People say that running eases anxiety and stress, and now I believe them.

"You're almost as good as me. Almost." Great, Ironfall, but it didn't make me feel less tired.

I laughed. "Thanks, but, yeah, no. You've been training since you were what? One month old?"

He crossed his arms. "That's not fair. But you're a pretty good rival right now."

"So you feel threatened by me, huh?" I said. Something panged in my chest. Did he actually believe that? "Mr. 'I can lift twice as much as you.'"

"Well, let's test that theory out."

Ironfall took a step back, raising his fists. And then we sparred. I thrust my fist at his head, but he ducked. His fingers clamped around my forearm, but I twisted it away. My foot connected with his knee.

Now I was in a completely different headspace. I was no longer here to have fun, I was here to train.

He groaned and melted to the ground. Now all I had to do was get him on the floor and hopefully he would tap out.

The next second, he whipped out something I'd yet to learn

and I was pinned to the ground. No, I wasn't going down so easily.

This was only practice for the time he inevitably fought me for real. When I defended my parents.

I shoved him off of me and scrambled to my feet. Stay low. Keep a good core. Fast feet. Anticipate.

Inhale. Exhale.

He threw himself toward me, but I deflected, twisting him around. But he maneuvered out of it. He was stronger. Quicker. Better. My breaths came heavy as I tried and tried to get him on the ground.

If I could just find his weak point. Something. Anything.

I needed to focus.

Then he stepped back, nodding. "See, I said you were good."

It took a few moments to recover. To remember that my life wasn't actually in danger right now. "Not good *enough*."

"You're getting there," he said, a grin sliding across his face. Now, I started slipping back into our normal routine. The one where I didn't have to think about him being a supervillain.

"Can I ask you something?"

"Sure." A mischievous gleam in his eye.

"Who's the 'they' you talked about at rehearsal?" That sounded casual, right?

He sighed, averting his gaze. "I...it's complicated." The look in his eyes told me there was more to it. Why didn't he want to tell me?

Why didn't he want to talk about it? I needed to know.

"You can tell me," I said.

He looked away, shoulders falling forward. "Okay. But I can't. Not...not right now."

I nodded, then turned and swept my water bottle off the ground. I gulped. The cool water refreshed my throat and gave me time to think—

A heavy hand tackled my shoulder. Liquid spewed all over the floor as my chest caved inward.

I whipped around, body poised for a fight. But I only met now-laughing Ironfall.

"Ha. Ha. Very funny." I forced my body to relax. Not funny at all. *He's just messing with you.*

He seemed upset the second before, but now...

Why did he want to take my mind off that topic? Why didn't he want me to know?

Did ANTE choose me? And why?

"Couldn't resist." He whipped out a dagger. Like a full-on Renaissance Faire prop. "Okay, what do you do when this happens?" We'd practiced this move a million times. Fighting with knives. Fighting with swords. Fighting with fists. He'd taught me it all.

I glanced from him to the blade. My body still electrified. But this was *my* Ironfall. The one who never quit teasing. I raised an amused eyebrow.

"What do you do?" he repeated.

Now it was my turn to give him a hard time. "Pull an Indiana Jones"—I bent his wrist and grabbed the blade from his hand—"and bring a gun to the knife fight. Or, you know, do that." I pointed at the blade now in my grip.

"Hilarious."

"I know. It's what I'm best at." Then we both broke down in laughter.

Just then, Sam walked in, balancing his laptop in his left hand. "Am I interrupting something?"

"No." I still giggled.

"Yes."

"I don't even want to know." Sam shook his head, now laughing with us. "Actually I do. What's going on?"

"Inside joke," Ironfall said, pulling himself together. "Don't you have hacking to do or something? Keep working on our fake clearance badges."

"I was coming to tell you I finished them," Sam said. "Everything is ready to go for the heist."

"Everything except..." Ironfall's voice trailed off as he turned toward me.

Sam glanced from him to me.

Awkward silence. My gaze snagged on Ironfall's laptop. It sat there on the desk, out in the open. All I needed was a few moments alone with it to slip in Ver's thumb drive. Then VIGIL would have all his secrets, and maybe the CIA would finally let us arrest him.

"Why don't you go home and shower. Then put on something nice."

I blinked. Wait, what? "Why?" I couldn't wipe the hint of a smile off my face.

He looked at the floor. "We're going to need it when we spy on the CIA tonight." Okay, that still didn't answer my question. "We need to go undercover, and we, uh, need to look nice."

"Oh, yeah." I stood there a bit breathless for no apparent reason, trying to keep a blank face.

Still, his avoidance bothered me. Why did he genuinely seem upset talking about it?

Sam just stared as Ironfall silently moved away.

"Did he just ask you on a date?" he asked once Ironfall was out of earshot.

I rolled my eyes. "No, it's an undercover mission." Okay, but he was right, it sounded like a date. Was it a date? "He said we're just going to spy on the CIA."

"Uh-huh. If you say so." He was still smiling. Oh, he totally thought this was a date. Great.

BESTVIGILMEMES.BLOGGINGLIFE.COM/IRONFALL
FEATURING THE BEST VIGIL & ANTE STUDIOS POSTS
(DON'T @ ME)
– UNAVERAGEVIGILFAN2002

justvigilfangirlthings:
Imagine Ironfall staring at you like you're literally the only person in the world who matters to him...because you are.

---

ironDIDNTFALL:
Dude when Ironfall finally gets a girlfriend he's gonna be unstoppable
Comments:
ironfallsarmy: I VOLUNTEER

---

thevillainwasbetter:
Ironfall needs a soft TM cinnamon roll who shows him the world. And then they slowly fall in love.
Comments:
'tiltheendofthemovie: Someone write a fic
Antefan231: TAKE MY MONEY
DegreeSurgeIsFire: WAIT and she's a normal girl outside the superhero world
rhettwickfordstanaccount: Brooooooo

---

vigilmerchcollection:
Coffee shop au where Ironfall orders black coffee but you accidentally take his drink. Now you have to return it...

APRIL 14 – 6:18 P.M. EDT

I reached for the door handle as an uncontrollable smile caught my lips. Me, in a beautiful dress. My hair somehow cooperated, and for once a makeup tutorial worked. I stood taller (and not because I was wearing heels).

My pulse fluttered.

"Where are you going?" Mom's harsh voice cut through the apartment.

I jumped, then turned, fingering the trim of my pale blue dress. "Uh, I have something to go to for a project. I'll try to be back by eleven." I glanced at Dad sitting at the dining room table, hunched over paperwork. He didn't even glance at me.

Mom raised a disapproving eyebrow. "Looking like that?"

"Is it bad?" I shrank back, resting a hand on the door handle.

"Yes. You aren't going out in that."

"Listen to your mother." Dad continued jabbing calculator keys.

I wrapped my arms around my waist as if hiding the delicate beaded design from her view. "But you were fine with it when I went to homecoming." Maybe...maybe it wasn't actually a flattering dress.

"Well, I'm not fine with it now." The same harsh tone. "And stand tall. You won't impress anyone without confidence." But I *did* feel some sort of confidence before she criticized my favorite dress.

"I have the perfect thing to wear." She glided into her room and returned with a long black dress (gown?). Golden leaves were embroidered into the tulle skirt, lessening as they drew nearer to the V-neck.

"I think that's a little much."

"You can never do too much."

I touched the hem of my skirt. "But I love this dress."

She thrust her gown toward me. "Change. Now."

"She's trying to help." Dad groaned. "If only someone would do the same with these stupid finances. I need to hire someone," he muttered. Wasn't he a banker?

I sighed, looking down at what was apparently a potato sack, then went back to my room and changed into my mother's gown. I twisted to close the back. Red waves swept from my haphazard updo. I brushed a strand away from my face.

Why did Mom even have this in her closet?

It *was* prettier than my cheap homecoming one. What if Mom thought this looked worse on me?

What would Ironfall think? No, no, that shouldn't have even crossed my mind. This was just a part of planning.

Nothing to worry about.

Then I went out, but she didn't even comment on my appearance. Not even to say I looked like a princess or "when did you grow up so fast?"

I pressed my lips together.

The weight of their lives rested on my shoulders. If I did one thing right, it had to be this.

"He's not picking you up?"

"It's just a project. Something for our play." Right. Just a project. Which was why my stomach was in knots.

"Trust me, I know what this is *really* about." No, no, you *really* don't.

"I think you have the wrong idea." On so many levels. Little did she know this was all about a heist I planned with a supervillain she thought was a movie character.

"Okay. You think that," she said. "Now go."

"Do I look...look pretty?" My voice wavered. It was a stupid thing to ask. How I looked didn't even matter.

"You need a necklace."

Dad said nothing.

I dug fingernails into my palm to keep from tearing up. "I think it's fine. And I'm running late," I said. Maybe I did need one though... "Do you have a particular one?"

"I do." She retreated to her room, then came out with a delicate gold chain. "Turn around." She clipped it around my neck, then turned me around. "That will do, I guess." She *guessed?*

I looked away from her hollow eyes. "I need to go. I love you." Then I grabbed my clutch off the counter and went out. The door shut behind me and I leaned against it, closing my eyes. I just needed to pull myself together to do this. The last thing I needed was to be upset about my mom and self-conscious of this overdramatic dress that looked like it came straight from the red carpet.

"Whoa. You look…"

My breath caught as I saw him down the flight of stairs. There Ironfall stood, outside my apartment, staring at me. His thick dark hair was combed back, a few rogue strands brushing against his temples. He wasn't in disguise, he was himself. The crisp collar of his pressed black dress shirt accentuated his chiseled jawline, and the sleeves hinted at the strength in his arms.

Heat rose in my cheeks, and time seemed to stop. My hands lifted the front of my skirts as I descended the stairs. Oh gosh, I hoped I wouldn't fall. Not while he was looking at me like… well…like that.

What was he doing here? I thought we would meet wherever we were going.

And then we were on the same level.

If I met his gaze much longer my knees might go weak, so I glanced down at my dress, rubbing my palms against the black tulle. "You're the one who told me to look nice." The corners of my lips threatened to perk up into a smile, but I suppressed the urge.

"Well, let's go. Do you have a notebook?" Whew. He seemed to have snapped out of…whatever that was.

"In my purse." My fingers clutched the small bag. *See, Sam, it's not a date*, I told myself.

Then we were off. We took an Uber back to the CIA building. The NYC lights glittered through the car window as we passed them by. This new situation didn't sit right with me. Up to that point, I'd been so used to our routine of planning the heist and rehearsing the show, but I'd never have predicted this.

The driver let us off nearby, and we walked a couple of blocks to our destination. I saw the CIA building. I was familiar with this route by now, as we'd cased the building from different locations many times. We had almost every agent's routine memorized at this point.

Ironfall took my hand. "Part of our cover," he whispered. My heart wouldn't slow. He led me under a small overhang with a red carpet underneath. What had I signed up for?

"Where are we going?" I asked.

"You'll see." Did I imagine the waver in his voice? His hand burned against mine.

Ironfall led me inside, into the most lavish lobby I'd ever seen. Ornate textured wallpaper covered the walls and the large columns placed around the room. Whoa.

"Welcome, Mr. Johnson. Please follow me to your table," a man in a white tux said. Oh my gosh. Were we going to eat here?

This was the nicest place I'd ever set foot in. Couldn't we have cased our target from another place?

We went up to a rooftop restaurant right across the street from the CIA building. Upon arriving, the waiter immediately took us to a small wooden table lit by three candles. A band played a slow waltz which made the candles and décor and everything...romantic. The thrum of the city pulsated, and skyscraper lights twinkled like stars in the background. A warm April breeze rustled through my hair. This was all so overwhelming. And now on a rooftop, well, that was a lot for a girl to handle.

Finally, Ironfall dropped my sweaty palm to pull my chair out for me, as if he was a perfect gentleman.

I sat down and glanced over at the CIA building. Perfect view. *Beautiful* view.

Waste of a lovely night.

The waiter took our drink orders and handed us the menus embossed with gold-leaf lettering. I'd never heard of most of the dishes on here, and let's just say that the descriptions were not very helpful. Ah yes, the Caesar salad looked like a safe option.

He paid for this with stolen money. Money he shed blood for. No. I shoved it from my mind. Now was not the time to think like that.

I glanced back at the building. No one had entered or left since we got there, at least from what I'd seen.

"Seems to be a quiet night," Ironfall murmured. Yet it was always quiet. That was the point of a secret headquarters.

"Yeah, I guess it is." I didn't take my eyes off the street, partly because I didn't want to miss any vital piece of information, and partly because I couldn't face what was before me right now. Tonight I just couldn't keep myself in check, could I?

Everything he did was a test. We weren't friends, he said so himself. Many times.

"You're nervous about this, aren't you?" And then there was that. He thought I was nervous. And I was. About everything. "Don't be." Our eyes met, my gaze melting into his dark eyes, eyes that seemed to stare deep into my soul. "No matter what happens, I'll be right there. We'll do it together. Side by side."

"Side by side," I repeated. *Soon my parents will be safe.* And Sam and I would be free.

The waiter came back with our drinks and took our order, offering me a break.

The sky turned from pink to purple to black, and I felt a little more like what was my new normal. The candles flickered at a small breeze, casting more strange shadows across Ironfall's face.

I glanced over at the CIA building. Someone exited. Tall, male, gray hair. Not unlike most of the other agents who frequented the place. That was all I could make out.

"Well, there goes Frank," Ironfall said. "Now there should be only Ed, Jake, and Karen in there. And security."

"Karen must be staying late to speak to the manager." I giggled quietly, fearing I'd draw unwanted attention to our conversation. Also, was it appropriate to giggle in an esteemed establishment? "How can you even see that far?"

He winked. "Magic."

My smile lingered. "Oh really?"

"Yep. Dead serious," he said as he was on the verge of laughter.

"Right. Right." I sighed and glanced back at the CIA building, the initial reason for us to be here. Yet I felt like that reason was slowly slipping away.

Another waltz picked up as more couples got up and started dancing. Everybody here was on a romantic date and just—sigh—so adorable. I couldn't take my eyes away from the dancing couples.

"You want to dance?"

My eyes widened as they darted toward Ironfall. "What? Oh, no, I was just watching them. I didn't mean…" But he was already up with his arm stretched out. I glanced back at the building we were supposed to be watching. "What about…?"

"I think we know enough." His voice was calm, deep, and sure.

My gaze traveled from Ironfall's eyes down to his hand. "Are you sure?" Nope. Nope. Nope. We definitely needed to take more notes.

"We've been observing their schedules for weeks."

Then why were we here now? This was becoming more and more like a date.

My hand slipped into his. He drew me onto the dance floor and our arms slid into position. Seemed like they were meant to fit that way. We swept across the dance floor as if we were the only ones there. I could hardly hear the murmurs of the dancers around us, all I noticed was Ironfall's hand caressing mine.

And it was suffocating.

This wasn't real. Both of us were pretenders, here to get something we needed. I was here to protect my family and save the world. He was here for some other reason. Why try to get into my head? Why bring me up here if he'd already scouted the area? Why choose *me*?

"Ironfall?" I whispered.

"Hmm?"

Was I really going to ask this?

Yes. "Why me?" I couldn't look him in the eye. "I'm nobody."

His grip tightened as if he was trying to keep me from running. "I guess I have to tell you."

"What are you afraid of?" I said, lines of concern creeping across my face. If Ironfall was scared of something, the world should be terrified.

"Remember how I said I haven't had contact with my father?" He looked away, but his hold on me didn't loosen, it only tightened. "That wasn't entirely true."

"Oh?" I couldn't breathe. What did his father have to do with this other than molding Ironfall into the monster he was today?

"He sent me a single message with no details, no reasons, just a name." He pressed his lips together and met my gaze. "Rosemary Collins."

I stopped dancing. "Your father knew about me?" Which meant ANTE did. They had my name on a list before all of this started, when I wasn't a double agent or even an agent. Just a fangirl trying to cope with life and maybe, just maybe, do something her mom wouldn't criticize her for.

"Yes," he said. "But I don't believe ANTE wanted to harm you. I think somehow they believe you're the one who can turn the tables in their favor."

The music got louder.

"Why didn't you tell me this sooner?" My chest rose and fell.

"I—I couldn't." Why was this so hard for him? What was I missing?

"Why not?"

"I didn't want you going over to their side before..." He stopped, shaking his head. "Everything ANTE does has a purpose. Choosing you wasn't an accident. So, when I got the name, I figured if I wasn't good enough to take over the world by myself, maybe you'd be good enough for both of us. I could do what my father hasn't been able to do yet, and then he'd be prouder than if I–" He averted his eyes. "Than if I simply delivered you to him."

"But I don't have any powers. *Nothing.*" I'm just a good liar. Too good. I wanted to get away, anywhere but here. Yet I needed to hear the rest.

"Something about you caught ANTE's eye." His hand burned against my back. "My father gave me the simple task of recruiting you, and...and I couldn't do it. I failed again."

"Did the message say anything else?" I gripped his hand tighter. I had to know.

"Nothing."

"It doesn't make sense. What was so special about me?"

"You're right, it's strange. You have a strong moral compass, and clearly you support the heroes rather than the villains. And you care about others. To even get you to help me I had to... motivate...you with threats. You had no combat skills, no hacking skills, no espionage skills."

And now I'm a double agent trained as a supervillain's weapon. My body tensed as I stepped back, lengthening the distance between us as we continued to slow dance.

"You're still scared of me." Yet that didn't seem to alarm him, he just looked sad. His shoulders fell as his brown and blue eyes reddened.

I couldn't lie this time. "Yes."

"I promise, I won't hurt you or your family." The earnestness in his tone... "Please. I'm not forcing you to be here. To help me."

"But there's no way to know whether or not you will follow through." I gulped. If I betrayed him right now, would he storm off to murder them with his dagger? Slice their throats... Suddenly a Caesar salad sounded like poison. I thought about mentioning it, but then it might give him the idea that I would betray him.

Because I already had. So many times.

He couldn't find out.

Ever.

"I know," he said.

I took a deep breath, looking away. *VIGIL agent—I'm a VIGIL agent.* "But I will continue to help you." Because there was no way he'd let a promise get in the way of his goal, no matter how sorry he pretended to be.

Was it pretend?

TRANSCRIPT OF THE INTERVIEW PROCEEDINGS
WITH IRONFALL
SOME NAMES AND LOCATIONS REDACTED FOR
SECURITY
INTERVIEW CONDUCTED ON MAY 20
LOCATION OF INTERVIEW: **[REDACTED]**
CASE #: **[REDACTED]**

AGENT LIAM BLAKE: How did you find out about Rosemary?

IRONFALL: ANTE reached out to me with the task to recruit her for them.

AGENT LIAM BLAKE: But you didn't tell her that for a long time. Why?

IRONFALL: I had bigger plans for us. And I couldn't lose her to them...not yet.

AGENT LIAM BLAKE: But it was what your father wanted.

IRONFALL: I wanted to give him his end goal instead of something so small.

AGENT LIAM BLAKE: So whose side were you really on? ANTE's?

IRONFALL: My own.

AGENT LIAM BLAKE: It sure seems like you were on ANTE's side.

IRONFALL: That is true, but they weren't exactly on *my* side.

AGENT LIAM BLAKE: Can you elaborate on that? Because it sure seems like you had a lot of access to their organization, which they liked to keep a pretty tight grip on.

IRONFALL: They contacted *me*.

AGENT LIAM BLAKE: But you took the job. Why?

IRONFALL: So I wouldn't fail them again.

AGENT LIAM BLAKE: Wouldn't fail ANTE? So your loyalties did lie with them.

IRONFALL: It's more complicated than that.

AGENT LIAM BLAKE: Well then, why don't you uncomplicate it?

CHAPTER 11

APRIL 15 – 1:59 A.M. EDT

My eyes hurt whenever I tried sleeping that night. My mind raced with nightmares. Reality seemed stretched and bent so now I couldn't see the truth.

Finally, I got up to get a snack or do something that would take my mind off of everything for a little while. The apartment was dull but filled with the ever-present sounds of a busy New York midnight. A siren echoed in the distance, but I was desensitized to it. Yet when my foot landed on a creaky floorboard, my pulse and mind raced.

Had someone heard? Who was there? Was someone poised to attack me?

My hands shook as I opened the fridge. Grabbing the milk jug, I poured myself a glass.

Nights were the loneliest.

"Rosemary?" Mom flipped on the lights. "What are you doing?"

I jumped. The glass slipped through my fingers and shattered. "I was j-just getting something to drink." It was only Mom. No need to panic. Even if it wasn't Mom, Ironfall had trained me well. "I couldn't sleep." Then I leaned down and picked up a couple of the larger shards, careful not to touch the sharp edges.

Go back to bed, Mom.

I still felt her eyes on me. Why was she standing there? Oh no, I didn't make her mad, did I?

She plastered on her glittering dress-to-impress smile. "Why not? Does it have anything to do with what he told you tonight?"

I froze. Oh no. "What?" Did that sound casual enough? I forced my fingers to keep picking up glass. "I told you, it's just a project." Why was she so adamant about this whole thing? And for once in her life why did she care so much? She needed to go away. I was in this mess because I was trying to save her, and she couldn't jeopardize that.

And why didn't she scold me for shattering one of her precious glasses?

"Just a project, hmm?" She narrowed her eyes. "I'm your mother. You're supposed to tell me these things. It's what *good* daughters do." How would she know that? She never even tried.

"I'm telling you the truth. Really." *I'm sorry.* I wanted to say something, to stop the lies, but I couldn't because I was on a top-secret mission that everyone—including her—thought was part of a movie. And if Ironfall somehow found out I was a double agent…

"Okay," she said. She didn't buy it. A floorboard creaked as she shifted.

"Don't you believe me?"

"You make it sound very convincing." She rested against the countertop. "You sure there's nothing else you want to tell me?"

"Yes, I'm sure." I placed another shard into the trash can.

"I'm trying to help you here." Was that…desperation in her voice?

I hesitated. "There's nothing you can help with." I was the one there to help her.

"You know I love you, right? You might not understand it now, but I'm trying to *protect* you."

"From what? There's nothing you can do." I looked up. Her face remained blank. I didn't need protection, I wanted her to love me. To hold me.

"There's so much you don't know about the world." She made it sound like I was a helpless, naïve five-year-old. But it was the other way around. Did she know that my fandom came to life and blew up in my face? No. I knew more about this strange new world than she did, and even then, I didn't know much. "You never know what the boys you like are keeping from you. What's hidden on their computers." *Computers.* That was oddly specific.

No, I was just paranoid.

"Mom, please just stop. I don't need a lecture about boys right now." A lump formed in my throat. *Don't cry.* It would give too much away and she'd pry even more.

She sighed and walked away. Did she really give up that easily? I was glad to see her go, but the conversation seemed more like she wanted to convince herself she was a good mother than actually love me.

"Are you going to help me get the glass off the floor?" My voice cracked.

"Clearly you prefer to clean up your own messes. But I'll be here when the real mess comes. And I do believe that will be sooner than you think."

My eyes stung. Nothing anyone did would fix this. She didn't even know it was real. And if she did...would she have cared?

APRIL 15 – 6:27 P.M. EDT

It was show day. My stomach was in knots and I couldn't stop thinking about last night, so things were going great for me. Sam walked to the theater with me, wearing all black, ready to run the tech booth.

"So how did last night go?" Ah yes, the question I'd been dreading. "Did he kiss you?"

My eyes widened. "What? No!" I smacked his arm to drive

my point home. "I told you, it wasn't a date." But he did dance with me and now I was more confused than ever.

"What intel did you gather, then? Learn anything we didn't already know?"

"No, we just wanted to be thorough." My stomach flipped. "He told me something, though. Something important."

Should I tell Sam? He'd kept my secret so far, but something told me last night was just between Ironfall and me.

"Important to the mission important? Or relationship status important?"

"He told me why he chose me," I said. "And he promised not to hurt my family. I think he trusts me."

"Oh my gosh, he fell in love with you."

"No, he didn't." I shook my head. "But that's not the point. He's connected with ANTE, and they told him to get me to join them. He doesn't know why, but he thought it was because I was some sort of secret weapon. So he planned to double-cross them and use me first." I left out the part about him not wanting to tell me. Sam didn't need to know that.

"Wait, *ANTE* like the top-secret villain organization thing from the *Cloaker* movie?"

"One and the same," I sighed. "I'm having a bit of a life crisis right now, if you can't tell."

"Well, just get through today, and then we'll worry about your feelings for Ironfall," Sam said.

"I think you mean the fact that ANTE wanted me to join them," I said.

Sam shrugged. "That too."

We made it the rest of the way to the theater, then went inside to prepare for the production. Backstage buzzed with activity. People traded eyeshadow palettes, put makeup on each other, and rehearsed a few lines. Showtunes blasted in the background on shuffle, switching between *Hamilton*, *Phantom of the Opera*, *Wicked*, *Dear Evan Hansen*, *The Lion King*, *Aladdin* and many others.

Was everyone as nervous as I was? Did everyone have that close to vomiting feeling? This was way more than I signed up for.

Josie did my makeup and hair.

"What happened to the costumes?" an ensemble actress shouted above the haunting chords of "The Music of the Night." All the girls in the room gasped at once.

As Josie wrapped the last of my red hair around a curling iron, I glanced over at the dressing room costume rack. What in the world? Our low-production-value costumes were gone. In their places, vibrant gowns that felt and looked extremely expensive. Straight off of Broadway. Ironfall didn't steal them...did he? Oh gosh, we didn't need *this* to incriminate us.

Incriminate *him*.

I thought back to the people he killed during his bank robberies. Did he...? I blinked. No.

"Josie, are you done?" I said.

She wasn't paying attention to me. "Oh, yeah."

I left the main dressing room, entering the small common room behind the stage. Ironfall leaned back in one of the chairs as he ate a granola bar while talking to Sam. He looked so innocent. No one would ever think he had killed anyone.

Wait, was I hallucinating or were the two of them laughing together?

I raised my eyebrows as I walked up. "Did you actually forgive Sam for shooting you?"

"A temporary truce," Ironfall said, now leaning forward. He sat between two large cardboard boxes storing props from previous years.

"I'll leave you two alone, then," Sam said, backing away. Please don't leave. I didn't want to have to do this.

Be brave and ask him. "Did you steal those costumes?" I whispered, glancing around to make sure none of my castmates heard. That would put them in danger. More danger than being in close proximity with him.

He raised his eyebrows. "What? No." Then he stood up, set the half-eaten bar down, and walked closer.

"How did you do it?" My voice fell into a whisper. "I know you had something to do with this because our costumes didn't have that many rhinestones at dress rehearsal." I hoped that didn't sound accusatory. "And some of them literally came from Walmart."

He sighed, looking away. "There's something I have to tell you."

Uh-oh. Here it came. "Hmm?"

His eyes suddenly looked so much younger than eighteen. Was he…scared? "I was going to wait until tomorrow, but I think I should tell you now." My heart thrashed against my chest, and I searched his face for some other clue. "You wanted to know what was on my computer." I froze. Did he know about the thumb drive? What did this have to do with costumes?

Still, I nodded.

"They're plans—disguise plans. 3-D mask renders. Clothing sketches. Costume patterns. Special effects programs." He pressed his lips together, eyes searching mine.

"I don't understand." My forehead creased. Why would that be his big computer secret? Couldn't he just create illusions? Shift reality to create the disguises and costumes and everything VIGIL & ANTE Studios portrayed him to be? "Why would you need—?"

He sighed, eyes cast downward. "My powers…they aren't what you think they are."

"What?"

Ironfall sighed again, taking a step toward me. Then he scanned the area before turning back. I gulped. Without taking his eyes off me, he reached into a box. His fingers wrapped around an open pocketknife. A chill ran through me.

What was he doing?

"Watch," he said, as if reading my mind. I stared at the tiny blade. It was so small, but in his hands, it could do so much damage.

He lifted his other hand and turned the knife towards it.

Before I could say anything, he pressed the blade into his hand.

I gasped.

Ironfall didn't even flinch.

Blood pooled in the palm of his hand as he pulled out the bleeding...

"What did you—?" But something cut me off. Because the skin on his hand...it knit back together. Blood still stained the knife and his now unbroken skin.

But the gash was gone.

He gestured toward his hand with the bloody pocketknife. "This...this is all I'm capable of. Healing myself, others. The whole changing realities thing is nothing but a facade of cheap magic tricks and elaborate disguises."

I brushed a finger across his hand. It was perfect. No incision. Not even a scar.

Nothing.

Speechless.

"I told you my father experimented on me until I got powers, but I didn't tell you something went wrong. I was supposed to end up strong, but instead I ended up weak, my power virtually useless to his plans. So I invented a new identity. A new power so people would fear me. I learned magic tricks, the art of disguise, sewing, 3-D printing, makeup, special effects, and just about anything else you can think of. And the answers to years of research are all on my computer." His computer. Was that really all that was on it? I needed an opportunity to use Ver's thumb drive.

I...I didn't know what to say. "So the movies—VIGIL—got it wrong."

"I wanted them to." He looked down once more. "I made them believe I was more than I am. Made you believe so too, but everything was a lie." Was it? Or was it his way of manipulating me? Still, the way he couldn't even look at me and how his voice wavered...

Why reveal it now? Why do any of this?

And his hand...the way it healed. "That's why after Sam shot you..." I breathed.

He nodded. "I healed myself. But healing doesn't make a villain strong. I'm such a fraud."

I gasped. "Why would you ever think healing is weak? You could *help*—" Oh no. I said too much.

"You don't understand. I *need* people to think I'm more powerful. If I can't manage that, how will I finesse the government from their hands? I need supporters to help fight."

"How many people know that you're faking powers?" A lump formed in my throat.

"Just you and my father." At this, our eyes met. Tears welled up in his eyes, but he blinked and they were gone. "No one else can know."

"I—I don't know what to say," I breathed. My chest tightened. He really couldn't do this without me. He needed someone to work tech, to follow him, because he had to keep up his notorious image. Sure, he could create elaborate costumes and use special effects, but he couldn't truly hide everything.

Which meant I had his weak point. So, so many weak points.

VIGIL needed to hear about this.

"Side by side?" he suggested.

I swallowed. "See you on stage." I started back toward the dressing room, my mind racing. Ironfall wasn't as powerful as we thought.

"Oh, I made you something else." His voice stopped me. When I turned around, he held out a beautiful brown wig. Just like what Belle would wear.

I glanced from him to the wig, and back again. "You made that?"

He shrugged as if it was nothing. "I have a 3-D printer. It's a special one."

I laughed simply because I didn't know what else to do. Between nerves and a supervillain spilling his secrets, every part of myself was on overload. "Are you sure that isn't your superpower? Because it's still pretty cool."

Once more, his face turned serious. Apparently, that struck a tender cord. "Trust me, I'm sure."

"I'm sorry. I didn't mean it like that..." I said.

Before I realized what I was doing, I threw my arms around his neck. His body tensed, but slowly his arms relaxed around me. A moment later, I let go, and hurried back into the dressing room.

I dressed in Belle's blue-and-white outfit. It was stunning, with delicate golden threads woven in, and a beautiful seventeenth century style blouse underneath the dress.

Mrs. Rodriguez entered. "All right, I need everyone on stage for pictures!" Butterflies fluttered in my stomach. "Wait a second, would someone like to explain these costumes?"

My fellow cast members looked at each other, bewildered.

"They were just here," Josie said. "But they're better than any I've ever seen."

"Well, they're beautiful," Mrs. Rodriguez gasped. "I don't know how they got here, but we'll use them."

After the first three pictures, my cheeks cramped up. I was afraid to smile too big, because I didn't want to get lipstick on my teeth. The weird position made my cheeks cramp even more. Fun, fun.

Finally, we finished pictures, and the curtain closed. Soon, the backstage was filled with echoes of people filling the auditorium. What if I slipped up? Would my parents even show up... and what would they think? What if I forgot a line? What if I forgot *all* my lines? Would I mess up on the stage kiss and make it more awkward than it already was?

Should we have practiced the kiss before now?

I positioned myself downstage left where the curtain met the wall. People in the audience murmured and hugged, slowly taking their seats.

Did Mom and Dad decide to come? My gaze swept across the part of the audience in my field of vision, but I couldn't see them.

A pang hit my chest. They didn't make time to come. I didn't know why I expected them to, but there was still that hollow part of my heart.

I knew they loved me, but they really stunk at showing it. Still, I couldn't imagine life without them.

Nope. Don't focus on that.

Lights flickered once, twice, three times.

Showtime.

Oh no, I wasn't ready.

My parents weren't here.

"Thank you all for coming out here tonight to witness the hard work of this incredible cast. These students are so talented..." Mrs. Rodriguez gave the director's speech in front of the curtain as we got into our positions backstage.

Someone nudged me. "Ready?" Ironfall.

"Not really," I whispered back. The knots in my stomach tightened.

What was my first line? My mind scrambled, but thankfully I caught it.

I had to sink into Belle's character.

"...Manhattan High School presents *Beauty and the Beast*." Then everything went dark.

Inhale. Exhale.

The lights came up.

The music began. All of the garbage of the past few months melted away.

And I started to sing.

TRANSCRIPT OF THE INTERVIEW PROCEEDINGS WITH IRONFALL
SOME NAMES AND LOCATIONS REDACTED FOR SECURITY
INTERVIEW CONDUCTED ON MAY 20
LOCATION OF INTERVIEW: **[REDACTED]**
CASE #: **[REDACTED]**

AGENT LIAM BLAKE: I thought you said you didn't trust anyone but yourself.

IRONFALL: Yes, well, I trusted her enough to keep my secret.

AGENT LIAM BLAKE: Remind me what that was again.

IRONFALL: Well let's all just go around spilling my secrets to the world.

AGENT LIAM BLAKE: Remember, you're the one who volunteered to have this conversation. I could put you right back in that cell to rot for the rest of your life and still have a clear conscience.

IRONFALL: But *I* wouldn't have a clear conscience.

AGENT LIAM BLAKE: So let me ask the questions.

IRONFALL: [inaudible] I can heal people.

AGENT LIAM BLAKE: Why did you create another power for yourself?

IRONFALL: The world wouldn't fear someone born to do good, but they'd fear someone with deception in his veins.

CHAPTER 12

APRIL 15 – 8:36 P.M. EDT

Intermission came too soon. Adrenaline rushed through my body. I sang my heart out. Lines flowed as if they were my own words. Everything was just...perfect...and we made it to intermission!

Before we knew it, Mrs. Rodriguez was backstage again.

"You all are doing amazing!" she said. "Mike, you need to project more, even though you have a microphone." Mike (a.k.a. Lumiere) nodded.

The little meeting ended, and people went to change into their next costumes and look over lines one final time.

"Ready for Act 2?" Ironfall said.

"I'm still in shock we made it this far," I laughed. "I was so scared going out there the first time, but now I'm having a blast."

"Me too."

"And just think. We get to do this two more times."

"There really is nothing like it," he said. "That rush of excitement as a song starts."

I jumped up and down as more nervous/excited energy built up than I could handle. "I know!"

Josie bounded around the corner. "You guys are coming to eat tonight, right?"

I glanced over at Ironfall. "Did you know about this plan?" He shook his head.

Josie's lips twitched upward. "It's tradition. You're coming. Sam already agreed."

He grinned, then nudged my arm. "We wouldn't miss it."

Josie giggled. "You're killing it, by the way." She twirled a strand of brown hair (which she dyed exclusively for the show).

"Oh my goodness, you are too!" I said.

She shrugged. "Ehh, my voice cracked during the opening song, but hopefully no one noticed."

I offered a sympathetic smile. "If it helps, I didn't."

"Thanks," she laughed. "It's probably fine."

"I didn't hear it either." Ironfall stepped closer to me. My cheeks flushed. It wasn't noticeable under all this makeup, was it?

"Now we're talking." She winked. Still not over her crush on "Nolan."

Mrs. Rodriguez walked past, tapping her manicured fingers against her iconic *Cats* clipboard. "Ten minutes before lights up." Oh my. Blood rushed through my ears.

Ten minutes.

"I'd better get ready. Let's hope the second half goes even better than the first," I said, then went back to the dressing room.

APRIL 15 – 9:29 P.M. EDT

Fog shot up from the floor. Two stagehands ran on and helped Ironfall transform from a beast to a prince.

My knees felt weak.

This was it. The one moment for which I was glad my parents decided not to come. And we'd never practiced it. *Don't mess it up.*

White mist rolled away as "my prince" stepped forward in a billowing white top. Our eyes met. Fire. Adrenaline surged through my body. His soft fingers found my cheek and I placed my hand on the side of his face. He furrowed his brow and rubbed his thumb against my cheek.

Could he feel my beating heart?

Why did he suddenly look like he'd always wanted to do this?

My head tilted to the side. And his lips found mine. My eyes slipped closed.

It was wrong. So wrong.

He held me hostage—my parents hostage. Playing along was my job. I lied to him as much as he lied to me. *It's not real.* He wouldn't go falling in *love*, especially not with me. But the way he opened up to me, the way he looked at me, the way he was kissing me, seemed like so much more to him.

This wasn't right.

I pulled away, breathless. And I smiled.

APRIL 15 – 10:38 P.M. EDT

Curtain call was a blur. Person after person came up to me, congratulating me on my performance. Soon enough, I was swept into the dressing room to change back into my clothes. Everyone floated on the success and adrenaline of performing, the atmosphere electrified with excitement.

How had I never been in a play before?

I packed my stuff and left the dressing room.

Josie came up to me. "Hey, are you walking to the restaurant now?"

I nodded. "Yep. Are you going now too?" I glanced around. Ironfall was nowhere in sight. I couldn't face him.

"Yeah. Want to walk together?" She rocked back and forth in her Converse.

"Can I tag along too?" Sam ran up and leapt to a stop.

"Sure," Josie said.

Ironfall walked over, backpack on and everything. My breath caught. "I'm heading out too." I shrank closer to the others.

Josie grinned, then yelled. "Anyone else ready to go eat?" She waited, but no one responded. "No, okay! See you guys there!" Her bubbly voice echoed throughout the backstage. "I think we're good."

We made our way from the theater onto the busy New York streets. I moved closer to Josie and Sam, but I couldn't think of anything to say. Was I right? Did he think of me as more than a friend? How was that possible? He was a cold-blooded killer. A villain. And charming. And different than I expected.

Ironfall touched my arm and held me back until we were a few strides behind the others. "Are you avoiding me?"

I froze, forcing a small laugh. *Yes.* "No. Of course not." Pause. "You did awesome tonight."

"Thanks. I think I owe a lot of that to you. It's easy to slip into character when you're so deep in yours."

My chest caved. What was I supposed to say to that?

"You might say she tells *a tale as old as time,*" Sam said. Apparently they could still hear us. Oh my gosh. Stop. But I couldn't hold back a chuckle. It was so bad…yet so good.

"I literally hate you." Josie elbowed him, but grinned. "But *be my guest* to make more."

Ironfall leaned in. "Do you think she's gotten over her crush on me now? Because I think she just fell in love." I could definitely see them together.

I flashed a grin. "You might say there's *something there that wasn't there before.*"

"You're part of the problem, you know that?" Ironfall's brown and blue eyes glittered.

"Yep."

"Hey Nolan!" Josie ran back to meet us. "You sure didn't hold back with that kiss. Should we get a wedding announcement soon?"

He rolled his eyes. "Hilarious."

Please kill me now.

"Ehh...I give it a 5.5 out of 10," Sam chimed in.

Josie slapped his arm. "You *rate* kisses?"

"You *don't* rate movie kisses?" Sam crossed his arms, lifting his chin as if impersonating a critic.

"This is why you're still single." Josie shook her head. They quickened their pace, still arguing about noteworthy movie kisses.

"They're made for each other," Ironfall said, laughing.

"Just to be clear, it didn't mean anything, right?" Please don't answer that. Please don't answer that. I stared at the VIGIL & ANTE Studios billboard as if trying to shoot lasers into it. "The umm..." Yeah, I couldn't say it out loud for fear of melting into a puddle of embarrassment. My cheeks were already the color of that stoplight up there.

His eyes remained dead serious. "It's called acting for a reason." He paused, then flashed a mischievous smile. "It was like kissing—"

I cut him off. "Okay, let's agree to never bring this up again."

"Pinky promise." He extended his hand, holding out his pinky finger. "Not even a villain breaks a pinky promise."

I shook my head, laughing, then hooked my finger around his. "You think you're so cute, don't you?"

"You know I am." He let go, thrusting his hands into his pockets.

"I'm not one of your fans, remember?" And things were back to the way they were before.

Relief washed over me.

APRIL 18 – 4:57 P.M. EDT

That Monday, there was definitely some post-show depression. You know, those few days after where you keep asking yourself what you should do with your life. And wondering whether or not it's appropriate to keep quoting lines from the show that became inside jokes.

I sat on the floor of the hideout, scrolling through Instagram pictures from the show while I waited for Ironfall to finish up whatever he was doing on his computer. I glanced up toward it, my hand feeling the thumb drive in my pocket. If I could just find an opportunity to plug it in.

But he wouldn't even let Sam touch his computer.

I sighed, looking back at my phone.

"I want to show you something," Ironfall said. Oh no. That was a scary thing to hear him say.

"Can you give a hint?" I laughed. "If this involves a pizza eating contest again, I'm out."

He winked. "Don't worry, excessive amounts of food are not involved."

I followed him outside and we walked a few blocks to an apartment complex. He let us inside and we climbed the staircase to the second floor. The thumb drive burned in my pocket as I stared at the laptop in his hands.

"Wait, is this where you live?"

He nodded.

And when he went inside the apartment, I thought I'd entered a clothing store. A rainbow of costumes and clothes hung on racks that covered the entire living room.

"Oh. My. Gosh." Was this even a realistic thing to have? How? Why? What?

"These are all of my disguises and costumes," he said.

"You made all of these?" My inner fangirl was *living*. Just think of the things I could cosplay for when I eventually went to comic con.

His smile grew even wider. "I did."

"This is...incredible," I gasped.

"Now, let's find your supervillain costume."

"What is this, prom dress shopping for superheroes?" I said.
"Well, supervillains, but whatever."

"Oh, you know it."

"I think this is an appropriate time to quote that one iconic line from *The Incredibles*," I laughed.

"Well, I am officially the Edna Mode of supervillains," he said.

"Yes, of course you are."

He leapt over to one of the racks and ran his fingers through the clothes with the largest, most dramatic gestures known to mankind. "Ah yes, I think this one will do." Out came a black leather suit with red accented seams and obnoxiously pointy shoulders.

I held a hand over my quivering mouth in a pathetic attempt to hide my giggles. "I literally can't with those shoulder thingies."

"It's fireproof, bulletproof, and something, something, what does Edna Mode say again?" Ironfall was too much sometimes.

"Not that, but good try."

He shook his head, but his eyes still smiled. "Whatever, I'm a better designer than her anyway. Now try this on."

I rolled my eyes. "Fine. But this is not in the running to be my official look. Those stupid shoulder thingies will not be my brand."

He thrust the strange costume toward me and tilted his chin up in mock haughtiness. "I have spoken." So I took the suit from his hands and went in the other room to change.

Once I zipped everything up and wiggled the fabric into place, the costume felt awesome. I could move around with ease (did I try a few cool stunts in the bathroom? You can't prove it.) and felt ridiculously cool. The only annoying things were those black devil horns protruding from my already bony shoulders. Yeah, this wasn't it.

Still, Ironfall would tease me forever if I didn't go out and show him.

Before going out, I slipped the thumb drive into the new

suit, just in case. Couldn't leave it lying around. I took a deep breath. He'd never know I had it on me.

One last glimpse in the mirror, and a forced smile. *Forget about the thumb drive.*

So, as one does, I went out strutting like a model on a catwalk.

"Ooh, that looks good," he said. Thoughts of espionage fled my mind.

I struck an I'm-about-to-punch-someone superhero poster pose. "I feel like Agent Manda from *Project Safeguard* in this." My copper waves swished around as I changed to a different pose.

"But a much cooler, darker version." Don't tell her that.

"I'm not feeling these though." I pointed at my shoulders.

"Why not? They're awesome."

"They're a safety hazard." I shot him a wry look.

He raised an eyebrow, but the corners of his mouth kept twitching and his eyes shone. "On what? They aren't even sharp." Aww, the poor child was trying so hard to keep a straight face. How cute.

"On my eyes, Ironfall," I laughed. "They're hideous!"

He stuck out his bottom lip in an overdramatic pout. "Okay, fine. You win." Then his temporary defeat dissolved into his boyish smile.

"Do I get to pick the next round?"

He gestured toward the many costume racks. "Be my guest. I made them for you when you joined my team." Then, I started combing through the pieces. Red ones and green ones and even hot pink ones were all lined up, neatly placed on hangers. They all felt of different materials, some leather, some spandex, and some with actual metal armor on them.

I looked around. There, buried in the middle of the clothes was a table. But it wasn't the table that caught my eye...it was a computer. *The* computer. I glanced over at Ironfall, who was rummaging through more clothes.

The thumb drive burned against my thigh.

This could finally be my chance.

My heartbeat quickened.

Did I have a five-minute opportunity? We'd have to see. I took a deep breath and forced myself to look back at the clothes.

On the second rack, I found a white suit with a golden accent around the waist. It didn't feel quite like leather, but wasn't as thin as spandex either. To me, this looked more like a superhero outfit than a villain outfit. And obviously I didn't want to look like a villain. So I pulled it out and ran into the bathroom before Ironfall could start another round of banter.

Don't think about the computer.

But all thoughts left my mind when I slipped on the white outfit. Oh my goodness, this was perfect. It was the most comfortable thing I'd put on my body. I stood a little straighter and looked at myself in the tiny bathroom mirror again. My grin couldn't be suppressed.

I put the thumb drive in the new suit and went out to show Ironfall. He'd hate it. I knew he would.

Instead he grinned. "Ooh, I like that one. The white is unexpected, but I could get used to it." Ironfall laughed. "What do you think?"

"Yeah, this is the one."

"Now we both have majestic outfits to take over the world in. Let's get our disguises for the heist."

An idea popped into my head. I resisted the urge to make sure the computer was still there.

"Wait! I—I think you need to try on a few things," I said. Did that sound too desperate?

"Oh, you do?" He laughed.

I nodded. "You need to be part of this fashion show too." *So I can clone your computer when you're in the other room.*

"As you wish." He rolled his eyes and dramatically made his way over to another rack, plucked a lime-green spandex suit off the rack, and half danced into the other room. I watched him until he shut the door behind him. Then I raced over to the computer.

Please, don't change too fast. Give me time.

I pulled the small device from a pocket on my thigh and slid it into one of the thumb slots. Then I glanced at a clock. Now I wait.

And wait.

And wait.

Halfway there.

Come on, stay in there for a few more minutes.

If he caught me...I'd be dead in a minute and my parents would soon follow. My chest tightened as a chill rushed down my spine.

"How do I look?"

I jumped back. Shoot, there was still a minute left. I looked up and forced a laugh. Did he notice I was next to his laptop? "Fashion icon." Was the tremble in my voice noticeable?

He winked. "That's the look I was going for. Having second thoughts about the white one?" Yeah, he looked like he stepped off a behind-the-scenes bonus feature.

"No, I just wanted to look through the rest. Thought I might find something over here," I said. *Definitely not near your computer.*

"Makes sense," he said.

I stepped forward, running my fingers over more hangers. They tapped against each other. I glanced up at the clock. Thirty more seconds. I stepped slightly to the right, looking through a few more hangers without actually looking at the clothes. I gulped.

Fifteen seconds.

"What should we do to celebrate a successful heist?" he said.

I stole another glance at the clock. Still a few more seconds.

"I'm not sure," I said.

Five. Four. Three. Two. One.

"Think about it. I'm going to get out of this suit. No idea why I even made this one." He shook his head, laughing.

I smiled too.

The moment he shut the bathroom door, I yanked the USB and thrust it into my pocket. Now, I could breathe.

APRIL 18 – 9:30 P.M. EDT

I stared at my superhero costume laid out on my bed as I dialed Agent Liam's phone number. Thank goodness he picked up instead of having to go through that security code nonsense I still didn't understand.

"Agent Liam speaking."

I stared at the small device in my palm. "I have the thumb drive."

"Good," Agent Liam said. "I'll send Ver over to get it. Do you have anything else to report?"

"Yes," I said quietly, glancing at my *Project Safeguard* poster as if Ironfall could hear me through it. "I think he trusts me, at least as much as he's capable of trusting. He told me he's been faking his powers."

"What do you mean?"

"He can't change reality. That was all special effects and elaborate disguises," I said. "He can heal."

"Do you believe him?" I couldn't read the tone of his voice.

"Yes," I said. "There were small hints since I've known him, and I saw him heal himself twice." Once when Sam shot him and again when he cut himself. How had I missed it before?

"Okay, I will make note of that. Ver will definitely be interested. Is there anything else?"

"He's planning to break into the vault in two days." I hesitated. "Well, the three of us are." I hated saying it.

"I know," Liam said. "We still don't fully know what his plan is. The CIA won't authorize us to bring him in until we do. I need you to stay undercover."

"Isn't stealing a valuable asset from a top-secret facility a bad enough plan?" I said. Please, get me out. "We already know he has bad intentions."

"They want the big picture. That's why you're going to help him steal whatever he's after. We moved the real assets to another secure location. Ver cooked up some replicas you will steal," he said. "He'll never have access to the real technology." So I'd have to go through with it. My stomach knotted.

"What if he knows they're fake?" I said. This could blow up in our faces.

"He won't."

APRIL 20 – 9:32 A.M. EDT

Today was the heist. Things were going well. Ver was in the middle of decrypting the thumb drive. Maybe she'd find enough evidence that we would be able to stop Ironfall before the heist even took place.

I dressed in a navy-blue business suit of Ironfall's creation, then glanced at myself in the mirror. The shoulder-length, wavy red hair was all right, but my face didn't look old enough to be a CIA agent. So I grabbed my makeup bag and spruced myself up. Then, watching a YouTube tutorial, I pulled my hair up into a secure French twist (that didn't look terrible).

Okay, now I could pass for at least twenty-five.

I grabbed a sophisticated-looking purse, adding in an extra change of clothes and the earpiece communicators Ver gave me. It wasn't until I walked out the door and headed for the hideout that the nerves really began to hit me.

Even though it was early on Saturday morning, people bustled around the city streets. No one stared at me and my business attire, which made me feel a little better. They were too obsessed with their cell phones or music playlists.

Ironfall and Sam were already at the hideout when I got there.

"Is everything in place?" Ironfall asked.

I nodded. "I believe so. Sam?"

"Yep." He nodded. "Here are your ID badges. You should be able to access everything."

Ironfall narrowed his eyes, but it was more playful than anything else. "Should?"

"C'mon, it's my work we're talking about. Of course it will work," Sam said. "I'll handle back end from the hideout, so you have nothing to worry about."

"You have the earpieces, Rosemary?"

I carefully took one tiny earbud from the case and handed it to him. "Yeah." Ver mailed them to me a few weeks ago, and I told Ironfall I found them online. "According to the Internet, this brand doesn't show up on metal detectors."

Ironfall slid the comm device in. "Then let's get going." He smiled.

What if something went wrong? This was totally illegal (in order to eventually catch the bad guy, but security wouldn't know that). The room seemed too hot. Sweltering, even. Sweat soaked parts of my clothing. Hopefully no one could see how nervous I was. What if—

Inhale. Exhale.

I was only following VIGIL's orders.

"See you on the other side." Sam nodded in our direction. "Don't get arrested."

"That's the idea," Ironfall said. I took a deep, shaky breath. He placed a hand to my back, rubbing softly.

"Thanks, Sam." I offered a terrified smile.

Ironfall and I took an Uber over to Broad Street. The ride took an hour, and we didn't talk to each other. If I spoke right now, I might throw up.

We exited the car about a block away from the secret CIA

building. This was a busy part of town, a place tourists often flocked.

"I'm going to survey the area." Ironfall's voice echoed back to me through the comm device.

I nodded, and he walked away. I glanced around, and even though I couldn't see anyone watching me, it felt like everyone was. Like everyone knew I was here to steal something.

Breathe, Rosemary.

Before I knew it, we stood outside the CIA building.

"All right, guys, you there?" Sam said.

"Yes," I said.

"Unfortunately I can hear your voice," Ironfall said.

"I'm touched. Okay, you're clear to go in. Wave to the camera," Sam said. "Just kidding, that would blow your cover."

"I'll go first," Ironfall said.

"When you meet, head to Level 001," Sam said. "The vault is blurred out because apparently it's a secret from security, but we'll figure out how to crack the lock when you get there."

"We already planned this," Ironfall said.

"Just checking," Sam said. The line went silent for two minutes before Ironfall confirmed he was inside.

"I see you," Sam said. "Head on in, Rosemary."

"I'm coming your way." I pressed a finger to my comm device.

I walked to the entrance. Were people suspicious? Would my badge work? I had faith in Sam, but still, a small part was scared this would be his one mistake.

I looked right; I looked left. No one seemed to spare a second glance, but my chest still tightened.

Now or never.

I entered the building. A large metal detector, like the annoying ones at airports, guarded the doorway. A conveyor belt x-ray machine stood to the side for bags.

The guard, who didn't look strong enough to stop someone from barging in, motioned for me to step forward.

Confidence was key, as my mom would say.

Soon you'll be safe, Mom. Soon you'll be safe.

I handed him my badge. Moment of truth. I tried to smile. "Good morning." The guy didn't even give me a pleasant look in return. He scanned the badge over something and motioned me through the metal detector, which produced all green lights and no loud, mission-ending beeps.

Once I was through security, the guard thrust my badge toward me. I nodded my thanks and clipped it onto my blazer.

Though the heist had hardly begun, I breathed a sigh of relief. I felt like security was the biggest risk. (Gosh, it even made me nervous going through the airport, when I wasn't planning on doing anything illegal.)

"Hello, Rosemary, you're in." Sam said in my ear.

I gave a small nod, walking farther into the large lobby before communicating with Ironfall. "I'm in the lobby." Hopefully that wasn't too loud. I casually glanced toward security, but they didn't seem to notice anything.

A few people walked around, but everyone seemed to have a place to go.

"I'm in the bathroom right now," Ironfall said. "Meet you right outside."

"Copy that," I responded.

"Keep going straight, and you'll run right into it," Sam chimed in from his very safe desk in our hideout. I followed his directions. Thankfully, the people I passed didn't pay attention to me.

I was so focused on acting natural that I nearly ran into Ironfall.

"Hi," I whispered.

"Elevators are that way." He pointed behind him. I nodded, and together, we walked toward it in silence.

"You're doing great, kids," Sam said.

"Thanks for the pep talk." Ironfall rolled his eyes. "Let's try to keep this line as clear as possible." His words echoed in my earpiece.

The elevator didn't have anyone else inside, thankfully. Once the doors closed on us, I breathed a sigh of relief.

I scanned my badge and pressed the button for the bottom-most floor. The elevator started moving, so at least my badge worked for this.

Down, down, down the elevator went.

"The guards aren't by the elevators right now, so you're good with that," Sam said. "There aren't any by the vault either." Even though we knew as much as there was to know about schedules and routines, there was always the chance that there was a random guard somewhere we didn't expect him to be. Thank goodness we had someone watching.

The elevator beeped, and the doors slid open.

I stepped out and motioned for Ironfall to follow.

"Right, then left," Sam directed. We followed his instructions. "Don't worry, the guards are still out of the way." I tried not to panic about them potentially rounding the corner at any second.

A circular steel trap door protruded from the floor. A blue square tile sat next to it. Was this the vault?

Ironfall rushed forward. "Biometric security, just like we planned. Looks like we need a handprint and voice activation." His words echoed through my comm.

Oh great. Worse than we thought.

"Well, not easy to crack, but you can pull it off," Sam said. Was he going to give us any more than that? "Thankfully I researched that one the most. Franklin Dower has the highest security clearance here so—"

"We'll need his handprint and voice," Ironfall said. Why did he have to look so serious...like he jumped off a *Project Safeguard* poster? He was the most intimidating when he looked like this. Where was the boy who played dress up with me?

"You get the handprint and I'll get the name," I said. "Sam, keep us updated."

"Got it." Ironfall looked at his watch. "We have thirty seconds until security walks by."

"I see them." Sam's voice sent adrenaline coursing through my veins.

I started walking briskly back towards the elevator. Ironfall caught up to me, and we ran the rest of the way. I scanned my badge and pressed the button for the ground floor.

I bit my lip, turning toward him. "Let's not kill this guy, okay. That would let the CIA know we were here." And the thought of someone dying because of my undercover mission sent a wave of nausea through me. Hopefully he believed stealth was the smartest move.

He broke free of his classic villain face. "No killing people. Got it." Was he planning on it before I said something? Please tell me no.

"Ironfall, head to the lab and make a silicon hand model. I'll walk you through it when you get there," Sam said.

"I already know how," Ironfall said. "The lab is on Level 20, right?"

"Yep," Sam said.

He pressed the button for the twentieth floor. "I'll meet you at the vault in thirty minutes, right after security passes through."

I nodded. "Half an hour. Got it."

His signature grin showed itself. "See you in a bit."

I offered a nervous smile in return.

The elevator doors slid open. My stop. The doors closed with Ironfall still inside.

TRANSCRIPT OF THE INTERVIEW PROCEEDINGS
WITH IRONFALL
SOME NAMES AND LOCATIONS REDACTED FOR
SECURITY
INTERVIEW CONDUCTED ON MAY 20
LOCATION OF INTERVIEW: **[REDACTED]**
CASE #: **[REDACTED]**

AGENT LIAM BLAKE: At this point, did you still trust Rosemary?
IRONFALL: 100 percent. I trusted her with my life.
AGENT LIAM BLAKE: I thought you didn't trust anyone.
IRONFALL: I wish I hadn't trusted her as much as I did.
AGENT LIAM BLAKE: Was she ready for the heist?
IRONFALL: I wouldn't have gone through with it if she wasn't.

CHAPTER 13

"Rosemary, you're heading to weaponry, but it's on Level 22 not the ground floor," Sam said.

"Copy that." Weaponry? Why on earth would it be there? Well, maybe if someone was on a special op and needed a recording device. I don't know, I didn't make the organizational system here.

I returned to the elevator. An agent wearing a gray suit and red tie stood nearby, hands thrust in his pockets. Did he know I wasn't supposed to be here? My fingers straightened the badge clipped to my chest. Yes, dude, I *was definitely* supposed to be here. See, I had a badge.

Should I say something to him? "Good morning." That wasn't incriminating and would possibly calm any suspicions.

"Morning." The man's response was curt but civil.

The elevator arrived, and a few people stepped off. Gray suit guy and I walked on.

So, the thing about elevators is that they, by their very nature, create awkward situations. (Especially when they break down. That's the worst.) At least this one didn't have weird music playing.

I scanned my badge and pressed the button that led to the twenty-second floor. The circle illuminated, and the screen above turned green. My badge still worked, so that was a good sign. Thank you, Sam.

Gray suit dude scanned his badge and selected Level 19. The screen glowed green for him too.

The elevator started moving, then stopped. Level 004. Did the CIA know Ironfall and I were here? Had we been found out? *Please don't let this be like that one scene in* The Winter Soldier. The doors slid open, and in walked two more CIA agents. They scanned their badges and selected their destinations. Levels 15 and 17.

I pressed my back against the wall to prevent someone attacking me from behind.

When the doors shut, nothing bad happened. Everyone minded their own business, but my chest still felt tight until I was the only one left in the elevator.

Finally, I arrived at Level 22. I half ran off that death trap.

This floor didn't look like the armory I originally thought it would. It wasn't a room full of machine guns, pistols, assault rifles, knives, and whatever other kinds of weapons that existed. It was a white hallway that looked eerily like a hospital wing. Fluorescent lights flickered overhead, and the white tile floors were spotless. At least the CIA had a good janitor.

"Second door on your left," Sam said. "That holds the supplies for undercover missions." Like those supply rooms you see in spy movies?

I kept walking until I reached the door...which didn't have a handle? Okay, that was weird. Next to the door was some sort of scanner looking thing. Hopefully it wasn't a handprint scanner.

I held my badge up to it. A moment later, the door slid open. Oh, thank goodness. This room appeared to be some sort of laboratory. A couple of tables stood in the center of the room, and counters lined the walls. There were a lot of computer screens and electrical outlets, but everything seemed to be in order.

"Someone's walking down the hallway. ETA one minute," Sam said. Oh gosh.

Uh.

"Fifty-five seconds."

I ran to the back of the room and opened a random drawer. Circuit boards. Okay, not helpful. I pulled open the next drawer and the next and the next. Nothing appeared to be an audio recorder.

"Hurry up. Fifty seconds."

Come on.

More drawers and more drawers. Still nothing.

Come on, Rosemary.

I opened another drawer.

Inhale. Exhale.

Not enough time.

The next drawer slid open. Inside were a bunch of small, silver recording devices.

"Thirty seconds. Get out of there because she's ready to turn the corner," Sam said. Sam sounded as anxious as I was, and that wasn't comforting. I snatched one of the devices, slammed the drawer shut, and raced out.

The door slid closed behind me, and I slipped the small device into my pocket.

The scientist rounded the corner. I walked slowly past her, and she didn't spare me a second glance.

I didn't breathe until I was well away from her.

"Close one," Sam said. "Mr. Frank Dower's office is on the top floor." Okay.

"I found a recording device. Beginning phase two now." At least I sounded professional.

I headed back to the elevator and pressed the button. A few moments later, the doors opened, revealing two guys with more muscles than weightlifters. Oh no. Not today, people. They must have been field agents, or the CIA equivalent of Navy SEALs. My feet shuffled back.

"Get in there. There's nothing more suspicious than running from these guys," Sam said. "That's right, I've seen a lot of action movies, so I'm an expert. Don't freeze up now."

Okay. I could do this...right? I gulped and stepped inside.

These were probably the guys who would notice the sweat on my forehead and that thing with the way your pupils dilate to see whether or not you're guilty.

My hands shook as I scanned my badge and pressed the button.

Deep breath.

A few floors later, the elevator stopped and the two guys got off. When the doors slid shut, I slumped back against the wall.

They hadn't noticed a thing.

I pressed a finger to my earpiece, making sure it hadn't moved. "I'm in the elevator heading up to Franklin Dower's office."

"Do you have a cover story?" Ironfall answered. Right. A cover story. That would probably be important.

"Yes," I lied. "I'll just tell him that I'm from the science div —" The elevator stopped, and the door opened. Some guy walked in. Oh goodness, did he hear part of my conversation?

"Rosemary, you okay?" Ironfall asked. Obviously, I couldn't answer.

The stranger smiled at me, then scanned his badge like everyone else had. "Good morning. How are you?"

I forced a smile, which hopefully looked genuine and older than a seventeen-year-old. "Good. How are you?"

"Fabulous, thanks for asking," he said. "Just got promoted to level seven yesterday." I had no idea what level seven meant.

I opened my mouth as if I was going to say something, but couldn't think of anything to say. So I smiled awkwardly again. "Uh...congratulations. That's great." And now he would be suspicious.

He smiled at me again. He seemed like a pleasant man and reminded me of a fun grandfather. "Sorry, do I know you?"

My breath caught. I shook my head. "No, we've never met." And I was *definitely not* stealing something from this building. Nothing to see here, sir.

"Oh, I know why I recognize you. You look like one of my coworkers," the man said. Whew. He didn't suspect me. But I really didn't need to hear his life story.

"I guess I have one of those faces." I really don't, though.

"You have the same eyes," said the stranger. "Sorry if that sounds weird." Yeah, uh, he was being a little weird.

People always told me I had my dad's eyes.

"Maybe you two are related. His name is—" The elevator door opened. "Sorry, this is my floor." He nodded, then stepped out.

Well, that was a strange conversation, and I hoped not to have any more. Two undercover operations at once was already more than I could handle.

Once more, the elevator rose. Finally, I arrived at the top floor.

"Turn left. Dower's office will be the last one on your left," Sam said. Okay, this mission was somewhat almost finished. Yeah, okay, not really. "It should have big, frosted windows. There aren't cameras inside, so you're on your own with this one." No cameras? That meant anything could happen.

"Be careful, Rosemary," Ironfall said. Was that a break in his voice?

A few minutes later, I stood before the office. This door had to be opened by scanner just like the one down in Weaponry. I pressed my badge against it. Red. Access denied.

Sam.

"Try knocking," he said. Knocking? That seemed weird.

"Really? Knocking? Can't you hack it or something?" I hissed, pressing a finger to my earpiece.

"Just knock," Sam said. "It will make you look more polite."

I sighed and tapped against the glass. Hopefully that wasn't too intrusive.

"Who is it?" A man's voice came from inside.

I glanced down at my badge. "Jane Smith." Way to go for originality, Sam.

"Scan your badge again," the man said. I did as he said, only this time the door slid open.

Dower was shorter than I imagined a top level CIA agent would be, but he held an intimidating presence in the room. His pressed gray suit, expensive shoes, and pristine posture commanded the atmosphere.

He turned toward me, stone-faced. Suddenly he seemed like a giant. "Explain yourself." Was it possible for someone shorter than you to look down on you?

My chest tightened. He knew.

Okay, now time for more lying. "I'm Agent Jane Smith from the science division. I was told to give you a report about—"

He raised a hand. "Stop right there. I know you're not from the science division." Suddenly my clothes felt too tight as my chest constricted. Oh my gosh...he knew about us. He knew I wasn't supposed to be there.

"Yes, I am."

"No, you're not."

"Rosemary," Ironfall interjected, "get out of there." His tone sounded urgent.

"Yeah, I'm with Ironfall on this one," Sam said. "You're about to go to jail."

There wouldn't be camera evidence, but Ironfall had audio on all of this. And if I got caught, Ironfall would disappear, Sam too.

Not to mention I would go to jail.

And my parents would suffer for my failure.

But if I made Ironfall lose, wouldn't they be harmed anyway?

"I am from the science division, sir. I got in, didn't I?" With his help, but whatever. With my hands, I made a writing motion. As Dower stared at me, a hand reaching into his jacket, I pulled a small notepad and pen out of my pocket. "Dr. Johnson wanted me to inform you that the recorder models should be ready for testing next week. However, I brought one for you to look at in the meantime." I clicked open the pen and began writing.

Ironfall is listening. I am undercover with VIGIL.

I shoved the paper his way, my hand shaking.

He paused. I couldn't read him. He would call security on me for sure.

"Well, then, let me see it. And tell Dr. Johnson I will be down there sometime today to check on his progress on production," Dower said.

Hopefully there wouldn't be any gaps in our conversation that Ironfall would notice.

Dower held out his hand. "Let me see the recording device for a moment, please."

I reached in my pocket and handed him the stolen item. He didn't look at it, however, he reached into the front of his suit and pulled out a pen. He wrote a message underneath mine and handed it back to me.

Where is Ironfall?

I scribbled under his pristine handwriting, then passed the paper.

No time. We'll meet at the VIGIL vault soon. Agent Liam replaced the real items with decoys. VIGIL needs to know what Ironfall is after.

"So do I press this button to record?" Dower said as if this was the next natural thing in our vocal conversation.

"Yes, sir. It was developed to help us crack voice-activated safes in enemy territory," I said. "It can reproduce the exact frequency of the speaker's voice."

Dower fiddled with the device a bit more, then pressed the recording button. "Franklin Dower." Whew. He decided to help us in this small, but significant way.

But he could have arrested Ironfall here and now, before anyone got hurt...or killed.

TRANSCRIPT OF THE INTERVIEW PROCEEDINGS WITH IRONFALL
SOME NAMES AND LOCATIONS REDACTED FOR SECURITY
INTERVIEW CONDUCTED ON MAY 20
LOCATION OF INTERVIEW: [REDACTED]
CASE #: [REDACTED]

AGENT LIAM BLAKE: What was your job during the heist?

IRONFALL: We had everything planned out except the layout of the floor. Quite frankly, according to the CIA, the vault doesn't exist. Only a few know about it. It isn't even listed on VIGIL records. So, once we figured out how the lock opened, I had to get a handprint to unlock the vault.

AGENT LIAM BLAKE: Whose handprint?

IRONFALL: Franklin Dower.

AGENT LIAM BLAKE: Did you blame Rosemary for ruining your plan?

IRONFALL: No, I was just glad she was okay.

CHAPTER 14

"That shouldn't have worked," Ironfall said through my comm device. He sounded breathless. Had he been running?

"I told you my fake badges were convincing," Sam said through my earpiece.

"He saw through the badge immediately," Ironfall groaned.

"Thank you, sir," I said to Dower, then left the office. I made my way to the elevator and rode it down to the vault.

"So far, the coast is clear," Sam said. I hated that all we had to work off of was "so far."

"Be careful," Ironfall said. "Something is up."

I stayed low and close to the walls.

"Rosemary, wait a sec, the guards are coming." My stomach leapt into my chest. They weren't supposed to be here. "Turn. Right now," Sam said.

The only reason they were here was—oh my—because I told Dower where we were headed. He didn't believe I was on a deep cover mission for VIGIL, he thought I was a terrorist in league with Ironfall. And he probably didn't arrest me earlier because he wanted to catch us both.

I lunged around the corner and pressed my body against the wall. Then I kept moving.

"So, uh, don't hate me but I think they know you're here," Sam said. "Oh no, this is bad, this is really bad."

"I'm on my way," Ironfall said. "It's going to be okay."

"Please don't rat me out when they interrogate you," Sam squeaked.

"Shut it, Sam," Ironfall growled.

I wanted to call for help, but that would immediately give me away. I would have to fight my way out of this. It was time for Ironfall's training to come into play. But I wouldn't kill them. I definitely wouldn't kill them. They weren't the real enemy.

Two guards rounded the corner. They wore all black, though their shirts were lumpy from bulletproof vests. Both had helmets and carried machine guns pointed to the ground.

Oh no.

Act like you belong. These guys weren't going to buy that though.

I gulped and stepped toward them. I kept my eyes trained on the ground and attempted to conceal my terror. My confidence wasn't there, but I hope that didn't show in the way I walked. Could confidence even be detected in the way someone walked?

"You don't have clearance to be down here," one of them said.

I froze, but didn't raise my head. My breaths grew shallower and shallower as the tension built in the small hallway.

"Explain why you're on this floor," said the other guy.

"Remember what I taught you." I could almost hear Ironfall encouraging me to take them out. No, that wasn't an option. I couldn't kill anyone...could I?

I stared. *Snap out of it, Rosemary.* Say something.

I could pull the VIGIL agent card, but would the mention of it make Ironfall connect the dots that I was a double agent?

The alternative was to claim I got turned around looking for the bathroom. No one in their right mind would believe that, and I already blew it upstairs with Franklin Dower.

The left soldier raised his weapon an inch. "Start talking or we arrest you."

I moved my arms forward as if to deescalate them. "Right. Sorry. I'm here on VIGIL business."

They glanced at each other but kept their guns trained on the ground. Oh no, they didn't buy it.

I gulped. "Agent Liam Blake sent me to collect something from the vault. I should only be a moment." Not forceful enough. I could lie to Ironfall but not them?

Eyes narrowed through the headgear. "Only two people have access to this floor, and spoiler alert, you're not one of them."

My shoulders pressed back. *Look more confident.* "Three people, actually. Do I need to report you to Agent Liam? If I have to get him on the phone he won't—"

"Dower alerted us to a security breach, and we are under strict orders to protect that vault by any means necessary."

"I have *permission* to be here." I stepped forward, keeping my hands in sight.

"You have five seconds to get on your knees with your hands behind your head." They raised their guns.

One guard placed a hand to his ear. "Sir, we have one of the intruders in custody. Waiting for the second now."

I could surrender. Let them finally arrest Ironfall. VIGIL would set me free, and life would go back to normal. But Ironfall wouldn't come to save me then, he'd run. My parents might die, no matter what he told me the day we spent at Central Park. Agent Liam had operatives stationed near my home, but would they get there in time? It was too risky to take the chance. Ironfall wouldn't leave Sam as a loose end either. He'd probably clean up and drop off the grid to complete his evil plan in secret.

And all this time planning together, getting to know each other, would end. Why did that send a pang through my chest? I should *want* to get away from him.

I took a deep breath, trying to clear my racing mind.

There was only one option: fight.

I hated it.

I looked up at them, slowly. Their fingers didn't rest on the triggers, but these guys could lift them, aim, and shoot me in seconds. There was no way that I could take them both down. I had to at least try.

I lunged for the guy on the right, wrenching the gun from his hands. If I were Ironfall, or what he wanted me to be, I would have blasted both of their brains out, but instead I chucked the weapon as far down the hall as I could.

Left Guy pointed his gun at me, but I pushed it away so I wasn't looking down the barrel. The guy didn't release his grip. Someone grabbed me from behind and pulled me down on the ground. I thrashed around, but his grip was iron.

Not strong enough. Not strong enough.

Ironfall hadn't taught me how to get out of this position: both arms pinned to the ground with a SEAL's (or the CIA equivalent's) machine gun trained on me.

"Where is your partner?" said the guy with the gun. "Dower told us you would meet him here." Guns almost always worked as motivators.

If I could just lift my legs up and kick both of them off of me. He shifted to the right. Clear shot. I thrust both my legs up and to the side at the same time. He toppled over. The guy pinning my arms down looked over and loosened his grip, so I knocked him off.

Adrenaline coursed through my body like I'd never felt it. They wouldn't take me. Ironfall wouldn't get away. I'd see this mission through.

The guy pointed his gun at me and—
BANG!
I'm...not shot.
Blood pooled at the man's mouth and—
BANG!
Both guards fell to the ground.
No.
I couldn't breathe. I only saw blood—so much blood.
My legs no longer supported me; I sank to the floor. No, they

couldn't be dead. They couldn't. I hadn't wanted to kill them. I hadn't killed them—this mission killed them.

I glanced back. Who fired? The smoking pistol lowered. Ironfall.

"You..." *killed them*. I couldn't say it all aloud. I couldn't. Stop. Stop. Stop.

"We weren't supposed to kill anyone!" The gunshots replayed and replayed in my mind.

They were on my side. And Ironfall just put bullets through them.

"How..." I gasped but didn't feel the air rush into my lungs. "How...could...you?" Tears. The dead men's bodies blurred into tears. "How could you?" That was the only thing I could say. "How could you?" There was another way, but he...murdered them in cold blood.

"I saved your life." He spoke slowly and softly, like one would talk to a scared child. But he'd just *killed* two people. Was he that unfazed by it? "You should have...never mind. I saved your life. That's all that matters."

"No—no." My voice shook as much as my body. "You *killed* them."

"Rosemary..." He placed a hand on my back and knelt beside me.

Suddenly my head felt as if it was going to explode. Here I was, playing him at every step of the game, just like he played everyone, and I felt betrayed by *him*. Had I somehow expected him to act honorably? Oh... "I can't do this," I whispered. He murdered someone. Why did it hurt *so much*? How could he do this?

"Yes, you can." Then his arms were around me. "We can finish this mission. Side by side, remember?"

No. Not side by side. Not anything like that because he betrayed me. As if I expected something better of a villainous *monster*.

He'd do the same to my parents.

"Ironfall..."

"What?" His voice was still soft. Too soft for a murderer's.

My voice was quiet and shaky. "You're a monster."

Two words. "I know."

My heart cracked.

"The first time I saw death was the first time I killed someone. My father locked me in a room and told me I couldn't come out until I—" His voice broke. "Until I took care of the prisoner inside. I was ten." His warm breath touched my ear.

"Your father made you...?" No. No, I couldn't finish that.

"It was a necessary cost."

A tear streaked down my cheek, leaving a wet spot on his shirt. "Is it ever truly necessary?"

"After a while you have to learn to block it out in order to stay sane."

"Why? Why do you do it?"

"I have to finish my mission." His grip on me loosened as he backed away and checked his watch. "We should get this over with well before the next round of guards arrives," he said. "We're almost done, Rosemary, and then we can take over the world. Together. You and me and the army we build." *You and me.*

He was just playing me again. He didn't care about anything, but why did it sound like he did?

Where did the lies end?

Where did *my* lies end?

Sam said nothing.

"Are you all right now?"

No.

I couldn't meet his gaze. I was going to win this. He wouldn't get close to me again. I nodded.

I don't need you, Ironfall.

He. Just. Murdered. Someone.

What if he did this to me? My family? VIGIL? The whole world? It was then that I finally looked at him—a murderer.

I was going to make sure he was brought to justice because

he sure as anything deserved it.

Ironfall took my hand and pulled me to my feet. I didn't jerk away.

He pressed the hand model to the scanner and played the recording, and the vault door raised. He went inside first, then I followed down the ladder. A few lights flickered on overhead, and dust swirled through the air.

I sneezed. The sound echoed off the thick metal walls. Did someone hear that?

Shelves, shelves, and more shelves. Some were empty, but most were filled with strange gadgets reminiscent of *Star Wars*. I didn't know what any of them did, but they all had to be dangerous to be locked in a vault within a secret CIA building.

How lethal was whatever Ironfall was looking for?

I glanced around but couldn't see Ironfall. He had disappeared into the maze.

"It's fine. It—it's probably fine." Sam's voice shook as he spoke for the first time. Had he seen those men die too?

A few moments later, Ironfall returned holding a leather case in his hand. It seemed like a normal old-fashioned briefcase, but obviously it wasn't.

"What is that?" I whispered.

"Something my father built. Now let's get out of here," he said, then he climbed out of the vault. For a second, I thought he would lock me in here to bury the evidence, but he waited for me to reach the surface.

Both of us lowered the door and ensured the vault was locked.

The two dead men lay on the floor. I retched as their faces morphed into my parents'. He'd do the same to them.

I ran to catch up to him.

Minutes later, we were out. No one said anything about the briefcase Ironfall carried, not even the security guards.

The chilly air felt good, though soon goosebumps rose on my skin.

"Y-you made it out," Sam said through my earpiece. He was still shaken.

Ironfall killed two people in there.

I steeled against the sadness. I'd only have to be undercover for a little while longer. Hopefully I could fool him until then.

He turned to me. "We did it!"

No. I forced a grimace. "We did." My hands quivered.

"Yes," Sam's voice echoed.

Then he grinned. That stupid, endearing, Ironfall smile.

"Get some rest and we'll meet in the hideout tomorrow," he said. "Are you going to be okay?"

I had to get away from him. I had to get out, to tell VIGIL I couldn't do this anymore.

But my parents. The dead men's blank stares flashed before me again. Ironfall would do the same to Mom and Dad.

I nodded. "T-tomorrow." I could avoid him until tomorrow.

"Sam, you're free to go as well," Ironfall said.

APRIL 20 – 11:47 A.M. EDT

Mom and Dad were out when I got home. I closed my eyes and locked the door. No one could hurt me right now. I didn't have to pretend to be someone else, I didn't have to watch my back.

I could just...breathe.

Ironfall's victims flashed through my mind. My breath caught. What if he did the same to me, to my parents? What if tomorrow, we were the ones lying on the ground, hearts no longer beating?

My entire body shook, my breathing uneven. Ironfall was going to kill me. It wasn't a matter of if, it was a matter of when.

I sank to the floor. Sobs wracked my chest. Why, Ironfall? Why?

And I wept.

Slowly, fewer tears came, but my body still felt weak. I couldn't do this. My parents were right. I wasn't good enough.

I fumbled for my phone and dialed VIGIL's number.

"This is Agent Liam." His voice sounded so good.

"I need help." My voice shook. "H-he killed people…" My mind raced. No longer could I form coherent sentences.

"I know."

"CIA building. The heist thing." My chest hiccupped. "My parents…he'll kill them. He'll kill me…"

"Slow down and take a deep breath. When do you see him again?"

No, I didn't want to see him again. "Tomorrow morning." A wave of nausea washed over me.

"We know what he stole, now we need to figure out what he has planned," he said. "You need to get a confession."

"I can't do this alone."

"And you won't. There will be agents stationed nearby. If he acts aggressive, call us."

I nodded, momentarily forgetting Liam couldn't see me. "Thank you," I whispered.

"Well done, Agent Rosemary."

Immediately after, I called Sam.

"Rosemary, I think this just got real." His voice was low and shaking. "It felt like a game for a while, but now—"

"It's like there's blood on our hands. On his hands. He killed them…" The image flashed in my mind. I tried not to gag.

"The movies, they make it look so easy," he said. Was he crying? "What do we do?"

I didn't know, didn't want to think about it. Still, I took a deep breath. "We have to go back. If not, he'll know about us and hurt my parents."

"I'm not going back," Sam said. "I helped him hack, my job is done. I'm out."

"Sam, please," I pleaded. "I can't go back alone, and Agent

Liam promised his agents would be stationed close."

"I'm done," Sam said. "I know it's not what the Safeguarders would do, but after what happened..."

"Please, don't leave me alone with him." A lump forced its way into my throat.

"He cares about you too much to hurt you, but he wouldn't hesitate to kill me like he did those guards."

"You're wrong. He'd rip away everything I care about in a heartbeat." His promises that day in Central Park would be void the moment he discovered I worked for VIGIL.

"No, I've seen the way he looks at you," he said. "If the fans knew about this, they'd ship you from like day one. He may not want to admit it, but I think he'd give up anything for you."

Blood rushed my ears. "No." I didn't want to be associated with him. That monster. Murderer. And I knew he'd throw my life away if it meant he won. "Sam, I need you to come tomorrow."

"You're on your own."

"Sam!" Tears streamed down my cheeks as I felt more and more alone.

Why me? Why did it always end up just being Ironfall and I?

APRIL 21 – 10:43 A.M. EDT

I couldn't see Ironfall today. I just couldn't.

Deep breath.

I was almost to the hideout.

Just a little bit longer.

I took a deep breath and walked inside.

Ironfall was already there. He grinned. "Hi, Rosemary."

I smiled, but didn't say anything. Okay, he was happy, so he probably wasn't about to kill me. (Or was this an act to lure me in again?)

He took my hands in his and stepped closer. "Today's the day we take over the world."

TRANSCRIPT OF THE INTERVIEW PROCEEDINGS
WITH IRONFALL
SOME NAMES AND LOCATIONS REDACTED FOR SECURITY
INTERVIEW CONDUCTED ON MAY 20
LOCATION OF INTERVIEW: **[REDACTED]**
CASE #: **[REDACTED]**

IRONFALL: She almost died.
AGENT LIAM BLAKE: Because of the guards?
IRONFALL: Yes.
AGENT LIAM BLAKE: Were you worried you made a mistake with her?
IRONFALL: No, I was terrified for *her life*.
AGENT LIAM BLAKE: So what did you do?
IRONFALL: I killed them. Both of them.
AGENT LIAM BLAKE: Do you enjoy killing people?
IRONFALL: No.
AGENT LIAM BLAKE: When you fought the Safeguarders a few years ago, you seemed disturbingly excited about it. Want to elaborate on that?
IRONFALL: It's a defense mechanism. I couldn't let it get out that I was weak.
AGENT LIAM BLAKE: How do I know you're not lying to me?
IRONFALL: Ask Rosemary.
AGENT LIAM BLAKE: And how do I know all of this isn't an act?
IRONFALL: Well, Agent Liam, I suppose you don't.

CHAPTER 15

I didn't know what to say. Should I call VIGIL? No, Ironfall would get suspicious and...kill me like those two guards. *Come on, Liam, I need you.* I couldn't even look into Ironfall's eyes.

"Now the first step is to film a message for the world, which the device we stole will forcibly project onto every screen in the nation." He spoke softly, turning into the gentle Ironfall I remembered from all the times I forgot he was a villain.

I couldn't pull away from him. "Okay." I knew his plan, and if he was ready to use the device, he'd soon find out it was fake. I needed to call VIGIL.

He stepped back and reached into a bag, producing the suit he'd helped me pick out the other day. At least it wasn't a weapon. "Put this on." He handed it to me. "It's for the thing we're filming."

Gold and white. Like stardust.

I held it up, forcing a smile.

"Are you okay?" he said, peeking around the fabric.

I gulped and nodded.

"I know yesterday was a lot." He took a hesitant step toward me. "But I'm proud of you. You should know that."

My eyes bored holes in the floor. "Thanks." I needed to get away from him.

A soft hand brushed against my arm. Heat radiated from his brief touch. "Really, I couldn't have done it without you."

At that, I met his gaze. My breath caught. Of course he could have completed the heist solo. If it weren't for me, he'd have done it long ago, so what did he mean by that? "You don't mean that."

"I do, Rosemary."

I chuckled nervously. "Come on, training me only slowed you down."

"No, I don't mean tactically. I mean...we're so much more than that. We're..." Ironfall trailed off, eating the room's oxygen.

"Friends?" I whispered, heart thumping in my chest. Surely he didn't mean to suggest something else.

He pressed his lips together, looking away. "Yeah. Friends." A lump rose in my throat. "Right, umm, I'll give you time to change." Then he left the room.

I stared after him for a moment before the horrific images of the people he killed flashed before me. That would be me if I didn't act quickly, whether Ironfall considered me a friend or not.

How long would I have alone? Long enough to change and call Agent Liam? I ripped my clothes off and pulled on the bodysuit. Then I dialed Agent Liam's number.

"This is Liam," he said.

Whew. I glanced at the door. Nothing.

I spoke in a low voice. Was Ironfall listening to make sure I didn't call for help? "You have to come. I know his plan. He...he's about to take over the world. He stole some machine from the vault, and now he's filming a video. I have no idea how that means taking over the world, but—"

"We're en route. Keep your phone on." Agent Liam's voice was the most serious I'd ever heard it sound, including in the movies. "Is your cover intact?"

I glanced at the door again. "Yes."

"Distract him. Don't blow your cover. We'll be there in nine minutes." Nine minutes. Would Ironfall find out the device was fake before they got here?

Such a long time, yet so short.

"You can do this, Rosemary. Nine minutes. Stay strong."

"Okay," I whispered.

Nine minutes until everything would be over.

My vision blurred with tears, and my arm sank to my side. Only nine more minutes. Then the world would be safe. My parents would be safe.

Ironfall entered the room, sporting a 100 percent accurate cosplay of himself. I stepped back. Now, he was truly dressed the part of Ironfall, the villain from *Project Safeguard*. He wore a black and silver leather shirt with signature asymmetrical seams and black leather pants. No mask hid the face every fangirl was in love with.

We're so much more than that.

I gulped.

The villain's face twisted with concern. "Is something wrong? Was what I said back there okay?" Suddenly he was right there beside me.

I gulped and tried to nod, but I found I couldn't move. Everything was wrong. *Everything.*

His eyebrows knit together as if he actually cared about me. If he ever did, he wouldn't after these nine minutes were up.

I couldn't look him in the eyes because he'd see right into me. Into all the lies I fed him. He'd see the monster I really was.

"I don't think you're telling me the truth." Ironfall's fingers brushed against my arm. "You can trust me, I promise."

Speechless. The knife. The blood. *Mom and Dad.*

"Rosemary?"

Soft, quick, and harsh breaths. In. Out. In. Out. Tears. Shaking. VIGIL, hurry up. It was like I couldn't breathe and my heart kept thrashing against my chest.

My fingers loosened. My phone slipped to the ground. The screen was on.

Ironfall looked down. "No..." he breathed.

I slowly followed his gaze. The phone number. It was still up. I sucked in a sharp, shallow breath.

Run.

My feet wouldn't budge. "This...this isn't what it looks like. My family, please." My voice was soft and high-pitched and pleading. "You can't."

For the first time since he saw the screen, he looked at me with big, brown eyes.

Run.

So much pain tormented his face. His eyes narrowed. Rage. He shifted into the evil Ironfall from *Project Safeguard*. The Ironfall I had known was gone, cast off like an act. "You." His tone was so accusing that it was as if he was stabbing me a thousand times, and I was dying a thousand horrible deaths.

I still couldn't move.

"You betrayed me." The same accusing, heartless tone. The Ironfall I knew was only an act to lure me in. His eyes were so... empty. Heartbroken?

"You betrayed me." He stood between me and my exit. "You're with VIGIL."

He knew. Something snapped as my head cleared.

Save Mom and Dad.

Save myself.

I had to be ready—

Ironfall lunged.

I leapt out of his way, but he seemed to have expected this, as he rolled into a somersault and landed on his feet. He drew two black daggers.

"Please..." I breathed. He knew my fighting style because he taught me. But I knew his too.

He didn't seem to hear my faint cry for help. I should be prepared for this. I should be ready. No longer was I a normal girl.

I was an agent.

I attacked first. I threw a punch at his face, but he deflected, sending my arm out sideways. His knife sliced toward me, so I used the momentum to yank his arm my way and pull him off his feet. I somersaulted, pulling him the rest of the way to the ground.

Ironfall may have been on the ground, but he had both knives. Before he could move, I pressed both knees on his arms to hold him down. But his legs thrust me off him.

I wrenched my body around and saw him already on his feet.

His jaw flared.

I had to win.

I had to hold him off.

I couldn't die.

Mom and Dad.

Fighting.

Fighting.

Fighting.

I wasn't strong enough.

He kept attacking; I kept deflecting, but each time I had to take a step back.

I wasn't strong enough. I kept retreating and retreating and retreating. My whole body ached, but the adrenaline and will to live kept me going. He was so much stronger and more experienced than me.

I had to live. Just a few more minutes now.

He kept attacking and swinging his knives at me, and I kept deflecting. I made a quick move and one of his knives flew across the room. He didn't even look to see where it went. Ironfall's eyes were fixed intently on me and only me. Deep into my eyes; deep into my soul.

I didn't want to die.

My foot shuffled back, but it wouldn't go anymore. *The wall.*

I couldn't retreat, and it would be my downfall.

Swing; deflect; swing; deflect.

Ironfall pointed the knife at my head. I grabbed his forearms and held the knife away. My grip was the only thing keeping him from killing me, but I couldn't hold them for much longer.

I gritted my teeth, and I fought the pain. I pressed back as hard as I could, with every muscle that I could. Ironfall was the stronger one. He would kill me before VIGIL got here. He'd escape. And my parents...

I wouldn't be there to protect them.

Tears leaked from my eyes. "I can't beat you." My voice was soft and barely audible. Defeated. Scared.

Ironfall's face only hardened. "I have to kill you." His tone was deep, emotionless, and resolved. I knew he wouldn't hesitate to...to do it, but I also knew I could only last a couple more seconds under his persistent pressure.

"Please...Ironfall. I'm sorry I lied to you," I said. My voice shook almost as much as my tiring arms. "Don't touch my family. You can't...please." No. No. No. "I'm not strong enough to beat you." *Don't lose focus.*

"How did I miss this? I thought we—" He stopped, shaking his head as if in pain.

"I'm sorry, I had to." There was nothing else I could say. Nothing else I could do. I wasn't strong enough. My arms gave out. The knife didn't move.

He leaned forward, pinning me to the wall, his hard, guarded face only inches away.

"How long?" His blade hovered over my throat. "How long have you been a double agent?"

"J-just after you f-forced me to join you." A tear slipped down my cheek, then another, as pressure built inside my chest. Mom. Dad. *I'm sorry.*

His jaw tensed as tears pricked his brown eyes. And that sliver of blue. "And to think that I thought...that you...that I—" He stopped, pressing the knife into my throat.

Can't breathe.

Sharp.

I squeezed my eyes shut. I couldn't see the look on his face as my blood spilt.

Tell my parents I love them. Tell them I gave my life for them.

Tiny breaths so the knife wouldn't dig deeper.

Why hadn't he done it yet?

My eyes opened.

His face was torn, eyes puffy as a tear slipped down his own cheek. "I have to kill you." Now his voice was barely a whisper. "I have to." But he pulled the knife back, leaning closer, eyes narrow. His gaze flicked to my lips.

Then he buried his face in my shoulder. More tears slid down my cheeks as I stood frozen, my hands hanging by my side. Sobs wracked my chest, and I cried into him.

Would he kill me and hold my body as life slipped away?

But something clattered to the ground. His other arm wrapped around me.

Then he pulled back, brushing a hand across my cheek. And he whispered, "Go."

TRANSCRIPT OF THE INTERVIEW PROCEEDINGS
WITH IRONFALL
SOME NAMES AND LOCATIONS REDACTED FOR SECURITY
INTERVIEW CONDUCTED ON MAY 20
LOCATION OF INTERVIEW: **[REDACTED]**
CASE #: **[REDACTED]**

AGENT LIAM BLAKE: When you discovered she was a VIGIL agent, what went through your head?

IRONFALL: Anger. Betrayal. And then dread because... because I knew I'd have to kill her.

AGENT LIAM BLAKE: What stopped you?

IRONFALL: I was weak. My emotions got in the way.

AGENT LIAM BLAKE: Are you implying that you had feelings for her?

IRONFALL: What does this have to do with—?

AGENT LIAM BLAKE: Answer the question.

IRONFALL: Yes.

AGENT LIAM BLAKE: You sure have a messed up way of showing someone you care.

IRONFALL: I know. Believe me, I know.

AGENT LIAM BLAKE: Did your feelings for her blind you to signs that she was a double agent?

IRONFALL: I spent every second locked up in that cell asking myself the same question.

AGENT LIAM BLAKE: What was your conclusion?

IRONFALL: Rosemary always seemed just a little too good to be a supervillain. So innocent, yet so knowing. It was little things like the way she made sure we protected life and the sad looks I sometimes caught her giving me. I think that was what drew me to her the most. She hated that I killed people when we broke into the vault. I truly saw myself that day I don't know why, but I did. She always had a fierce light that I didn't, and though it exposed my darkest shadows, I still lo—

AGENT LIAM BLAKE: Why did you stop?

IRONFALL: It's nothing.

AGENT LIAM BLAKE: Do you love her?

IRONFALL: [inaudible]

AGENT LIAM BLAKE: I'm sorry, I didn't get that.

IRONFALL: Never mind.

AGENT LIAM BLAKE: Do you think it was all a lie?

IRONFALL: I don't know.

AGENT LIAM BLAKE: Do you blame her for lying to you?

IRONFALL: I'd lie to me, too.

CHAPTER 16

Ironfall backed up slowly. I still couldn't move.

"Go, before I change my mind." He still spoke softly.

I ran. I didn't even think about tying him up or arresting him. I just ran.

The sidewalk was as crowded as always, and they didn't even pause to look at my superhero outfit.

Liam, Ver, and Manda hurried toward me, their guns drawn and pointed at the ground.

I glanced at the doorway. "He's in there."

They rushed inside, but I didn't follow. I couldn't face him again.

How did a cold-hearted, manipulative murderer change his mind? Why did he spare me?

A few minutes later, they emerged with Ironfall in handcuffs. He glanced my way, then averted his eyes. His face was hard, and his lips pressed together, once again the *Project Safeguard* version of himself.

Agent Liam nodded at me.

Manda and Ver each held one of Ironfall's arms and pushed him into the black Mercedes.

I stepped closer.

"Good work, Agent." Liam nodded, slipping on his sunglasses, which with his suit made him look even more like a spy. "You're one of the best."

I sure didn't feel like it. I shook my head. "Ironfall let me go.

He was going to kill me. We fought, but I wasn't strong enough. He just...let me go."

Agent Liam glanced at the car. "Well, what do you know." He thrust his hands into his pockets. "I need you to come to the base for debrief, but I'll try really hard not to need you after that. You need rest."

I was too tired to say anything else but, "Thank you for saving me."

Shivers traveled down my spine.

Agent Liam nodded. "Anything for my agents." *Anything for his agents—me.* Dad-Liam strikes again.

"How's Sam?" I said.

"He's fine," he said. "We're still debriefing him, but he's cooperating."

"Has Ver gotten into Ironfall's computer yet?" I said.

"She believes she's close. With Sam's help, it may only be another couple days. He's a bright kid. I'll call you when they do."

The corner of my lip turned up a little. He smiled back. Then he got into the car.

I was safe. Free. But I didn't feel an immediate weight lifted off my shoulders like you do after the last day of school.

I stood there on the sidewalk like that for a few minutes. Still, no one noticed me. My head drooped, and I went inside to change.

Our—Ironfall's—empty hideout sent a pang though my chest. It used to feel so full of life, like when we would spontaneously belt out *Wicked* or *The Little Mermaid*.

Now it was nothing more than another abandoned building, and the world would never know its favorite supervillain was here.

I sighed and changed back into what I was wearing before, the glitter falling to the floor in one last hurrah. Then I stuffed the costume in my bag and went back to the VIGIL headquarters.

I told Agent Liam everything.

APRIL 21 – 6:39 P.M. EDT
When I got home that night, I was the only one there. The apartment was dark and hollow. My keys echoed when I set them down on the counter.

It's over.

My knees suddenly grew weak, and I leaned back against the door. The lump in my throat grew until a single tear streamed down my face. Then two. Then three. My chest heaved as I sank to the ground sobbing.

It's over.

They're safe.

Sometime later I moved to the couch. I'm not sure how long I cried. This sinking weight inside was drowning me, and I couldn't find a way to get free. My chest heaved with sob after sob. Nothing could ever go back to the way it was before.

"...if that idiot boy had just done what we told him to..." Mom's voice echoed outside our apartment. I jumped. "We even checked his little hideout to make sure he was doing his job."

"I knew we should've said something," Dad said.

"But that would have made things worse!" The hairs on my neck raised.

"Shh. You knew better than to trust Jasper's son with something so important. He was bound to double-cross us." What were they talking about? *Double-cross.* That sounded too much like...like something in the spy world. Oh goodness, what was I thinking? It couldn't be that. But could it? None of this made sense. VIGIL not arresting that...that villain the moment he contacted me. The CIA preventing them from doing anything. Ironfall letting me go. My parents talking about someone double-crossing them. Life itself.

"We'll finish this discussion in a minute," Mom said.

The lock jiggled. My first instinct was to raise my fists, but no, that was dumb, it was only my parents. Mom came in first. The sight of her brought both relief and more pain. The lump in my throat throbbed as I tightened my jaw to hold back more tears. I turned my red bloodshot eyes and wet cheeks away.

They said nothing to me before heading to their room. Only then was I able to look up again.

I let out a breath.

No more tears flowed. I was too dry. Too exhausted.

But I wanted—needed—answers to have at least some grip on reality.

I tiptoed to the doorway and pressed my ear against the wood. They talked in low voices I was barely able to make out.

Inhale. Exhale.

"This is our daughter's *life* at stake. Not to mention our reputation." Dad's voice. My heart stopped. Their daughter as in...me?

"But what good will it do if she hates us for it?" That was Mom. Why did she even care if I hated them?

"At least she'll be alive and our standing will remain intact."

I froze.

Alive. Hate them.

Something was wrong.

The voices grew more hushed. "...CIA..." Wait. Ironfall and I robbed the CIA building yesterday. Was it really only yesterday? More importantly, was this robbery all over the news? Did the world know about the guards Ironfall murdered? Was I a wanted person?

Or...or...they...

No.

I wouldn't think about it.

"...signal to initiate phase..."

They were hiding something from me. Something big. Something about the CIA, signaling someone, and my life.

Footsteps.

No time to think now.

I ran and threw myself on the couch. No, Mom and Dad, I definitely wasn't listening to your conversation.

Another lie, even if it was only one in my head. I still hid the truth from them. So many truths, actually. But were they hiding even more from me?

Or maybe the robbery was all over the news and they were worried about my safety because of it.

My gut twinged. Something told me it was so much worse than that.

When they came out, my attention snapped to them. Dad was stone-faced as always. Mom's eyes were red as if she'd been... crying. Though she still looked put together (no, she didn't have mascara running down her cheeks), I'd never seen her such a mess. The only time she showed emotion was when she was mad at me. So what was serious enough to have her in tears?

What good will it do if she hates us?

Dad stood by the door. "How was your day?" he said, his voice the same dull monotone. Okay, why was he asking that? Did he want some sort of confession? Why had Mom been crying? What secrets were they holding on to?

"Weird." Vague, but accurate. What was going on? They were free of Ironfall's threats, but there was now something else sinister.

"Okay," he said, then walked away. Was that his way of playing it cool? Something was up. Why were they being like this?

Please don't let the robbery be on the news.

My heart beat against my ribs as I shut myself in my room. I read every single news site. NBC. ABC. CNN. All of them. Nothing showed up about Ironfall and me. Not so much as an article about VIGIL & ANTE Studios.

I slammed my laptop shut and went out into the living room.

Mom cooked dinner, and Dad watched the news. Still, nothing about the heist.

I glanced back and forth between them.

Something in my stomach sank.

What was going on?

As much as I hated it, there was only one way to find out.

My phone rang. Mom and Dad didn't look up. I sighed, looking down at the screen. It was Sam. As much as I didn't want to talk to him, we'd just been through a traumatic experience together.

I went back into my room and answered. "Hey."

"So it's over. We're done," he said.

"Yeah, we are." I glanced at my door as if my parents were about to walk in. They were acting so weird. "I have a weird question. Does anyone know about the heist?"

"Besides VIGIL?" he said. "My house hasn't been swarmed by the FBI, so I'm guessing not. Why?"

"Nothing, just something my parents said."

"The same parents who ignore you?"

"Yeah, but I overheard them talking about the CIA. Something about my life being at stake," I said. Had I heard them right?

"You sure they weren't watching TV?"

"They were talking outside our apartment," I said. "I heard them through the door."

"Oh good, another mystery." I could feel him rolling his eyes.

"I'm not dragging you into this one," I said. "Besides, I don't think I'll need a hacker."

"I could break into their bank account and make sure they aren't laundering money. Not that I actually know what money laundering looks like."

I laughed. "Haven't you done enough illegal things for Ironfall?"

"I'm basically a full-blown VIGIL agent now," he bragged.

"You'd still need a warrant." Wasn't he the one who claimed to watch *Criminal Minds*?

"Not if I'm good enough to hide it."

"It's probably nothing anyway. If I need your help, you'll be the first to know."

APRIL 22 – 3:04 P.M. EDT
Today was my eighteenth birthday.

School was torture. Every time I tried focusing on the teacher, thoughts of Ironfall flooded in. I trudged through the halls in a daze wearing a baggy black hoodie in an attempt to make myself invisible. No one looked at me; no one even said a word. Except Sam, who droned on and on at lunch about VIGIL & ANTE Studios and Ironfall and how bad today's food was.

My heart was shattered, and I didn't know how to put it together again. Yesterday my world fell apart, and today wouldn't fix it.

Going directly home after school felt weird. Almost every day for the last couple of months I went to the hideout or drama practice. Sam texted me saying he was headed to VIGIL to work with Ver on sifting through Ironfall's computer.

Mom and Dad weren't home, though that wasn't a surprise.

What were they talking about yesterday, and why did they bring up the CIA? And why were they arguing about me?

I found myself at their closed bedroom door. It was probably unlocked, but somehow going in there felt like a violation. Even though VIGIL put Ironfall behind bars, I was terrified.

My fingers grasped the cool metal handle. I turned the knob slowly, degree by degree, trying to eliminate as much noise as possible. The hinge creaked. I cringed. *Remember, no one is home.* Once again, I was in spy mode, but this time, my parents were the persons of interest.

I had no idea what I was looking for, but I needed something to give me a clue as to what was going on. A diary? A computer file? Something that would say *something* and explain their strange actions.

Yet their bedroom appeared normal. Fresh linen scent misted through the air. Their mattress was positioned against a hideous black accent wall in an attempt at something classy. Two thrift store lamps with lampshades from the '80s stood guard on either side of the bed. A built-in wooden wardrobe was on the left, and a few sparsely decorated bookshelves were on the other side. Sometimes I wondered if Mom even tried in her designs, which was ironic because she always scolded me when I didn't perform perfectly.

Maybe something would be on the shelves, but a quick scan proved otherwise. There weren't any books, just a few dusty faux plants and a couple of perfect Instagram-worthy wedding portraits positioned throughout the hollow cubes.

Gosh, I didn't even know what I was trying to find. Was I being hypersensitive to their actions after...? Maybe *I* was the one going crazy.

Why were they talking about the CIA? I had to know.

I checked under the bed. The only thing under there was an extra table leaf.

The wardrobe. Something had to be in there.

I wasn't imagining their suspicious behavior, right?

I opened the large wooden doors, revealing a cavity with hanging clothes. The bottom held three large drawers. I tugged on the top one, and it glided all the way out.

It felt wrong to be going through their things.

But I had to know.

Each item was folded perfectly, so not messing them up would be the most difficult part. I pulled back the silky top layer, then the next, and the next, and the next.

Nothing.

Not even a spare apartment key.

The second drawer would have to yield *something*.

Was I crazy?

Yes—

Then I noticed something dark at the back. A seam in the wood? I pulled the drawer farther. It was so faint I could barely see it, but there was definitely a small rectangle cut into the center.

I gulped.

I pressed in on it. Something clicked. I jumped back.

The compartment opened, revealing two things: a gun and a badge.

TRANSCRIPT OF THE INTERVIEW PROCEEDINGS
WITH IRONFALL
SOME NAMES AND LOCATIONS REDACTED FOR
SECURITY
INTERVIEW CONDUCTED ON MAY 20
LOCATION OF INTERVIEW: **[REDACTED]**
CASE #: **[REDACTED]**

AGENT LIAM BLAKE: Why didn't you talk when we first brought you in?

IRONFALL: Well, Agent Liam, I didn't want to give away all my secrets.

AGENT LIAM BLAKE: You successfully avoided every interrogation technique.

IRONFALL: Maybe you should have tried asking nicely.

AGENT LIAM BLAKE: You sure don't sound like you want to be here right now.

IRONFALL: I don't. But I have to.

CHAPTER 17

A CIA badge.

I froze. Were they secret agents...? Sweaty fingers brushed against the metal center of the badge.

The badge wouldn't be hidden in a secret compartment if it wasn't real.

My vision blurred. They had double lives. How could they lie to me about something that drastic? How could they keep up the pretenses of being an interior designer and banker?

They were terrible at what they claimed were their jobs. How had I not figured this out?

I picked up the badge.

Betrayal. Did they know I was a VIGIL agent? That I had the most dangerous job in the organization? That I agreed to help Ironfall in order to save them because no matter how much of a failure they thought I was, I couldn't live without them.

This only made the tears flow more freely. My body sank to the floor, but I couldn't peel my eyes from the badge in my hands. My dad's name stared back at me. All I could do was look at it and cry. They betrayed me in more ways than one. They *failed* me.

I blinked and tried to clear my head, but it didn't work. All I saw was the proof in my hands.

The front door opened.

A shock surged through me.

Voices.

I closed the drawer and climbed on top, pulling the wardrobe doors shut behind me. Darkness swallowed me as Mom and Dad's clothes wrinkled against my body. Hopefully nothing would fall.

"...she needs to — " Mom's voice stopped.

Silence.

They knew I was here.

My clammy palm still clutched the CIA badge with Dad's name on it.

Footsteps.

A single line of light from the seam in the doors shone on my face, allowing me to peer into the room, but then something covered it. They were just outside.

My body dissolved into sweat.

Dad threw open the wardrobe.

My eyes widened. I couldn't breathe. *No.*

Say something.

His eyes flicked to my hand that held incriminating evidence.

"Is it true?" My voice wavered.

"Yes," Dad said. "We are both CIA agents." No emotion. Nothing to indicate that he was upset I found out.

Both.

They worked for the CIA. The people who didn't want Ironfall arrested.

Did they know? My pulse quickened. Wetness still pricked my eyes; I blinked it away. My fingers ran across the leather wallet.

I glanced over at Mom. She nodded. "It's...it's true." Something flickered in her eyes.

"Why didn't you tell me?" I gripped the badge tighter.

"It was top-secret information. So it's not that we didn't *want* to tell you, but that *you* weren't ready." Mom pressed her fingers on top of my white knuckles.

I jerked back. "So it was my fault that you didn't think I

could handle it? I'm your daughter. You've been lying to me my whole life."

Her forehead wrinkled. "We've wanted to tell you for so long." Her voice rose as each word became more passionate. But to me it rang hollow.

Did she really mean it? Or was she putting on yet another show? Did she want me to feel guilty for her actions?

"Did you know? About me? And that the VIGIL & ANTE Studios movies are real?"

Mom nodded, her brown eyes wide. "Yes, we did, and we made sure you were safe the entire time."

Safe? *Safe?* "Do you know why I joined Ironfall?"

She stepped closer as her painted lips curved up in a sickening smile. "Because he's a character in your favorite movie."

I shook my head, shrinking away. Why would she think that? "Because he threatened to kill you."

"He wouldn't have hurt us," Mom said.

"I joined VIGIL because I realized Ironfall would throw us away once he got what he wanted. I risked everything because of you." A scream lodged in my throat, but I refused to let it out, I couldn't show them how much this hurt. Not right now. "And here you could have gotten me out the instant Ironfall approached me."

Dad cleared his throat. "You were protected the entire time—"

"If I wasn't 'ready' to learn about you being CIA, how was I 'ready' to become a double agent?" My muscles tensed.

Dad crossed his arms. "You weren't supposed to—"

Mom cut him off. "I swear, we only have your best interests at heart. You have to trust us. We're your parents. We know what's best for you, just like I've always told you. You aren't ready to do things on your own. You know we love you, right?"

How could there be more? Unless... "Wait, what was Dad going to say? I wasn't supposed to *what?*"

I didn't tear my gaze from him.

"Nothing, he wasn't going to say anything. Were you, *dear*?" Mom's tongue spewed fire. No, he was about to say something *very* important. "Why don't you come out of there and we can talk about it somewhere more comfortable?"

"Why don't you answer my question?" My eyes narrowed.

Mom clutched her hands together until her knuckles turned white. Did I detect fear?

"There's more you don't know," Dad said. "Once you have the full story, you'll change your mind." His voice was calm and collected, yet unfeeling. Did they have any idea the trauma I went through? The trauma I was *still* going through?

Moreover, what was the full story?

"Let me guess, that involves you 'protecting' me. I don't buy it. You could have told me the moment I became a VIGIL agent, right?" This didn't add up.

"It's not that simple..." Mom stepped closer.

I maneuvered out of the wardrobe but stood my ground even though my back pressed against a wall. "I think it is. You work for the CIA, could have protected me, and didn't because you were too concerned about yourselves." I dug my nails into the wood at my back.

"We *are* protecting you!" Mom's voice had every mark of an emotional performance. Perfect like her clothes, like her hair, like she wanted *me* to be.

"But you already failed at it." *Don't cry, Rosemary.* "Just like you think I do."

"You *need* to trust us," Mom pleaded. "You know we love you."

"Why would I trust you if you've never even been there for me? My whole life, you ignored me and shoved me to the side. You always put yourselves first."

"Honey," Mom soothed. "I know you must be going through a lot." She reached out and placed a manicured hand on my shoulder. It burned.

An unwanted tear spilled down my face. "You don't know anything." I pressed my lips together.

"Remember that conversation the night you went to dinner with Ironfall? I told you that you don't know everything about the world." Her voice got sharper.

"You always say that! And you're right, I don't. But I don't trust you enough to help me through it," I said. "You *always* find ways to tell me how I failed, but I was ready enough to survive a supervillain without you, so I think I'll be all right on my own."

Mom crossed her arms. "Okay, you know what? I'm done having this conversation with you. When you want help, come find us. We're only trying to save your life."

"You already failed at that," I said.

Mom stormed out. Dad lingered for a moment, then followed her.

I looked around one last time. The black walls, the white sheets. My whole life, I never knew the secrets this room held. My parents were secret CIA agents. And, somehow, they were trying to save my life.

The bad design of their bedroom made sense now, and the black wall seemed almost symbolic.

How many more secrets?

APRIL 22 – 7:38 P.M. EDT

I spent the rest of the afternoon in my room trying to rid myself of the sickening grief embedded in my soul. Doubts ran through my head at a mile a minute, but I pushed them away. I needed to be able to think clearly.

The one productive thing I did was shoot Sam a text.

Me: I found a badge. They confirmed they work for the CIA.
Sam: Wait WHAT?!

"Yep," was all I could think to reply before I sank into my mound of pillows and watched a random Disney movie that's now a blur. My phone wouldn't stop vibrating, so eventually I shut it off.

When I finally left my closet-sized room to get a glass of water, I felt nothing. Empty.

No more tears would come, even though I wanted them to.

Whispers came from my parents' bedroom.

If I could just hear what they were saying, maybe I'd find out whatever Mom stopped Dad from saying. What could be worse than them hiding their lives from me and leaving me in a supervillain's clutches? I crept closer. Shadows disrupted the light filtering underneath their door. The knob twisted. They came out, and I shuffled back.

Dad strode toward me. "We need to talk."

My stomach dropped. Oh no. Here it came. I clutched the old couch to keep myself upright.

Mom glanced over at Dad, her eyes narrowing. I'd rarely seen them like this before today.

"Your life is in danger," Dad said. Mom nodded, but still didn't tear her laser-focused gaze from him.

That could only mean one thing. "Ironfall escaped," I breathed. Oh my goodness, I should have known. He was too smart to be captured.

And now he was on a war path for revenge. I was his target.

"No, he's in VIGIL's custody for now. This is a much more dire situation." Dad crossed his thick arms. "And you will do as we tell you." Chills.

"You have no idea just how serious this is. If you don't listen to us, you *will die*." Mom's voice shook, her brown eyes wide. What was she so afraid of? "And there's nothing we would be able to do to stop it."

"Not to mention our lives would be ruined," Dad said. Because of my death?

A door slammed. I jumped. Dad's hand went into his jacket. It was probably the tenant downstairs.

I clutched my quivering fingers behind my back to hide my nervousness. "Just tell me what's going on." My chest tightened.

"We are only trying to protect you." Mom reached out a hand as if to warn me to remain calm. "You can't handle this on your own."

Why were they dancing around the problem? What was so serious that they felt the need to approach the topic so delicately? "Mom, who is trying to kill me if it isn't Ironfall?"

"Well, it's not so much that someone is trying to kill you specifically," Mom said. She stepped to the left, blocking my only exit. "But we can't guarantee your safety when—"

Dad cut her off. "Your mom and I are high up in the CIA, but we are loyal to a subset group that has a much better strategy for a peaceful world."

No.

No.

No.

No.

No.

They're ANTE.

My throat closed. Tears stung my eyes, but no, I couldn't cry now. I had to keep my head.

My parents were ANTE. I missed all the signs. How could this have happened? Why didn't I realize before? How had everything I'd ever known collapsed *again*?

The air conditioner sputtered to life, but uncomfortable heat radiated around me.

The breath left my chest. I stepped back, eyeing both of them. "You're ANTE."

Dad nodded. "Yes. And soon you will be too." That was why the message Ironfall got had my name on it. ANTE knew about me because my parents wanted me to join them.

This couldn't be happening.

I shook my head, staring. "No. You can't..." I was VIGIL, they were ANTE.

Dad's teeth clenched. Mom widened her eyes.

"We tried telling you slowly, Rosemary. Really, we did. You were never supposed to join VIGIL, and once again, Ironfall didn't recruit you like he was supposed to."

"So you set a supervillain on me?" I couldn't breathe. Air. I needed air.

"We told him to recruit you. That's all, I swear," Mom said. "Ironfall would never really have hurt us, he must have seen it as the only way to get you on his team. *Everything* we've done has been for your own good. We love you, so, so much."

"How is getting a deadly killer to recruit me 'for my own good'?"

"Rosemary, I don't think you understand. When ANTE wins, they won't leave anyone who opposes them alive," Mom warned.

"You mean *you* will kill me." My chest heaved. I couldn't join them.

"We thought Ironfall would be perfect because he was a character in your favorite movie. He would make you see the truth. Can't you see? We did all of that because we love you. Someday when you're a mother, you'll understand the lengths parents go to for their children," Mom pleaded.

"I didn't need protecting, I needed you to be there for me. To be honest with me. To cheer me on. To support me when I messed up. All my life, I tried to earn that. I joined Ironfall to save your life and earn your love, and what do I get? More manipulation." My chest felt hollow.

"If you want to please us that badly, join us. Then we can be together as the family you pictured in your mind," Mom said. "You just have to do this one thing."

"No." I blinked. "And to be clear, I didn't just become a VIGIL agent to protect you. I did it to save lives." My hands formed into fists. "I won't join you."

"Please. You have to listen to us. We are trying to protect

you," Mom said. "You *have* to join us. If you want our love, renounce VIGIL."

I straightened, stepping back, trying to seem as confident as Mom always told me to be. "I said no."

Dad gave her a warning glance, then stepped forward. "Rosemary, we're not giving you a choice." He reached into his coat. I flinched. Here it came. Their true colors. "You will be loyal to ANTE. End of discussion." They didn't want *me*, they wanted a compliant version of me. That was the girl they loved.

"Now wait just a..." Mom placed a hand on his arm.

"You will do as we say or suffer the very severe consequences." He reached behind him, retrieving a small black pistol.

Was...was he willing to kill me? His own daughter?

The fire that ignited in my abdomen screamed at me to get out of there, but they blocked my path. The windows, if they even still opened, were too high to jump from. I looked around. Bulky couch. Enormous TV mounted on the wall. Short cabinet underneath. Small dining room table on the other side of the room. Kitchen from the '80s. My windowless room. Bathroom. Their master "suite." I had to figure out another exit. Yet there wasn't one. I'd have to fight my way out of this. All of Ironfall's training came flooding back.

Keep yourself calm and sharp.

I'd learned from the best. Let's hope it was enough.

I moved away from the couch so I was evenly spaced between it and the table. I needed as much range of motion as I could get.

"I helped stop a supervillain, and I will stop you too." I clenched my fists. Would I be able to?

"You *will* join ANTE." Dad raised the gun. My spine prickled. "Getting out of this is not an option."

"Please don't do this." I gulped, pressing my lips together and tightening my fists. A sickening feeling stirred in my abdomen, mixing with the adrenaline coursing through my body. *Don't lose it, Rosemary.* I had to at least keep my emotions at bay until I saw where this was going.

"Come with us," Mom said, tears filling her wide eyes. They had to be fake. "Rosemary, come with us willingly, and we will love you forever." As much as my heart pulled me toward them, I couldn't betray the world for something so selfish.

I tilted my head to the side, eyes wide. "Does that line work in the movies?" I couldn't just hand over the world to ANTE.

Dad didn't lower his gun. Mom probably didn't want a fight, but Dad wouldn't hesitate to use that weapon of his. Would the fire escape work? No, I'd have to smash a window to get out there. No time for that. My pulse thrummed. I couldn't change their minds. Would they spare me like Ironfall did?

I searched their faces, but only found a manipulative desperation in Mom and a stone-cold indifference in Dad.

Again, I swallowed down my emotions. "I won't join you." I planted my feet into the ground.

Dad's finger found the trigger. I leapt to the side and charged. My hands grappled for the gun. I twisted, wrenching it from his steel hands like Ironfall taught me. Mom slipped out her own pistol and fired it in one motion. Miss.

Was she not aiming for a lethal area?

I pointed the gun at them, stiffening my arms. I breathed heavily. "Let me go or someone gets hurt."

But Mom only raised her gun back at me. That left Dad open. They still had the upper hand.

"We can't do that, sweetheart. This is what's best for you," Mom said. "Drop the weapon."

This wasn't good.

I somersaulted to the ground, rolling to my feet just inches from them. My fists hardened. I swung upwards, shoving my mom back, but she still clutched the gun. Dad came from behind. Elbow. Knee. Bone connected with bone.

Ouch. He stumbled back as Mom recoiled from another attack. I turned sideways so I faced both of them.

If I could distract both for a few seconds, I could run. *Throw them off balance.* That's what Ironfall would do.

I thrust my knee forward, pounding Dad's abdomen, then I kicked out his knee. Mom rushed forward, but I threw out my fist, knocking against her jaw. She stumbled back.

Run, Rosemary, run. I swung around and sprinted.

BANG.

Something pricked my leg.

What the—?

All went dark.

TRANSCRIPT OF THE INTERVIEW PROCEEDINGS WITH IRONFALL
SOME NAMES AND LOCATIONS REDACTED FOR SECURITY
INTERVIEW CONDUCTED ON MAY 20
LOCATION OF INTERVIEW: **[REDACTED]**
CASE #: **[REDACTED]**

AGENT LIAM BLAKE: Let's talk about how you discovered Rosemary.

IRONFALL: My father told me to recruit her to ANTE. That's all. An encrypted message sent to my phone.

AGENT LIAM BLAKE: How long had it been since you'd heard from him?

IRONFALL: Years. Though, it turns out the order actually came from Rosemary's parents. They impersonated my father and sent me a message.

AGENT LIAM BLAKE: And why didn't you do what you were told to do?

IRONFALL: I had a better idea because I thought the reason ANTE wanted her was because she could tip the scale in their direction, and I needed someone that powerful on my own team. And then I got to know her, and I didn't want to lose her.

AGENT LIAM BLAKE: I thought all you wanted was to please your father. Given you believed he sent you the message, didn't your plan go against him?

IRONFALL: Wouldn't he be more pleased to have his own son hand the world to him?

CHAPTER 18

DATE AND TIME: UNKNOWN

The white walls of this cell were solid, and no matter how much I banged on them, nothing cracked, no hidden doors opened. Trapped.

So I lay back down and fell asleep, but this brought nightmares about Ironfall attacking me and ANTE finishing me off. I woke up screaming. Fabric clung to my sweaty skin. My lungs fought to take in more air as my pulse raced out of control.

The door to the cell slid open. I jumped.

Mom and Dad.

Betrayers.

Liars.

Manipulators.

They'd tranquilized me and brought me here. My leg still stung from the dart.

If I'd let Sam help me investigate, would they have kidnapped me?

My teeth clenched. No. I couldn't face them. I fixated my gaze on the blank wall.

The hard mattress shifted. Heat burned my left side. They were too close. Beads of sweat rose on my forehead. My chest tightened. *Get away.*

"Talk to us. We're finally allowed to," Mom said, her voice soft. "You can tell us anything."

"You locked me in a cage." I still couldn't look at them. Goodness, I could barely stand being this close.

"Well, you haven't proven you can be let out." I tried not to flinch at Dad's harsh tone.

My hands clenched into fists. "I'm an adult." White walls. White floor. White everywhere.

"Honey, that may be true, but you need to trust us right now," Mom said.

I looked over, staring her straight in the eyes. "In case you missed every movie ever, ANTE is evil." That was all I said. I gritted my teeth and clenched my hands.

"The things VIGIL does don't add up. Think about it." Mom placed a hand on my knee, but I jerked away. "Come on, you have to admit to that." Not really.

"You're joining ANTE whether you like it or not." Dad crossed his arms, narrowing his dark eyes.

"Is that a threat?"

"Absolutely." He tilted his head to the side.

"No, no one is threatening anybody. Your dad and I are both aiming for the same thing." She glared at him. "We will do what we can to save you." Her forehead creased in unfamiliar spots.

"You're trying to save me from your own terrorist group. That's a fun one to think about if you'd like to consider things that don't add up," I said.

"We aren't terrorists, but if you don't join us, you're the one who will be considered one," Dad said. "And we have ways of making you do anything we want, so I suggest you stop this rebellious act." This time I didn't feel bad about not living up to my parents' expectations. If I'd have known those lofty standards included "terrorist," maybe I wouldn't have tried so hard to make them love me.

"Radicals. Really, we should be called radicals," Mom jumped in.

"Did you see the movie *Cloaker*? You're terrorists." My breath shook. How would I get out of this? Would I even be able to get out?

Wait. Cloaker. He was supposed to be undercover in ANTE. If I could just find him...

"See, VIGIL pulls the strings. They pitted you against us." No. I joined VIGIL to *protect* them.

"I think you did a pretty good job of that yourself when you told me who you really work for," I said. "No government organization did that." Nails clawed into my palms, a momentary distraction from the rising panic.

"I'm sorry you feel that way, but we were high level agents. We weren't allowed to tell you for your safety," Mom said. "And if something happened to either of us in the field, it would make the loss easier for you. We did it because we loved you."

"That may be, but right now you're trying to manipulate me." I shifted toward the edge of the bed. "It's not going to work." Leave.

"That's why we have plan B. Like I said, you *are* joining ANTE." Dad looked at my mother. "See, I told you my plan was better."

But once again, Mom swooped in to soften his threat with gaslighting of her own. "I promise, we aren't trying to manipulate you. We're *here* for you." Mom's voice rang hollow, yet to the untrained ear sounded sweet. It sickened me as much as the cleaner fumes that hung in the air. How could she act like she genuinely loved me while she was so disappointed in me?

"You've never been there for me before. Do you even love me?" I didn't want to know the answer.

"Yes," she said. Were her words really as empty as I thought they were? Maybe they did want me to switch sides so ANTE wouldn't kill me. But what if it was another one of their sick games? What if they always dangled their love just out of reach on purpose? Or maybe everyone felt like this towards their parents.

How had I missed their double lives? Maybe their lifelong

criticism of me was correct: I wasn't good enough at life. I should have seen this coming. I could have stopped it. I could have—

Stop. Think clearly. *I need to be Agent Rosemary right now.*

I needed to find Cloaker. I needed Sam to tell VIGIL everything we'd talked about.

Dad stepped forward. "This isn't going to work. Get up. Now."

I resisted the urge to jump back, but I obeyed, just this once. My shaky legs pushed me to my feet. Mom stood too, and the two of them flanked me. We left the cell. I shivered.

Flickering lights cast a green-ish glow across the concrete walls of the bunker. This place might be anywhere. The only thing I knew for sure was that this could be my only chance to escape.

Maybe they were taking me somewhere to brainwash me. Or execute me. No, they had to love me deep down. They brought me here instead of icing me when I said no. And even if I suspected they had ulterior motives, that could still be love, right? Somehow? Maybe.

They couldn't spend their whole lives with me and not love me.

Why was I still thinking about this? Escape first, existential crisis later.

Right or left. I glanced down both sides of the hallway, but they looked the same. They both had the same strange lights and dingy concrete walls.

I'd just have to pick a direction and go.

Hoping was better than nothing.

I wrenched myself from their grasp and bolted right. Thank you, Ironfall, for making me run so many laps.

Ironfall...

"Stop!" Mom shouted after me. No, I wouldn't. I had to get away. Adrenaline pumped through me. I ran and ran, but it didn't feel fast enough. Too...slow...to...make...it. Someone almost had me, I felt it. Legs burned as they pushed harder.

The long hallway forked, and again, I thrust myself right.

I glanced back. Not. Far. Enough. Away.

Someone grabbed my arm. I stumbled forward, then turned and kneed him in the stomach. He doubled over. How old was he? Eighteen? Nineteen? Not much bigger than me with his twig-like figure swimming in black protective gear. I punched him again. He swung his fist, but I deflected.

This guy was barely trained.

I needed to get out of there.

I twisted his arm and threw him over my back. His head slammed to the ground. Blood. Too much of it. Oh no.

I pressed a finger to his too-crooked neck as more blood spilled from the gash.

Nothing.

Dead.

No.

He couldn't be. I couldn't live with myself. *Monster.*

He was so young. So new.

Run.

I had to get out of here. I bolted from the dead man. Right. Left. Left. Right. Which way was the exit? I had to get out. Away from the lies. I needed help.

Run.

I took the next right and ran straight into an armed guard.

"Stop!" he shouted, pointing a machine gun at me.

Images of Ironfall shooting those two men flooded through me. "N-no, d-don't shoot!" I screeched. The gunshots. Their blank faces. The blood. *Him.*

I froze.

But I had to get out.

Gulp. I lunged. His biceps were larger than my thighs, but I had to get away. I tried wrenching the gun from his hands. He didn't even watch it clatter to the floor. Fists swung at my head, but I deflected.

Okay, maybe this wouldn't be so bad.

Wrong. He grabbed at me. I twisted around, but his iron grip still clawed into my flesh. I kneed, kicked, and twisted with every bit of my adrenaline-boosted strength. He didn't so much as let out a frustrated grunt. This wasn't a matter of skill, it was a matter of strength.

He pinned me to the floor within seconds. Strong fingers crushed both forearms into the concrete and a knee pressed into my stomach. The soldier wouldn't look at me.

Footfalls pounded against the floor until a tall, silhouetted figure towered above. "Don't *ever* try anything like that again." *Dad.* I'd never heard him so angry, not even when I refused to join ANTE. My heart thrashed against my ribcage, trapped just as much as I was.

"Remember who the enemy is, Rosemary. See, you need us to tell you." *Mom.* I couldn't breathe. The soldier's grip grew tighter and tighter, carving into nerve endings until I cried out.

"You...are...the...enemy." *I would have died for you.*

Mom leaned down and brushed a hair out of my face. I couldn't shrink away. "You're not thinking clearly. Trust us. Once you accept your new position, life will grow so much easier. Make me proud, Rosemary."

"Are you threatening me?" I whispered.

"I'm promising you. I *do* love you," Mom said. She said that all the time, but all of this: the captivity, the lies, the manipulation, everything. She had such a twisted definition of love.

Or could it be called love at all?

She turned to the tank of a man. "Take her back to her cell."

The guard got off me and yanked me to my feet. His thick arm wouldn't let go as he dragged me across the concrete. I glimpsed blood pooling around the dead man's bashed head and more panic flooded my nerves. Then I was back in my cell. I stared at my hands. Was I as bad as Ironfall? As my parents?

Did that man have parents? Siblings? A girlfriend?

I stepped back from the door as my knees weakened, more sobs wracking my chest.

I just killed someone.

I sank to the ground, burying my head between my knees. I didn't mean to kill him...it just happened.

It's part of being an agent.

But was being captured by your evil parents part of that deal? Did they even love me? Was this love?

My stomach turned.

The door slid open. I jumped.

Dad.

Oh no. I couldn't deal with him. Not now.

I tugged my knees closer.

"Hello, Rosemary." He seemed cooled off. Frosty, even.

Silence.

"I didn't come to talk, so that should be a relief." His emotionless voice echoed against the plastic walls. "Your mom thinks she can talk you into joining us, but that isn't going to work, is it?" His eyes glinted in the florescent light. "I see a lot of myself in you. Strong. Resolved. You aren't easily manipulated; it's going to take more than desperate pleas to convince you of something. But we'll break you eventually. It just requires something stronger than words."

I resisted the urge to flinch. "You think you know me, but you don't." My voice shook. I didn't sound that strong. And I wasn't. Images of the man's lifeless body flashed through my mind.

I killed someone.

He chuckled, stepping closer to my cot. "Every teenager says that when they don't agree with their parents."

"But this time it's true."

"No, I don't think it is," he said. "But I won't let you ruin it. You have no idea how much your mom and I have at stake, and nothing is more important than protecting that. Not even you."

This confirmed what I already knew. It was never about saving me. They just wanted me to comply. I almost died for them. I put my life on the line for them because the thought of their death was so much more painful than my own. And they kept me in a cage because they thought I'd jeopardize their position in a terrorist organization?

It was as if something inside clicked. Something I thought was true but didn't know for sure.

This *wasn't* real love.

They might think so, but it wasn't. It couldn't be.

Love wasn't manipulative. It wasn't cruel. It didn't go away when someone failed. It didn't get cast aside in favor of ambition.

Mom and Dad didn't love me. They wouldn't die for me. They wouldn't sacrifice for me.

They only abused me and called it love.

I kept this realization to myself and straightened, forcing back tears. "Why are you trying to manipulate me if I can't be manipulated?" I said.

He chuckled. "All right, let's take a field trip." He seemed so much larger than six feet tall. *He doesn't love me.*

How had I missed this? That everything they claimed to do for me was really done for themselves? Guilt settled over me.

"Get up." He grabbed my arm and yanked me to my feet. I stumbled forward, shoes squeaking against the white tile. His fingers clawed deeper into my skin.

I sucked in a harsh breath. "You're hurting me." A tear brushed down my cheek.

"Dying will hurt a lot worse." Then he dragged me from the room into the maze of identical concrete hallways. "You have no say in your future. You have no authority. You *will* submit."

"Why does ANTE need me?" I gritted my teeth.

He just laughed. Loud and menacing, as if he was putting on a show. "We don't *need* you. Aside from what Ironfall taught you,

you're hardly a valuable asset. So get it out of your head that you're some special chosen one."

"Then why not kill me? It would save a lot of trouble."

"It's my job as a parent to keep you alive. That's why you will join us."

By the time he threw me into another dull concrete room, a purple splotch crept up my arm where his hand had been. There was a single man inside, and he was basically a giant. Like the one muscly bad guy in every action film that's twice the size of the good guy.

A lump formed in my throat, but no more tears came.

"Have fun," Dad said. "And welcome to ANTE. Don't mess up." Then he left, slamming the door behind him.

I should have seen this coming. I believed their lies for *years*. *This isn't love.*

"We will have you take a physical assessment and then begin your training." The towering man stepped forward. Florescent lighting cast harsh shadows across his cruel face. "Are you ready, operative?"

"No." I shook my head, gingerly touching my injury. No. I wouldn't join ANTE. I wouldn't train with them. I wouldn't do anything. Lies, so many lies here. I looked behind me at the steel door. It had to be at least six inches thick, with a large dead-bolt securing it closed.

I didn't have a choice but to obey. If I'd only realized sooner...

"Good. Good. Let's get started," the man said.

DATE AND TIME: UNKNOWN

The next few weeks of captivity were a cycle of combat training, eating, sleeping, and thinking too much. Every day held the same numbing routine. ANTE gave me no opportunities to escape. And no one *ever* gave me a chance.

I still didn't know where Cloaker was or if he was even here. Hope that Sam had told VIGIL enough for them to piece together what happened slowly drained from me.

I grew stronger with training but was never strong enough to escape the two armed guards who clutched my arms every time I wasn't locked in a room. And the dead man's face burned into my mind every time I closed my eyes.

Ironfall always told me to anticipate. I should have seen this. My parents were right about one thing: I wasn't good enough. They were so much better.

And it looked like ANTE would take over, maybe because I wasn't there to stop them.

If the number of scratches on the wall were correct, it was now sometime mid-May.

My cell door slid open. It wasn't time for training yet. I looked up. Mom stood in the doorway holding a comforter and a small cardboard box.

What was she up to now?

"How's training going?" She stepped inside. The white door sealed shut.

I didn't respond.

"Well, I brought your bedding and a few of those programs you have hanging on your wall at home." She didn't even know some of my most prized possessions were called Playbills. Looks like someone missed that in Convince Rosemary We Care 101. "Thought they might make you feel more at home in your new room." She placed my things by the cot.

"You mean my prison cell," I sighed. Look at this place. With the harsh white walls, the bleach I never desensitized to, the reflective floor, and this lumpy hospital-like cot. Nothing could change the way I saw it.

It was the same conversation we always had. She tried to persuade me to give in and join them. To have a relationship with them. Why did she even try anymore? My answer was always the same. Besides, she never meant a word of it.

Because it wasn't real love.

"Think of it more as a dorm." She motioned at the sterile walls. "This is probably as close to college as you're going to get."

"See? Prison." I looked away, folding my hands.

"That isn't what I meant," she said. "But you're starting to come around."

I gritted my teeth. "I will never join you." She only wanted me there for her personal gain. If I stayed in this bunker much longer, I'd go out of my mind. I missed the sun.

"When are you going to accept that we only want what's best for you?"

I groaned. "The day you admit that ANTE is evil. And for the record, my answer will never change." *This isn't love.*

"We aren't evil, you only think we are. All we want is peace. And I know because I'm good friends with the man who started it. Sweetheart, we know exactly what this organization is about." I didn't doubt that.

"Then you have a very twisted understanding of good. I'm done talking about this." My lips pressed together. I clutched the mattress.

"I only pushed you because I care," she said. No, she pushed me because she wanted me perfect for herself. "It's a rough world, and you have to be ready for anything. There is no room for error, and no perfection without sacrifice."

No perfection without sacrifice. Where had I heard that before?

She sighed. "Would you like help making your bed?"

"No." I looked away. Things were so much simpler when VIGIL & ANTE Studios was just that: a movie studio.

"I thought so." She left without saying anything more.

TRANSCRIPT OF THE INTERVIEW PROCEEDINGS
WITH IRONFALL
SOME NAMES AND LOCATIONS REDACTED FOR SECURITY
INTERVIEW CONDUCTED ON MAY 20
LOCATION OF INTERVIEW: **[REDACTED]**
CASE #: **[REDACTED]**

AGENT LIAM BLAKE: Were you aware that Rosemary's parents worked for ANTE?

IRONFALL: No.

AGENT LIAM BLAKE: I have a hard time believing that.

IRONFALL: It's true. Check your scanners. I haven't lied to you once.

CHAPTER 19

MAY 15 – around 10:30 A.M. EDT

An armed guard came in. I shrank back, balling my hands into fists. He was large and bulky with pale skin and light hair.

It wasn't time for training, so what was he doing here?

He pressed a finger to his lips, motioning me toward him.

My forehead wrinkled in confusion. "Who are you?"

He looked behind him, then turned to me again. "Cloaker. Now move quickly, I just learned what ANTE's planning."

My eyes widened. "Where have you been?"

"Believe me, it wasn't easy to work my way into this base, even as a shapeshifter," he said. "Took me months to find it. Now come on."

This propelled me into action. I ran toward him, and he grabbed my arm as if he was a real guard. He pulled me into the hallway, quickly turning left.

That was when we saw my dad walking down the hallway. His peach-colored suit looked out of place in the damp hallway.

I averted my gaze.

"She's not supposed to be moved yet." His harsh voice echoed in the dismal hallway. I flinched. "Training isn't for another hour, and she's not even going today."

Don't look at him. Don't look at him.

"Sir, I was given orders by—" Goodness, Cloaker didn't even sound like he did in the movies. I guess he also took on the voice of whoever's body he copied.

"This prisoner is in *my* care. She's my daughter," Dad said. I gulped. He saw right through Cloaker's perfect shapeshifter disguise. *Just go away so we can escape.* "Orders pertaining to her only come from me."

"Sir, these orders came directly from—"

"Return her to her cell." The edge in Dad's voice grew sharper. "Now." Blood rushed into my ears as I finally looked up to meet his eyes. The lack of fire sent my stomach into knots.

Psychopath.

"Yes, sir." Cloaker's grip loosened.

"Actually, I'll take her from you." Dad narrowed his eyes at me as if he hated me. Probably did.

"No," I breathed, my gaze darting to Cloaker. "I'm not giving him a hard time."

Dad stepped closer. "Is there a reason you want to go with him more than me?"

"Other than you're a terrible father?" *Leave me with Cloaker, please.*

"Our leader wants to see you in his office," he glared at me. "I'm taking you there myself."

"Wrong answer," Cloaker said, now letting go of me. "But thanks for the intel." He punched my dad in the face. Dad reeled back, then struck back, but Cloaker expertly deflected the blow.

"I knew there was something off about you. Who are you?" Dad's voice could be a weapon right now.

Was that a smirk on Cloaker's face? "I'm whoever you want me to be." In a series of lightning-fast moves from Cloaker, my dad fell to the ground, limp. I ran over, pressing a finger to his neck. A steady pulse vibrated beneath my fingertips. Though I shouldn't have, I breathed a sigh of relief.

Cloaker had only knocked him out.

He then touched my dad's face. The guard's features melted into the harsh ones of my dad. Hair shifted color, clothes changed.

He was now a perfect copycat of my father.

"Get him into the cell, then let's go pay the head of ANTE a visit."

I could only blink at him. Even his voice sounded like my dad. Just hearing it and seeing his face made my chest tighten. *It's Cloaker*, I reminded myself. The man standing before me wasn't my father, he was one of my favorite superheroes.

"Come on." He tugged at my arm, and I followed him. He led me from one dismal cave-like hallway to the next. Overhead flickered tubes of white florescent lights. Metal doorways were spaced every ten feet. But since there was nothing distinct about each passage, I was soon lost, and no matter how hard I tried, the pattern escaped me.

Questions raced through my mind. Why did the leader of ANTE want to talk to me?

Calm down.

"They're planning to attack the Capitol in two days. That's when they'll come out of hiding and take over. They have their claws deep within government intelligence agencies and the military. Once they take out Congress, it's over. Congress is calling a major vote, and everyone is attending," Cloaker said, quickening his pace. I practically had to run to keep up with his long legs. My dad's long legs? Wow, this shapeshifting thing could be mind-boggling.

More turns and more metal doors. Something wet dripped on the top of my head. I shivered.

Just when I thought this maze couldn't get any more confusing, we approached a half-open door on the right.

"This is it," Cloaker said. "Let me do the talking. Once we confirm this man is the leader, we take him out."

I nodded, heart pounding. Could I help kill someone? I already had one life on my hands; could I handle another?

We stepped closer, and he pushed the door the rest of the way open, revealing a dark office. His jaw clenched, and he dragged me inside. My stomach lurched as I saw him drop into character. He stood to the side, hands resting on a large oak desk, a contrast for the industrial vibe the rest of the bunker had going on. He glanced at me, then grabbed my wrist and dragged me into the large office.

A tall middle-aged man sat in a large, cushioned office chair like a crime boss in an old black-and-white movie. His skin was deathly pale in the soft yellow lamp light. He wore an ANTE pin on his suit, and he had this hardened look on his face. Was he the leader of ANTE?"

"Don't make me regret giving her an assignment, James," said the man.

Cloaker shot me a glare, falling into my father's mannerisms. "You won't. Get on with it."

"You're edgy today," the other guy muttered. "You haven't had coffee yet, have you?"

"There's more pressing business."

The man smirked, now looking at me. "If you were just any prisoner you would have been killed for all the trouble you caused me, but your dad helped me see some of your...benefits. And as the leader of ANTE, I love benefits." Oh no, what could that mean? I stole a glance at Cloaker.

We had confirmation that this man was the leader.

"Jasper!" The door burst in with my real father tumbling through. "That man isn't me! He's Cloaker!"

Oh no, this was bad. My heart palpitated as Cloaker and I leapt into action. I lunged for my real dad as Cloaker attacked the leader of ANTE. I cut toward his stomach, but he deflected, kicking my legs. I stumbled, but attacked again.

Bang! Cloaker crumpled, shriveling into a face I'd never seen. A dart stuck into his back. Just a tranquilizer. He had tan skin and dark hair. It made sense, though, that his actor persona wasn't his real face. My dad quickly placed my hands in cuffs.

No, Cloaker. I needed to get out of here. We needed to tell VIGIL what we knew.

We had to stop ANTE.

"Well, VIGIL is a problem again," the leader—Jasper—said.

I gulped, glancing frantically between them.

"Which is why we have her." Dad pulled out a chrome-colored bracelet. It was thin, about half a centimeter wide. He shoved it on my left wrist and clasped it together. It was tight against my skin and wouldn't slip off. His wide eyes bored into me as if warning me not to ruin his life.

Then he unlocked my handcuffs. This was bad. I rushed to Cloaker, shaking his unconscious form. Come on, wake up. Do something!

ANTE's leader leaned his elbows on the desk. The desk lamp cast strange shadows across his face. "He won't be waking up anytime soon. I wouldn't bother."

"The bracelet carries a lethal injection," Dad said. "If you don't follow our orders, we will press a button, releasing it into your system." Gulp.

No. "I...I can't join you," I whispered, standing up.

The leader's intense blue eyes met mine. "Do you know what supersedes all? The human instinct to *survive*." He took out a black fob with a bright red button—red buttons are never good —and brushed his hand over it. An intimidation tactic.

The crimson shade was too bright for the room's wooded vibe.

I tried to slip the bracelet off, but it was too tight. Oh gosh... they could kill. I tugged on the device, but it was locked. My chest caved in as I pulled harder and harder, feeling as if the circlet drowned me.

"Now you will see just how important it is to be loyal to ANTE." Dad's jaw flared. "I told you the consequences for not complying would be severe."

"I risked my life to save you, Dad," I said. "What makes you think I won't disobey orders to save people again?"

"Clever girl," clucked ANTE's leader. "We also have your hero here. Cloaker, I believe he likes to be called. A silly superhero name, if you ask me. His life is also in your hands. You obey us, you both live. If not, you both die. The choice is yours."

I gulped. My vision blurred as I tugged harder against the bracelet. *Harder.*

"You are to go to Liam's base and from there, we will give you instructions. Make it seem like everything is normal. If you so much as give them a hint that we sent you..." ANTE's leader fingered the crimson button. Slowly, I nodded. Because what else could I do? If I refused to cooperate now, Cloaker would die and VIGIL would have no chance to stop the attack. And...they'd kill me. What they claimed was love wouldn't stand in the way of that.

An ANTE agent I didn't recognize wrapped a blindfold around my head and led me through a complex maze until I felt warmth wash over my face. A soft breeze tickled my hair. Never had the city smelled so good.

The guard took off the blindfold, and I squinted from the sudden bright light. *The sun.*

"Put this in your ear." The agent held out his hand, revealing a small comm device, similar to the one Ver gave me. I slipped it on. Then he left.

I twisted the silver death bracelet around my wrist. They wouldn't hesitate to kill Cloaker if I betrayed them. But if I didn't betray them...

This was far worse than lying to Ironfall because if I even thought about escaping, they'd flip the kill switch. I wouldn't even have the chance to tell VIGIL about the attack. They wouldn't know about it until it ended, and Cloaker would die.

Invisible walls seemed to close around me, pressing me to choose. Cloaker's life, or VIGIL. And all the crap that came from that.

Focus. I pressed fingers into my temples. Now wasn't the time to panic or make impossible decisions. *Get your bearings.*

Where was I? Cars whizzed past. A siren blared a couple blocks over. I shifted my weight. After so long in silence, the city noise was unsettling.

Okay. I needed a street sign or something.

After a few minutes, I finally figured out that I was close to the VIGIL base. But that meant if something went wrong, ANTE would be here in a moment. I took a deep breath to clear my mind, but I didn't start walking. No. I couldn't go. If I did, they'd make me...

A man jostled against me and continued walking. People all around cluelessly making their way to wherever they needed to be.

What could I do to get out of this?

VIGIL needed to know about the Capitol attack. But if I told them, ANTE would kill Cloaker. And me. If I didn't go to the base, they'd end me as well. If I went to the base and listened to them, my friends would probably die. By my hand.

"Get moving," someone barked through the earpiece. My chest tightened, tears rising. *No, don't cry here and attract attention.* I couldn't let ANTE know I was conflicted. So I trudged forward.

The kill bracelet seemed to weigh a thousand pounds.

I wouldn't make any rational decisions if I didn't stop freaking out. I sucked in another deep breath, but it did nothing to calm me.

I arrived too soon. My breath shook as my feet shuffled close to the door. The building's chipped painted brick and black front door seemed so normal and unassuming. If I went inside, who knew what ANTE would force me to do. Maybe VIGIL had an idea? Maybe there was some way I could stop this.

If it took me eighteen years to figure out my parents worked for ANTE, how would I stop this without them realizing? That thought was like a punch in an already bruised chest. I couldn't save VIGIL, and I couldn't save the world. So what was I to do?

My hands fidgeted until they cramped.

"Go inside." The handler's deep voice jolted me.

Adrenaline coursed through my veins, and without thinking, I spoke. "Rosemary Collins." And the door clicked open.

I stepped inside, and the door shut behind me, sealing VIGIL's fate. Every muscle in my body tightened.

Ver and Sam stood in the corner, typing on their computers. Blue light from monitors lit up her face. She looked over suddenly, her eyes growing wide. "Rosemary!"

I fiddled with the bracelet until the metal left red marks on my skin. I used to be able to respond with something that sounded legit, but now... "I...I..." I glanced up at the black surveillance camera tucked in the back corner.

"Hey, it's okay," she said. Then she pressed a finger to an earpiece of her own. "Liam, can you come in here?"

Maybe I could get Liam a message that ANTE was holding me hostage and planning to attack Congress before they flipped the kill switch. But would that only get everyone killed?

And that meant Cloaker would die.

TRANSCRIPT OF THE INTERVIEW PROCEEDINGS
WITH IRONFALL
SOME NAMES AND LOCATIONS REDACTED FOR
SECURITY
INTERVIEW CONDUCTED ON MAY 20
LOCATION OF INTERVIEW: **[REDACTED]**
CASE #: **[REDACTED]**

AGENT LIAM BLAKE: Did you know about ANTE's plan to attack the Capitol?

IRONFALL: No.

AGENT LIAM BLAKE: Let's talk more about your relationship with them.

IRONFALL: My father started training me to serve them when I was three.

AGENT LIAM BLAKE: To serve ANTE?

IRONFALL: Yes. I started out as a disappointment because my father's experiments left me with a power that wasn't very useful to them.

AGENT LIAM BLAKE: He created your powers?

IRONFALL: Yes. It wasn't an even playing field. VIGIL had super soldiers, and ANTE didn't.

CHAPTER 20

MAY 15 – around noon EDT

How could I ask for help without ANTE knowing? If I could just do that, Ver could probably figure out how to hack this bracelet and maybe trace it to the base, if given enough time.

But we didn't have enough time. And ANTE would take over the world in two days, and the moment I disobeyed, Cloaker would be dead.

Agent Liam's commanding presence brought a sense of relief. Like always, he wore a pressed black suit and red tie. How many of these did he own? "Agent Liam, it's so good to see you." I tried my best to sound calm. Was it the right thing to say?

"Cloaker contacted us saying you were ANTE's prisoner." He stepped away from the frosted glass wall, eyes wide. "But you just...walked in."

"I'm just glad you're safe. He's glad too, he's just being himself about it," Ver laughed.

"Did Cloaker help you escape?" Agent Liam said.

Silence from ANTE.

"Y-yes." *Cloaker.* I pressed my lips together, glancing around the room, trying to think of something else to say. Computer monitors. Bulletproof glass. Oddly placed windows behind me. A cell in the hallway (Ironfall's?). Cameras.

Wait. Cameras. There were cameras here, and the CIA—probably infiltrated by ANTE—was watching. I had to get him outside, but in a way ANTE would think was normal. No, who was I kidding, ANTE would see right through it. But it was my only shot at warning them and getting help.

Agent Liam's eyebrows scrunched together. "Is something wrong? Where is he?"

I glanced into a corner at a shadowed camera, then nodded. My breath became ragged. *Pull yourself together.* Warning them was the right thing, I told myself. These people were there when my parents weren't. I couldn't let them down because I failed to see through Mom and Dad's facades. Not to mention our country was at stake. "Can we go outside, maybe?" Real smooth, Rosemary. "I need to talk to you alone." Well, that was a dumb excuse.

"What are you doing?" I recognized the voice coming from the comm device. The leader of ANTE. Oh no, this was bad. He was already suspicious.

Did I imagine Liam's shoulders falling? "Of course. Whatever you need." I nodded and forced a smile as if everything was fine. Then we got out of sight of the cameras. Agent Liam would find a way to help if I could stall ANTE long enough.

Once we were a block away from the base and the busy sidewalk outside, I stopped and turned to face Agent Liam. He stopped too but said nothing. No one else in earshot. A small convenience store stood on the corner across the street, and a weathered apartment complex on the other. The hot May sun beat down on my face, but I welcomed it.

This was it.

I pointed to my ear and mouthed, "ANTE is listening."

Liam pressed his lips together, but again didn't say anything. His phone. I could type. I made a writing motion with my hand. This was just like what happened during the heist.

He withdrew his iPhone and opened the Notes app.

"They have Cloaker and sent me to spy on you. They'll kill him if I don't do exactly what they tell me to. This bracelet will also inject me with poison," I typed, then handed the phone over. I glanced down at my wrist. Was ANTE wondering about the silence?

His lines of concern crossed his forehead as he placed a brown hand on my shoulder, giving me a reassuring squeeze. It didn't make me feel better. This was *my* fault.

A woman walked past. I tensed. She didn't even glance at us.

Agent Liam typed a message and handed the phone back. "We'll fix this."

There was still only silence from ANTE. They'd probably get suspicious if I didn't say something out loud soon, like when I talked to Franklin Dower during the heist. Shivers ran down my spine, even though the air was hot.

"You've been through a lot," Agent Liam said aloud. How was he not absolutely freaking out? Clearly, he was the better spy. "It's okay to feel scared."

"Thanks," was all I could manage.

Tell him about the attack.

Then two words came through my earpiece. "Kill him."

I sucked in a breath, adrenaline electrifying my body. I shouldn't have said anything. Blood rushed from my face, and my heart stabbed against my ribcage.

"Something wrong?" Liam asked. Oh no, now ANTE would know that he knew... I couldn't respond.

"Kill him, or we'll kill you. This is a chance to show your loyalty," said the evil voice in my ear.

But I'm not loyal to you.

The poison would probably kill me within seconds. Who knew how long Cloaker would have.

This situation was my fault. If I realized sooner that something wasn't right with my parents, maybe I wouldn't have to choose between my life and warning VIGIL.

Liam typed into his phone. I'd only known him a few months, and between that and watching his movies, he was more of a father figure than my real dad ever was. And I couldn't live with myself if I didn't speak up.

That seemed to fuel me, somewhat. I took a deep breath and readjusted the earpiece.

But was there a way to save everyone? Including me and Cloaker?

"Is it done?" said the voice in my ear. *So they can't see.* I gulped. I could buy us a little time.

A car rushed by.

"Yes, it's done." My voice cracked. *Agent Liam, help*, my eyes pleaded.

"Good. Now head back to the base. We'll take care of the body." *Take care of the body.* I'd have to get this bracelet off before they found him not dead.

I took a shaky breath. I'd get out of this alive just like I did with Ironfall.

"Why aren't you moving?" said the gruff voice.

I had mere seconds before they killed me. Forget Cloaker, VIGIL had to know or a lot more people would die. I turned to Agent Liam. *Win. Please win. Fix my mistake.* "My parents are ANTE. They kidnapped me. They're attacking Congress in two days. Ihavenoideawhattheyhaveplannedbut—"

"No!" Someone's voice penetrated through the earpiece.

Prick.

Something poked into my wrist. It only stung for a second. Everything started to get cloudy. My surroundings blurred and my legs wouldn't support me. I collapsed. Being carried. Bouncing around. Eyes rolling. Some guy screaming and clutching my hand—I couldn't focus.

The world faded to black.

Exhale.

TRANSCRIPT OF THE INTERVIEW PROCEEDINGS WITH IRONFALL

SOME NAMES AND LOCATIONS REDACTED FOR SECURITY
INTERVIEW CONDUCTED ON MAY 20
LOCATION OF INTERVIEW: **[REDACTED]**
CASE #: **[REDACTED]**

AGENT LIAM BLAKE: When I carried Rosemary in, you screamed for us to let you out, claimed that you could heal her.

IRONFALL: Yes, I did.

AGENT LIAM BLAKE: Why?

IRONFALL: I couldn't let her die. Not in front of me. I was desperate.

AGENT LIAM BLAKE: You still cared about her.

IRONFALL: I couldn't make it go away. And believe me, I tried. She lied to me. She betrayed me. I knew I had to push my feelings aside and focus on my own goals, but at the time the pain of her death seemed much more than the pain of my own failure.

AGENT LIAM BLAKE: And you didn't escape after. Why?

IRONFALL: I couldn't return to my father empty-handed.

CHAPTER 21

There was blackness, then a long gasp for air.

My finger twitched. A warm pressure enveloped my hands like someone...no, multiple people, held them. The unusual coolness of the metal circlet disappeared. The kill bracelet was...gone?

My eyes fluttered open. Ver, Manda, Sam, and Agent Liam were there...and Ironfall? His blue and brown eyes stared back at mine, then he suddenly seemed very interested in Ver's monitor wall. My heart quickened. Wait, what was he doing outside a *cage*?

My strength was returning. "W-what happened?" My mind worked backward. Bracelet. Kidnapped. Mom and Dad. ANTE.

"Oh my gosh, you're alive!" Sam gasped.

My chest tightened as a sudden thought crossed my head. "ANTE's coming. Their base is close."

"Liam explained," Manda said.

"They—they have Cloaker," I said. "After months of digging deeper he finally made his way onto the base. He tried to help me escape, and we almost took out the head of ANTE, but they knocked him out and put that cuff on me. And now he's dead because of me."

Agent Liam pressed his lips together. "Rosemary, it's not your fault. You did the right thing telling us about the attack. It's what he would have wanted."

"The chances he's actually dead are slim," Manda said. "They'll want to interrogate him first."

That didn't make me feel better.

Then Manda stood up and yanked on Ironfall's arm. He glared, then rose to his feet. He didn't fight as Manda grabbed his other arm and tugged him into the hallway.

Ironfall put on his smug grin but went along with her without issue. "You're welcome for saving her life." Wait. He... healed me? My pulse quickened. "It won't happen again." He looked me dead in the eyes then, as his gaze hardened.

"Yeah, somehow I think it will." Sam rolled his eyes.

Manda didn't respond as she shut the cell door and double-checked the lock. "That's enough of him having the opportunity to escape." She glared back at him. "Not that he'd have made it past me."

A surge of relief coursed through my body. I sat up and felt more awake and alert than I ever had. "Did he really save me?" Why was Ironfall helping me *now*, after I betrayed him? Why had he spared me the first time? Did he...actually care about me? So many questions.

"He wouldn't shut up until we let him," Manda said.

"But *why*?" I said, eyes flicking to his hallway cell.

"That's the first time he's said anything other than a snarky comment," Sam said.

"What I want to know is why he responded to you *and* why he didn't run," Manda said.

Sam only shrugged. "I don't think that's very much of a mystery."

Agent Liam pressed his lips into a thin line. "What do you mean by that?"

"The guy is clearly head over heels for her," Sam said. "Don't tell me you can't see it."

"Ironfall doesn't just fall in love," I said, shaking my head. After the rooftop date and the times he'd opened up, he might like me, but he wouldn't let emotions get in his way. "I don't know why he saved me." *We were so much more than that.*

"How are you feeling?" Agent Liam said. "Is anything hurt?"

My entire body felt new, like it'd been refreshed, and not because of all the physical training ANTE put me through. "No."

"Looks like Ironfall's secret superpower did the trick," Sam said.

"Did ANTE hurt you? Torture you?" Agent Liam said, concerned.

I shook my head. "They were training me to be their soldier. I'll be okay." After years of therapy, probably. But I was good enough for the moment.

Then Agent Liam spoke in a lower voice. "Good. I need you to talk to Ironfall. Find out anything you can about ANTE and what they're planning."

No. I couldn't face him again.

My breath became shaky. "I—I can't. I wouldn't even know what to say." And I was admitting this in front of my heroes.

"It isn't a coincidence you were the only one to cause a reaction. I wouldn't ask unless it was crucial," he said.

I gulped. "If you think so." *You can do this, Rosemary.* But what was I supposed to say? Talking to the man who tried to kill me then let me go was the last thing I wanted to do. Maybe Agent Liam was wrong about me. I was wrong about my parents.

That was when the alarms went off. Sam shrieked. Before anyone could say anything more, Ver leapt back to her computer.

Agent Liam stepped closer, back in all business mode. "Talk to me."

Ver slammed her fingers across the worn keyboard. "The entire system's down. There's nothing I can do."

Sam leapt to her side. "Let me help." Now they were both typing furiously.

Oh my gosh. *ANTE.* "They've started taking over. They wanted me to kill everyone, and now they must be sending in backup," I said. My parents sent backup, only reinforcing my knowledge that they didn't really love me.

Liam kept calm. "Get a distress signal to Commander Vigil." The name sparked a familiar excitement. If she came, we'd have nothing to worry about. Except maybe me fangirling too much.

Ver shook her fist at the blinking red screen. "The whole system's shut down. I can't even access the internet to send an email." Each wall monitor shifted crimson, then blackened. "Phones are shot too."

I looked at Sam, who only nodded in agreement.

Then Liam turned to me. "Do you know anything?"

I shook my head. "They have an underground bunker nearby, but I don't know exactly where. Cloaker was captured trying to get me out. They killed him because I told you... And they have sleeper agents, at least I think that's what they're called, throughout government agencies. I assume they're going to be activated during the Capitol attack. I'm sorry that's all I know. I should have seen this coming. I'm so sorry." I should have known. Should have realized my parents only fought for themselves.

Manda shifted her weight to her other hip. "Well, if any of you are ANTE, might as well start shooting." I glanced at the four people in the room—possibly the only members of VIGIL left. No, they weren't the last. The superheroes *had* to still be alive. Even if I spent most of my life thinking they were only my favorite movie characters, I couldn't imagine a world without them in it.

"Manda, lock down the base. Ver, Sam, get that system back online. Rosemary, see if you can get anything out of Ironfall. All right, let's get to work," Agent Liam said. "Rosemary, come with me." I nodded and followed him into his glass-encased office. He reached in a desk drawer and pulled out a pistol and holster.

He handed them to me. "Do you know how to fire a gun?"

I shook my head. "I haven't gotten there yet. Ironfall... prefers other weapons."

Then he drew his own handgun. "Get in a fighting stance like you would in hand-to-hand combat. Grab the grip with both hands. Keep your index finger off the trigger until you're ready to shoot. Pull the top part back and release it. Keep the top of the gun level to shoot accurately. Then squeeze the trigger. Understood?"

Uh...not really. "Sort of?"

He nodded, then put his gun away. "It'll be good enough for now. Now go talk to Ironfall. See if he knows anything about ANTE's immediate plan; anything else can wait. You have three minutes."

I strapped the holster to my waist and went to guard Ironfall's cell. I really didn't want to do this. Would Ironfall try to manipulate me into letting him escape?

"And Rosemary, you can do this," Agent Liam said.

I nodded, forcing a smile. "I hope so, sir."

I stationed myself outside the chrome bars. The room was small, clean, with a cot positioned on the back wall...the wall closest to whoever lived next door.

"Agent Liam sent you because he thought you would be able to get something out of me, didn't he?" No, I couldn't look at him.

"ANTE's plan is to attack Congress in two days. What do you know?" I gulped, backing away so he wouldn't reach through the bars and steal my pistol.

"Only as much as you've graciously let me hear through these lovely bars." His fingers curled around the metal as he stuck his head through them, glaring at me.

I studied the floor. "Really? Because I find that hard to believe."

"I could say the same about you." His voice was ice. "But if you let me out, I can help you."

My stomach turned.

Liam walked by and motioned for me to follow him. I still wouldn't look at Ironfall as Agent Liam and I returned to the main room. Monitors previously on the desk now pressed against the wall so the desk could block the front door. The back door was the same.

"Ver, status update," Agent Liam ordered.

She shook her head. "Nothing. ANTE corrupted the entire system, and Mr. I-broke-into-your-system-in-five-minutes can't fix it either."

"Hey!" Sam shot her a glare before turning back to Agent Liam. "You know it's bad when I think it's bad. And it's bad."

"Rosemary?"

"He claims he doesn't know anything, but I don't know if he's telling the truth," I said, clasping my hands behind my back.

Someone banged on the front door. Three loud raps. My heart pounded, my gaze whipping toward it. No. Not yet.

Agent Liam smacked the wall. "We need more time." They'd be able to get past the desk within minutes, most likely. That door had to be stronger than it looked, right? A top-secret base would not have a generic door from Home Depot.

More banging, along with shouts. "CIA! We have you surrounded. Exit the building unarmed with your hands above your head, and you will not be harmed."

My heart pounded.

"Yeah, that's not the CIA." Ver shook her head. "Or it's ANTE cells within the CIA."

Sam's eyes were filled with both terror and excitement. That guy was a mystery.

"Both exits are blocked, so we're going to have to fight our way out. Manda, what's our strategy?" Liam said.

Manda nodded. "I'll seal the back door shut so we don't get an assault from both sides. The front door should buy us about fifteen minutes. Thankfully it's only disguised to look weak. We'll put furniture in here to act as cover. It won't completely stop bullets, but they won't get in as many clean shots."

Agent Liam straightened. "All right, it's time to save the world...again."

I'm not exaggerating (much) when I say that my entire life led up to that moment. "Did you just quote the second *Project Safeguard* movie?" The grin on my face couldn't be suppressed as sudden excitement burst through me.

"I'm dead. Literally dead." Sam grinned.

Agent Liam gave a rare smirk. "It's like the movies are based off real life or something. Crazy. Now let's move!"

Then the team split up. I headed for Liam's office.

Moving this desk to the other room would be interesting. Thankfully, Ver joined me. Together, we carried it into the main area.

"I could help with that, you know," Ironfall said as we passed his cell. Ver and I both ignored him. "And I could help you fight ANTE, too."

Ver ran out to help Manda with a thick mattress. They slid it inside and then turned it so it nearly touched the ceiling. It swayed back and forth a little, then steadied.

"That's the last of it," Ver said.

Manda brushed off her hands. "Does anyone want to shut Ironfall up? He keeps making snide remarks."

"With pleasure," Ver said. "What are we going to do with him anyway?"

Agent Liam crossed his arms. "He's our prisoner, and could turn out to be an asset, so we protect him. When we have a way out, we bring him with us."

Manda held up a pair of thick handcuffs, though I had no idea where they came from. "I'll put him in these." She walked toward Ironfall's hallway cell.

"I don't think that's going to do much to shut him up," Sam laughed. "Might need a gag for that."

"Can we get something to shut *him* up too?" Manda called out, pointing at Sam.

Sam rolled his eyes. "Being annoying is what I'm here for."

ANTE rammed against the door even harder. The walls shook. Everyone froze, the gleam in Sam's eyes slowly draining away. By now, they'd most likely gotten something heavy duty to crack it open.

Manda reentered the room.

Agent Liam crept up to the window which was awkwardly placed close to the ceiling, then he stood on the shaking desk. For a split second, he peeked out, then jumped down.

"I'm getting too old for that," he laughed.

"Should've let me do it." A smile broke through Manda's usually emotionless face, then it disappeared. "What are we looking at?"

"Twelve strike team operatives, all fully geared," Agent Liam said. "Everyone get in position." No one hesitated.

Sam nodded at me before hiding. Ironfall hadn't trained him. Had VIGIL in the weeks I'd been held captive? Would he survive this?

Get in position.

Right. Get in a good position. I moved away from the door and crouched behind a desk pushed on its side.

That was when the door blew in.

Heat. Ringing. Silence.

Oh my gosh.

I reached for my gun.

My heart thudded against my chest as if it was going to escape without me.

Would I have to kill someone today? Blood iced as my heart punched my ribcage.

I peeked around the corner. The first operative leapt across the stone desk pressed against the doorway. I breathed deep, trying to calm myself enough to think rationally. If I didn't think rationally, I wouldn't focus on my technique, and I'd definitely forget what Liam said about firing and reloading a gun. I would spiral out of control, slip up, and let down the team.

Bang!

Someone shot at the first operative just as the second one tumbled across the entranceway. The agent wasn't fazed. Great.

Bulletproof vests, helmets, and bulky pants that may or may not have had armor underneath.

Gun out. Pointed in a safe direction. Safety off. Then I'd aim, shoot, and hide before they had a chance to return fire.

Okay, here goes.

I whipped around. The sights lined up with the guy, and I squeezed the trigger. The recoil jerked my wrist, but that didn't matter. I shoved myself back against the mattress, heaving for more air. Bang! Another gunshot. Something whooshed past my ear. If I was an inch to the right…

The room grew hotter. My knuckles turned white around the pistol.

Now was not the time to think.

I peeked around the mattress. At least five more soldiers all dressed in bulky, midnight-colored protective gear. Helmets and goggles obscured their identities.

One raised a machine gun. I jerked back behind the shield. Heartbeat. Heartbeat.

I looked back around and fired, then jumped back to safety.

Had I hit something?

Probably not. I gasped for a shallow breath.

I peeked again. Seven overpowering men in such a little space.

More bullets flew toward the VIGIL side, and we returned fire as much as we could. They were too heavily armored and had rapid-firing weapons. I reloaded a couple of times, but soon I was out of bullets.

"Liam, this isn't going to work!" Ver shouted.

My head spun.

"On it!" Liam shot, then hid again. "They're moving closer. Prepare for hand-to-hand combat." At least I was a little better at that, but first I'd have to get through the guns the other guys were holding. They obviously had more ammo than us. And, unlike me, they could hit stuff.

No, I wasn't going down like this.

Yet now there was one exit, and twelve highly trained men stood in our way. We couldn't make it.

A guy showed up next to me. Scary helmet. Stiff bulletproof vest with "CIA" printed in white. Dark clunky pants. Automatic weapon.

I launched myself at him, shifting to the side as quickly as possible to avoid any bullets. Okay, step one, get where the gun wasn't pointed at me.

My ribs ached.

I grabbed the cold metal and twisted. The agent grunted but still held fast. My muscles burned. Adrenaline electrified every cell in my body. It wasn't enough. Our hands intertwined against the metal.

If only I had a superpower.

I tugged down on the gun, hanging my entire body weight on it. The guard lurched forward at the sudden shift in weight. His grip on the weapon slipped, and I smashed it against his head.

He sank to the ground.

Everyone was fighting hand-to-hand now. Oh gosh, there were too many to count. Wait a second, there was a guy over there with his gun trained on—

I leapt as far as I could.

BANG!

No pain. He missed? But now I had *two* guys with guns trained on me. Where did the other one come from? Didn't matter. Another burst of adrenaline exploded in my stomach. *Don't panic.* Two incredibly trained agents with guns pointed at me. No big deal at all, right?

No time to think. No time to act.

They both had clear shots.

I had to *focus* and remember Ironfall's training.

Ironfall.

I leapt to my feet and sprinted towards them, zigzagging as much as I could in the three-foot space. The distance shrank to inches. The first guy made the mistake of glancing over at Manda. I knocked him out.

The second guy moved his finger over the trigger, but I ducked behind the desk. A spray of bullets rushed past.

I just needed a—

Pain seared my cheek as someone punched me. My head jerked to the side.

The guy raised a fist again, but I eyed the gun in his other hand. I attacked.

He grabbed my arm as I threw a punch. Then the guy *talked*. "You chose the wrong side." Deep, husky voice.

"Oh, really? 'Cause you're the one who chose a cheesy villain line." I thrust him against the bedframe. He grunted. My hand clamped around his right arm—the one clutching the gun—as I pushed it against the wall. He tried to resist, but I threw my entire body weight against him.

Okay, headcount. So far there was only one man unconscious and a heck of a lot more people left to handle.

"I could use a little help over here!" Ver screeched.

We were going to lose.

TRANSCRIPT OF THE INTERVIEW PROCEEDINGS
WITH IRONFALL
SOME NAMES AND LOCATIONS REDACTED FOR
SECURITY
INTERVIEW CONDUCTED ON MAY 20
LOCATION OF INTERVIEW: **[REDACTED]**
CASE #: **[REDACTED]**

AGENT LIAM BLAKE: When ANTE attacked, did you expect them to break you out?

IRONFALL: Not in the slightest. I knew I was on my own.

AGENT LIAM BLAKE: Did ANTE know you were in our custody?

IRONFALL: They infiltrated most government organizations, so I assume so.

AGENT LIAM BLAKE: Then why would they ignore you?

IRONFALL: Remember when I said it's complicated?

AGENT LIAM BLAKE: Then uncomplicate it, please.

IRONFALL: As you wish.

CHAPTER 22

"Keep...fighting..." Liam said with labored breaths.

Pain burst through my midsection. Couldn't. Breathe. As a gasp wracked my body, the guy was free and moving the gun's barrel towards me. I knocked it out of the way and threw a punch at the guy's face.

Painful vibrations traveled up my fist from his plastic goggles, but I barely felt it. The agent tumbled back against the wall once more. Burgundy blood dribbled from his nose.

Two cries of anguish and two guys dead on the ground.

"We need some backup over here," said some ANTE agent. My body electrified.

Without taking my eyes off the guy who was just stumbling to his feet, I picked up the gun, cocked it, but hesitated. Could I kill him? Blood rushed through my ears.

He grabbed the barrel, trying to wrench it away from me. No. No. No. He couldn't.

Bang!

My finger squeezed the trigger before I could even think about it. What had I done? The blue fire in his eyes snuffed out. Lifeless on the ground with a bloodied face and a whole lot of armor. Dead. Dead like the man I...I killed at ANTE. I shuddered. Dead like the people Ironfall killed.

Ironfall.

Wait a second, he would provide more power, and he was one

of the most skilled fighters...well...ever. "I have a terrible idea," I murmured.

I aimed the gun towards one of the guys fighting Manda. She was the most tactical agent. Honestly, she was probably stronger than most men. Once she was free, she could help the others.

The gun clicked. Empty. Hopefully she'd be able to handle her two opponents. I dropped it and snuck around the perimeter of the room and into the narrow hallway.

This was such a bad idea.

Ironfall stood in his cell in the fight-ready position, fists raised but wrists bound. He flashed a smile but didn't lower his hands. "So, turns out you need my help after all."

If this went south, he would kill all of us. I was wrong about my parents; was I wrong about this too? But if we didn't even try, ANTE would win. And that would be even worse.

"Yes," I hissed, glancing at the battle in the main room.

"Why let me out?" His jaw flared.

My heart skipped a beat. "Now isn't the time to discuss that. You might not make it out of here alive if you don't help, though."

"Aren't you afraid I will betray you?" Was he teasing me?

I gulped. *Yes.* "Should I be?" In his mind, I shattered his trust. Switching sides would only be to his advantage. This was a terrible idea.

Move.

I glanced back at the war scene. Agent Liam took someone out, then glanced back at me and reached into his pocket, drawing out something that glinted in the florescent lights.

"Catch!" Liam launched it toward me. A shiny golden object clanged to the ground. The key. I had Agent Liam's approval. I gulped and scrambled to pick it up. I fumbled with the lock, and the cell door swung open. Ironfall stepped out until we stood inches apart. Breath wouldn't come.

He was free.

What have I done?

I could only envision this backfiring. And it would be my fault. Again.

Dark movement in the corner of my eye caught my attention. Someone barreled towards us. Ironfall ran to meet him. The large guard skidded to a halt, but Ironfall was already there. The two wrestled to the floor. Ironfall launched the man off him then crouched over him.

Snap.

My gut wretched, chest tightening. The agent was dead.

Ironfall stood up with ease even though his hands were still restrained by Manda's handcuffs. If he could do *that* handcuffed, he must have gone easy on me. Which led me, once again, to wonder why he spared me. And why he saved my life half an hour ago.

Did he still need me for something?

Did he want me to still help him take over the world?

Would he try recruiting me to ANTE like he was originally supposed to?

Ironfall brushed off his hands, then slipped out of the wrist restraints as if they were a child's toy. How did he do that? More importantly, why didn't he take them off sooner? He could have easily...

More sounds of fighting from the main room.

We weren't out of the woods yet.

Both of us turned towards the action. I stole a glance at him. His sharp features were hard with concentration. Then once again, our eyes met, his soft and familiar with their warm brown and that distinct blue sliver. Why weren't they cold? He always had a plan to execute and could do so without feeling. Betrayal wasn't tolerated. So why was he acting like this? "Side by side?"

I froze.

Why had he spared me, a traitor, a betrayer?

Why hadn't he turned to ANTE yet?

Why did I feel like he was exactly where he wanted to be?

And yet I was backed into a corner. I had no choice. Deep

breath. "Side by side." It felt strangely intimate. Reminded me of how things used to be. Just me and the supervillain as if we were back sparring in our hideout or goofing off belting showtunes. Like him kissing me on stage. Yet my stomach turned.

He'd betray us. I couldn't let that happen.

Together we strode down the hall, adrenaline powering each bold step. My shoulder brushed against his arm. Ironfall balled his hands into fists.

Manda let out a war cry as she battled against three operatives. The remaining four pounded against Agent Liam, Ver, and Sam.

"Hey!" Ironfall's voice crashed through the groans and grunts of the fight. Silence. His muscles flared. "You looking for a challenge?"

I raised my fists.

Three of them launched toward us, but we didn't move. One guy motioned for his buddies to get on either side of him, blocking our path to the exit. We could only retreat farther into the hallway.

We stood our ground.

Beat.

Beat.

Beat.

I took a deep breath and let it out.

For a few moments, I was calm. It was just me and Ironfall against the world.

Now.

I turned, pressing my back against Ironfall's. Then I lashed out. Kick. Punch. Deflect. Block. Twist. Kick. The other soldier grabbed my side, but Ironfall elbowed his chest and threw him to the side. My head whipped back around as the guy wound up for another hit. Deflect. Deflect. Deflect. Three leg blows and a head shot. The soldier grunted and collapsed.

I turned back to Ironfall. His second target fell.

"You help Sam and Ver, I'll head to Agent Liam," I said. He nodded.

An operative smashed Agent Liam to the ground. Liam grunted and the attacker pulled back a punch. I grabbed his fist and yanked him toward me. I met his dark eyes. The eyes of a killer. He yanked me forward. I stumbled. Liam maneuvered his legs and threw the guy off him. Then the attacker stumbled backwards. Agent Liam scrambled over and smacked the side of his head before the man could fight back.

All enemies neutralized. But they had backup coming.

Ver pressed a hand to her bleeding nose. Manda leaned against the stone desk, arms crossed as if she'd spent the last few minutes sitting there instead of fighting for her life. Sam had his head in his hands, but he was still alive.

Where was Ironfall? Oh no, this was all my fault. I shouldn't have let him out, because now he'd go wreak more havoc.

But then he reappeared at the edge of the hallway and leaned against the bulletproof glass wall as if he too was part of the VIGIL team. A chill ran down my spine, even though sweat poured over my skin.

Manda produced yet another pair of handcuffs and held them up in front of Ironfall. Did she always carry an extra pair? "Are these a joke to you?"

Ironfall smirked. "Yes." I shook my head. If this scene went in a movie, it'd become an iconic meme. Surprisingly, Sam had no sarcastic comment.

She narrowed her eyes, strengthening her laser sharp glare, then grabbed both of his wrists and slapped the restraints on. She tightened them until even I could see the surrounding skin was white. Ironfall didn't even flinch.

"All right, ANTE has backup coming. Ver, grab some sunglasses, baseball caps, and your laptop. We also need more firearms and ammo. Everyone has two minutes to be in the car," Agent Liam said. "Manda, guard Ironfall."

"With pleasure." Manda shot her prisoner another glare, which again, he ignored.

I stepped toward Sam. "You okay?"

He brought his hands away from his face. Was he crying? Still, he nodded. "That was a lot less cool than the movies."

I nodded, my gaze falling to the floor. "I know."

Ver returned a few moments later with obnoxious "I <3 NYC" hats for everyone.

"Ah yes, the superhero-in-disguise staple." Sam smirked before putting his on. This warranted a chuckle from around the room.

As Ver walked by Ironfall, she jumped up and slapped one on his head. She smirked, brushing a platinum curl behind her ear. Then she reached into her bag and produced a small handgun, which she gave to Agent Liam. He holstered it inside his suit jacket (yes, he was still wearing a suit).

"Let's roll out," Agent Liam said. He peeked through the doorway, then climbed over the desk and went outside. "We're clear." I followed him, then came Sam and Ver, and finally Ironfall and Manda.

The black car parked on the curb beeped.

Ironfall leapt over the desk and sprinted.

Manda took off after him. Her legs, though short, quickened with each stride. The gap between them closed. She threw her body against him. They tumbled, clawing at each other. She landed on top.

She jerked him up and dragged him back to the car. He didn't fight against her, just kept that smug look plastered across his face.

Tires skidded on the pavement. I whipped my head around to see two black SUVs about a hundred feet away.

"Get in the car." Agent Liam got into the driver's seat. I tumbled into the back. Ver clutched her bag and got into the passenger seat.

Bang! Bang! Bang! Gunshots.

Ironfall was pushed into the back row of the SUV, Manda sitting next to him. Sam sat in the middle row.

Glass shattered. I flinched, ducking my head as debris from the back windshield hit me.

"Everybody down!" Agent Liam shouted. There was no way I was going to do anything else.

The car engine revved and lurched forward.

More shots echoed.

Agent Liam swerved the SUV left. I crashed into Ironfall, who fell into Manda.

Seatbelt. I needed my seatbelt. I reached up for the strap, keeping my head pressed against my lap. My fingers latched around it, and I pulled, maneuvering it under my abdomen. It clicked, though I wasn't sure how much good it would do right now.

"Hang on, another turn." Now we went right. Ironfall rammed into my side.

Bang!

The sound of shattering glass resounded. I glanced up. Left sideview mirror. My chest tightened.

The car lurched left.

"Manda, return fire," Agent Liam said.

"If you hold the car steady," Manda said.

I looked up again, and now Manda was hanging out the side, one arm clinging to the open window frame and the other hand clutching a gun.

She fired two rounds.

Crash!

"Got 'em," Manda said.

The car slowed.

TRANSCRIPT OF THE INTERVIEW PROCEEDINGS
WITH IRONFALL
SOME NAMES AND LOCATIONS REDACTED FOR
SECURITY
INTERVIEW CONDUCTED ON MAY 20
LOCATION OF INTERVIEW: **[REDACTED]**
CASE #: **[REDACTED]**

AGENT LIAM BLAKE: Rosemary has in her report that you disappeared for a few minutes. Would you like to explain where you were?

IRONFALL: I needed to grab my dad's device. The one we went through so much trouble to steal in the first place.

AGENT LIAM BLAKE: Why didn't you take that opportunity to escape?

IRONFALL: Like I said before, escape would be useless if I didn't have it. The real thing, not the decoy you let me steal. And I already failed at one mission ANTE gave me. If I failed my own mission...let's just say my father would be more than a little disappointed.

CHAPTER 23

MAY 15 – 2:32 P.M. EDT

We ditched the car a few miles later and flagged down a cab. Hiding in a taxi wasn't exactly my idea of "lying low." Sure, people in movies did it all the time, but 80 percent of the time the taxi driver was the bad guy. Also, five agents, a prisoner, and a civilian driver don't exactly fit well in a car designed for six people. Yes, it was a tight fit (and slightly illegal), but we paid the driver a little something extra.

What could go wrong?

The taxi driver let us off at a shady car rental place tucked under a rundown brick apartment building in Brooklyn.

Agent Liam took off his jacket and placed it over Ironfall's handcuffs so it looked like he simply carried it. Manda gripped his arm and glared.

The two of them walked in first. With her free hand, she tilted down her baseball cap. "We need a big car." She smiled and changed the way she carried herself. Suddenly, she seemed happier and bubblier like Jana Anthony, her actor alias. This was so different from the Agent Manda I knew who almost never sounded happy. How long would it be before this guy recognized her? Or any of them, for that matter. Four of the people with me were big name movie stars for crying out loud.

If only Ironfall made us disguises.

But the guy wasn't even looking. He was sucked into a game of solitaire on his ancient desktop computer. "Okay, whatever."

This guy was clearly more interested in his lame solitaire game. "Hang on, I need to beat this."

Ver leaned close to my ear. "Wow, he gets paid to play solitaire. I should work here instead of being shot at working for VIGIL. Not that I don't like working for Agent Liam, just not the almost dying part." She chuckled. A smile tugged at my lips.

A couple moments later the guy looked up. His bloodshot eyes widened as his jaw dropped. "You're..."

Agent Liam grinned. "You caught us."

Manda jabbed Ironfall in the side before he could make a remark, but the guy seemed to notice this. Once more, his eyes bulged. "Wait. Are you two dating? Teaaaaaa. I never thought about the two of you together before, but now I kinda like it."

"This is what I live for," Sam whispered my way.

The smile that appeared on Manda's face looked so pained. "No, we're definitely not dating. Just good friends. Right, Rhett?" She throttled his arm. Ironfall nodded.

"We do need a car, though," Agent Liam said. "Do you mind?"

"Right, right, sorry." He turned back to his computer and exited his solitaire hand. As he pulled something that looked like paperwork up on the computer, he stopped. "Is it crazy to ask for a picture with you guys?"

Ver stepped forward. "You know, we're actually trying to keep this reunion thing on the down low, so we'd appreciate it if you don't tell anyone about this."

"I'm dead," Sam whispered as he attempted to conceal his growing grin.

"Is this about a new movie?"

"It's top-secret," Ver said with a nod.

Then he pointed at me. I froze. "Ooh, are you two in it?"

"Us?" I said, glancing at Sam. "Uh..." Was I really just asked if I was an actor in my favorite movie series? New level: unlocked. That was certainly something I never thought would happen.

And Sam looked like he was about to explode with excitement. "This is literally the coolest thing that's ever—"

"That's another secret," Agent Liam said. "Now please, we are on a tight schedule." We had to get to Washington, D.C. as soon as possible.

After an insane amount of paperwork (and even more of the guy's understandable fanboying), the VIGIL family (and Ironfall, the prisoner) went into the garage and picked out our car: an "ultra-stylish" 1999 Ford something-or-other truck. The most average car in the garage. Liam drove, and Ver and Sam took the two other seats on the front bench, leaving Manda and I on either side of Ironfall. I stared out the window, but his piercing gaze seared into me. Now that I wasn't fighting for my life, being so close to him was only painful. Emotions flooded through me in the silence.

Finally, we started moving.

This truck smelled weird, like a mix between a new car and an entire gallon of essential oils.

"I think we have some catching up to do. Care to start talking, Ironfall?" Agent Liam glanced into the rearview mirror. There was no way he'd give away anything now after these agents interrogated him for weeks.

Ironfall laughed. "Aww, are you finally letting me join the team?"

"No, this is an interrogation," Agent Liam said. Manda shook her head as if she was 1000% done with Ironfall's shenanigans.

Ironfall cleared his throat. Would he actually start giving us information? "Then no, I'll keep my business to myself, thank you."

"Well, we're all entitled to our opinions. What is ANTE's plan?" Agent Liam said.

"They're attacking the Capitol Building in two days."

Manda sighed. "Can you be any more vague?"

"I only know that much because you told me," he said. "You

told me a lot of things actually, whether you meant to or not. Maybe you should have soundproofed that cell."

My blood ran cold. He was manipulating us, just like my parents manipulated me. I failed to see it then; I wouldn't fail to see it now.

"What's your plan?" Agent Liam tried again. Ironfall didn't even respond to this one.

"Is healing your only power?" But Ironfall didn't answer Manda's question either. He sucked all the air from the truck. I was too close, too close now. I thought I could handle it, but now, every muscle in my body screamed at me to run.

But I couldn't.

"I'm still shook that you faked your powers all this time," Sam said. "Honestly it's kind of impressive." No one said anything.

Tension could be cut with a knife.

I pressed my lips together. This was going nowhere. Maybe he would answer my question, but what if that made things worse? What if I asked the wrong thing and he stopped responding to anyone? What if he lashed out and jumped out of the truck? And could we even trust anything he did say?

I ran my palms over my face. I would only make things worse.

I glared out the window only to glimpse a VIGIL & ANTE Studios billboard as we passed by.

MAY 15 – 5:46 P.M. EDT

We pulled off the Interstate at an obscure exit that appeared to only have a run-down off brand gas station and a McDonald's. Agent Liam parked, then everyone but Ironfall got out. We all made sure the doors remained locked.

Manda leaned against the car door, and Ver stood to the side, her arms crossed. Sam brushed hair out of his eyes as he stood next to both. Honestly, I think he was just happy to be there.

Agent Liam stepped forward, closing the makeshift circle. "The first order of business is figuring out what to do with our prisoner."

"I saw him slip out of those handcuffs as if they weren't even there," I said.

He nodded. "Right. With our lack of resources, it's going to be difficult to stop him from running."

Manda stepped forward, firmly planting both feet on the ground. "My thought? He wants to be here."

"Interesting theory." Agent Liam crossed his arms.

"He doesn't seem to be trying very hard to get away. Look at him." She glanced through the tinted windows. "He's just sitting there."

"Why would he want to remain our prisoner?" Ver said. "That's just dumb." But Ironfall was never stupid. *Ever.*

"It's because he's in love with Rosemary." Sam grinned. I sighed, looking away.

Manda ignored his comment. "Or we're taking him exactly where he wants to go."

"He already said he didn't have any helpful information about ANTE," Ver said. "Unless he lied, which isn't improbable given his track record."

"My parents wanted him to recruit me," I said. "But for some reason, Ironfall didn't do it. At least, not all the way."

Ver sighed. "Then we must be missing some other connection between him and ANTE."

"He also said he wants to take over the world to prove something to his father, who we know is involved in ANTE, and I really don't think he was lying about that," I said. "So who is his dad inside ANTE?"

"He never told me any of this," Sam said. "I think he's still mad I shot him." The team ignored him.

Ver tapped her fingers together. "When *Project Safeguard*—

a.k.a. World Domination Part 1—happened, we were able to snag a DNA sample. The CIA tested it thoroughly before handing it over to Cloaker so he could make himself look like Ironfall for the movie. And, quite simply, Ironfall doesn't exist. There is nothing on him or any potential relatives. Essentially he's a ghost."

Agent Liam turned to me. "Do you remember anything else that could help?"

I shook my head. "When I was ANTE's prisoner, they never mentioned him. Unless you count my mom cussing him out for not getting me to join them." The thought of my mother stung. I couldn't make the same mistake with Ironfall.

"Let's look at this from a different angle. I wanted to arrest Ironfall as soon as he contacted you, but the CIA threatened to shut me down if I did," Agent Liam said. "Now that we know ANTE has people on the inside, maybe they made that call."

"To protect him?" Manda said.

"Or to give him time to do his job," I said. "My parents wanted me to join ANTE so I didn't ruin their standing. Apparently, I was never supposed to work for you guys. Holding off arresting him would give him more time to get to me. My parents were desperate for me to join them, so their reputation remained intact."

"Let's come back to this. I'll fill up the car and guard you-know-who. You stretch your legs. Meet back here in ten minutes," Agent Liam said. He turned to the gas pump as Ver, Manda, and Sam went inside the gas station.

I started to go inside, then turned back to the car. I couldn't get Ironfall out of my head. Why wasn't he running? I had to be missing something, and I couldn't afford to do that again.

Go talk to him. I didn't know where that sudden urge came from, but the next thing I knew, I stood right outside the car. My hand brushed against the warm door handle, then gripped it, pulling it open. Ironfall looked up from his lap, then back down, shoulders sagging. Was he...upset? Or was this a tactic to manipulate me?

"Here to interrogate me again?" he said. His voice was ice.

I shook my head. "No. I mean...yes...I mean...I don't know. Agent Liam didn't send me, if that's what you're asking." My fingers pressed into my forehead. What was I even supposed to say to him?

"Oh," he said. That was it. Cold and disinterested. "So *you* want to use me."

My breath caught. *Use him.* Like my parents used me. "You know what? Never mind. I can't do this." I reached for the door handle.

"How could I have missed *Agent* Rosemary coming?"

I gulped back tears and set my hand in my lap. No. Stay on mission. "What do you know about ANTE? Did you know about the Capitol attack before you heard it from us?"

Nothing. I glanced over. Stone-faced. Cold. Not the Ironfall I remembered, but maybe I didn't know the real Ironfall. How much of our time together did he fake?

No more than I had.

I looked away. "Is healing your only power?" Could he hear the uncertain waver in my voice?

Silence.

"Explain how you invented a power. How did you manipulate people into believing it?" Beat. Beat.

"The same way you manipulated me."

Like Mom and Dad did to me. Everyone manipulating each other for their own gain. But I *had* to do it. Yet I couldn't say that now. The lump in my throat threatened to strangle me. "How—" My voice cracked as emotion overwhelmed me. I had to get out.

I couldn't do this.

I jumped out of the car and slammed the door behind me. I pressed my back against the door as sobs wracked through my empty chest. Tears streamed down my face.

I ruined everything.

"Are you okay?"

I jumped, then sighed with relief. It was only Agent Liam. "Not really."

"You talked to him, and I'm guessing it didn't go well."

I shook my head, which only made more tears flow down my face. Then he leaned forward and wrapped me in his arms. His warm embrace only made me cry harder.

"I'm...sorry," I sniffled.

"I'm actually used to it. You'd be surprised how often this happens at comic con."

I leaned into him, wetting his pristine suit with my tears as I sobbed. But his fatherly arms never faltered, never even moved. He held me; no strings attached.

When he finally let go, the tears became fewer and fewer until I no longer felt like my heart was unable to be mended.

I brushed away the remaining tears. "You know that the fandom calls you the team dad for this very reason, right? You take a while to show it, but eventually it comes through." I smiled as if to thank him for being there.

"Huh, the team dad. Don't ever call me that again." But he still grinned, the smile shining across his dark face.

I laughed a little as the hollow feeling started to dissipate. "There's even this one fanart comic where all the VIGIL heroes are toddlers and you're the adult trying to wrangle them."

He chuckled, brushing his chin. "Well, sometimes my agents act like children. I still hate it though. I'm a *professional*."

"Don't pretend you don't care about us." I shook my head. "Because you do. You'd give your life for any one of us."

He nodded, looking down. Oh, my goodness, was Agent Liam Blake *embarrassed*?

"And don't tell Manda, but everyone calls her the team mom," I said.

"Don't let her hear you say that." His eyes sparkled. "But she *is* very protective and loyal. So maybe it's an accurate description."

"Careful, you don't want her to hear you say that." Now I smiled.

"Hey guys!" I looked over as Ver ran out of the gas station, hands full of chip bags and soda and Sam in tow. Oh no...running with soda. "We brought snacks." A bag slipped off the pile, bringing the mountain down.

I turned to Agent Liam. "And she's the big sister of the family. Sam is the annoying little brother."

He shook his head, placing a hand on the driver's door handle. "This *team* needs to move out."

MAY 15 – 7:35 P.M. EDT

We drove and drove, only stopping for short bathroom and food breaks, until we ended up at a secluded motel twenty miles away from Washington, D.C. that looked like it came straight out of *Stranger Things*. The outside had traces of a once bright yellow paint job. Now it was mostly brown with dirt and grime. The motel seemed even creepier since it was late at night. We were in the middle of nowhere and picked the only vacant motel around. (Yeah, this was a last-resort kind of place.)

We checked in, then crashed in the room, which wasn't any better than the outside. The walls were made of that ugly '80s fake wood paneling, and stained sheets probably disguised bed bugs in the mattress. The floor would be more comfortable if I was willing to brave that puke-green carpet. Every time I inhaled, the air stank of mildew.

Manda got in the shower, leaving Ver and I alone.

I lay back on one of the beds. A spring dug into my back, but I was too exhausted to move. Still, questions flooded my mind.

How long until Ironfall betrayed us? Why did he save me? How deep did that loyalty lie?

Did he actually care about me?

Too many questions.

I took a deep breath.

A door slammed shut. I bolted upright, but no one stood there. Manda came out of the bathroom in a robe, wet hair cascading down her back. She hadn't slammed that door. Who had?

"If you make one wrong move, if you hurt anyone on my team, I will take you down." That was Liam's voice from the next room over. Whew. No one came in our room. "I'm a very light sleeper." He and Sam were going to *sleep* with Ironfall in the same room?

"So am I," Manda said. Someone laughed. I wasn't sure if it was someone on the team or a random stranger in another room. These walls were apparently made of paper.

I lay back down knowing sleep wouldn't come.

Ver turned on the small black box TV that was probably from the '90s.

"...prison break from Attica Correctional Facility three days ago. The escaped prisoner has been identified as Jasper Emmerling, convicted of domestic terrorism and multiple counts of first-degree murder. He was serving a life sentence. Emmerling is considered armed and very dangerous."

Ver sat up. "Manda. Look."

Manda got up. "I'll tell Liam to turn on his TV." Then she ran out of the room.

I turned toward the TV and stared. The mugshot on the tiny screen was none other than the man my dad told me was the leader of ANTE. His dark brown eyes looked even more evil in the picture. My heart pounded. "I know him."

"Wait, you know this man?" Ver said. "How do you know him?"

The door burst open before I could answer. In came Manda, Agent Liam, Sam, and Ironfall.

I looked back at the TV. The scene changed to a press conference. "We will update you when we have more information. If you are in the Attica area, we advise you to be alert..."

"So Jasper Emmerling must still be running ANTE," Agent Liam said.

His face flashed back up on the screen. I shivered and looked away. "He was at ANTE's base this morning." I stole a glance at Ironfall, then averted my gaze.

Wait a second.

Jasper Emmerling's picture still showed on the TV. I tilted my head to the side and studied Ironfall's face, then the image, then Ironfall. The same hair. The same jawline. And very similar eyes.

"He's your father," I said.

TRANSCRIPT OF THE INTERVIEW PROCEEDINGS
WITH IRONFALL
SOME NAMES AND LOCATIONS REDACTED FOR
SECURITY
INTERVIEW CONDUCTED ON MAY 20
LOCATION OF INTERVIEW: **[REDACTED]**
CASE #: **[REDACTED]**

AGENT LIAM BLAKE: You were right where you wanted to be, weren't you?

IRONFALL: It wasn't the most ideal situation, but yes.

AGENT LIAM BLAKE: Then why did you try to escape before we left New York?

IRONFALL: Well, it would've been easier to finish my plan without you guys.

AGENT LIAM BLAKE: Let's talk about your conversation with Rosemary at the gas station. What did you two discuss?

IRONFALL: She tried to get me to talk about ANTE.

AGENT LIAM BLAKE: What did you tell her?

IRONFALL: Nothing.

AGENT LIAM BLAKE: She came out very upset.

IRONFALL: That's what she wanted me to believe.

AGENT LIAM BLAKE: Why would you say that?

IRONFALL: Her goal in everything was to save the world. Knowing I could get away was a threat to that. It was all a game to pretend that she truly cared about me while she was undercover so I would have a reason to stay.

AGENT LIAM BLAKE: Was she the reason?

IRONFALL: I don't think so.

CHAPTER 24

Everyone fell silent. Ironfall didn't twitch, didn't move. What was going on inside his head?

Agent Liam turned to face Ironfall. "Is that true?"

"Yes." He didn't seem upset that we found out. In fact, his entire body was completely relaxed. Was this something he wanted us to know? Or did he not want to show his frustration?

"Manda, stand guard. Ver, Rosemary, Sam, come with me," Agent Liam said.

We followed him out into the fresh night air. Gosh, it felt so good to get away from the mildew stench. Flickering yellow streetlights cast eerie shadows. I shivered, even though the thick humidity encased my body in a layer of moisture. My eyelids drooped in the heat, but I blinked the exhaustion away.

"Okay, so his father is the leader of the terrorist group," Ver said. "That's...not what I expected, though I'm not sure why I didn't see it coming."

"I've seen your movies more times than you want to know, and that man isn't in any of them," Sam said.

"We sometimes change people's identities," Ver said. "Since Jasper was already in prison, the public would know his name and face."

"Got it." Sam grinned. "Please use my face in at least one movie. I'm begging you."

Agent Liam cleared his throat and rubbed his cleanshaven

face. "Moving on. We can assume two things: Ironfall wants to be here and pleasing his father is his goal."

"And now we know his father is the leader of ANTE," I said. "Great."

"How do we know he's not just using us as a ticket back to ANTE? I mean, that *is* where we're going," Ver said.

No, something about that didn't feel right. "He helped us fight against them at the base. If he was truly working for them, they would have rescued him." Fingernails dug into my sweaty palm as I wracked my brain to figure out what Ironfall was planning.

"I agree. It's safe to assume he's working independently," Agent Liam said.

"So why would Ironfall want to take over the world for himself? That seems counterproductive seeing as his *father's* goal is world domination." Ver tilted her head back, tapping fingers against her leg. "I mean, if I wanted to please my dad—which, love my dad by the way—I wouldn't go take the world from him."

A lone car pulled into the parking lot.

I thought back to my parents, how they always told me I couldn't do things, yet here I was and—

It clicked.

I gasped. "To prove he can do it. Ironfall said his father doesn't believe in him, so if he takes power right out of his father's grasp…well…he *has* to respect him."

Sam shook his head. "Guys, he could just up and leave and do that now. He's not an idiot."

Good point. Hmm…how else did all of this fit together? Or were we completely wrong? Maybe I'd misinterpreted every interaction I had with Ironfall.

I leaned against a column. "Unless he knows we'll help him. If we take over, we beat ANTE at their own game. It's about public support. He thinks that from his popularity in the movies, he can gain some loyal supporters willing to turn radical. Maybe enough to tip the scale."

"And he has less resistance because he doesn't have to worry about beating us." Ver nodded. "So he needs us. Wow, never thought I'd say that out loud, though I guess we kind of need him too. There are like four of us and who knows how many ANTE agents and supporters. If Ironfall has a way to get us an advantage..."

"You're saying we make him part of the team. It's a risky move." Agent Liam crossed his arms. "But we're limited on options." Well, this certainly wasn't how I thought today would go. This was a terrible idea.

"Conning the con-artist. I like it." Sam grinned. "Right out of a spy movie."

"How do we know he won't betray us?" I said.

"Oh, he will. That's why we'll be ready when he does," Agent Liam said.

"And if we're wrong about his motives?" I said. "Shouldn't we find a safer option?" My gut screamed at me. This couldn't be the solution.

He sighed. "We have no backup, few weapons, and five people. This is the only shot we've got."

"And we're not throwing it away." Ver grinned. Silence. "Come on guys, it's a *Hamilton* reference. No? Okay." I wasn't in the mood to laugh.

"Yeah, not a musical theatre fan." Sam shrugged. It was only VIGIL & ANTE Studios with him.

"If you guys think so," I whispered. They were way more experienced agents, so they must know what they're doing, right? They cared about the world. They cared about *me*. Who was I to question them? Besides, I was too tired to think clearly.

But this felt wrong.

Ironfall would betray us.

And could we get the world back from him when we were done?

How would we keep this a secret from the public?

Too many questions, but I kept them to myself. The other agents probably already had the answers worked out. I took a deep breath, trying to calm my racing heart.

"I'll bring Manda in on the plan. Can the three of you keep an eye on Ironfall?" Agent Liam said.

MAY 15 – 8:01 P.M. EST

A clunky air conditioner and the Food Network broke the room's silence. I kept my exhausted eyes fixated on the TV. I wanted nothing more than to crawl under the covers and fall into the clutches of a dreamless sleep, but no. I couldn't.

Manda and Agent Liam returned a few minutes later.

"All right, everyone, team meeting." Agent Liam stepped forward. Ver and I scooted to the edge of our bed. Sam looked over. "Ironfall, that includes you. You've been upgraded; welcome to the team."

"Me?" His eyes widened and he pointed toward himself. But the surprise on his face was only a flicker. Did we actually get a step ahead of him, or did he want us to think we'd figured him out?

Manda unshackled him. *They know what they're doing. Trust them.* My gut twisted.

Ironfall stepped into the circle, right next to me. My body tensed. "I must say, this is a twist," he said.

"Don't let it go to your head." Manda crossed her muscular arms.

"I think we can work together to achieve the same goal," Agent Liam said. The air conditioner rattled to life.

A knowing smile played at Ironfall's lips. "And what exactly would that goal be?"

"We both want to get ahead of ANTE, and Rosemary said

you have a way to do that." Agent Liam stood tall, making himself more intimidating. "We're going to take over the world, just like you originally planned."

Ironfall turned to me, narrowing his eyes. "I see you took my advice. You learned to anticipate." It was one of the first things he taught me. Know your opponent so you can predict them. Use them. *Exploit them.*

I said nothing, only focused harder on Agent Liam.

"But are you sure you anticipated correctly, *Agent?*" The words rolled right off Ironfall's tongue. My gut twisted. Someone was still mad at me.

"Yeah, probably. She's usually right," Sam said.

Then why save my life?

Manda's eyebrows raised. "Is there a reason we should question it?"

"No," Ironfall said. "Your assessment was correct."

"Then don't bring up more reasons we shouldn't trust you." Manda raised an eyebrow.

"Fair point. But why should I trust that we truly share the same goal? Aren't you supposed to be the *heroes*? Taking over the world seems a little unorthodox."

"You could settle for being our prisoner," Agent Liam said. Now I stole a glance at Ironfall.

His eyes bored daggers into my soul. "But you can't call me part of the team while you hold me hostage, now, can you?"

Manda grabbed his arm, sizing him up. "I'll handcuff him." She stood a few inches shorter than him, but her warrior presence made her seem like a giant.

Ironfall just looked over and smirked. "You've seen how much I struggle getting out of those."

"Then we'll triple handcuff," she hissed. "Maybe add duct tape."

"Your concerns are noted, but I make the final call. We're doing this, and Ironfall is on the team. End of discussion," Liam said. "Now, seven a.m. is coming early, so I suggest everyone get some rest. Ironfall, Sam, with me."

Ironfall raised his eyebrow, tilting his head sideways as if amused. He didn't look at me again as he left the room.

MAY 16 – 7:06 A.M. EDT

The next morning we met outside near the dirtiest swimming pool I'd ever seen. Green algae mixed with leaves, bugs, and I didn't even want to know what else. Three plastic tables that probably used to be white sat on the dirt-covered deck.

Agent Liam and Manda were already seated next to each other. Though the air was hot, Liam still wore his signature suit and red tie, though they needed ironing. The white shirt beneath had creases from where he'd clearly slept in it. Sam's hair stuck up in all sorts of places, and he looked ready to fall asleep in his seat. Ironfall stood a few feet away at the edge of the pool, still wearing his Ironfall suit, complete with every hair in its place. He and Manda were the only ones who didn't look like they'd just rolled out of bed.

I quickly took the empty seat between Agent Liam and Ver so I wouldn't have to sit next to Ironfall. I was too tired to think about him right now. He came and sat down between Sam and Manda right across from me. I gulped.

"Tomorrow, the attack on Congress begins at ten a.m. That means we have just over twenty-four hours to prepare. Ironfall, I can't believe I'm saying this, but take it away." Agent Liam leaned back into the chair as he folded his hands together.

Sam's eyelids drooped, but Ver elbowed him. He flinched, sitting up straight with his eyes wide.

Ironfall's brown eyes flashed. He pulled a small black box out of his pocket. *The device we stole from the vault.* Did he have to look so smug cradling it?

"It's a fake," I said. "They switched the real items in the vault for decoys."

"I know." Ironfall grinned. "I recently came across the real one."

Agent Liam leaned forward, narrowing his eyes. "Where did you find it?"

"Your office. Now, this hijacks every video and audio feed and plays whatever message we tell it to. So, ladies and gentlemen, we're going to make a movie." Ironfall ran his fingers along the smooth cube. Yeah, he let his new power position go to his head.

Sam instantly perked up. "A movie? Like a VIGIL & ANTE Studios movie?"

Manda crossed her arms. "That's the dumbest plan I've heard in a while."

"Isn't that what we do for a living?" Ver chuckled. "Besides saving the world from homicidal maniacs, that is." Like the man sitting with us? She rubbed her puffy eyes then tried smoothing down her frizzy blonde curls.

Ironfall didn't seem fazed. "The video is an illusion that will accomplish two key things. It will act as a red herring for ANTE and cause people to panic, making them much easier to manipulate."

Ver turned around her laptop, displaying a map of the area. "There's a local news station thirty miles from here."

"Wait, we're actually doing this?" Sam's eyes glittered.

"We could use their equipment for the shoot," Agent Liam said.

"The video will feature each of you so ANTE believes you are fighting against me in another location," Ironfall said. "While we broadcast the video, we disguise ourselves and sneak into Congress, and, well, I think you can guess what happens from there."

"Okay." Agent Liam nodded. "We'll go with your plan. Ver, where is the best place to get disguises?"

She stopped clacking the keyboard. "Already on it. There's a small shopping center by the station."

Agent Liam scooted his chair back, standing to his feet. "Meet at the car in ten minutes."

"Can we stop at a drive-thru?" Ver said. "I'm starving, and I ate all my snacks."

Agent Liam chuckled. "Have I ever not fed you on a mission? Actually, don't answer that. Yes, we'll eat somewhere."

"Okay, good, because I'm hungry too," Sam said. "And I want one of you to autograph my kid's meal toy."

MAY 16 – 8:49 A.M. EDT

We pulled up to a very small local TV station. My new pin-striped blazer itched, and the pants pinched my waist. I smoothed down my red waves, but I was ready. Well, maybe not mentally, but I looked the part.

"You know what you have to do," Agent Liam said. "We'll be right there as backup."

I ran my fingers along the leather CIA badge wallet. I could do this...right?

Right.

I was an agent. I would have backup. All I had to do was convince the news station I was a legitimate CIA agent. And who wouldn't want to do that? Come on, everyone dreamed of being a super-spy at some point. A thrill surged through me. This was just like a movie. I could almost hear the *Mission: Impossible* soundtrack playing in the background.

As I made my way toward the building, Agent Liam and Ironfall trailed behind me wearing matching suits and large sunglasses to mask their identities. They even had those clear earpiece coil things to make them look more official.

Then we went inside. Ouch. These shoes were rubbing my heels raw.

"Hello. How can I help you?"

I turned my head to a middle-aged woman behind the desk. She wore a bright pink dress accented by matching lipstick.

I stepped forward and thrust back my shoulders. That made me look more official, right? I'd seen this done a million times in movies, and now it was my turn. "Hi. I'm Deborah Hart with the CIA. This building is key in a case crucial to national security. I'm going to need you to evacuate the building immediately so my team can investigate." I held up Agent Liam's CIA badge, covering his name and photo with my hand.

"I'm sorry?"

I glanced back at Agent Liam. He didn't budge.

"Ma'am, this is a national security matter. I'm going to have to ask you to evacuate the building immediately." *Don't smile. Don't smile.*

Her eyebrows knit together. "Has someone done something wrong?"

I looked her dead in the eyes and said the classic line. "That's classified."

"Okay. Okay. I'll do it." The woman stumbled out of her chair and scurried into the hallway. Wait, did I go too hard? Maybe I was too intimidating...

But oh my word, I felt so cool. I turned back to my "backup." "Not gonna lie, I've always wanted to do that." I almost squealed. *Almost.*

Moments later, people started filing out. I straightened. *Keep in agent mode.*

Reporters gave us quizzical looks as they fidgeted with pens and pencils. Oh no, they were dying to figure out what was going on. *Great.*

"Make sure everyone's gone." Agent Liam motioned for us to follow him. The three of us combed through every room, searching for gutsy journalists sniffing for a national security secret. (If they discovered this one it would probably be the most shocking find of their lives.) We found no one, so we called Sam, Manda, and Ver in from the car and headed into the newsroom.

The studio was huge with bright lights and a lot of screens. There were a few fancy desks with the network logo printed on the front. Special stage lights hung from the ceiling, and a big black TV camera faced the desk. The back wall was mostly black except for a large green screen painted in the center. I assumed they did the weather there.

Ver and Manda set down the bags of clothes and makeup we bought.

"Let's make a movie," Agent Liam said.

"This is the coolest thing that's ever happened to me." Sam looked around, eyes wide.

"Here's the general plot. Ironfall stands on the rooftop of a New York skyscraper giving a convincing 'you're now under my control' speech. Manda, Ver, and I come in, but he defeats us. Then Rosemary enters. This will be the climax. Ironfall ends up defeating her too. End scene."

"Sounds perfect." Ironfall grinned.

Oh. My. Gosh. I was about to become canon in the VIGIL & ANTE Studios cinematic universe.

Me. A character. With my own poster. My own everything.

I could cry.

"Okay. Ver, you're on editing and effects. Manda, work with her to nail down lighting and sound like we did on set for *Illuman*. I will make sure the camera is all set up. Ironfall and Rosemary, head to the greenroom and get ready. Sam, you just... you just hang tight with your computer and see if you can find any new information on ANTE."

Sam nodded. "That's cool, but could I maybe have a small part? Just an extra or something?" Sam said. "It's literally my dream, and as your biggest fan—"

"Tech is more important right now." Ironfall's eyes flashed his way. Clearly he was still mad at Sam.

Agent Liam ignored this. "Do you think we can start in an hour?"

My chest tightened. I'd have to be alone with Ironfall.

Ver turned to Ironfall and I. "Yeah. We'll need you guys back here in about thirty minutes so we can do lighting and sound tests."

Sam left to find a computer.

I nodded, and Ironfall and I grabbed the grocery bags.

MAY 16 – 9:35 A.M. EDT

The greenroom was a small space with a couple of couches and mirrors, a mini fridge, and a TV. The warm scent of coffee permeated the air.

Ironfall ran straight to the small fridge and took out an iced coffee. He twisted open the lid and took a long sip. Strange, I'd never seen him drink coffee.

I turned away and started opening the makeup we bought. The thick silence choked me. The only thing to break the quiet was the crinkling packaging.

Then I turned to the mirror and slathered on some concealer. Goodness, I looked like a raccoon with my dark circles and sunken eyes. A bit of foundation, blush, and bronzer should do the trick, or at least help.

Ironfall's gaze burned through the back of my neck. My hands shook as I twisted open the mascara wand. Nope, not a good idea to use now unless I wanted to enhance the glam raccoon look.

"I thought we were supposed to be on the same side," Ironfall said. I froze. What? Why say something now? Because we were alone.

I stared at him through the mirror, ready if he tried to attack. "We are. For now." He didn't move. He just stood there.

"I mean before." His voice lowered as if trying to sound more mature. "I thought we both wanted the same thing."

"No, we didn't." I shook my head. What was this about?

"You yourself said you wanted your parents' approval, and they're on my father's side, which made us on the same side."

Oh. Pain burst from that too-fresh wound, but I forced it down. "But I wasn't on their side," I gulped.

"I thought you loved them," he said. "Wanted them to be proud of you." I did. More than anything, but nothing would make that happen.

I sighed. "They don't love me." And they never did, not really, anyway.

"How do you know that?" He almost sounded like he was trying to prove me wrong. Was that what this was about? The glory of beating his betrayer?

"With people like them, nothing you do will ever be enough. That can't be what love is. Not real love, anyway," I sighed, looking away. "True love is always selfless." Something he would never understand. Something my parents wouldn't realize.

He raised an eyebrow, an amused and annoyed look plastered across his chiseled face. "Where'd you get that? A Disney movie?" Now he was toying with me.

I shook my head, closing my eyes. "I realized it when they locked me up in a secret base and threatened to kill me if I didn't take out my team." For my parents, having me in ANTE was purely prestige, and they were willing to do whatever it took. My own parents. A sob rose in my chest, but I dug my fingernails into my hand to stifle it.

"Everyone has a selfish agenda," he said. "And to think you once fooled me into thinking you were different."

"Of course I had an agenda," I said. "Protecting my parents was the only reason I agreed to be your partner. If I said no, you'd carve them with your blades, so I had no choice."

"If you loved them so much, why risk their safety by secretly working against me?" Clearly he didn't buy my motives.

"Everyone was at stake, not just my parents. I couldn't follow blindly knowing that the cost of my safety was the world." I hesitated.

What was going on inside his head?

Why did he need to know?

And why was I telling him?

"I see." He nodded, but a defensive smile played at his lips.

Finally I set down the mascara tube, then turned to look up at his towering form. "So do you think your father will welcome you with open arms?"

Now his mischievous grin grew, but never reached his haunting gaze. "Oh, he'll love my plan. When it works, and it will, everything will be too flawless to ignore."

"Or will he only tell you 'what took you so long?'" The realization struck me that his father never loved him either. I knew that pain, felt that pain right now. Broken families, broken trust…where did the broken things end?

He stepped back, splaying his hands out as if shrugging off my words. "That was convincing, but I know better. You just want me to give up."

No.

In that moment that wasn't my top priority. Because he needed to realize the same truth I had. But he still saw me as a liar. A traitor. He wasn't wrong. But if he labeled me a hindrance to his plan, why keep me alive?

The oxygen seemed to disappear from the room. I wished I could hear his thoughts. My next question slipped out before I could stop it. "If all I do is lie, why did you save me?"

The smugness disappeared. He didn't move, didn't breathe.

We were so much more than that.

"Rosemary? They need you for lighting tests." Ver.

I gasped and reached for the mascara tube.

"And I'm supposed to do Ironfall's makeup," she continued.

"Right," I said, then scrambled out, still reeling.

I heaved open the studio door and stepped onto the film set. What had just happened? My parents. His dad. Everything.

Ironfall hurt as much as I did.

"Does this sound better?" Manda stood in front of the large lime-green wall. Over her towered a long boom pole and mic set up on a tripod.

Agent Liam took off a large headset. "I think we're good."

"You needed me?" I said, blinking away remnants of the conversation. *Time to focus, Rosemary*.

They both turned.

"Yes. While Ver keeps Ironfall busy, we're going to film an end credits scene. Ironfall doesn't need to know about this special addition. You and Manda will play your actor personas and invite everyone to see your new movie, *I Am Stardust*, in theaters a month after *Project Safeguard 3* releases."

Wait a second. It was like I stepped into some fictional world. This couldn't be real. "You mean I'm going to be the *star* of this movie? I get my own VIGIL & ANTE Studios *movie?*" My grin grew until my entire body tingled with excitement.

"Yes," Agent Liam said. *Me*. A normal girl with no special powers. A fangirl thrust into her fandom which is actually real.

"Forget dreaming of being an extra, I'm a main character." Was it childish if I squealed right now? I thought I might explode.

I was going to be in a movie in my favorite franchise, acting with my favorite characters who were now my family. For now, I felt as if nothing could go wrong.

Though Ironfall was sure to prove that feeling wrong. Unless...unless he was still searching.

Focus.

TRANSCRIPT OF THE INTERVIEW PROCEEDINGS
WITH IRONFALL
SOME NAMES AND LOCATIONS REDACTED FOR SECURITY
INTERVIEW CONDUCTED ON MAY 20
LOCATION OF INTERVIEW: **[REDACTED]**
CASE #: **[REDACTED]**

AGENT LIAM BLAKE: So, we asked you to be on our team. Did that take you by surprise?

IRONFALL: Yes, it did.

AGENT LIAM BLAKE: Yet you still wanted to be there. Why?

IRONFALL: I figured you would see my plan as the best option, I just never thought you would trust me that much.

AGENT LIAM BLAKE: For the record, we never trusted you.

IRONFALL: For good reason.

CHAPTER 25

MAY 16 – 10:23 A.M. EDT

"Remember, you're on the roof of a tall building in New York, so if you go back too far you will fall off the ledge," Agent Liam said.

Ver held up a toy clapboard we bought at Walmart. "Scene 1, Take 1, marker." She ran off the set, leaving Ironfall in the center of the shot.

"Action!" Liam said.

"My name is Ironfall, but you probably already knew that. I assume I'm already trending on Twitter. By now you have realized that I've hacked every cell phone, laptop, TV, and radio signal. And how would I be able to do such a thing unless I took over the one thing you hold most precious: your government? Yes, that's correct, I overthrew the United States government."

"Enter Manda." Liam waved a hand at her.

She ran onto the set aiming a handgun, eyes narrow. "You can't rule if you're dead." Was she acting? No, probably not.

Ironfall turned toward her, that award-winning devilish grin across his face. "Then I won't die."

"Move in," Agent Liam said, leaning over to watch the scene play out on a monitor.

Then they fought. Ironfall threw her around, but Manda gave it her all. She was definitely trying to hurt him.

Right on time, Ironfall had her pinned, just as they planned.

"I need backup on the roof!" Manda shouted into her invisible ear comm.

Thirty seconds later, Agent Liam and Ver entered the stage, guns drawn. Almost my cue.

Acting with my favorite actors. Gosh, I could barely act on a stage. But I wasn't that girl anymore. So much had happened since then.

"On your knees with your hands behind your head," Agent Liam ordered. Of course, Ironfall didn't, and soon all of them were in one confusing, action-packed battle.

But Ironfall pulled ahead. Soon, the three VIGIL agents were "unconscious."

I leapt onto the set, then stood firm with my gun trained on Ironfall's heart. "Stop right where you are." Yeah, that sounded legitimate.

"You think you're going to stop all of this with a single gun?" Then he gave a deep, throaty laugh. "You can do so much more than that."

"You're the one who taught me how to fight." I stepped toward him, trying to keep my hands steady. "So yeah, I think I'll take advantage of the gun while I have the chance." My muscles tensed. Stay in character, just stay in character.

He raised his hands slowly in the air, in the typical surrender position like he was supposed to.

I took a deep breath and once again focused on my aim. My eyebrows scrunched together in concentration. But I didn't pull the trigger. I didn't make a move; I just stood there, waiting.

My mind jumped back to earlier. Why couldn't he see that his mission was wrong? My chest tightened.

Focus.

"You can't do it, can you?" His voice was almost a whisper. I responded by placing a finger on the trigger and let it linger.

Two beats.

"I'm taking you in, Ironfall," I said. "We can do this the easy or the hard way." I *hate* it.

I couldn't believe I just said that. Giggles bubbled up until I couldn't control myself. "I'm so sorry." The laughter wouldn't stop, even when I buried my now red face. "That was the dumbest thing I could have said."

"Cut!" Agent Liam shot up off the ground, laughing himself. "It happens to the best of us. You should have seen Manda on set of her first movie."

Manda shot daggers with her eyes. "We don't speak of that." Then she got up too.

Ver leapt to her feet, laughing at me too. "Well, this is definitely going to have a, umm, memorable blooper reel." Ver looked directly at Ironfall. Yes, that was an understatement.

I glanced over at Ironfall, still trying to stifle my embarrassed laughter. He smiled back. And for just a moment, things seemed like they used to be when we sang showtunes and ran around New York City.

Please don't betray us.

I knew he would.

He moved closer to me. "This is definitely different from stage acting."

"Yeah, but at least if you say something stupid you can do it over." I shrugged. Was my face still red? "Also, we get a green screen."

"So?"

"So it's cool? It's pretty much an official movie set." I pointed around at the studio. Being in here still felt fake. All of this felt fake, if I was being honest.

"Very true." He nodded. I couldn't read him. "Guess you're an official movie star now."

"So are you." I looked away. "And this time it isn't just your face."

"I see what you're trying to do." His voice iced over. "It's not going to work. You won't distract me again."

My chest caved. I didn't know what to say.

"All right, let's review the footage and reset," Agent Liam said.

Ironfall flashed another frosted look my way, then walked back onto the set.

MAY 16 – 9:47 P.M. EDT

Back in a new motel room (this place didn't smell like mold!), the six of us hovered over Ver's computer studying the schematics of the Capitol and its surroundings. A wire-framed model of the grandiose building hovered center screen. Lawns and roads fanned out, creating circular fortresses of open space. On either side, buildings formed grid-like patterns.

Manda pointed to a street a block away from the building. "If we park here, we get easy access to this entrance while remaining inconspicuous."

I should be used to planning stuff like this by now, but the thought of sneaking into the United States Capitol was much more daunting than your friendly neighborhood top-secret CIA vault. Okay, I do realize that both are terrifying, but the Capitol... well...the stakes were so much higher. Hundreds of variables could tip the scale. Would Ironfall betray us or take our side? How many guards would there be? Would we actually take ANTE by surprise? Could we take them out and reinstate the government?

Just thinking about it made my gut twist.

"That spot will get the least attention, and I could easily run back end from there." Ver zoomed in, then dropped a pin on the street.

"What about civilians?" I said. "Will they be safe with us there?"

"I'm not sure we have a choice," Agent Liam said. "Right now keeping the government afloat is our top priority."

I gulped. But how many innocent people were in danger? Even more if ANTE won. So we had to beat them. We *had* to. I glanced at Ironfall, the one hole in our plan.

He was planning something. He had to be with that mischievous grin plastered on like a mask.

Agent Liam reclined against the bed's pillows (these weren't stained!), running his finger back and forth along his smooth chin. "Rosemary can go undercover to scout while the video plays. Once she confirms the location of the attack, we move in."

Oh no. Me? "Are you sure I'm your best option?" I said. *Please don't make me go in first.* What if ANTE caught me, and I ruined everything?

"They won't be as quick to recognize your face, especially if you're in disguise," Agent Liam said.

Ironfall nodded. "I agree." If only he knew I hacked my way through our heist instead of being capable. But I couldn't admit that to him now.

"Okay. Ver, we need IDs," Agent Liam said.

"I got you." Sam raised his hand. "I made all the IDs when we broke into your vault. Sorry about that, by the way."

"All right, Sam, you're on the clock. What's your progress on the movie, Ver?" Agent Liam said.

"Our special program is almost done rendering the New York skyline. Then I only have to color grade and send it to the 'Cube of Wonders.'"

Ironfall raised a finger. "Make sure it isn't too heavily color graded—"

"So it looks real. Got it," Ver finished. He stared back at her, eyes wide. "What? You think I'm an amateur?"

"Why can't all movies be made this quickly?" I shook my head. "It'd make my life so much easier." I felt Ironfall's eyes on me again. What was going through his head?

Ver laughed, shifting her position on the bed. "Because they don't have our signature technology. I'm half tempted to give it to Disney because I'm dying to see the new Star Wars movie."

Sam's head popped up. "Star Wars? I'm dying to see *Project Safeguard 3!*"

"Moving on, tomorrow we leave at seven a.m. That gives us wiggle room to account for traffic and a drive-thru. The movie will premiere at ten a.m. Ver, see if you can contact the Safeguarders," Agent Liam said. "Everyone make sure to get some sleep."

MAY 17 – 9:59. A.M. EDT

I walked up to the Capitol's entrance. Last time I was here, I was a fifth grader on a safety patrol trip. Now, as I went to the historic structure, I wore a navy-blue business suit, heavy makeup, and flats.

"Approaching the entrance now," I said. My heart hammered louder with each step toward those two doors.

"All right. When you're through security, I'll start broadcasting," Ver said through the comm. "Good luck. Not that you need it, but still, it's nice."

Two armed guards flanked the entrance. Black padding made them seem even larger than life. Dark masks and reflective sunglasses hid their identities. They stood tall and intimidating —both over six feet high. The "POLICE" made my stomach clamp up. *They'll find you out in a second.* But if I hesitated, they would know I wasn't supposed to be here. And I didn't even have a gun to defend myself. If I did, ANTE would know we were here, and all would be lost.

I flashed my badge. *Please don't look too closely.*

Could they hear my erratic heart?

"Proceed through security." They moved aside.

It worked. Oh my goodness, I actually made it through. A new burst of adrenaline gave me the courage I needed to step through the doors.

Inside was a metal detector with a small table next to it. The security guard seemed nice enough. His smile could welcome just about anyone, and I didn't even see a gun on him. Was he ANTE? Would ANTE kill him?

"Please empty your pockets and place personal items on the table," he said.

"I don't have anything on me," I said. Would he find that weird?

He nodded, then maneuvered around the table to the other side of the metal detector. "All right, please step through." Moment of truth, even though nothing would set off the alarm.

I hoped. My breath caught as I stepped through the silver arch.

"You're all clear." He nodded.

I let out a breath and forced a smile. "Thanks." Did he notice the waver in my voice? I walked away before he could say anything more. My shoes clacked against the slick stone floors. Security probably cleared out all visitors and unnecessary personnel hours ago. Dark carved wood accented the walls, and a lemon-cleaner scent hung in the air. I glanced back. The guy still wasn't suspicious.

"I'm in," I hissed.

"All right. Broadcasting video in three, two, one."

I needed to move fast so the rest could make it in without being noticed. I sped up as much as I could without being suspicious.

"Attention all personnel. Due to Ironfall's broadcast, this building is now under lockdown," someone's voice boomed over the intercom. Oh no.

"It's working," I hissed. "So far, only two SWAT team looking guys guarding the entrance. They let me in, but now the building is locked down. You need to hurry."

Silence.

"Guys?" Still no response. Oh no. ANTE knew we were here.

I continued down the hallway, quickening my pace with each step.

After ten minutes, the movie would end. Then ANTE would turn its full attention to us...assuming they didn't already know I was here.

Move faster.

What if we didn't win? What if Ironfall betrayed us too soon? How many people would ANTE slaughter?

What if Ironfall was even worse than ANTE?

Another thought sparked goosebumps. I was alone in here.

Footsteps. Two distinct heels tapping on the marble floor. Someone rounded the corner. Black suit. Tall red heels. Long fresh-from-the-salon blonde waves. I gulped, then straightened to match her rigid posture.

She turned her fierce blue eyes on me. "Where is your pin?" Pin? What was she talking about? My eye snagged on a gold "A" pinned on her chest. The line across the A tipped down in the middle to create a diamond. A for ANTE. So they already revealed themselves.

My breath shook. "I..." Oh no, I couldn't freeze up now. Uh... oh! "Someone pickpocketed me on the Metro this morning. Shame you can't just order one on Amazon." That sounded fake, but she had to believe me. My chest tightened.

The woman rolled her eyes. "Well, I guess I'll have to fix that."

She nodded, then walked away. Phew. I passed inspection. But this wasn't over yet.

I glanced back, and the woman was gone.

"Ver, ANTE started the attack," I said.

She didn't respond. My gut twisted. Something was wrong. Okay, I couldn't panic. Just find where ANTE was and what they were doing, and I would be good. I glanced at my watch. Five minutes until the message at the end of the video played and the window of surprise would be over.

I continued down the empty hallway, then turned again. This

would lead me to the House Chamber, which was big enough to hold everyone. All ANTE would have to do was get the Senators in there.

"Ver? Agent Liam? Anyone?" Silence on comms.

Why weren't they answering? I *needed* them.

What if...oh no. What if Ironfall betrayed us?

He was so close to being on our side.

Two heavily armed guards stood in front of the large wooden door. Tall. Muscular. Bulletproof vests and tactical gear. Helmets. Assault rifles.

"Stop right there!" The guy on the left raised his weapon. "No one has clearance to enter this room." That was a sure sign that the chamber was exactly where we wanted to be.

Why had my team not responded?

Were the guards ANTE or Secret Service?

"Do you want me to report you?" I said.

Then the other guy started talking. "We are under strict orders to keep everyone out." ANTE pins flashed on their vests.

ANTE must have the entirety of Congress held hostage in this chamber.

I stepped closer.

"Don't make us take you out," one of the guards said.

All I could do was stand there, giving them as many threatening "Karen looks" as possible.

VIGIL needs to get in here.

"Don't move." The voice came from behind. It sounded like—

My breath caught in my throat.

Mom.

TRANSCRIPT OF THE INTERVIEW PROCEEDINGS WITH IRONFALL

SOME NAMES AND LOCATIONS REDACTED FOR
SECURITY
INTERVIEW CONDUCTED ON MAY 20
LOCATION OF INTERVIEW: **[REDACTED]**
CASE #: **[REDACTED]**

IRONFALL: I had to complete my mission. No matter what.

AGENT LIAM BLAKE: What stopped you from killing us?

IRONFALL: Rosemary. I was going to, but...the way she cares for her team...it isn't one of her perfectly crafted lies. She almost *died* for you. I'd never seen anyone do that before. Something felt wrong about killing you.

AGENT LIAM BLAKE: And then what happened?

IRONFALL: I told ANTE right where you were.

CHAPTER 26

Slowly, I turned around. There stood my mom, pointing a gun at me. Her auburn hair sleeked back in a military bun and black suit pressed so it fit her figure. She looked like a congresswoman.

My eyes connected with the man standing right next to her. I sucked in a breath. "Ironfall."

No.

He sold us out.

Betrayal stabbed me like a knife. Chest constricted. Throat closed. Eyes stung.

No.

I knew we couldn't trust him.

Were the other VIGIL agents okay?

I'd had so many doubts, I should have said something. I should have known.

Mom pointed to the guards. "Leave us." They obeyed.

My mom and Ironfall. All I could do was stare at both of my betrayers.

Time slowed.

I couldn't take my eyes off Ironfall. My knees weakened. "You betrayed us." I knew it was coming.

His eyebrows knit together. "I had to." I barely heard his low voice. Was that regret? No, just more manipulation.

Somehow that made everything hurt more.

This was what they did. Deceive people. I knew this going in.

I knew Ironfall was a villain. I knew my mother was...well...I didn't know.

But I...

I...

A tear slipped down my cheek.

Mom stepped forward. "Your father was right. I can't talk you into switching sides. I should have told you sooner. At least I'd have been able to save you." Her words echoed in the majestic hallway.

"I don't need saving." *Except from you.* My voice shook. Fear crept through me as my chest tightened.

"It doesn't matter. You're my daughter. I should have done whatever it took to never let this happen." Her jaw quivered. "As soon as we win, you'll be the first traitor they execute. And I know it won't be painless. I am *so sorry* I failed you." Were her eyes shimmering with tears, or was it a trick of the light? "You shouldn't be the one to pay for my mistakes."

What was she trying to do now?

"Is my team dead?" I said.

"No," Ironfall said, then lowered his head in silence. Why didn't he kill them?

So many questions, not enough answers.

It was up to me. I stood between them and the entire world.

But I felt too beaten down. Still, I had to at least try. "We are taking ANTE down today whether the two of you like it or not." My voice sounded too weak to threaten.

Ironfall didn't meet my gaze.

"You won't get very far on your own," Mom said. "It's too late for you. Too late." She shook her head, her face screwed up as if she was deciding something important. "I'm so sorry. This is how it has to end." Her finger inched toward the trigger. My eyes widened. Instincts took over. I grabbed the gun, twisted out of the way, and wrenched it from her hands. Then I tossed it away. She smacked me. I reeled backward, my cheek stinging.

Ironfall only stood there.

She attacked, I blocked, I attacked, she blocked. Punch. Block. Kick. Block.

Though she always claimed she was trying to protect me, she wasn't holding back. When the time came, would she kill me? Was I willing to kill her in self-defense?

I loved her. She betrayed me, but I loved her. No, I had to shove that out of my mind. It would make me sloppy.

Fighting. So much fighting.

I couldn't tell what was going on anymore.

Numb.

Ground. I was lying on the ground and she was on top of me. Hands pinned at my sides. Gun pressed against my forehead. Finger on the trigger.

She'd do it. Each of the last beats of my heart seemed to confirm it. She thought my death was better than a life outside her vision.

Mom's chest heaved, a tear splashing against my face. "If...if I don't kill you, your death will be so much more painful." The metal shook. She sobbed. "You were supposed to be on my side. The right side."

Mom.

"I would have given up my life for you." My voice shook as my vision blurred

Fight.

"This is the right thing to do. I'm sorry, I'm so, so sorry. This is best."

I closed my eyes, tears dripping down my cheeks.

"It's only best for you." Ironfall's voice rumbled in the background. Mom didn't even flinch.

Bang!

Suddenly weight crashed on me. I couldn't breathe. Eyes still closed. Suspended in a moment of time.

Was this what death felt like?

The weight lifted. A low groan.

I wasn't the one dead.

I opened my eyes. Ironfall stood over me, rolling something —someone—off me. Blood smeared across my face, my clothes, my hands, but it wasn't my own.

Mom. "No!" I sat up and stared at her body. Her breaths came shallow. Blood coated her teeth. I reached over, taking her hand.

I glanced up at Ironfall. He stood like a statue staring down at my mother's figure.

The dying light in her eyes burned holes in him. "*Traitor.* If you'd have been smart enough to convince her to join us..." Mom wheezed, then sputtered. Red dribbled down the side of her perfect face. "Y-you failed us...just like...my daughter. I see why... your father...calls you...his...failure."

"You were right." Ironfall looked at me, eyes now narrow. "They only care about us if we do what *they* want."

Mom stilled in my arms. No more subtle movements. Her cheeks didn't quiver. Eyes didn't move. Muscles relaxed.

"She's gone," I whispered. What just happened? She tried to kill me, then the next thing I knew she was dead. Gone. Rage. Loss. Relief.

Ironfall rested his hands on my shoulders, but I jerked from his grasp. "She's gone. She's gone."

He put his large hands on my shoulders once more, and I couldn't crawl away. "Rosemary. She was about to kill you; I had no choice."

"You killed her." It was all I could say, all I could do to keep from sinking to the ground and sobbing. My mom's blood was smeared across my face, now mixed with salty tears. "Y-you killed her."

A gentle hand brushed against my cheek. "Right before she killed you." His voice was soft and tender. I tried to replay what happened in my mind. Sobs wracked through my chest. "You were right. They only cared about themselves." He cupped my face.

What was he doing? He—? "She was going to kill me. You..."

"I know, Rosemary. I know. But you need to focus," he said. "There's still a chance."

My mind jumped back to reality, though the weight of death still hung heavy. He *betrayed* us. Images flashed of him standing beside my mom.

I was the last line of defense.

Every part of me screamed to curl up in a ball. It would be so easy to run. I was outnumbered. Outgunned. Outwitted.

I couldn't do this.

Mom's bloodied form seared into my brain. I gagged.

Still a chance?

My garbled thoughts came up with only one plausible solution. He still wanted to take over the world.

Bricks weighed down on my shoulders, hands, and feet. But I jerked back and pushed myself off the ground. My knees quaked as I forced myself to stand in front of the door, blocking Ironfall's path.

"I can't let you go inside." My hands turned to fists.

He held a hand out toward me. "Rosemary, I'm going in there to *stop* my father."

"You're lying."

"You have every right to think otherwise—"

"I know you." I gritted my teeth. "You'll say anything to get what you want. You're just like them." Was he willing to fight to get past me? *Can I even do this?*

"I see now. You were right about love," he said. "However my father treated me, it wasn't...it wasn't love, and nothing I do will change that. He cares about his own agenda more than anything or anyone, and we have to fix it. Once you were willing to die for your parents—use that now. It's time to use that, Rosemary. I may not trust you to be loyal to me, but I trust you to stop my father. We're the last hope."

Focus. Don't look at Mom. Don't think about her. Focus on saving the world.

Inhale.

Exhale.

The smooth wooden doors rubbed against my back.

My breath caught.

I'd been taken in by false promises before, and I wouldn't make the same mistake this time. He was partially right, though. I was their last hope. And I couldn't miss the warning signs this time.

I launched toward him. I swung an arm, but he deflected. I rammed my knee into his chest. He stumbled back, but returned even stronger. Punch. Deflect. Kick. Deflect. Deflect. Kick. Kick.

"Rosemary..."

He wasn't even trying.

Wham. His leg dug into my stomach. Lungs burned. I couldn't breathe. Pain punched through my abdomen. Falling. I clutched his arms, bringing me down with him. My side collided with the door. It burst open.

We tumbled inside.

TRANSCRIPT OF THE INTERVIEW PROCEEDINGS WITH IRONFALL
SOME NAMES AND LOCATIONS REDACTED FOR SECURITY
INTERVIEW CONDUCTED ON MAY 20
LOCATION OF INTERVIEW: **[REDACTED]**
CASE #: **[REDACTED]**

AGENT LIAM BLAKE: Did you plan all along to turn us over to ANTE?

IRONFALL: Yes.

AGENT LIAM BLAKE: Your goals still seem tangled

together. You were helping ANTE, but you also saved Rosemary after compromising VIGIL's mission at the Capitol.

IRONFALL: Something Rosemary said about my father clicked. The pieces all fit together. My whole life was a lie.

AGENT LIAM BLAKE: You believed her, even though she was the enemy?

CHAPTER 27

As I wheezed for air, cool metal handcuffs clamped on to my wrists. Blurry vision. Couldn't focus. Someone jerked me to my feet, shoving me forward. I stumbled, blinking, trying to clear my woozy head.

Once I stood still, the haze faded all at once. The vast chamber was filled with hundreds of well-dressed men and women contrasted by terrified and threatening expressions. Bright blue carpet covered the floor. The room was set up in a semicircle, with the many wooden chairs all facing a hierarchy of trapezoidal desks at the front of the room. An armed militia of snipers lined the balconies above, pointing their weapons down into the crowd of hostages below.

At the center of the tallest desk stood Jasper Emmerling, Ironfall's father.

Ironfall. Where was he?

I looked around. My eyes landed on Liam, Manda, Sam, and Ver, handcuffed in the far corner. Sam's eyes were wide with fear as he took in everything. My gut twisted. But at least they were alive.

We had no chance.

ANTE had won.

People I didn't recognize sat a tier lower. The bottom layer was empty. My dad was nowhere to be seen. Why wasn't he here?

"Father." Was that alarm in Ironfall's voice? I craned my neck to see him making his way down the center aisle as if all this was planned. Each comfortable step left more dread inside. He lied. Again.

If only I was stronger, maybe VIGIL would've had a chance.

Jasper leaned forward against the wooden podium. "I don't need your help, Ironfall."

But Ironfall didn't back away. He kept moving forward, step by step, and no one stopped him. "Really? You taught me how to play the long game, so guess what this is? This is the endgame."

His father only laughed, motioning at the chamber's grandeur. "We're doing just fine without you."

"Ah, I see." Ironfall didn't slow his pace. "But I had a plan."

"Which clearly you failed at. Again."

"Who says I ever failed?" A smile played at Ironfall's lips as he continued swaggering toward the podium. Step by step, complete with a villain monologue. "You reached out to me and ordered me to recruit someone: Rosemary Collins. When I found her, she looked like just a normal girl. But clearly you wanted her for a reason, so I figured out a way to get your attention. And then my master plan began to unfold. We could work together to take over the world *for* you, which you have yet to be successful at. That was something you couldn't find fault with. Thanks to your device, my video played to the entire nation. And if you check Twitter, I'm sure you'll find that they are excited about it."

What would happen? Ironfall was a loose cannon right now, and Jasper, well, who knew what he would do.

Jasper stroked his chin. "That's interesting, because I never gave that order."

Ironfall didn't seem fazed, he almost looked...amused. Because he already knew. "Really?"

"My two top agents went behind my back to get you to recruit their daughter, Rosemary, so she would be spared when we took over," Jasper said. "You couldn't see through a fake order? I thought I taught you better than that." So my parents went rogue. They really were desperate to "protect me." To have me by their side. So desperate my mom thought killing me was the best way to do that. I pressed my lips together. That wasn't love.

Mom.

"Even if I had given you that task, you failed me." Jasper pressed a hand to his chest as if feigning hurt. "If you only put more effort in, you'd see better results." His chuckle reverberated through the chamber. "And then I'd be able to trust you." Chills crept up my spine. "Be able to call you my son."

Now Ironfall stood just feet from his father. He paused for a moment. Silence filled the chamber. "But would you really?" My breath caught. What? "Or would you only keep me hoping so I'd follow your orders?"

Our conversation in the greenroom.

What was he doing?

I could only watch, wide-eyed.

Jasper's eyebrows raised. "Disrespect only digs your grave deeper."

"You only care about me if I do exactly what I'm told," he said. "Is that right?" What was he doing?

"I don't have time to waste on disobedient soldiers." Jasper reached into his coat and withdrew a handgun. "Now you're becoming a hindrance. Certainly not doing you any favors if you're trying to make me happy."

"Someone told me recently that love is selfless." Ironfall looked back at me. "Turns out she was right." I stared into his eyes, and he stared into mine. Those same blue and brown irises that followed me through New York all those weeks ago when I was scared and defenseless. They were the eyes that met me every day at the hideout to train me. The same eyes that laughed whenever he was truly happy. The eyes that craved love.

The eyes of a killer.

What was Ironfall's plan? Was he really on our side?

"Don't be ridiculous. Everyone has an agenda. Love and

approval are only a means to an end, a way to manipulate." Jasper didn't lower the handgun.

I couldn't move.

"Or maybe love means putting someone else before your own agenda, no strings attached." Ironfall straightened. Tears pricked my eyes.

Jasper laughed. *Laughed.* Cruel and dripping with disdain. Psychopath. "I think you have unrealistic expectations."

"Then I don't want it." He stood square against his father, rising to his full height.

"Good." Jasper's new smile matched Ironfall's. The resemblance was striking.

"But not good for you," Ironfall said. Now he stood just feet away from his father. "I've learned a few things since you last saw me, and because of that, I'm right where I want to be."

Jasper's face hardened. "Really?" He aimed the gun and fired. I jumped back. Ironfall dropped to the ground, somersaulting out of the way. His face hardened, and he looked at me again, broken but set. Set in what? Helping VIGIL? Or taking over the world for himself?

Ironfall rose to his feet.

What was his play?

"You're going to regret that," Ironfall quipped, then slowly moved to the side of the desks, right where the walkway was.

Jasper raised his eyebrows. "You dare threaten me, boy?"

"I think you underestimate my abilities." The devilish grin was back. He rushed over and then leapt up the steps.

Snipers on the balcony leaned forward, preparing to shoot him.

"Don't fire! He's mine." Jasper fired again, but Ironfall dodged, then reached forward and grabbed the barrel, twisting upward. Jasper let go and thrust a white knuckle forward.

Every muscle in my body tensed.

Ironfall dropped the gun and grabbed an arm, landing a punch to the abdomen. His father reeled backward, but Ironfall moved forward, then wound up his arm as if to throw something. In a quick movement, something silver flew, landing near my feet.

I looked down. A key.

Ironfall...

Adrenaline pumped through my veins.

We could beat this.

I unhinged my handcuffs and threw the key as hard as possible toward the VIGIL agents. Then I turned my attention back to Ironfall. Jasper had him pinned against the back wall, a knife pressed to his throat.

With everyone's attention on Ironfall, Manda slipped into the room's shadows like a wraith, then scaled the wall, climbing onto the balcony. She came up behind one of the snipers, tightening an arm around his neck. He collapsed.

Ironfall let out a strained groan. My attention snapped back to him. *Mom.* He killed her to save me. His gaze flicked to me, screaming for help.

He saved my life so many times.

Could I let him die?

I rushed forward. Jasper narrowed his eyes, then turned. Ironfall shoved the knife away and leapt towards me.

We stood right next to each other against the enemy.

"Side by side?" He breathed heavily.

I glanced over. He killed my mom. He's a villain. But he was on our side. I narrowed my eyes. "Just this once."

That was when the VIGIL team attacked. Manda shot the rest of the snipers with the first one's rifle. The congressmen shrieked as they ducked under their seats. Jasper's gaze snapped up, a new fire burning in his eyes. Sam threw a punch at a nearby guard. The guard stumbled back, hardly dazed. Then Ver stepped in.

As if in sync, we started fighting. Ironfall swung for Jasper's face, while I kicked out his legs, but he deflected both. Again and again. How was he better than both of us? Our arms connected. He kept going.

I thrust my fist at him, but Jasper grasped and twisted. Pain ripped through my arm. A groan escaped.

The arm dropped to my side.

Ow. Ow. Ow.

Tears stung my eyes.

Jasper hit me with a gut punch. My lungs expelled air, but I couldn't catch my breath. Oh gosh. This was it.

Ironfall scored a punch to Jasper's face. As he recovered, Ironfall turned to me, brushing a hand against my arm. Instantly, everything felt so much better.

His healing power. "Thanks."

I attacked again so Jasper could focus on me. Ironfall grabbed the forgotten gun and pointed it at his father.

And then pulled the trigger.

Jasper collapsed. Blood splattered on the ground. He thudded to the carpet. His dead eyes remained open. Everything went silent.

I couldn't concentrate on what was going on behind me. But the screams of hostages made me not want to see. Soon, what few ANTE agents remained alive lowered their weapons in surrender.

This was the end.

"Wow, that happened." Sam's voice burst through the silence, but it sounded far away as if I was in a dream.

My heart beat inside my hollow chest.

Ironfall dropped the gun. "It's over. It's over."

My legs gave out.

My mom tried to kill me.

Ironfall betrayed me.

Everything was blurry.

We won.

But it wasn't as glamorous as a superhero movie ending.

Blood splattered across my clothes. Bruised body. Shattered

heart. Broken mind.

Ironfall sank to his knees, placing empty hands behind his head. Surrender.

Soon security swooped in. Men and women in bold FBI jackets swarmed in the slow-motion aftermath of a crime thriller. Except no one would hear about this when VIGIL & ANTE Studios dropped their next movie.

Handcuffs. Questions. Debriefs. Reports. Paperwork. Strict nondisclosure statements.

I floated through the scene, taking in nothing and everything for hours. All I could do was stare as a forensics team zipped my mom's bloodied form into a body bag.

Paperwork was thrust in front of me, and I signed it with glazed-over eyes.

So this was truly the end.

My mom was dead.

My father was missing.

Ironfall was in custody.

ANTE was gone.

The world was safe.

MAY 18 – 4:23 P.M. EDT

The VIGIL team stepped back into the destroyed bunker. Torn mattresses, battered furniture, cracked glass, shattered computers, and brown blood stains covered the floor. I stood there, staring at the mess. Was the fight only three days ago? It felt like a hundred years.

And now my mom was gone.

I took a deep breath. This was all over, so why didn't I feel relieved? "What happens now?" What was I supposed to do, now that my parents were gone? What about high school? Ironfall?

Agent Liam turned. "We make that movie we announced."

"Oh my gosh." Sam grinned like that was the best news of his life.

"I think we may want to clean up the base first," Ver said. "This even puts my apartment to shame, and believe me, that's saying a lot."

"That's a yikes from me," Sam laughed. I couldn't help but chuckle along with everyone. Why did they seem okay? Maybe I should act like them.

"You might want to clean it up, Ver, because Rosemary is going to stay with you until we move to the L.A. base next week," Agent Liam said.

I tried smiling and acting like my heart wasn't strewn across the floor. "L.A. base?"

Agent Liam's lips perked upward. "You do realize we have three months to pull off a blockbuster film, right? Of course we have an L.A. base."

"It's more of a studio, really. The best part is we have an In-N-Out Burger a block away." Ver grinned.

I shook my head. "I've never had it—"

"Oh, don't worry, we'll change that," Ver said. "I may or may not have eaten it three times a week when we filmed *Project Safeguard*."

Agent Liam chuckled. "You're not the only one."

"We all did it." A rare smile crept across Manda's face.

"Well then, it will have to become our tradition." I grinned. "Maybe a post-credits scene? Like the Avengers with shawarma?"

Sam's eyes sparkled. "Ooh, yes!"

"We already tried," Agent Liam said. "Didn't get approved."

Ver crossed her arms. "In case you haven't noticed, ANTE doesn't run the CIA anymore. No one can stop us now."

Two FBI agents walked Ironfall through the doors, each keeping an arm captive. His solemn face formed into a grin. "Except me."

Manda glared.

"I'm just kidding," he said.

"Take him into the interrogation room. Don't bother cuffing him to the desk, he's not going to harm anyone," Agent Liam said. "Right?"

"Yes, sir," Ironfall said, not a hint of sarcasm in his voice. Then he looked right at me with his brown and blue eyes.

He seemed…calm.

The agents escorted him out.

"What happens to him?" I said. Why hadn't the CIA taken him with the other ANTE agents?

"He wants to give a full confession. We'll see how that goes and move from there," Agent Liam said. "I for one want to know why he kept switching sides."

I stared at where Ironfall had just been. "I…I think it's me."

"We'll know his reasons soon enough," Agent Liam said.

TRANSCRIPT OF THE INTERVIEW PROCEEDINGS
WITH IRONFALL
SOME NAMES AND LOCATIONS REDACTED FOR
SECURITY
INTERVIEW CONDUCTED ON MAY 20
LOCATION OF INTERVIEW: **[REDACTED]**
CASE #: **[REDACTED]**

IRONFALL: Rosemary was right.

AGENT LIAM BLAKE: About what?

IRONFALL: Nothing I did for my father would ever be enough.

AGENT LIAM BLAKE: Do you believe he loved you?

IRONFALL: No, I don't. Or if he thought he did, it wasn't real love.

AGENT LIAM BLAKE: But clearly you wanted it.

IRONFALL: For most of my life, he was the most important person in the world to me.

AGENT LIAM BLAKE: Yet he repeatedly put you down, is that right?

IRONFALL: Yes. Sometimes if you want someone to change bad enough, you fool yourself into falling for the same lies over and over.

AGENT LIAM BLAKE: Is that how you felt about your father, or how you want us to feel about you?

IRONFALL: That's how I convinced myself that I could earn my father's...love.

AGENT LIAM BLAKE: So why did you decide to fight on our side after you betrayed us?

IRONFALL: I realized I didn't want to be as much like my father as I thought I did.

AGENT LIAM BLAKE: Did you do it out of revenge? He did threaten you.

IRONFALL: No.

AGENT LIAM BLAKE: Because he wouldn't accept you?

IRONFALL: I know you have a hard time believing it, but it's true.

AGENT LIAM BLAKE: I do have a hard time believing it.

IRONFALL: I wanted what Rosemary had with you, with everyone. I couldn't get that from my father, because he'd never be able to see anything outside of his selfish goals. Whenever I didn't measure up, he cut me out. As much as I can't trust Rosemary, she risked her own happiness to save *everyone*. That seemed about as far from my father as I could get, so I thought I'd give it a try.

AGENT LIAM BLAKE: So you admit that you were wrong before?

IRONFALL: Yes.

AGENT LIAM BLAKE: Ironfall, I need to know, do you regret the horrible things you've done?

CHAPTER 28

MAY 20 – 8:57 P.M. EDT

I stepped back from the mirrored window that overlooked the interrogation room, pressing my lips together.

"I...I..." Ironfall hesitated. Had I ever seen him this vulnerable? This broken? "Yes." The quiet desperation in his voice made a lump form in my throat. So...so...genuine.

"Do you think he's telling the truth?" Ver said.

"I don't know." I shook my head. He lied and manipulated. Just like me. If he thought he could get off free by pretending to have a change of heart, he would do it.

It would take so much more than the right words to change my mind.

It was hard to believe him. He betrayed us every time. Except when it mattered the most.

"I guess we'll find out when Liam's done," Ver said.

On the other side of the glass, Agent Liam looked up from the iPad in his lap and folded his hands on the desk. "Is there anything else you'd like to say?" He seemed somber and contemplative, not as hard as he was when coordinating the Capitol attack aftermath.

"I don't think so."

"Okay." Agent Liam kept a stone face, got up, and walked out.

Ironfall didn't move, didn't even look over at the one-way mirror which he had to know we watched him through.

The door opened and Agent Liam walked in. I couldn't read him.

He set the tablet on the desk and cleared his throat. "He's telling the truth."

"What?" My chest tightened. How could he...? The base's AC unit kicked on. I jumped.

"He never lied," Agent Liam said. All those things. All those words about me. They had to be false. "He passed our lie detection system, and I couldn't catch him in anything."

"Lie detectors can be wrong, right?" My eyebrows knit together. This would be so much easier if every word was false.

"That's true, but in all my years as an agent, I've never been wrong in the interrogation room. My instinct says he's telling the truth." He leaned against the desk, gazing through the window at our prisoner. "So we're going to have to decide what to do about this."

Ver nodded. "The transcript will be included in Rosemary's report to give to our screenwriters."

"Good. Maybe they will give a second opinion. Include the video and lie detector report as well."

Ver nodded as her fingers danced across the keyboard.

"How could he be telling the truth?" My breathing became shallow. What did he hope to accomplish from this? What was his angle?

What if he *was* telling the truth?

"We'll figure this out. If he really had a change of heart, maybe he could help us out. He's a good actor after all," Agent Liam said. "If you're okay with that."

"You mean put him in my movie?" Could I handle that?

"It'd sure make editing a lot easier," Ver said. "Since we lost Cloaker, we would have to deepfake Ironfall, which would take forever, even with our special software. Not that I'm complaining, because I'm not, but it would be easier."

I pressed my lips together, shoving Cloaker's death out of my head. "Well, he loved being in *Beauty and the Beast*. Maybe this would do him some good. Help him with the transition if he really does want to change and join us." My voice shook. Were we really considering this? "But I don't trust him."

"Neither do we, but right now, we're short on people and he's too good to waste. The moment he steps out of line, he's done," Agent Liam said. "And think, we don't know how deep ANTE goes. There could be sleepers embedded in high places in case the Capitol attack went south. Ironfall isn't on their side anymore, that much we know."

"So we share a common enemy." Ver nodded. "Smart."

"My thought exactly," Agent Liam said. "It makes him our secret weapon."

This would end badly.

And the fandom would eat it up.

"Do you want to be the one to break the news to him, Rosemary?" Agent Liam said. "Out of all of us I think he trusts you the most."

"I can." I nodded. No...I couldn't. "Though he doesn't trust me, sir. Not after I betrayed him."

"But you're the most familiar. It should help," Agent Liam said, pressing his dark lips together. "And I think you've gained more credit with him than you realize."

"You sure you're up for it?" Ver said.

No. "I think I can handle him," I said. Key phrase: I think. "Can I borrow your iPad?"

He placed the thin tablet in my hands, then pointed out the controls and indicators. Green meant truth; red meant lie.

Could he see the iPad shaking in my unsteady hands? I took a deep breath to slow the pounding in my chest. It didn't work.

"Wish me luck," I said. Then I left for the other side of the mirrored glass. I paused before turning the knob. Out here in the hallway by myself... As much as I hated it, I had to talk to him.

Ironfall looked up, his eyes widening. "Hi, Rosemary."

My breath caught. "Hi." Every word in the English language

escaped me. What was I supposed to say? How was I going to break the news to him?

"Did you hear...?"

I nodded. "Yes. I listened to the whole thing."

Silence.

"Anything else you want to add while I'm in the lie detector seat?" He didn't look at me.

This kicked me into action. I glanced down at the iPad. His heart was beating just as fast as mine was. How did it know that? Was he wired to invisible heart monitors?

Focus.

I sat on the opposite side of the table, resting my iPad on my lap so he couldn't see it.

Deep breath. *You can do this.* "Do you still want to overthrow the government?"

He leaned forward. "No."

I sucked in a breath and studied the screen. All green.

Ironfall wasn't lying.

"Good." I gulped. "What about killing people? You finished with that?" This would be a lie. It had to be.

"Only in self-defense." Green light. Heart rate and pupil dilation within the allowed range.

How was he passing this?

"What about my mother?" I said.

"She was about to kill you," he said. *I know.* He did the right thing. But she was...gone. "I-I'm sorry." Green light. "We both lost parents that day. I pulled the trigger on both of them. I have to live with that. I know there's nothing I can do to make it up to you." The screen turned green again.

A lump formed in my throat. "Actually, there might be. I have a deal for you." My own pulse raced.

"A deal?" His forehead wrinkled as if suddenly he was listening more intently. The sliver of blue in his eye seemed brighter than normal.

"Yes," I said. "How do you feel about working for VIGIL? I

know I haven't exactly given you any reasons to trust me, but you haven't given us any reasons to trust you either." Lying was what got everyone into this mess in the first place.

"What's your angle?" His eyes narrowed. "Why are you doing this? If you think I'll trust you, you're sorely mistaken." Green light again, but I needed no lie detector to tell me that.

An idea popped into my head. I knew how to prove that all my cards were on the table.

"Switch seats with me," I said.

"What?"

I stood. "Switch seats. Ask me anything you want and see for yourself whether or not I'm telling the truth."

He pushed himself up using the armrests, then stepped around the table. As we passed, my stomach turned. I never took my eyes off him. Then I handed him the iPad and sat down, ready for my secrets to be spilled.

"Okay. Ask whatever you want." Did he hear the waver in my voice?

"Is this deal legitimate?" His hands grew white around the tablet.

"Yes."

"Will you or VIGIL betray me?" Fair question.

"Not unless you break the law." I let out a breath.

"You're not...lying." He sounded...surprised? And knowing all at once. What was going through that man's head?

"I hate lying more than just about anything," I said. "Without trust...there's nothing. Am I telling the truth?"

"Yes." His voice wavered. "Yes, you are." Everything inside me screamed. What was going through his complex mind? "Was any of it real for you? Did you care about me? Or was it all manipulation?" *Did.* Past tense.

I gulped. "Y-yes. The whole time, I was scared that if I misstepped, you'd kill my family. But sometimes I could forget all that and just be us. I cared about you." I bit back rising tears. "We have a common enemy now," I said. "You can help us fight.

You said you wanted to be the opposite of your father. Now's your chance." Again, I wasn't lying.

"Can I ask one more question?" he said.

I nodded.

"What do you think of me?"

"I think..." My voice cracked. Murderer. Liar. Manipulator. But I'd seen so many other sides of him. He showed me why he became what he was. And maybe...maybe he wanted to be different. "I think you have nothing left, and you're still trying to find the answers."

"But what do you *think* of me? Am I a bad person?"

I closed my eyes. "Yes."

"Do you think you could learn to trust me?"

My chest tightened. Could I? All those things he said. All those maybes.

Maybe he wanted to change, to be different. But like my parents, like his father, he only used people as means to an end. Sure, he said he viewed love differently, but was he willing to act on it? Was he really willing to be selfless?

Did *I* want him to?

Before he found out I worked for VIGIL, we had fun. We laughed. We shared things with each other. Sometimes I could forget who he really was. And...I think he really fell in love with me.

"We're done with this." I stood. "Will you accept VIGIL's deal and work for us? Even when our mission goes against your personal agenda?"

He rose to his feet and sat back in the lie detector chair, placing the tablet on the table. "Yes."

The iPad turned green.

And it terrified me.

BESTVIGILMEMES.BLOGGINGLIFE.COM
FEATURING THE BEST VIGIL & ANTE STUDIOS POSTS
(DON'T @ ME)
– UNAVERAGEVIGILFAN2002

shutupandvigil:
WE'RE GETTING MORE IRONFALL CONTENT THIS IS NOT A DRILL

Yourfriendlyneighborhoodvigilagent:
Me every day: Let me tell you about VIGIL & ANTE Studios
Me when they announce a new movie: VIGILLLLLLLLLLLLL

CommanderVigilisLyfe:
Hello yes it's high time we added another female superhero. Stardust is gonna be freaking amazing.

VIGILfanboy27:
Okay so I know the movie doesn't come out for 3 months but I kinda ship Stardust and Ironfall. Think of the enemies to lovers. Think of the BANTER. The SHENANIGANS. The eNeMiEs tO lOvErS. *chef's kiss*
Comments:
IronfallDidWhatNow: WAIT YESSS
VIGIL'sBiggestFan19293: I can get behind this
CommanderVigilFan28: @katykat8689

Katykat8689: *@CommanderVigilFan28 I feel called out XD*

IAMSTARFALL: *Starfall is now their official ship name don't @ me*

---

ironDIDNTFALL:
That moment when you're low key disappointed Ironfall didn't actually take over the world during the I AM STARDUST reveal vid

---

StardustIsMy(new)Hero:
Ironfall: *takes out VIGIL agents*
Stardust: *swishes cape* My time has come

MAY 26 – 3:30 P.M. EDT

Sam closed out of the BestVIGILMemes page, grinning as he sat back down at his new desk at VIGIL HQ. "See, I told you the fans would ship you. It's scientifically proven. And also he's totally in love with you."

"Sam." I shook my head. "Science needs more credible sources."

"I always check my sources." He grinned. "Who do you think created this site?"

I blinked. "*You* run BestVIGILMemes?"

"Yep. I'm kind of a big deal."

Why was I surprised? Now I was grinning too. "As much as it pains me to admit, that's pretty cool. I love that site."

"Note to self: change tagline to 'the official favorite site of'...

whatever your stage name will be." He brushed his bangs away in mock haughtiness.

I glanced over at Ver, who was too glued to her own computer to pay attention. "Let's not do that."

"Okay, fine, but can I interview you? I'm your biggest fan."

I rolled my eyes. "I've been famous for ten days."

He shrugged. "Still your biggest fan."

"You're the worst."

Sam plowed on. "But the interview would get some serious traction. I know the site is already huge but imagine if I could interview an A-list actress. That's you, by the way."

The fact that this conversation was even possible blew my mind. Just a few months ago we were talking about waiting for the *Project Safeguard 3* announcement, and now I was a star of my own superhero movie.

"I'll think about it." My lips tipped upward. Knowing him, he'd get his way.

He didn't have time to think of an annoyingly witty response before the room's color shifted to an eerie flashing red. I whipped around to face Ver.

Sam jumped up, racing over to Ver. "What did you do wrong?"

The wall of screens blinked from red to black, red to black.

"Nothing." Ver's eyes were wide as she looked up from her laptop. "It's like someone is taking over the system." As she spoke, the screens shifted colors. Some now flashed magenta, some orange, some blue.

"Is it ANTE?" My stomach dropped.

"I don't know," Ver said. "Wait, hang on. There's some sort of code on my screen now. Keep Ironfall in the interrogation room and get everyone else in here." Since we didn't fully trust Ironfall, he was pretty much banished to the one soundproofed room.

My heart pounded as I gathered Manda and Agent Liam.

They glanced at each other as they walked into the main area. Manda's hand balled into a fist.

"Talk to me," Agent Liam said.

"I figured it out!" Sam said. "The code on Ver's screen is a message."

"I knew you were a genius." Ver grinned. "Have you cracked it yet?"

Don't feed his ego, I thought about saying, but now wasn't the time.

"Well, apparently my code-cracking skills need work because I think it says 'root beer.'" Sam smirked. Ver and Manda looked just as confused as he was.

"Ver, do you have a more educated opinion?" Manda rolled her eyes.

Agent Liam rushed over to the computer, leaning against the desk. "It's Cloaker's distress signal."

Cloaker? I thought ANTE killed him when I wouldn't kill Agent Liam. "He's alive," I breathed. "They kept him alive."

"You're sure? This could be a remnant of ANTE setting a trap," Manda said.

Agent Liam shook his head. "I was the only one who knew the code. He's injured, likely still held at the base. Just because we took out the head of ANTE doesn't mean we took out the body."

"And we start with Cloaker," Manda said, stepping forward.

Agent Liam nodded, then looked at me. "You're the only one who's been there. I want you and Ironfall to take point."

My blood froze at the thought of working with Ironfall on something this dangerous. "Are you sure we can trust him?"

"He hates ANTE as much as we do," Agent Liam said. "He will want to be there, and we need his disguises."

I nodded. "Yes, sir."

"Ver and Sam, I want the exact location of the base."

The tech geniuses nodded before getting to work.

Agent Liam then turned to Manda. "You already know what to do."

"On it." A rare smile slipped onto her face, but was gone an instant later.

Agent Liam then handed me a cream folder. "Brief Ironfall and have him prep your disguises. I want the two of you in and out before what's left of ANTE knows what's happening." He pressed his lips together, worried. There was still so much to do.

I nodded, gripping the folder as I walked toward the last place I wanted to go. The interrogation room loomed before me. I took a deep breath before stepping inside.

Of course, Ironfall already had a smug grin on his face. "Finished your meeting already?" Ironfall said, eyes flashing. "Or are you finally ready to clue me in to your secrets?"

I stepped forward, placing the folder onto the table.

"Well?" he said.

I slid the folder towards him, meeting his gaze. "We have our first mission."

ACKNOWLEDGMENTS
(a.k.a. The End Credits)

To quote Nick Fury, "There was an idea." A single question asked by a scared and lonely teenager that changed everything: "What would happen if the Marvel movies were secretly real?" This question branched into an idea which transformed into an original novel I desperately wanted to share with the world. Now, years later, it's here, and I couldn't have done it without these amazing people by my side. Each one is a superhero in their own right.

Mom, thank you for always being there. Words can't describe how grateful I am for you. You are truly the strongest woman I know. Thank you for always fighting for me.

Savannah, thank you for being my favorite sister and partner in crime. You're going to do amazing things! (P.S. I hope this book was much better than it was when you read it the first time.)

Grammy, Grampy, and Uncle Brian, thank you for supporting me in everything I do. You're all officially hired as my publicity team. I love you so much!

Dad, thank you for taking me to my first writer's conference and for wanting my author journey to be successful.

I am also grateful to the incredible people who taught me

how to write. Mom, you were my first teacher, and the one who gave me the gift of reading and writing. Mrs. Hunt, you may not remember me, but I fell in love with writing in your fourth-grade class. I did, however, ignore your advice to only write what I know. What can I say? I'm a sci-fi/fantasy author at heart. Mrs. Hassen, I still ask myself whether or not one of my written works meets to your high standards (usually quoting one of your catch-phrases in the process). As much as I hate to admit it, I'm grateful for your brutal-but-necessary essays. Clearly you did something right, because I'm not ready to blow the writing popsicle stand just yet.

I can't forget to thank all of my incredible writing friends as well. Thank you Hosanna Emily and Savannah Grace for your wonderful feedback as this story took shape. It wouldn't exist without your encouragement, critiques, and brainstorming sessions. Each one of you is a gift, and I can't wait to see where your own writing takes you! Erica Davis, thank you for suggesting that I make Rosemary an ordinary girl without powers. I am forever grateful for that advice. Thank you to all the lovely writers who helped me with my query letter and first few chapters. To my Mitchtam ladies: thank you for all the NaNoWriMo encouragement and word wars. Last, but certainly not least, thank you McKenzie for being a wonderful publishing sister.

Thank you Micaiah, Makayla, and Katie for being some of this book's biggest cheerleaders. I love you 3000. Micaiah, rooming with you has been an honor. Thank you for sticking with me through the ups and downs of rewriting, querying, rejection, and success. Makayla, in the short time I've known you, you have become one of my dearest friends. I'm pretty sure I can say you're Sam's biggest fan, and quite possibly the whole book's biggest fan. Katie (a.k.a. my "twin"), I'm not sure where to even start. You've been there since we first met on Go Teen

Writers, and you've impacted my life in so many ways. I truly don't know where I (or this book) would be without you.

Thank you Micheline for taking a chance on this story. You are an incredible artist, editor, storyteller, mentor, and friend. I am so blessed to call you my publishing mom.

Above all, thank you to my Lord and Savior Jesus Christ. You are the main reason this book exists. Thank you for giving me a passion for storytelling and the desire to share your Truth through the written word. You helped me persevere through long hours of editing and months of waiting for my publishing "yes." This book, and all my future ones, are yours.

ABOUT THE AUTHOR

Megan McCullough wanted a superpower, so she picked up a pen and became an author. Living in Florida, the theme park capital of the world, only fuels her love for storytelling. When she isn't writing, you can find her designing a book cover for someone else's literary masterpiece, fangirling over the Marvel Cinematic Universe, or wishing she was at Disney World. Join Megan's adventures through her Instagram (@meganmcculloughbooks) or at meganmccullough.com.